CRASH
INTO ME

Reader reviews for *Crash into Me***

'If you're looking for your next best rom-com, look no further'

'The book works on so many levels and I thoroughly enjoyed!'

'Such a fun rom-com that I really loved. Not sure how this is a debut!'

'From the first chapter, I was hooked on the main characters, Mia and Luca, and couldn't wait to see where their romance led'

'You can feel the heat between these race-crossed lovers as surely as if you're standing on a track with the motors revving'

'I enjoyed every minute of this fantastic rom-com. I can't wait to see what this author writes next!'

'If you love a fun lighthearted romance novel this is for you. Buy the book! You won't regret it!'

'Nothing beats finding a new author who knows how to write. *Crash into Me* propels the reader into auto racing, tight-knit teams and minds of the principals'

'Mia Rubie is the epitome of a woman rising to the occasion and realising she can be both a leader, a competitor, and a woman in love. I could not put this book down'

'The attention to detail and the cadence of the story made this book a hard one to put down for me. Great characters… a perfect unfolding and a lot of cheeky one-liners that made me laugh and keep reading'

'This second-chance romance has it all – clever banter, memorable characters, and a unique setting in the global world of elite racing'

DARCI ST. JOHN

CRASH INTO ME

Bedford Square
Publishers

First published in the UK in 2024 by Bedford Square Publishers Ltd, London, UK

bedfordsquarepublishers.co.uk
@bedfordsq.publishers

© Darci St. John, 2024

The right of Darci St. John to be identified as the author of this work has been asserted in accordance with the Copyright, Designs and Patents Act 1988. All rights reserved. No part of this book may be reproduced, stored in or introduced into a retrieval system, or transmitted, in any form or by any means (electronic, mechanical, photocopying, recording or otherwise) without the written permission of the publishers.

Any person who does any unauthorised act in relation to this publication may be liable to criminal prosecution and civil claims for damages.
A CIP catalogue record for this book is available from the British Library.
This is a work of fiction. Names, characters, places, and incidents either are the product of the author's imagination or are used fictitiously, and any resemblance to actual persons, living or dead, businesses, companies, events or locales is entirely coincidental.

ISBN
978-1-83501-189-8 (Paperback)
978-1-83501-190-4 (eBook)

2 4 6 8 10 9 7 5 3 1

Typeset by Palimpsest Book Production Limited, Falkirk, Stirlingshire

Printed in Great Britain by CPI Group (UK) Ltd, Croydon CR0 4YY

MIX
Paper | Supporting
responsible forestry
FSC® C171272

For Michael

Chapter 1

Mia Rubie's father once said that her smile could raise the dead. For the second time in her life, she wished it were true.

'How's my girl holding up?' Her dad's best friend opened his arms, and Mia collapsed into one of her godfather's famous bear hugs. His tweed sport coat was like sandpaper against her cheek, but she buried her face in all the same. It was the most comfort she'd felt all day.

'Hanging in there, I guess,' she lied, then took a deep breath in hopes of holding back another cascade of tears and turning into a blubbering mess for the thousandth time in four days. 'I still can't believe he's gone, Cliff. It doesn't seem possible.'

Not even a hundred hours had passed since her father exited this world. As each one of those three-hundred-thousand-and-some-odd seconds had ticked by, Mia's brain had been working overtime, trying somehow to process the inconceivable, how a man who'd always been larger than life could now be lying in the casket behind her.

'When my phone rang, I thought he was calling to say good morning. Poor Barb, having to—'

As if she'd been summoned from a lamp, her dad's longtime live-in house manager and unofficial wrangler of the Rubie family – a selfless job if there ever was one – appeared beside her. 'Oh, no, don't you feel sorry for me,' Barb said, her voice far calmer and several octaves lower than when she'd literally screamed into Mia's ear as her father was being loaded into an ambulance. 'I only wish I'd forced the paramedics to let him talk to you. If I'd known – well, damn. Here I go.'

Cliff pulled the now weeping Barb into their hug.

Even though the Chicago skyline had been in Mia's rearview mirror within a half an hour of hanging up the phone with Barb, her dad had died before she crossed the border into her home state of Michigan. When she'd rushed into the hospital lobby, ready to pounce on the first person she encountered with a stethoscope, she'd instead found herself looking into the eyes of a somber-faced Barb.

And she'd known.

'I wish I'd been able to say goodbye.' Mia sniffed. 'I wish I'd been able to say a lot of things.'

Not that she hadn't had ample opportunity to say all of the things when her dad was alive. They both had. But instead of sitting down and talking about why Mia had walked away from the sport she'd once loved like two rational adults, they'd chosen to dance around the central conflict in the drama they'd both played a part in creating, each of them waiting for the other to make the first move. Apparently, she'd won by default.

It was the hollowest of victories.

Now, it was too late. She couldn't apologize to a dead man. And although her dad had always accomplished whatever he set his mind to, admitting to his own wrongdoings or granting forgiveness from the hereafter was out of reach, even for him.

'Don't I know it, kiddo. But trust me when I say, he knew. The man knew everything.' Cliff gave them both a final squeeze before leading Barb away, leaving Mia to return to the task of greeting those gathered to say their final farewell to the great Robert Rubie, auto racing legend.

Five hours into the viewing, a line of people still wound through the funeral home, their feet shuffling along an invisible dotted line on the paisley carpeting. A line so long that she couldn't see where it ended, only where it began – with her twin brother and her. It was hard to believe that she and Jordan were here again, standing in front of a casket holding another parent taken too soon.

I wish I were anywhere but here. Mia closed her eyes and lightly knocked the heels of her boots together three times, only to open them to find a portly middle-aged man approaching her with open arms. She'd lost count of how many hugs she'd accepted from strangers.

'Mia, I'm so sorry to meet you under these circumstances, but... my gosh, do you look like your dad.'

Her teenage-self had always bristled at the comparison. Not that there was anything wrong with her dad's looks or, for that matter, hers. Blue eyes. Sandy blonde hair tousled in perfect just-stepped-off-the-beach waves. A permagrin that could best be described as 'resting happy face.' But when your mother had been a supermodel with a pout so famous that it had landed her on the cover of every fashion magazine in existence, it was hard not to resent not getting that gene. By luck of the draw, and genetics, the pout had gone to Jordan – although he mostly wore it as a scowl.

Her looks would forever be filed in the perpetually cute category. Just like her father's had been.

The man released her from his hug, only to grab her hands warmly in his. 'I own an Italian deli on the west side. Your dad couldn't resist my sub sandwiches. Was in a few times a week during the off-season.'

Between this guy, the Detroit-style pizza lady she'd met earlier, and Barb, a 'feeder' if there ever was one (even if it wasn't part of her official job description), her dad's heart attack was becoming less and less shocking.

'Of course.' Another fib.

Mr Sub beamed. 'Rob was so proud of his little girl in Chicago. Tell me, how's the job? That promotion working out? It sounded really great.'

They chatted for a few more minutes, during which Mia realized that there were few details her father hadn't felt comfortable trading for a little salami, capicola, and provolone. Her last boyfriend. Their disastrous vacation to Greece. The subsequent breakup. Apparently, her dad had thought she could 'do better.' No secret there.

After promising to stop in and try the newly named 'Rob Rubie,' which she learned was the old number four but with her father's favorite modifications, Mia managed to slide her hands from Mr Sub's vise-like grip and send him on his way. She scanned the line once again and spotted relatives mixed in with employees from Rubie Racing – her dad's second family – along with plenty of fans in team garb. At least twenty race car drivers were also waiting to pay their respects to one of their own. Ten she knew well from her childhood; men her father had raced against who were more like brothers than his own flesh and blood. The others were younger, from the current generation lapping the world's tracks alongside her brother. Like Jordan, they possessed an air of subtle arrogance that set her teeth on edge, even though she knew it was key to them confidently maneuvering cars hurtling a couple hundred miles per hour.

Without a doubt, Jordan would deal with each of the drivers himself, as he had all day. And that was just fine by her.

The only race car driver she'd allowed herself to give a damn about in the last fifteen years was lying behind them. She turned toward the casket and straightened his favorite Rubie Racing jacket. The team uniform had been a spur-of-the-moment decision when the funeral home director called for clothes to dress him in, but she'd known instantly it was the perfect choice. Rob Rubie had lived and breathed auto racing. If the Angel of Death had owed him any favors, and he likely had, her dad was already driving the afterlife's longest and most winding road course.

A strong whiff of 'funeral home scent' from the wall of floral arrangements surrounding the casket brought Mia back to reality with a sudden tickle in her nose. She sneezed again and again.

'You OK, sis?' Jordan asked, the concern in his voice a mismatch to the annoyed look in his eyes.

'You bet, bro,' she said, rubbing her nose with a tissue she'd tucked up her sleeve like a ninety-year-old woman, then gently dabbing her puffy eyes before searching the line again.

Jordan followed her gaze. 'Looking for someone in particular? A certain Italian driver, perhaps?'

'Luca?' she bristled. 'As if.'

Only to her chagrin, she sounded more like a sixteen-year-old girl denying a crush than the sensible thirty-three-year-old woman she'd become. Who, today of all days, was steeling herself for the moment when she came face-to-face with the man who once upon a time had broken her heart.

Like she needed one more piece of kindling to toss on the emotional bonfire blazing inside her. She gave the line another glance, knowing it was a matter of when, not if, her ex-boyfriend would appear to extend his condolences. Just like every other member of the Rubie Racing team.

Without another word, Jordan turned to greet the current world champion. A snippet of their talk about the upcoming season drifted into earshot, and it took all of the restraint she could muster to not shove her fingers in her ears to block it out. Racing was the last thing she wanted to think about right now, regardless of the fact that she and her brother were the sole heirs to the only American team in the world's most prestigious auto racing series, and the life she'd long ago sped away from was now crashing back into her.

Just a few more days, and then you can go home and back to your regularly scheduled life.

Mia's feet cramped in her new boots, and she curled and uncurled her toes in hope of finding some relief. Jordan passed an older couple off to her, and she accepted their hugs, listened to their memories, and prayed her feet would soon go numb along with the rest of her body.

Chapter 2

Luca Toscano placed his hands on the steering wheel, closed his eyes, and took a deep, centering breath. Just like he did before every race.

Only he wasn't sitting at the start line on a racetrack. He was in the parking lot of a funeral home, attempting to tie his goddamn necktie for the fifteenth time.

Luca could hardly believe he was about to pay his respects to the man who'd promised to make his dream of being world champion come true – twice – only to up and die before he did. That was why he'd felt like a Mack Truck was sitting on his chest since Brian, the team manager, had called him with the news of Rob's death. At least that's what he told himself as he gave the tie one final go and, miracle of miracles, lined up the ends enough to save the silken noose from the nearest trash bin.

He slammed shut the door of his silver Range Rover and made his way through the rows of luxury cars and SUVs lining his path to the door. An impressive showing considering the Apex racing season was about to begin, and an ocean stood between most of the other teams' home bases and Rubie Racing's. But then Rob had also made plenty of friends in every type of auto racing, and a couple of those series only ran stateside. Still, there couldn't be a single Ferrari, Mercedes, or Cadillac left at a rental car agency within a hundred and fifty miles of the Detroit airport.

As he suspected, the place was thick with fellow race car drivers and team owners from around the world. They hated to lose one of their own, especially an all-around good guy like Rob Rubie. Luca took his place in line and shared a nod with those he passed as he slowly snaked his way up to the casket, appreciating not having to engage any of his colleagues in conversation and address the question on everyone's minds. But their murmurs confirmed that they were all thinking what he'd been for the last three days: *What happens to Rubie Racing now?*

He wasn't a religious man by any means, but he sent up a prayer that the guy planted front and center of the casket wasn't any part of the answer to the question at the forefront of everyone's mind. While he was at it, he added a second prayer for when he came face to face with the woman he knew would also be there, even though he'd long ago given up hope of ever laying eyes on her again.

'Jordan, I'm very sorry for your loss,' Luca said to the man who was technically his teammate when he finally reached the end of the line. He accepted Jordan's outstretched hand, then pulled him in for a brief hug and a couple of taps on the back. 'Your father was a good man. He will be missed.'

Considering that Jordan had been doing his best to make him feel as if he didn't exist during their time as Rubie Racing's two required drivers, Luca shouldn't have been surprised when Jordan made a point of looking past him to see who was next in line. 'I'm sure you'll miss him more than most, Luca. I mean, you were one of his biggest accomplishments, without a doubt.'

Gone was the tiny flicker of hope Luca had had about Jordan leaving any animosity behind, at least for one day.

'Well, you and Mia.' Jordan jerked his head to his right. 'Surely, you remember my sister.'

'Yes, you know I do.' Luca allowed himself to follow Jordan's lead and finally glimpse the first – and only – woman he'd ever loved.

Jordan raised an eyebrow, then turned his attention to the next mourner waiting to talk to him, leaving Luca with the same impression he had after almost all of their interactions.

What an asshole.

Mia appeared deep in conversation with a grandmotherly type, giving him the perfect opportunity to escape. Only he couldn't stop himself from pausing to steal another look as he walked past her. One of her hands rested on the woman's shoulder as they talked; the other clutched a tissue she brought up to her face. To dab her eyes, which were open wide and looking directly at him.

Busted.

Luca shoved his hands in his pockets and, while he waited for Mia to finish her conversation, fully took her in. The stereotypical girl-next-door he remembered was all grown up. Still cute, as opposed to the model-type he now preferred, but gorgeous all the same. Especially in the soft grey cashmere sweater dress covering her from neck to knee and a pair of tall black leather boots. Before he could stop his brain, it pictured how those boots would look if she lost the rest of the outfit.

Since when did they keep funeral homes so warm? He was reaching to loosen his tie when Mia released the older woman from a quick hug and turned his way.

'My dad's high school English teacher,' she said, wiping away more tears as he walked up to her. 'Apparently, he was big into haikus.'

His puzzled look was met with the famous Rubie grin.

'C'mon, you know, the Japanese poem. Three lines? Five syllables, then seven, then five? Typically focus on nature, although Dad's, unsurprisingly, were almost always about race cars.'

He shrugged a shoulder. 'Nope. Can't say I've heard of it. But then I didn't exactly have a traditional education.'

She began tapping a single finger against her mouth and repeating, 'Five, seven, five.' Her eyes narrowed.

'Mia?' He swallowed, wishing she'd stop drawing his attention to her lips.

'Got one.' She paused. 'My father just died. He tried to walk on by me.' Another pause. 'After fifteen years.'

Bullseye. A direct hit to the heart. 'I'm not sure what to say, besides I'm sorry,' he said.

'I know, but it's ironic, right? Dad once said that I'd see you again over his dead body.'

Chapter 3

The cathedral was the only church in the Detroit area grand enough to host the funeral Mass, and a ridiculously generous gift toward its restoration had ensured the Gothic Revival-style space would always be available to the Rubie family. Regardless of the fact that Rob Rubie was a 'Chreaster' Catholic – only showing up on Christmas and Easter in his Sunday best.

'Trust me, I pray more than most people,' Mia could hear her father telling her whenever she'd asked why they had to go to church and he didn't. He'd always added with a wink, 'Someday, daughter of mine, you'll understand.'

That someday still hadn't arrived, and it most certainly wasn't today, as she sat sandwiched between Cliff and Jordan. Her brother had declined the car service Cliff arranged and instead made his way to the front pew just three steps ahead of the casket. She had half wondered if he'd show up with a date, but he was alone.

Not that he wasn't dressed to impress. His slim charcoal

suit was classic bordering on trendy, which was always a pricey combination. Mia assumed a stylist had paired it with the crisp white dress shirt and tie in the precise shade of navy as his car the previous season.

Not that she had room to talk. Since she left Chicago without a clue of what was in store for her, she'd driven straight to the mall after making the arrangements at the funeral home and handed her credit card over to the first consultant she saw. No doubt, the woman had taken one look at her frazzled state and the black American Express her father had insisted she carry in case of an emergency and thought, 'Jackpot.'

But her actions were more necessity than luxury. She'd declined the Fendi bag the stylist had paired with the simple black woolen dress for the funeral – albeit reluctantly, and only after an emergency call to her best friend Star back in Chicago from the dressing room. And she'd certainly done penance for splurging on those black boots with four-inch heels during the twelve hours she'd spent on her feet yesterday. Today's black patent leather Mary Janes were proving to be somewhat kinder to her arches, although the dull ache in her feet was a welcome distraction from the stabbing sensation piercing her heart in time to an invisible metronome.

Beside her, Jordan tapped his loafers on the marble floor to his own beat and glanced at this watch every few minutes. He'd never been the most patient or well-behaved person during Mass, and she'd be the one to know. The two of them had logged plenty of hours sitting side-by-side in wooden pews, with him always more focused on trying to get her in trouble than learning about kindness and compassion. As if she needed a second reason to be inexplicably sad, Mia realized that the days of them being siblings who teased yet still liked each other were now all but distant memories. They'd first faded when she and Jordan had started racing go-karts against each other. When Luca had joined Rubie Racing the first time, those days were almost completely behind them, and she and Luca being as thick as thieves had sealed the deal.

Near the end of the service, Cliff stood up and made his way to the altar, pausing briefly to rest his hand on the casket before ascending the stairs to the lectern.

No one was more qualified to eulogize her father. The two had grown up on the same street in northwest Detroit and had even raced karts against each other as boys. But by their teen years, it had become obvious that her dad possessed a one in a million gift. He'd raced his way up to the big leagues while Cliff went off to college and then law school. They'd lived the rest of their lives in different worlds but remained best friends, and Mia couldn't recall her godfather ever not being there. Her dad had trusted him more than anyone.

Cliff cleared his throat before leaning toward the microphone. 'Thank you for coming and, monsignor, thank you for your kind words about our friend. We can all agree that St Peter opened the pearly gates wide for Rob, and he happily raced through them to find his beloved Trish.' His voice faltered, and he paused to take a deep breath before continuing. 'Rob wasn't one for guesswork, as most of you here know. Once he made a plan, he stuck to it, even if he didn't let anyone else in on it, or it wasn't clear to anyone, and I mean anyone, but himself.'

A crisp white envelope appeared from the inside pocket of Cliff's sport jacket, along with a pair of reading glasses. 'Rob gave this to me at our last review of his will. Each year, he wrote a new letter to be read at his funeral. Like I said, no guesswork. God knows we didn't think his time would come this soon, but here we are.'

As Cliff unsealed the envelope and carefully unfolded the paper inside, Jordan increased the speed of his steady 'tap, tap, tap' on the marble. This letter was obviously a surprise to him, too. Mia considered moving her hand within his easy reach, in hopes that he might hold it. But the thought of being rejected by the only family member she had left kept it where it was.

'Hello, my mourners. Thank you for being here. My only wish is that I was sitting among you instead of at that big pit stop in the sky.' Cliff cleared his throat again. 'I certainly cannot complain about my life, so I won't bother to try.' Laughter bounced off the cavernous stone walls. 'But I am writing to let you know that my legacy is with all of you. And, so, it will never die. You and my children ensure that. My son, Jordan, who followed in my footsteps on the track, and my daughter, Mia, who will now lead Rubie Racing as its next owner and team principal.'

Jordan's foot stopped mid-tap as he stiffened next to her. This wasn't the plan.

He knew it.

She knew it.

And judging by the collective gasp that echoed from the marble floors to the stone ceiling, and the hushed murmurs that followed, all seven hundred people seated behind them knew it, too. A wide-eyed Barb grabbed Jordan's hand while leaning over him to pat Mia's.

Mia wanted to run up onto the altar, grab the paper out of Cliff's hands, and read it herself, but her legs were frozen. Only those wheels in her brain were moving, this time trying to process the bomb her father had managed to drop on his funeral from the hereafter.

This was a mistake, or a practical joke. The man had loved a good joke. Maybe he wasn't even dead but waiting for the right moment to pop out of the casket and yell, 'Gotcha!' Then, he'd laugh harder than anybody else, like he always had. She fixed her eyes on the casket's closed lid and waited. Nothing.

Damn.

Clearly, her father had been delusional. The signs were there. First, he had brought Luca back to the team, and now this. People should be concerned. Someone should say something. She should say something. She couldn't lead a racing team. Her path had been decided many years ago – by her. She'd created her own footsteps instead of following in his. And now he wanted her to sit in the driver's seat and steer Rubie Racing's future as team principal? She knew her dad had been a dreamer, but this was off the charts, even for him.

Her mind raced as her body remained paralyzed. Her hopes were raised when the priest stood up – then dashed when he only did some magical hand motion that quieted the crowd in about half a second before nodding to Cliff to continue.

'I announce this here, today, because I have one final request of each and every one of you. Please show my daughter the friendship and support you've provided me all these years,' Cliff read. 'But now, I want you to go and celebrate my death just as you did so often during my life. I've planned an after-party, make that an afterlife party, at the Rubie Racing complex. I will be there with you in spirit, always.'

Cliff folded the letter and placed it back in the envelope before descending the steps of the altar and returning to sit beside Mia. He put his arm around her as soon as he sat down and tugged her close to him. 'You OK, kid?' he whispered.

Mia could only shake her head no. Sweat was beginning to bead on her forehead, and she eyed the cool marble between the pew and kneeler. Would anyone notice if she pressed her cheek against the floor, just for a moment? Deciding that it probably wasn't ideal, she instead focused on matching Jordan's breathing. In through the nose and out through the mouth, in through the mouth... *come on, Jordan, out through the mouth*. After what seemed like an eternity, she squeezed his hand and he exhaled. And so did she.

The priest wrapped things up and let everyone know where they could find maps to the Rubie Racing complex. Since her father was being cremated, there would be no graveside service. The casket, with her father's body inside, was to be taken away once the cathedral emptied. This scenario – embalming, then cremation – wasn't typical but, as she'd learned when his funeral plans were revealed, he had considered this to be a fitting end. Probably because so many drivers of his generation had expected to burn to death in a fiery crash on the racetrack. Because so many of them had.

Mia assumed that she, Jordan, Cliff, and Barb would take a few minutes together after everyone left to say their final goodbyes. But Jordan rose from his seat with the rest of the congregation, walked straight up to the casket, and rapped on it with his knuckles.

'Hey, dad,' he said, his voice breaking. 'Go to hell.'

Mia spent the forty-five-minute drive from Detroit to the western suburbs pinballing from hysterical laughter to crying to seething anger and back again. It was a good thing her father was dead, because she would've seriously considered murdering him otherwise.

'What the hell was he thinking? How am I supposed to waltz into some weird afterlife party and mix and mingle like my life hasn't been totally upended?'

Cliff and Barb tried their best to console her, but they ultimately resorted to tough love when they pulled into the parking lot and Mia refused to exit the vehicle. Well, Cliff did, but then he was already on edge from rounds of defending himself for not telling her what he'd deemed 'not his news to share.' Barb was too busy performing an Olympic-level handwringing routine.

'This is what's going to happen,' Cliff said. 'You're going to walk in there with your shoulders back and your head held high. Because you're Mia Rubie, and it's time you started acting like it. Of course, you could also tuck tail and run, but I think you've done enough of that in this lifetime, don't you?'

Mia met her godfather's glare with a more intense one of her own. 'I would hardly call what I decided to do with my life fifteen years ago tucking tail and running, and I can't believe you of all people would—'

'But in all honesty,' he cut in, his tone softening, 'I don't think that's what you want. And I know it's not what your father would've wanted either, Mia.'

'If we're being honest, it doesn't matter what I want.' Apparently, as far as her dad was concerned, it never had.

Barb grabbed Mia's hand. 'I know you're upset, but sometimes, you have to push through and do what you don't want to do. This is one of those times.'

Mia sucked in what felt like all of the air in the vehicle and contemplated holding that breath forever, or at least until she blacked out. Unsure of how long that would take, she finally exhaled. 'Fine.'

The crowd parted as Cliff guided her straight to a fully stocked bar.

Within seconds, a shot appeared in front of her. 'Seriously?'

'Drink it,' Cliff said.

Mia pursed her lips and shook her head. 'Nope.'

'Mia, this is going to be a very long night if you don't

settle down and relax. I don't think you can manage it on your own. Take the shot.'

When Barb nodded her encouragement, Mia grabbed the glass and downed what turned out to be whiskey in a single gulp, enjoying the scorched path it left down her chest more than she expected. As soon as she set the shot glass on the bar, Cliff motioned for the bartender to fill it again. This time, instead of arguing, Mia welcomed the burning sensation. When her empty shot glass was replaced with a healthy pour of red wine the next round, she was almost disappointed.

'We circle the room once, make polite small talk.' Cliff handed her the wine. 'Deal? No one expects more, I promise.'

Considering that the Rubie Racing complex was as large as three football fields, and the party was in full swing in the expansive space where her father's private car collection was on permanent display, one round could easily take an hour.

To her relief, most of the guests were too busy stuffing themselves with smoked salmon canapés, bacon-wrapped scallops, caviar, and a perennial Rubie family favorite – miniature hot dogs wrapped in crescent dough – while sipping vintage champagne to commemorate her dad winning the Monaco Grand Prix in 1979, to offer Mia more than a quick hug or hello. It was hard to believe these same people were just at a funeral. The heavy, dark cloud of sorrow from the last few days had been lifted; the tears and long faces replaced with alcohol-fueled laughter and joy. But then Rob Rubie always could throw one hell of a party. The fact that his favorite catering company had pulled off his elaborate plan in a few short days was nothing short of a miracle. He'd somehow managed to go out one-upping everyone he'd ever known.

And then, of course, there were the cars. Even Mia couldn't help but gawk at her dad's collection, and she'd grown up climbing in and out of them — mostly when she thought no one was looking. Vintage and collector models and race cars made up the majority of the thirty on display, with a few random cars special to the Rubie family for one reason or another thrown in. Showcased together, they were awe-inspiring to even casual observers. And there weren't many of those in this crowd.

She felt less like the elephant in the room than she anticipated, but then this was largely the aristocracy of racing, for whom discretion and subtlety were second nature. It also helped that they were well on their way to being more than slightly inebriated.

When Cliff finally released her from her duties, Mia strolled through the cars, a second glass of wine in hand.

And that's when it hit her.

As owner of Rubie Racing, every single one of these cars belonged to her — from the 1926 Ford Model T Speedster to the DeLorean her dad had bought the summer she was more than slightly obsessed with *Back to the Future*. Although she suspected Jordan would fight her for the 1969 Chevy Corvette L88, his boyhood favorite, and the R25, his race car from his winningest year.

Also hers were the team's current race cars, which were

tucked away in garages elsewhere on the complex, far from curious eyes. The ones being readied to zoom around racetracks around the world in two short months and hopefully bring a long sought-after world championship home to the Motor City for the first time.

What in the hell could her dad have been thinking?

Of course, if he had told her flat out that he wanted her back in the Rubie Racing fold, she would've said no. Her career was important to her, and she was good at it. So what if marketing wasn't as exciting as cars traveling at breakneck speed? A life lived far from the edge had almost the same view and, as a bonus, no one got hurt.

Except, apparently, her dad had been harboring a secret agenda that ended up cutting off his daughter's nose and spiting his son's face.

These realizations had her searching for a place to inconspicuously sit down and tuck her head between her knees or, at the very least, a paper bag to blow into for the next twelve hours.

Instead, Mia resorted to draining her glass in front of a cherry red 1967 Porsche 911 Coupe while thinking about the first time she'd sat behind its wheel with her dad riding shotgun. Within seconds, the empty glass was lifted from her hand and replaced with a full one. She turned to thank her donor, only to find herself breathing the same air as Luca. Feeling heat race to her cheeks, likely turning them nearly the same shade as the car, she whipped back around after a quick thank you. It was the wine and the whiskey, she reassured herself, and took a long, steadying sip before looking his way again.

'I learned to drive in this car. I was twelve, and we were on vacation in northern Michigan during summer break. I wouldn't stop pestering Dad, and he finally took me to the parking lot of a grocery store after hours and let me have a go.'

Luca looked from the car to her, then back to the car again before deadpanning, 'You must mean one like it. Having an adolescent student driver behind the wheel would surely eliminate any automobile from future collecting.'

'Ha, ha.' Mia took another long sip of wine and allowed herself to take him in. Gone were the boyish looks she remembered so well, although his wavy brown hair still appeared finger combed. ('I've never owned a brush' took the prize for the oddest brag she'd ever heard.) Her own fingers flexed at the memory of running through his silky locks, and they fought an urge to do it again.

Overall, the past fifteen years had been more than kind to him because, of course they had. He'd always been slim, but like most drivers, it was all muscle from training strategically. The cut of his black suit was similar to Jordan's, but Luca pulled it off in a way that only a European man could – even one who no longer lived on the Continent. She raised her glass to her lips as she contemplated how this could be, only to realize that her eyes were lingering along with her thoughts.

For Pete's sake, stop ogling your ex at your father's funeral party.

Her gaze jerked up at the sound of him lightly clearing his

throat. 'So, what you're telling me is that your father was obviously out of his mind.'

Mia nodded. 'That was most definitely confirmed today, wouldn't you say?'

His eyes crinkled as he smiled. 'I meant because he let a twelve-year-old behind the wheel of a classic Porsche.'

'I'll have you know I mastered the clutch in ten seconds, which has to be some sort of record for a tween.' She paused to sip her wine. 'I was referring to the bombshell he dropped at his funeral. We both know I have no business in this business.'

He lifted a single shoulder in a shrug – a classic Luca move. 'Your father was no crazier than any other person in this room.'

'Well, that's not saying much.'

To prove her point, she glanced around the space, her hand following her eyes like a game show hostess, only to discover that the pair of them were attracting quite a bit of attention. Barb smiled and waved from where she stood next to Cliff.

Thankfully, a chair was ceremoniously plunked down in the middle of the room, and a former world champion climbed atop it and dinged his crystal champagne flute with a spoon. A hush fell over the room as he began sharing one of Mia's favorite stories, about how her father had managed to convince every driver to drop his name to a certain supermodel who, as the face of an Apex sponsor, was following the circuit that season. But they talked him up so much that when he finally spoke to her himself after the third race of the season, which he lost by a hair, she said with a pout, 'You're the great Rob Rubie? Not sure I see it based on today's performance, but buy me a bottle of champagne anyway.'

People laughed, and toasted, and laughed some more, and they didn't even know about her father's sweet tradition of treating his wife to the same pricey bottle every year on the anniversary of that night, even after she was no longer able to join him.

A line of sorts began forming for a turn at story time. They were in for a long evening; this was not a bashful group. Mia found herself looking for the nearest escape route.

As if he could read her mind, Luca swapped their empty wineglasses for champagne from a passing tray and whispered, 'Come with me. There's something I want you to see.'

Her desire to leave the spotlight trumped any hesitation about being alone with Luca. Add in the alcohol and he may as well have been the Pied Piper, given how readily she trailed after him. When they reached a door about fifty feet away, Luca handed her both champagne flutes before producing a security badge from his pocket and swiping it in front of a scan pad. After opening the door and allowing her to pass, he double checked that it had closed before heading on.

'Paranoid much?'

'I learned from the best.' He laughed as he passed by her to lead the way. 'Your dad was constantly updating security around here. Always seemed like overkill until the day we found a blogger sniffing around, taking photos of the new rear wing we were developing with his watch.'

'Wait, what? How'd he get into the building? What did my dad do to him?'

Luca shrugged. 'Never heard, but I assume he lived. Imagine he needed a new watch, though.'

The darkened corridors lit up as they walked deeper into the complex. The party noise faded away, leaving Mia with only her thoughts and the sound of their echoing footsteps. When was she last at the complex? Ten years ago? Definitely before she moved to Chicago and officially left Rubie Racing behind. Invitations to Christmas parties and end-of-season celebrations had arrived each year like clockwork and gone straight into the recycling bin. That hadn't stopped her father from continuing to send them. He was as determined as she was stubborn, and vice versa. It was amazing that they'd managed to have any sort of father–daughter relationship at all.

Granted, that had taken some time, once she'd taken away the one thing they'd always had in common. But eventually, they'd found other things to talk about – for a good while, at least. Until that horrible season when her dad had been especially down, and Mia hadn't been able to bring herself to change the subject when he'd called her to dissect what could be behind their losing streak. She had only started watching races again so she could hold up her end of those conversations. Now she couldn't help but think that it had all been part of some master plan for her to take over Rubie Racing.

Mia emerged from her thoughts just as she crashed into

Luca, who'd stopped at another scan pad. Although she managed to slow her momentum enough to cause only a minor accident, the champagne sloshed in the glasses she was carrying. Before their eyes, a single drop splashed to the floor.

'Uh oh, you're in for it now. If you're looking for Rob to come back and haunt you, the best way is to dirty his floor.' He turned and touched her wrist. 'I'm sorry. That was incredibly insensitive.'

'It's all right.' Her gaze dropped to his fingers, which slipped just beneath her sleeve and came to rest on her suddenly rapid pulse – the slight contact having apparently sent a ripple of awareness straight to her heart. She felt something besides numbness for the first time in days, along with a pang of guilt for enjoying it, considering she'd sobbed a final goodbye to the lid of a casket mere hours ago. 'And I should be so lucky.'

Her focus didn't leave Luca's backside for the rest of their journey, which didn't help slow her heartbeat, but did keep her from running into him when he stopped again.

'To be honest, until the break-in, I couldn't figure out if your father was extremely paranoid or protective,' he said, swiping his badge then holding the door open with his hip.

She handed him his glass as she walked into the darkened room. 'Knowing my dad, it was probably a little of both. But I guess he had a right to be.'

'Yes, I'd say so,' Luca murmured, and let the door close behind him.

Chapter 4

Luca wanted to see Mia's face when the lights went on over the new cars for the season – to see if she would light up like she once did. His hope was that whatever he saw written across there would tell him if her passion for the sport still ran deep, how she would lead the team, and whether he needed to go elsewhere to finally win the grand prize of racing.

Those were among the myriad thoughts swirling around in his mind since he'd learned, alongside everyone else at the funeral, that Mia would be his new boss. He hadn't allowed his mind to wander in her direction for years – the ability to compartmentalize inconvenient thoughts and feelings was a gift most race car drivers shared. Not that her absence on the circuit had gone unnoticed, especially those first few seasons after they'd broken up. But now she was back, and he had questions that needed answering. And soon.

At thirty-five, he was close to aging out of auto racing. Each passing season, there were fewer drivers from his generation and more younger drivers nipping at their heels. If the last few days had shown him anything, it was that life was precarious on and off the racetrack.

Luca certainly didn't envy Mia – he wouldn't have wanted to follow in Rob's footsteps. The man had achieved legendary status even before he died. Rob had been more involved than any owner Luca had driven for during his career. His mind ticked off those names, four in the thirteen years since he'd landed his first 'ride,' one of the two coveted driver spots on any Apex team. Most of those owners had only been there for the highs and lows, leaving it up to their team principals to call the shots on a daily basis. But then teams were increasingly owned by conglomerates and shareholders. Rob had occupied both the owner and team principal roles and had been in the trenches every day, working alongside the team manager and listening to his drivers, mechanics, and engineers. He'd known the business of every person in his organization, yet respected their talents and abilities enough to stay out of their way and let them do their job. It was a rare gift.

Yes, Rob had been one of a kind, a smart driver who had become an even smarter team principal. Luca couldn't think of a single person in the racing industry who hadn't had the utmost respect for Rob. When word had gotten out that Luca was leaving his last team for Rubie Racing, his former team principal had shrugged and said, 'I can't say I blame you.' That guy was among the throng of people from around the world eating, drinking, and toasting Rob's memory on the other side of the building.

Luca flipped on the light, and, to his relief, Mia gasped when she saw Rubie Racing's latest prototype – the R29 – come to life.

His and Jordan's cars dominated the immense space, which was bright white from floor to ceiling and cleaner than most operating rooms. Each car was allotted its own area, and offices for the engineering teams and mechanics lined the perimeter.

'Are we allowed to be in here?' Mia asked.

He leveled her with a look of disbelief. 'I don't know. Maybe we should ask the owner of Rubie Racing.'

Luca took her following him over to his car as a sign of approval.

Like every Apex car, it was low and lean; a sleek body flanked by four wide, smooth tires. The cockpit was nestled mid-car, and the bucket seat fit him like a glove, literally, since his body cast had been used to design it. But the front of the car was the *pièce de résistance*. Their engineers had toiled for months to create a more aerodynamic nose that still played by the series' governing body's rules.

'Oh, it's beautiful. Not that how a car looks has anything to do with how fast it can go, but being easy on the eyes certainly doesn't hurt, does it?' She turned toward him and raised an eyebrow, followed with her champagne flute up toward the ceiling. 'Dad, you did good.'

Luca raised his as well, then reached over and clinked his glass to hers. After they both took a long sip of champagne, he cleared his throat. 'Every season's car is a team effort, but your father was especially a driving force behind the R29. And he truly believed that we'd struck the right formula with this one, that this car would take us all the way.'

He took a deep breath and another sip of champagne to ease his nerves. Luca Toscano didn't get nervous, he reminded himself before continuing, 'But I've been thinking these past few days, and propose that we consider changing the name, starting a new tradition, a new era for Rubie Racing. What do you think about calling this year's car the RR1, in honor of your dad?'

'I think that would be very nice, Luca. Thank you.' Mia beamed at him and blinked away the few tears pooling in her eyes before walking around the car slowly, dragging her fingers lightly along the bright orange paint that matched Rubie Racing's largest sponsor. The color was a stark change from the silver, black, and blue cars he was accustomed to, but given that an Apex team needed many millions in sponsorship dollars a season to stay competitive, he'd warmed to driving an orange car.

'Interesting color choice,' she said.

'Shh, not too loud. You don't want to upset the turbo pumpkin.'

'An even more interesting nickname. I'll be sure to keep its location secret from a certain princess and her fairy godmother.' She chuckled at her own joke, just like Rob would have, then continued her tour, the clicking of her heels on the concrete floor silencing every few steps as she paused to examine one thing or another. First, it was the front wing, integral to controlling the airflow around the car; then the open wheels, which along with the engine made Apex race cars the fastest of the fast; and then the halo, the latest requirement the sport's governing body had added to protect drivers from flying crash debris. The decreased likelihood of having random car parts smash into his head far outweighed his personal dislike for how the halo looked.

As Mia studied his car, Luca couldn't take his eyes off her. She still bit her lower lip when she was deep in thought, like now, as she leaned into the cockpit. And she still mindlessly tucked her hair behind her right ear, only to have it fall back in her face seconds later. A sudden need to tuck that hair behind her ear again cropped up like an itch he couldn't scratch – or rather, shouldn't even think about scratching.

When she completed a full circle around his car, she came to stand next to him again at the nose. 'Thank you, Luca,' she said softly, turning toward him.

'You're welcome. Like I said, your father poured his heart and soul into this car. It's now yours, along with his hopes and dreams. And mine, of course.'

Especially mine.

'Wow, that's no pressure at all.'

Mia's gaze dropped to the floor, and Luca followed it to find her once again brushing away tears. He couldn't seem to stop himself from grabbing her hand and pulling her close. When she leaned into him, his arms wrapped around her as if they were on autopilot.

'I'm so sorry, Mia. I'm sure the last thing you need today is... any of this, really.'

Himself included, surely. Not that a single cell in his body was willing to break the hug. When it came to Mia, he'd always felt powerless.

To his surprise, her arms went around his waist as she rested her head against his chest. 'It's all too much,' she said. 'Being at my dad's house without him being there. The funeral, his letter, my brother, who is conspicuously absent from this damn afterlife party, in case you hadn't noticed. Honestly, I don't know whether to scream or cry.'

'Try both and then go with what feels best. Isn't that the Mia Rubie way?'

She laughed into his chest. 'I hate to break it to you, but that Mia Rubie doesn't exist anymore.'

Before he could ask what she meant by that, the door opened, and Cliff, security badge in hand, popped his head in. A petite woman with dark curly hair pushed past him into the garage.

'Whoa, fancy car,' she whistled. 'Too bad it's missing a roof.'

Mia shrieked and leapt out of his arms and toward her. 'Star! What are you doing here?'

'Well, my best friend's dad died, and I thought she might need some emotional support. Long story short, I caught the first flight out after the very important meeting I couldn't miss earlier because my co-presenter's dad died.' Although Star was talking to Mia, her eyes were fixed on Luca. 'I've been racing around town since I landed, trying to find you. Pun intended. Obviously.'

Within seconds of hugging her friend, Mia was all out sobbing. The sight was almost too much for Luca to bear.

'I see you've met Cliff,' Mia said when she'd calmed herself down. 'And this is Luca Toscano, one of the drivers for Rubie Racing. Luca, meet Estrella Martinez, my best friend in the whole world.'

That shouldn't have stung, but it did. At one point, the best friend title had belonged to him – now, apparently, he was just 'one of the drivers.' Luca extended a hand, which she accepted. 'It's nice to meet you, Estrella.'

'Oh, you can call me Star. Any friend of Mia's is a friend of mine, and you appear to be a very good friend who, surprisingly, I wasn't aware of.' She winked, then turned to Mia, who shifted uncomfortably next to her when she lowered her voice and said, 'This isn't a guy you kick out of bed for eating crackers.'

Cliff cleared his throat. 'Shall we rejoin the party, or are you done, Mia? I may have dragged you in here, but you can leave of your volition. Our driver is out front, at the ready, whenever you'd like to make your escape.'

Mia nodded at her godfather. 'That would be right now, Cliff. I hope you can navigate this maze of a building and find the back door. I'm feeling a little drunk and a lot emotional, and I'd like to avoid any further niceties today.'

She wasn't joking, Luca realized, as she walked out the door with Cliff and Star in tow, without even a backward glance at him or his turbo pumpkin.

*

Judging by the swaying of the man who now stood atop the chair, Luca guessed he'd missed more than a few toasts to the dearly departed while he was off touring Mia around the property. He was debating whether to attempt to catch up with his fellow 'mourners' or make his own hasty departure when a glass of champagne found its way into his hand.

'I must admit, I would much rather be spraying you with this, but maybe in a couple of months, yes?' The giver raised his glass. '*À votre santé.*'

Only a cocky bastard like Henri Aveline would toast to health at a funeral. Luca raised his glass to match the Frenchman's before him and instead said, 'To Rob.'

Laughter erupted around them, and Luca was thankful for a reason to turn his attention to the speaker, whose own laughter was increasing his swaying.

'But of course, to Rob. So shocking.' Henri took another sip of his champagne, then made a point of studying the golden bubbly. 'This is quite good. Such a nice surprise. But then the French vintages truly are the best.'

With a sigh, Luca returned his attention to the last person he felt like making small talk with, regardless of the situation. Why hadn't he dashed out the back door with Mia and her entourage when he had the chance? Oh, that's right. He hadn't been invited to their exit party.

'The timing couldn't be worse, I'm afraid,' Henri said.

That's fairly obvious. Luca grinned. 'I'm sure we'll muddle through all the same.'

Henri returned Luca's smile, as if the two of them shared

an inside joke instead of a twenty-five-year rivalry. He could hardly remember a time when the two weren't competing for something. The top spot on the podium. A ride. Once or twice, a girl.

'Mia is looking well,' Henri said in that nonchalant way he thought he'd mastered. 'Do you know if she's seeing anyone?'

Although Luca had wondered the same thing himself, he glared at Henri. 'No idea, *mon ami*. Given that she just lost her father, I'm also not sure if this is the appropriate time for that question or whatever it is you're insinuating.'

The hand that landed on his shoulder was a welcome weight even before he realized whose arm it belonged to.

'Ah, Monsieur Thomas,' Henri said, clinking glasses with the man most likely to be voted Mr Congeniality in Apex's tidy boys club.

Although the Welshman shot Luca a knowing look, Wyn gave his standard, 'What's occurrin'?'

'Oh, you know,' Luca said, then took a slow sip from his glass.

Wyn nodded.

The three of them stood in an awkward silence until Henri excused himself and wandered away. It was a scene they had repeated hundreds of times since they were mere ten-year-olds racing souped up go-karts at the beginning of their careers.

'Is it just me or has he somehow managed to become more arrogant since winning the world championship?' Luca asked.

'It's just you, mate,' Wyn said. 'You've always let him get under your skin.'

Luca decided to change the subject rather than admit, once again, that Wyn was right. 'Nice kilt. Rob would be honored.'

Wyn only broke out his Welsh kilt for special occasions, like his wedding. As a groomsman, Luca had even donned one that day. It had been a breezy afternoon in the Welsh countryside, to say the least.

'Only the best for Mr Rubie.' Wyn looked in the direction Henri had headed. 'Seriously though, are you OK?'

'The jury's still out, to be perfectly honest. It's a lot to digest.' Luca wasn't one to bare his soul to just anyone, but Wyn was more like a brother than a friend. 'When did you arrive? You should've called. You could've stayed at my place.'

'This morning, I did, and I am,' he laughed. 'I tried to flag you down earlier, but your attention was, shall we say, elsewhere. And then you seemed to be as well. Must've made for an interesting reunion.'

Luca knew Wyn's curiosity about Mia, unlike Henri's, was genuine. But he also couldn't ignore what the two men did have in common: They drove for competing teams of Rubie Racing. Plus, Mia wasn't just a woman he'd once loved, a fact known to only a small handful of people, including Wyn. She would now sign his paychecks.

He chose his words with care. 'You could say that. Went fine though, all things considered. Apparently, she learned the news about her new role when we all did. Seems a bit shell-shocked. Can't say I blame her.'

'Do me a favor and tread carefully, mate.' Wyn's simple cock of an eyebrow said that he remembered that long ago day when twenty-year-old Luca had appeared on his doorstep, brokenhearted and without a ride or a team. 'Besides, you have no reason to go around repeating past mistakes. Not when you have one of the most beautiful women in the world at your disposal. Where is Julia, anyway?'

Luca shrugged a shoulder at the mention of the woman he'd dated last season. Julia Sullivan was the last person he wanted to think about today, or any day, for that matter. He placed his now-empty champagne flute on a passing tray, then headed to the bar to grab something stronger. Much stronger.

Chapter 5

Although Barb showed her to the guest room, a drunken Star decided bunking with Mia would be more fun. Only instead of falling right to sleep, she peppered Mia with a million questions about Luca.

Star yawned. 'Out with it, *mija*.'

The Spanish term of endearment for 'my daughter' had always warmed Mia, even if Star was only a few years older.

'Out with what?' Mia asked, as if she didn't know full well how futile playing dumb was. The woman possessed a superpower when it came to getting people to talk.

'The hot race car driver. Spill. And don't even think about skimping on the details.'

The truth was, Mia didn't know where to start, besides at the beginning. 'My dad recruited Luca as a reserve driver when I was sixteen. I was driving then, too, in the entry-level class, and I'd seen him around.'

That was an understatement. It had been love at first sight, at least for her. Even though Luca was older, and drove in the class above hers, she'd watched him from afar, intrigued by his quiet confidence and skill behind the wheel. She'd been over the moon when her dad had decided to add her crush to Rubie Racing. Although she'd prepared herself for him being no different than any of the other cocky guys she'd raced against, Luca had proven her wrong at every turn and, before long, they were spending every possible second together.

'He was my first... *everything*.'

'And yet you've never mentioned him, to me,' Star said, the hurt in her voice impossible to miss.

'It was a long time ago, and things didn't end well. There was an accident at a race.'

At that, Star shot up in bed. 'Oh my God, Mia, were you injured?'

The face of another driver flashed before her eyes. Her head shook, both in answer Star's question and to make the image go away. 'No, I wasn't in the car.'

But it was still my fault. Maybe not technically, but as far as she was concerned, a significant portion of the blame rested on her shoulders. The fact that she hadn't been behind the wheel was an inconsequential detail. Her life had crashed and burned all the same.

Even in the darkened room, Star's smug satisfaction was written all over her face when the past finally did spill out of Mia. How Luca truly had been everything to her – her best friend, as far as her dad and everyone else was concerned, and when no one was around, her boyfriend.

'Why the secrecy?' Star asked. 'Oh, wait. Was he the ugly duckling who turned into the world's hottest swan?'

Mia groaned, shaking her head again in an attempt to erase yet another image – this one of eighteen-year-old Luca. 'No, he was a hot duckling, too. This may come as a surprise, but I was an adrenaline junkie at sixteen. Sneaking around was exciting.' *Exhilarating.* 'Plus, if my dad had known what we were really up to, there's no way he would've let us spend so much time alone.' *In her room, with the door closed.* 'But it was mostly a turn-on, for me at least.'

'You *were* an adrenaline junkie? I hate to break it to you, but you're the most intense person I know. Present company excluded, of course.' The bed shook from Star's laughter. 'But honestly, I still can't believe you managed to keep him under wraps. Your brother had to have been wise at least.'

'Jordan and I have been the definition of sibling rivalry for as long as I can remember. If he'd known I was messing around with Luca, he would've blabbed. And we didn't get away with it. My dad caught us.'

That was one trip down memory lane Mia wouldn't take, no matter how hard Star pressed. Some things were best left in the past, which she realized wouldn't be an issue given the soft and steady breathing coming from the other side of the bed. She often suspected Star had an on-off switch hidden somewhere on her torso, considering how quickly she usually nodded off at night, even without a half bottle of wine in her, and then sprang to life the next morning.

Mia's own eyes soon began to close. She drifted off to

sleep, reminding herself that she didn't spend all those years getting over Luca to fall back in love with him the first time she saw him again. Even if he was still a sight to behold.

When Mia woke up what seemed like only a few hours later, it was to a pounding headache. She massaged her temples, trying to assess whether it was from days of crying, the copious amounts of alcohol she'd mixed at her father's afterlife party, or the red wine nightcap she and Star had shared with Barb.

Of course, there was also that tiny matter of her life suddenly veering off the rails.

An image of her dad lying in his casket in full racing regalia flashed before her eyes, and tears burned the back of her eyelids. She pulled the covers over her head and begged her brain to focus on something else, anything else.

It chose Luca.

Traitor.

She blamed Star for asking so many questions about Luca before they fell asleep. Otherwise, Mia's brain would be free and clear of the man. But Star had refused to believe that seeing Luca again hadn't surfaced long-buried feelings, considering, as she'd put it, 'I'm stirred up, and I only shook the guy's hand.'

'He was comforting me,' Mia had said, attempting to convince her best friend as much as herself. Because everything about that hug had taken her by surprise, but most of all, how the past fifteen years had melted away once Luca's arms had wrapped around her.

Flipping onto her stomach, Mia buried her head under a pillow and kicked her feet like a toddler throwing a tantrum.

'Stop. I don't know what you're doing, but stop it right this second.'

Mia looked across the king-sized bed to discover her best friend clinging to the far edge of the mattress.

'Sorry, I forgot you were here,' Mia said.

'I hope you don't say that to all your overnight guests.' Star caught the pillow Mia tossed at her, then slid up and placed it between her back and the wrought iron headboard.

Even if her head hadn't felt like it was filled with cotton, Mia would've had a hard time wrapping her brain around the events of the past week. Her dad had died, she'd been reunited with the only man she'd ever given her heart to, and she was suddenly being thrown back into a life she'd long-ago left behind.

'I apparently now own a racing team. "I" as in "me." How messed up is that?'

'What's the big deal?' Star asked. 'You're a master delegator. Put someone in charge and show up when you need to. You know, like when the weather's bad in Chicago. That gives you a good nine months of the year to work with.'

'Excellent guess there – the season is almost exactly that long but, unfortunately, includes those prime months when you finally get to ditch your winter coat and hang out at beer gardens and baseball games.' Mia sighed. 'Only Rubies aren't supposed to phone things in. To quote my father, "You're either in it to win it or you stay the hell out of the way."'

'So much about you is becoming clearer,' Star said. 'I mean, wow. I heard you say those exact words to an intern once.'

Given that the intern in question had steered clear of Mia for the entire summer, maybe the apple hadn't fallen too far from the tree. Not to mention, her dad had eaten, slept, and breathed Rubie Racing, and Mia also did those things in an unhealthy manner. Star knew this better than anyone, since the two of them worked side by side, often logging ten- to twelve-hour days launching brands around the world. Mia certainly hadn't been named the youngest senior marketing strategist in company history because of her insistence on work-life balance.

'Mia, your dad knew you had your own life. There's no way he expected you to drop everything.'

The mere thought of dropping *anything* was enough to make Mia break out in hives. It wasn't exactly the ideal time for an unscheduled detour from her career. She and Star had recently been assigned the project of their dreams – a global campaign for one of the firm's biggest tech clients. Although her boss had said and done all of the right things when she'd bolted out of town after her dad's heart attack, even tacking on a few days to the company's standard bereavement leave as a courtesy, Sarah expected her back at it sooner than later.

Of course, the timing hadn't been great for her dad's exit either. He'd have another heart attack if he knew he'd died just before the season he'd been counting on to be the penultimate of his Apex career was set to begin.

'OK, for the sake of argument, let's walk through what

this might involve,' Star said. 'I mean, the only race cars I've seen were nothing like what I saw last night. That thing was sex on wheels.'

Mia laughed. 'Looks like we're starting from scratch.'

The crash course she gave Star about all things racing would've made her father proud. How Apex was short for the World Apex Grand Prix Motorsport Series and the most elite of all the racing classes. How its cars compared to the ones Americans were most used to seeing – stock cars with roofs (much slower) and smaller versions of Apex cars (still not as fast). Both of those series stuck mostly to tracks in North America, unlike the Apex circuit, which spanned the globe. Teams like Rubie Racing earned points based on how well their two drivers finished each race, and the drivers accumulated their own points, too. At the end of each season, separate championships were awarded to both the driver and the team with the most points.

'My dad was never world champion, although he came close one year,' Mia said. 'So close, he could taste it. When he retired, he vowed to bring a world championship to Rubie Racing, either through a driver or the team.'

'And?'

'I guess you could say he died trying.'

'And now it's up to you to fulfill your father's dying wish? That's heavy stuff, *mija*.'

Besides Star, who'd met her father during one of his visits, no one else in the Windy City had a clue that teenage Mia had been a race car driver or that her family was basically racing royalty. They'd known each other for a while before Mia had divulged that information, and only during a drunken game of 'truth or truth.' Looking back, she was almost positive her friend had invented the game on the spot to stealthily learn Mia's secrets after seeing her condo. That gift from her dad was not the typical abode of a first-time homeowner.

Her former life had been surprisingly easy to leave behind. Auto racing wasn't something that came up in casual conversation. The only races her co-workers talked about incessantly were the ones they ran, like marathons and 5Ks. For the record, people who thought race car folks were obsessed had never endured the nonstop chatter of someone training to run a twenty-six-point-two-mile race they didn't have a chance in hell of winning.

'I honestly can't believe you once cared so much about racing. You never wanted to talk about it. Actually, you couldn't change the subject fast enough.'

'It's not who I am,' Mia said. 'Not anymore, at least.'

Disappointment washed over Star's face. 'Oh, you weren't any good.'

'The hell I wasn't,' Mia said, as surprised as Star at the defensive tone in her voice. 'That's not why I left.'

'So, why did you? Why would someone who's apparently amazing at every single thing she does walk away?'

'The person I became behind the wheel wasn't who I wanted to be.' That was an understatement. She'd been a teenage hellcat with an angelic grin and personality traits she'd worked hard to leave in the past and wasn't eager to revisit. 'Trust me, if you think I'm intense now, you definitely wouldn't have liked race car driver Mia. At least not as much as this Mia.'

'I doubt that,' Star said. 'Plus, Luca seemed to like both versions.'

She would bring him up again; the woman lived to poke the bear. As her friend pressed on, Mia learned firsthand why the last place people ever wanted to be was in Star's crosshairs.

'Is Luca the reason you're so set against this? Because if he is, I don't think that's a good enough reason.'

'There's way more to it than Luca.' Although he and his smoldering hazel eyes were reason enough, as far as she was concerned. Running what was essentially an empire took experience and passion, and at this point, she didn't have either for Rubie Racing. 'You know what? It doesn't matter. The more I think about it, I can't imagine anyone expects my level of involvement to match my dad's. I honestly don't think that's even possible.'

Mia glanced at the clock on her nightstand and frowned. They'd been talking for more than an hour, and Star would need to leave soon to catch her flight. A sudden wave of melancholy washed over her at the thought of saying goodbye.

'Why don't you switch your flight? Cliff's stopping by to go over the will in a bit, but after that we can hang out.'

With a shake of her head, Star bounded out of bed with a newfound energy she always seemed to have on reserve.

'No can do. One of us has a job to get back to — and a sinking feeling that her partner in crime is about to pull a serious disappearing act.'

Cliff had asked to meet with Jordan and Mia at noon. Once Mia loaded Star into a cab, she had exactly one hour to shower and muster some enthusiasm, any enthusiasm, for what her godfather would reveal beyond yesterday's bombshell letter that had her bouncing around the grief scale.

The steaming mug of coffee Mia found waiting on her dresser post-shower helped, although a few sips increased the rumbling in her stomach. She threw on the yoga pants and sweatshirt she'd left Chicago in — which she'd found washed and neatly folded on her bed the next day — and headed downstairs to the kitchen to discover her godfather pouring himself a cup of coffee. Mia thrust out her own mug for a refill.

'And how are we feeling today, young lady?' Cliff asked. He pulled out a chair for her at the island before taking the next seat and helping himself to a generous scoop of one of Barb's famous breakfast casseroles.

Her stomach rumbled at the sight of the mixture of hash browns, cheddar cheese, eggs, and bacon, and she grabbed a plate and followed his lead.

'I've been better, but if my memory serves me correctly, this will help.' She inhaled a few bites, then washed it down with coffee. 'Please remind me to never drink again.'

'Only if you make the same promise to me.' Cliff laughed. 'I can't imagine anyone is feeling great this morning.'

As if on cue, Barb walked in looking worse for wear as well. 'I will say, your friend Star seemed completely unaffected. Hair of the dog?'

'One would think so, but no. She's apparently immune from hangovers and always has been.' Mia stopped Barb for a hug as she walked by. 'Thank you for doing my laundry. That wasn't necessary. Taking care of me isn't exactly part of your job description.'

'Well, I don't exactly have a job description anymore,' Barb said, her voice breaking. 'My job was to make sure this was always a home for your dad. I keep thinking he's only out on the circuit and will be back soon, grumbling about one thing or another.'

In her whirlwind of grief, Mia hadn't stopped to consider how her dad's death had impacted Barb, who'd been managing the estate for so long that she'd become a permanent fixture of not only the house but also the Rubie family. 'That's ridiculous! You were more than just a glorified housekeeper to him, and everyone knew it.'

Although the implication wasn't clear to Mia until after it had left her mouth, Barb stilled. Her gaze darted from Cliff to Mia as her hands went to her hips.

'Your father and I may have shared a house, but we were strictly employer and employee. Roommates, if you will, perhaps siblings at worst.'

'Who's like siblings?' Jordan asked as he walked in.

Mia snorted. 'Not us.'

Jordan rolled his eyes at his sister, then shook his head

when Barb offered him a plate. 'If you don't mind, I'd rather get this show on the road,' he said.

Cliff piped in, 'Don't mind at all. Just let us finish eating, and we'll move to your dad's study.'

Her godfather shifted his attention back to his casserole and began shoveling in forkfuls at a snail's pace. Mia, too, focused on her meal, but more on chewing, swallowing, and praying it would stay down. After a few seconds, Jordan left the room in a huff.

Cliff gave Mia a wink. 'Take your time.'

Fifteen minutes later, the three of them walked into the study to find Jordan sitting behind their dad's desk, so lost in thought that his mask had slipped. But when Cliff cleared his throat and dropped a file folder on the desktop, the mask shifted back into place, bitterness overtaking sorrow as easily as paper covers rock.

'I think it would be easier if I sat there, buddy,' he said softly.

As Mia and Barb settled into the armchairs flanking the fireplace, Jordan moved across the room to the leather lounger. He immediately propped his feet up on the matching footstool in a sad attempt at looking relaxed.

Cliff opened the file folder to reveal a thick stack of papers stapled together and a handful of envelopes. 'Now then. As we all know, Rob was, in a word, organized. Intense. Strategic. Wait, that's three words.' He chuckled at his own joke as he retrieved his reading glasses from his shirt pocket. 'He approached his will with the same determination he did every race, reviewing it every year, tweaking it when he—'

'When was the last time there was tweaking?' Jordan interrupted. The intent of his question wasn't lost on anyone, but he added, 'To things like, I don't know, team ownership.'

'Fairly recently,' Cliff said, taking the document in hand and moving on as if he'd given Jordan the answer he was seeking. 'For the record, I told him that families no longer read wills aloud, except in the movies, but he insisted that I gather the three of you together and do it this way anyway.'

With that, Cliff began reading. Jordan actually muttered 'What the hell?' when he learned all that Mia was inheriting along with Rubie Racing: Essentially, anything and everything to do with the team's operation, including the complex and its contents, the private planes for the team and cars, and Rubie Racing's hefty bank account. In addition, she'd also receive about forty percent of her father's personal wealth.

Jordan was also unable to stay silent when Cliff revealed that Barb would get the Rubie family estate and a substantial reserve fund for its upkeep and taxes. As if her brother didn't have as much affection for the woman as Mia, or a house of his own. A nice one – or so Mia had heard. She'd never darkened Jordan's doorway. Family gatherings and holidays had always taken place at their dad's, and Mia had never had a reason, or an invitation, to visit her brother's home.

Barb shifted in her chair, her hands wringing again. 'Well, I certainly don't feel right about this,' she said.

'I think it's exactly right,' Mia said, purposely meeting Jordan's eye before catching Barb's. 'This house is a home because of you and, at this point, it's more your home than anyone else's.'

Jordan also wasn't pleased to learn he'd left Cliff the lodge and eighty-five acres of virgin white pines in Michigan's Upper Peninsula. Dad and Cliff had spent many a summer break there, on Lake Superior's shore.

'That certainly doesn't sound ethical to me,' Jordan said. 'Isn't there some conflict of interest rule against attorneys taking gifts from their clients?'

Cliff shut that right down. 'Actually, your dad had another attorney countersign his will to avoid any appearance of impropriety.'

A couple of charities were next. No one was surprised that the breast cancer foundation for which their dad had served as a board member since the disease took his wife would receive a significant chunk of change, as well as a foundation that provided scholarships to children of race car drivers injured or killed on the track.

The room held its breath when Cliff finally read, 'Lastly, to my son, Jordan.'

Jordan stood up and moved closer to the desk, his unconvincing relaxation performance over. 'This should be good. There isn't anything left.'

Mia couldn't help but roll her eyes. That wasn't the least bit true. Although what remained was likely not nearly what her brother felt he deserved.

But what Rob Rubie thought his son deserved was this: Nothing, for as long as Jordan kept his place on the Rubie Racing team, except for the salary and bonus structure specified in his contract for either he, Luca, or the team winning a world championship. Should he choose to resign from Rubie Racing, he would receive the remainder of his father's personal wealth – slightly less than half by Mia's estimates. But only then would those millions find their way into Jordan's pockets.

No one in the room dared to look at Jordan.

Once Cliff placed the document back in the file folder, he took out three of the envelopes and lined them up on the desk. 'Rob also asked me to give you these letters. You're under no obligation to read yours here, or to share the contents. I have no idea what's in any of them. As executor of the will, I'll be in touch with each of you to explain the legal process for inheriting your assets. Of course, feel free to call me any time.'

'Oh, I think I'm clear, but thanks, Cliff,' Jordan said, grabbing the envelope with his name on the front and stomping out of the room.

Barb rose to take her envelope and when she left, too, Cliff moved from behind the desk to her empty chair. He handed Mia an envelope before sitting down.

'You OK, kid?'

She shook her head. 'Still shell-shocked, Cliff. Maybe more so now.'

Tears sprang to her eyes when she glanced at the envelope

on her lap and saw her name in her dad's perfect handwriting. He'd always joked that his textbook cursive was about the only thing that would make the nuns at his Catholic grade school proud.

The last time she'd been home, she and her dad had sat in these very spots. It had been Christmas Eve, and the two of them had stayed up late talking. He'd sipped a glass of scotch in front of the fire and asked question after question about her job, her friends, her life. She'd fallen asleep thinking that, for the first time, her dad had actually seen her for who she was. A Christmas miracle. Except maybe not, depending on Cliff's definition of 'fairly recently.'

'Rarely am I on the same wavelength as my brother, but when exactly did Dad change his will to leave the team to me?' Mia asked.

'Just before the new year,' he said.

'Right. And did he happen to say why he decided to upend my life? Why he placed so little value in my choices?'

Cliff shook his head. 'I'm sorry, kid. All he said was that he'd been thinking about it for a while. Remember, for all we knew then, he was as healthy as a horse. He didn't think he'd be gone so soon. No one did. Man, do I miss that guy.' His voice broke and with a deep sigh, his gaze shifted to the letter in her hands. 'But maybe you'll find some answers in there.'

Mia looked again at the envelope and ran her finger over her name, picturing her dad carefully scripting each letter. 'I hope so.'

'I will say this, Mia. Your dad never second-guessed any decision he made – he was truly the most confident guy I ever knew. He put all of this on your shoulders because he was one hundred percent sure you could handle it. And for the record, so do I.'

Chapter 6

'Bloody hell. Is this a puzzle?' Wyn picked up an edge piece from the dining table and held it up to the light like he was inspecting a suspected counterfeit bill. 'Mate, I'd be lying if I said I wasn't concerned.'

Luca had forced his hungover and grumbling friend into running shoes and out the door before either of them were fully awake. He could've gone alone, but he'd needed someone to talk to so he wouldn't dissect every second he'd spent with Mia with each pound of the pavement. Between the biting cold and the wind whipping off the Detroit River, Wyn hadn't been impressed with Luca's adopted hometown. Back in Luca's loft, which occupied an entire floor in what was once a warehouse along the river, his former roommate had moved onto picking apart how Luca had spent his spare time during the off-season.

'*Och*. Is that a mixer?'

After placing a protective hand on the professional stand mixer in the same shade as his turbo pumpkin, Luca shrugged a shoulder. 'I'm the one who should be concerned. First, you're confused by a puzzle piece and now you're questioning what this girl is? Have you truly never seen a mixer before?'

Wyn tossed back the last of his espresso and shoved the tiny cup at Luca for a refill. 'Of course, I have. We got one as a wedding present. It's red. My question is, why do you, a single man who, to my knowledge, has never baked a thing in his entire life, have a mixer? And don't tell me it's because it matches your car, because that's only slightly less disturbing.'

Learning to cook hadn't been on Luca's agenda, but it had become a necessity in a city where he knew few people and had quickly tired of eating alone in restaurants every night – not to mention a waste of a chef's kitchen. He'd gotten into a routine of ending his Saturday morning runs at the farmer's market to stock up for the week. One day, while he was trying to figure out what to do with some of the vegetables, a memory of his grandmother's focaccia had surfaced, and a new obsession had been born.

'For the record, I can bake, and you should consider doing puzzles, too,' Luca said. 'They're a great mental workout, which you could apparently use. Now, do you want breakfast or not?'

When Wyn nodded, Luca got to work on a frittata to use the last of the week's roasted veg while his friend pressed him on whether he thought Mia was qualified to run Rubie Racing.

'I can have a talk with the Carvalhos, if you'd like,' Wyn

said. 'They may be looking to change things up next season. You'd be my number two, but then you always have been the *cachu*.'

Luca laughed along with Wyn, even though they both knew his dream team vision was more a dream than anything else. Wyn was a solid, consistent driver who finished in the top ten most races. The points he earned were valuable, but he rarely stood on the podium platforms. Those coveted three steps went to drivers like himself and, as much as it galled Luca, Henri.

It had been that way since he was a kid racing in figure eights in his kart. He wasn't sure if he would've had the patience to be in the sport for so long if he hadn't dominated. Never winning the world championship was tough, but at least he knew he had a shot.

Maybe that's why the decision to join Rubie Racing again had come so easily. Rob's hunger for the title had not only mirrored his own, but his boss had been confident that winning it all was within Luca's reach. Luca wanted to believe that, regardless of who now led Rubie Racing, it still was.

'I think it would be in poor form to bail on the team now,' Luca said. 'I'll see how things go, for Rob's sake.'

After Wyn left for the airport, Luca spotted a lone freighter slowly making its way down the icy Detroit River and sat in his favorite leather lounge chair, put his feet up, and watched its progress through his loft's massive windows. His thoughts drifted with the waves, thinking of Rob and all of the other people who'd walked in and out of his life. Sometimes, they stayed awhile; oftentimes, they didn't. It was the nature of the business. But none had departed as unexpectedly as Rob.

His eyes closed as his mind replayed their final interaction the night before Rob died.

On his way out of the building, he'd poked his head through the door of Rob's office to find his boss still at his computer, pecking at the keyboard with one finger.

Rob looked up to catch Luca shaking his head and the two laughed, neither having to verbalize their running joke about Rob learning how to type 'one of these days.' Luca swore that watching his boss craft an email one letter at a time was as painful as smashing into a wall at race speed.

Luca stepped inside and shared that his car had been blessed as ready to go for the upcoming season, and Rob got up from his chair and came around to lean against the front of his desk. Rob promised to stop by to see on his way out.

'This is going to be a great year, I can feel it,' he said, pulling Luca in for a hug.

Rob had been a self-professed hugger, which had taken some getting used to. Luca's own father had replaced hugs with handshakes when he was four. Even at the few bedtimes he'd been around for.

But what Rob had said next was what Luca couldn't quite shake. 'I'm proud of you, son.'

Son.

He could still feel the word deep down in his gut.

It was hard to believe that more than two years had passed

since he and Rob sat down for a pint in a small pub in England. After a frustrating race at Silverstone had ended with Luca finishing just off the podium, Rob had approached him on the side and asked for a meeting. Their relationship had grown cordial through the years, which was surprising enough on its own, given their history. But in a million years, he'd never expected Rob to come knocking on his door again, and nothing could've prepared him for the strategy Rob had laid out for the next three years.

Luca hadn't been considering switching teams. He'd been in the middle of negotiating his next contract and had already turned down other, more lucrative offers. But what Rob had offered him sparked his interest in a way that caught even him off guard — a seat at the table. Rob had emphasized that everyone at Rubie Racing, from the mechanics to the engineers to the drivers, were equals. Luca had left that meeting knowing that putting his career back into Rob's hands was his best chance at becoming world champion.

And so he'd gone all in. As soon as the season ended, Luca had shocked the racing world by packing his bags and moving to Detroit. And to his amazement, he'd walked into his loft looking for a place to rent, took in the view of the Detroit River, the exposed brick, high ceilings, and weathered, wide-planked wood floors, and bought it on the spot. Without planning to, he'd become a homeowner and set down roots for the first time in his life at thirty-three. Every nook, cranny, and cabinet had been filled in a single afternoon during a whirlwind shopping trip. The salesperson who'd unexpectedly earned the commission of a lifetime still sent him thank you notes.

Luca looked around his home and sighed. He wasn't ready to leave Detroit or give up on Rob's strategic plan. The car was ready to go. He was ready to go. The only wild card was Mia, and whether she was as determined as he was to carry on her father's legacy and make his dreams come true.

Unfortunately, the person he'd normally talk through this with was also the person whose death had caused the dilemma in the first place. Like a tanker making its way down an icy river in February. Unexpected, then gone in an instant, continuing its journey far out of sight.

Damn death anyway.

Chapter 7

The floral comforter had covered Mia's bed since the summer after she and Jordan turned twelve. The year she'd become a 'woman.'

'You're not a little girl anymore,' her mom had said through tears, and then began redecorating Mia's room with gusto.

Mia had cried, too, but only because becoming a woman proved to be a total pain in the ass when a one-piece racing suit was involved.

Her mom had ordered the pale turquoise bedding from France. When Mia's collection of posters of famous race car drivers had been taken off the wall with a tad too much glee, she'd realized her mother's excitement had nothing to do with the sprouting of breasts. Her mom had hoped her tomboy would magically transform into a 'normal' teenage girl. The kind who was interested in makeup, manicures, and designer clothes. Who carried a handbag instead of a backpack and didn't smell like fuel and exhaust.

It would be impossible to count the number of hours Mia

had logged under that toile comforter the next summer, after her mom had died. A thousand at least, she thought as she snuggled under the well broken-in cotton, missing both of her parents more than ever and trying to find some consolation in knowing they were now together again. Somewhere. Somehow.

She gazed at the framed photo of her parents on the dresser. The snapshot of the young, handsome driver climbing out of his race car, helmet in hand, stopping to kiss his blonde supermodel girlfriend, had always been one of her favorites, the gold standard for true love and romance. Only the younger version of herself had wanted to be the race car driver, not the pretty girlfriend waiting in the pits.

With a deep breath, Mia took the envelope off her nightstand and slid her nail under the flap to unseal it.

Daughter of mine,

You must be surprised by my decision, but did you think I would let you run away from your destiny forever? Your spirit, your passion, is with Rubie Racing and always has been.

My only request is this: Stay. Go back to the track. Lead our team. Swear on your dead father's grave that you will spend at least one season on the circuit.

I trust no one more than you. Now, you need to trust yourself. Remember, every good driver gets caught in the marbles at least once. The key is getting out of them. You can. You will.

I love you and I miss you always.
Dad

She reread the note a dozen times before setting it on the pillow next to her and surrendering herself to yet another good cry. When she finally managed to settle down, she glanced at the letter, heard her father's words again, and then sobbed some more.

In her mind's eye, Mia pictured herself as a girl, sitting on her father's lap at the Indy 500, like it was yesterday. A driver had found himself near the wall of the track, where the tiny pieces of rubber that wear off the cars' tires settle. He'd begun to slide around and lose control, and she, afraid of him crashing into the wall, had buried her face in the safety of her father's chest.

'It's OK,' her father had said, patting her back, his eyes never leaving the action on the track. 'He was caught in the marbles, but he's out now. Good drivers always find their way out.'

Only, she hadn't – or at least not in the way her father had hoped. It had been fifteen years since the night when her life hit the wall along with her driving career. She'd worked hard to pull herself back together and find a new path. And now her father was telling her, from beyond the grave, that she could still regain control and cross the original finish line?

The thought left her wanting to hide in her bed for another thousand-hour stretch.

As if there were time. The Apex season was a month out, with pre-season testing in Spain before the first race in Australia. Until the final and twentieth race at the end of October, the Rubie Racing team and cars would jet to racetracks around the world in what would be a meticulously planned eight-month whirlwind.

Without a doubt, every single thing was in place at this point. After all, she'd gotten her t-crossing and i-dotting from her father along with his permagrin. He'd handpicked Rubie Racing's several hundred employees. The team was on solid ground, even without him. Even without her.

Except her dad had chosen her to continue his legacy. And he expected her to actually do it, not just phone it in. Be there every step of the season as team principal. Hit pause on her life, her career in Chicago. It was a big ask, even for a dead man.

For perhaps the millionth time, Mia wished for a different relationship with Jordan. Close like siblings were supposed to be; closer given that they had shared a womb for eight and half months. Although by the stories their mother used to tell, they hadn't exactly coexisted peacefully in utero either.

No, Jordan wasn't the kind of brother she could call for a heart-to-heart talk. Especially not this one. He had his own decision to make; his own letter to digest. Considering what their father had felt comfortable having Cliff read aloud, she couldn't imagine what Jordan's letter said. The great Rob Rubie's power of persuasion would be on full display if both of his children were able to put aside past grievances in pursuit of ensuring their family's legacy.

While it seemed like a no-brainer for Jordan to take the money and run, Mia made a mental note to check her brother's contract, especially his bonus structure. Even from the periphery of the sport, only peering in on occasion, she knew the odds of her brother winning the world championship were low. He'd always been a decent driver, but he wasn't a solid podium finisher. Luca, though, he had a real chance of capturing the top spot – and giving her brother a serious payout.

She added pulling Luca's contract to her mental to-do list but already guessed her dad had shelled out big bucks to lure him back into the Rubie Racing fold.

Luca.

Spending months working alongside him would be far more challenging than dealing with her brother. Not that she was his type anymore, judging by the company he kept these days. His latest girlfriend was a supermodel, and the general assumption in the gossip magazines was that the two would walk down the aisle as soon as they were able to keep their clothes on for more than five minutes. Considering their noticeable absence from the public eye since last season ended, they had either been lying low or, more likely, lying in.

And for a reason she couldn't put her finger on, Luca's genuineness last night gnawed at her. The way he'd whisked her away from the party at the exact moment she'd needed an escape; how he'd suggested they name the turbo pumpkin for her dad; when he'd added his hopes and dreams into the mix, as if she needed even more pressure. She'd felt his eyes on her as she looked over his car, as if he was trying to figure out who thirty-three-year-old Mia was.

He'd have to get in line.

*

'I figured this is how I'd find you.'

Mia's gaze didn't need to shift from the ceiling to know Barb was standing next to her bed with mugs of tea. The steeping cinnamon spice gave her away.

'And for once, I'm going to join you.'

After Barb set one mug on Mia's nightstand, she made her way to the other side of the bed and stretched out. Mia could hear her fiddling with her tea, dunking the bag into the steaming water over and over again until the whole room smelled of cinnamon. Unable to resist the sweet aroma, Mia shifted until she sat up and leaned against the headboard, then wrapped her hands around her own warm mug.

'Dad wrote in his letter that he wants me to ditch my life and lead the team for the season. Be the boss of everyone, every department. Make decisions like I know what the hell I'm doing. Be the face of Rubie Racing to the world.'

'That's certainly a big ask.' Barb raised an eyebrow. 'How do you feel about it?'

'Like my life is spiraling out of control.' Only a week ago, she'd been going about her business, unaware that her entire universe had been about to change. The night before her dad died, she and Star had stayed late at work preparing a presentation – which Star had finished and given alone the morning of the funeral. 'I left all things racing behind years ago because I thought walking away was the best thing for me, for everyone.'

'I remember.'

Of course, Barb wouldn't have forgotten. She'd had a front-row seat.

'The thing is, I like my life. I know it wasn't what Dad had pictured for me, or even what I thought my life would be.' She took a sip of tea and let the heat and the spice warm her from the inside out. 'Did you know that I only found out how proud he was of me for my last promotion at his funeral? The guy who sold him submarine sandwiches told me.'

Barb nodded from the other side of the bed. 'For the record, he told me, too. He was plenty proud of you and your success, but he felt that the team was where you belonged, and he'd been waiting for you to figure that out on your own.'

Mia couldn't imagine a world where she would've voluntarily left her job, friends, the city she loved, especially considering it would've involved working with Luca.

'Is this about a certain guy?' Barb prodded.

'No, Luca and I are long over. Although if Dad wanted me by his side, why would he have brought Luca on again? He must've known I wouldn't come back with him around.'

Even though Barb tried to cover her smug smile with a sip of tea, Mia caught it anyway.

'Hmm. I wasn't talking about Luca. I thought maybe you were dating someone new in Chicago that you hadn't told me about, a relationship you didn't want to leave behind.'

'Oh.' In truth, Mia couldn't remember the last time she'd even been on a date. Since she'd earned her promotion, she hadn't had much time to meet someone new, let alone start a relationship. 'No, I wouldn't have to write any Dear John letters.'

And then something occurred to Mia that she'd never considered before — Barb's love life. 'Did you and my dad ever date? You know, on the sly?'

'God, no,' Barb laughed. 'Rob and I never had the feelings for each other that we'd had for our spouses. Sure, we cared for each other and enjoyed each other's company. It was nice, really, being with him here for all those years. When Jordan finally moved out, I figured I was done for, but I think he was used to having me around, too. He promoted me to "estate manager," gave me business cards and everything. A decent raise, too.'

'Well, I for one am glad you're still around. I'm not sure what I would've done these past few days without you here.'

'Ditto.' Barb smiled and set her empty mug on the other nightstand.

Mia drained what remained of her tea, too. 'What do you think I should do?'

'Besides getting out of this bed?' Barb asked with a smirk, even though she made no move to do so herself. 'Maybe let's start by not looking at this as a be-all and end-all decision. Doing what your dad asked doesn't mean your life in Chicago is over forever. You can just hit pause and then start again when the season is over.'

'Wait, there's a pause button?' Mia asked. 'You mean the best way forward isn't to burn whatever you're leaving behind to the ground?'

At that, Barb did get up. 'Smart ass. Before you pull out the matches, call Brian. If anyone can tell you what's going in with Rubie Racing, it's him.'

Chapter 8

Early the next morning, Mia found Brian waiting for her outside the back entrance of the Rubie Racing complex. As team manager, he was the person her father had trusted to not only know the nuts and bolts of the organization, but also make sure they were always in their proper place. Brian's name had come up so frequently that Mia felt like she knew him better than she did. Not that they were strangers by any means – Brian had been more consigliere than employee and had been invited to many a family gathering throughout his years with the team.

Barb was right – if anyone could tell her what was in store for her, it was Brian. Maybe that's why he hadn't seemed surprised to hear from her the night before and took no convincing to meet up with her on a Sunday morning.

'Ms Rubie,' he said as she walked toward him, coffee and doughnuts in hand.

'Mr Smith.'

He grabbed one of the cups of coffee off her so she'd have an arm free to return his hug. 'You all right?'

'I've had better weeks.' She gave him a half-smile. 'Still doesn't seem real, does it?'

He returned his own sad smile. 'Which part exactly?'

'All of the above,' she said. 'And honestly, you look as exhausted as I feel.'

'Thanks, I guess,' he said.

The lines around his eyes creased more than they used to, and his face was also well-weathered for a guy in his late thirties – likely from either too much stress and or too much sun reflected off asphalt. Probably both. Rubie Racing consumed Brian's life to nearly the same degree as it had her father's.

His head jerked toward the beige four-door sedan she pointed her key fob at to lock. 'I don't think you need to worry about anyone stealing that around here. You couldn't get a better rental?'

'Now, don't you be jealous, but that baby's all mine,' she said.

His jaw fell open. 'You have got to be kidding me.'

She wasn't joking. When it came time to shop for a new car, Mia had purposely sought the most unexciting drive she could find. The automatic transmission and lack of leather upholstery, sunroof, or an in-car entertainment system ensured she was comfortable but unable to experience even the least bit of fun.

'It's functional,' she said.

'It's a buzzkill on four wheels.'

'It gets me from point A to point B, and that's all you really need a car for.'

'I wouldn't say that too loudly around here.' Brian glanced around, as if to make sure no one had overheard their conversation.

There wasn't a soul in sight. The parking lot was empty except for her sedan and what she assumed was his tank-like SUV. Given the events of the past week, she'd banked on the two of them having the place to themselves, even with the Apex season right around the corner.

Still, Brian ushered her into the building like he was a federal agent and she was entering the witness protection program. The maze of hallways were still confusing even without an alcohol-induced haze and Luca's backside to distract her. After passing through several security doors with scan pads, they finally landed in the reception area surrounded by offices.

Brian paused in front of a door with a plaque reading 'Rob Rubie.' Mia stepped in front of him, turned the doorknob, and found herself in the space her father had spent more of his life in than the sprawling mansion ten minutes away. The stereotypical corner office faced a pond and had changed little since the last time she was in it more than a decade ago. Knowing her dad, he had probably decided that money for redecorating and new furniture was better spent on the cars, even if the massive U-shaped executive desk and matching oak bookcases were outdated.

The office looked like he had simply stepped out and planned to be right back. A coffee cup with the team logo was half full on his desk. His glasses were on top of his computer keyboard, so he wouldn't have to look for them when he arrived the next morning. Only he never made it to work again. The next morning, after the same jog he did almost every other day of his life, he'd died.

Mia wrapped her arms around herself and filled her senses with what remained of her father. 'I hate that he's dead. God, I hate it so much.'

'Me, too.' Brian walked over to a round conference table tucked in the corner of the room and pulled out a chair for her before sitting down himself. He pushed a stack of folders aside — one of the many stacks covering every flat surface of her father's office — and helped himself to a doughnut from the bag he took from her. 'So, let's talk.'

'You first.' She wanted to get out of the way the single question that had been burning a hole in her brain since the funeral bombshell. 'Did you know?'

'About you taking over Rubie Racing? Not exactly, but,' he took a bite of donut, 'I had an inkling. After all these years of working together, your dad and I didn't have many secrets, and he hinted once or twice that you were the heir apparent. But judging by the look on your face at the funeral, I'm going to go out on a limb and say you weren't privy to that information.'

'Correct,' she said, buying a few seconds with a sip of coffee. 'I was thinking I could manage things from Chicago, but that goes against his wishes. Of course, giving up my life for the season goes against mine. I'll be honest with you. I'm not sure what to do.'

'And you thought I could help?' he asked.

She nodded. 'Tell me what everyone here is thinking and be honest. Obviously, they got a double whammy, with Dad dying unexpectedly and then me, of all people, being named owner and team principal.'

Brian also used the sip of coffee trick to stall. 'They're upset and confused. About both.'

She exhaled heavily.

'Mia, it's no offense to you. They trusted Rob, and they loved him. He truly was the heart and soul of this organization. They don't know you. They only know your brother and, well, that doesn't entirely work in your favor.'

She couldn't help but roll her eyes. 'And here I thought my brother only treated me in that special way of his.'

'Oh, you're special all right.' He added gently, 'They'll come around once they get to know you, and the fact that your dad chose you will go a long way.'

It was easy to see why her dad had liked Brian so much, and why – of all the people who'd contacted him over the years – he had taken a chance on the skinny Black teenager who wouldn't stop writing to him about racing and cars. Brian had already been at the top of his class at Detroit's most prestigious technical high school when the two struck up their unlikely friendship and then became the recipient of the first Rubie Racing scholarship for automotive engineering. After interning every summer and finishing graduate school, Brian had worked his way up to the second most important position on a racing team.

But not the top. That position now belonged to her.

'How about you? Are you mad that it's me and not you?' she asked. 'I mean, if anyone at this table has earned it—'

'Stop. This is Rubie Racing, and you're Mia Rubie. Whether or not you believe it, this is all part of your DNA. I've told every person who's called me that Rob left us in good hands, and I know Luca's done the same.'

Mia chose to ignore that last bit. 'Well, that remains to be seen, doesn't it?'

'I don't know. If I were a gambling man, I'd bet on you taking this organization exactly where it needs to go.'

'But you're not a gambling man,' she said.

He shook his head. 'Nope. So here's the truth – you're not going be at the helm of an empty ship, and the cars aren't the only well-oiled machines in this place. The team, the season is already a go. What we need more than anything right now is a leader.'

Brian went to snatch the last bit of glazed doughnut from her fingers, but Mia popped it in her mouth before his fingers were anywhere near it. He raised an eyebrow at her still lightning-quick reflexes before grabbing his coffee off the table.

'Shall we then?' he asked.

Ten minutes later, Mia found herself sitting in Luca's turbo pumpkin. As Brian explained the changes to the engine and chassis design for the upcoming season, Mia's thoughts slid to a place they normally weren't allowed, to her race car from her seasons with Apex's entry-level series for teenage drivers. She could almost feel the steering wheel in her hands, the vibration of the tires, the heat from the track.

From her very first moment in a race car, there was nowhere else she had wanted to be. Her mother had done her best to discourage her infatuation with all things racing, while at the same time encouraging Jordan's interest.

'It's not ladylike, Robbie,' eight-year-old Mia overheard her mother stress during a fight with her father, after she'd pestered her parents about getting a go-kart. Jordan had one but refused to share.

'It's in her blood. You're going to have to deal with it.' With that, her father ended the discussion. The next week, Mia was the proud owner of a kart identical to Jordan's in every way except for the color. Hers was pink, which she later realized had been her father's attempt to pacify her mother. She couldn't have cared less what it looked like, as long as it was hers.

She and Jordan spent hours at the go-kart track near their house that summer, their mother watching and worrying from the stands. Even though he had a slight advantage from karting longer, she was beating him regularly within a month. When he began whining that her kart was faster than his, she swapped karts for a week and bested him in his. By the end of September, Mia and her pink kart had pretty much kicked every kid's ass in metro Detroit, to her mother's dismay. At least she relented and wore a pink frilly dress – justified only because it was the same color as her kart – to the end-of-the-season awards ceremony. Both of her parents were proud of her that day.

Mia drifted back to reality to find Brian smiling down at her. 'You miss it,' he said matter-of-factly.

'Nope,' she replied, accepting his help to climb out of the car. 'Not one bit.'

'You're not a very good liar, you know.'

Jordan's car was identical to Luca's except for the number – twenty-six as opposed to nine – and that it had been set up to fit Jordan's frame. She declined Brian's offer for her to sit in her brother's car, too, not trusting that it wasn't somehow booby-trapped or, at the very least, equipped with the dental floss 'alarm system' he'd perfected when they were kids to make sure she stayed out of his room.

They also saw the technology center and the wind tunnel, which the team relied on to ensure the race cars and their many parts were aerodynamic. They walked through a cafeteria, coffee shop, gym, and droves of offices before reentering the inner sanctum hosting the larger, more private spaces for Rob and Brian.

She couldn't believe how much Rubie Racing had grown. What her dad had accomplished was beyond impressive, and she felt a sharp pang of regret for missing the opportunity to let him show her himself. Maybe then this decision would've been easier.

As if he could read her mind, Brian leaned forward across the conference table they'd landed at again, looked her straight in the eye, and said, 'Do it.'

'You think it's that easy, do you?'

'No, of course not,' he said. 'But what do you have to lose?'

After he went back to his office, Brian's question echoed in her mind. She located a notepad and weighed the pros and cons. She quickly filled the pro column: Her condo wasn't going anywhere; she could probably take a sabbatical, given the circumstances, although she wasn't looking forward to having that conversation with her boss; her love life was nothing to write home about at the moment.

In the con column, Mia stopped after writing the first item and stared at the two words: Rubie legacy. What if she burned to the ground everything her father had dedicated his life to building up?

It wouldn't be the first time she'd disappointed her dad, but at least it would be the last. Mia thought back to Brian's question and realized the answer was nothing. Because when you've lost the one person in your life who would've done anything for you, regardless of everything, you have nothing left to lose.

Mia took a deep breath to prepare herself to rip off the Band-Aid, then sent a text to her boss. She wasn't surprised when her phone rang seconds later – Sarah worked as many hours as the team she led.

'Please tell me you're back,' Sarah said.

That's all it took for Mia's tears to flow again. How she had any moisture left in her body after the past week was surely a medical mystery. 'Sorry, but no.'

And she was sorry. Sorry to be walking away from a job she loved. Sorry to be leaving the life she'd worked hard to build for herself. Sorry her dad had died.

After stumbling through what had to have been the strangest reason for resigning that any boss had ever heard, there was only silence on the other end of the line.

When Sarah finally spoke, there was disbelief in her voice. 'Just so I'm clear, you'd like to take a leave of absence because you now own an Apex team and your dad's dying wish was for you to lead it? Which will involve you traveling around the world for the next eight months? Oh, and also, your brother is a race car driver, and you used to be?'

Mia couldn't help but laugh. 'I know it sounds crazy, but that's the gist of it.'

'Might this have come up at some point in the past five years we've worked together?' Sarah said. 'I mean, my husband is a huge Apex fan. He watches every race. I can't believe you're a Rubie, as in a Rubie Racing Rubie.'

'Sorry.' Only she wasn't, not one bit. She'd loved that nobody had been any the wiser about her family of origin, because it had allowed her to make it on her own. 'So, what do you think? Can I take a sabbatical of sorts?'

At that, Sarah sighed. 'I'll talk to the powers that be. But I have a feeling there's a better chance that I'll be asking you for a job in eight months than vice versa.'

Chapter 9

More mornings than not, Luca was the first person to arrive at the Rubie Racing complex. He contemplated the day ahead on a five-mile loop on the country roads around the complex then lifted weights in gym before showering, eating breakfast, and settling into his office. Rob would often track him down to chat about racing news and rumors. Those hours before the rest of the staff began filing in were his favorite of the day.

But everything was different now.

He was at the company espresso machine he'd contributed to the office his second day on the job when he noticed light shining from under Rob's door. Without thinking twice, he knocked and walked in, somehow forgetting for a split second that he wouldn't find Rob sitting behind his massive desk.

Instead, it was Mia, who jumped up from the leather chair with a start. 'Luca, hi. Good morning.'

'Mia, sorry, I, uh… sorry.' His hand dragged through his still damp hair, then settled on the back of his neck. 'I guess

I expected to see your father. My brain hasn't yet accepted that he's gone.'

'No need to apologize.' Her gaze softened, and she sat down. 'My brain has been having similar difficulties these past few days. I'm used to living in the Central time zone, and it seemed silly not to get started early once I was up. And let's face it, there's plenty to do before we all fly off to Spain.'

Noticing that her voice lacked the conviction of her words, Luca eyed the chair in front of the desk where he'd spent many an hour rehashing races and talking strategy. As he eased himself into it, Mia turned from the computer screen to face him, shuffling the papers spread out in front of her into a messy stack. His eyes locked on the legal document that ended up on top before she moved the pile next to other stacks that had long lived on the section of the desk behind her. He knew a contract when he saw one. He'd signed enough of them over years, including, from what he could tell from his glance, that one in particular.

With everyone asking whether he planned to stay with Rubie Racing now that Rob was gone, he hadn't stopped to consider that the team might not keep him. That maybe Mia would give him the heave-ho, decide she'd rather own a team that didn't include her ex.

'So, you're setting yourself up in here then?'

The infamous Rubie grin all but disappeared from her face and, after a long moment, Mia nodded. 'I have to admit that it feels a little strange, like I'm playing "work" in my dad's office. I keep thinking he's going to burst in and tell me to get the hell out of his chair.'

They both looked toward the door, as if they each hoped it could possibly be true. Considering how irrationally sad he was when no one appeared in the doorway, he couldn't imagine how Mia felt.

'Actually, it wouldn't surprise me in the least if he was already haunting the place,' Luca said. 'Aside from summer break, he rarely shut off. I found him asleep in that very chair more than a few times. Why do you think it leans back so far?'

'Truth be told, the apple didn't fall far from the tree. I've been known to burn the midnight oil every now and again, too.' Her eyes darted around the office before settling on him again. 'With the season only a few weeks away, camping out in here seemed like the easiest way to dive in.'

'You're actually staying?' he asked, cringing at the unintended harshness of his question. When her smile faded again, he added, 'Not that I think it's a bad idea.'

Although it may have been the truth, that didn't mean he necessarily thought it was a good idea. At least, not for him. When Luca had first arrived in Detroit, he'd fully expected to run into Mia. Although he'd noticed years ago that she never traveled with the team, he had no way of knowing that she didn't come around the complex either – until she hadn't. But now, she would be there every day. The thought of going suddenly from zero to twenty races in eight months with her along for the ride had him gripping the arms of the chair.

She coolly raised an eyebrow. 'What can I say, I'm a Rubie at heart. I'm in it to win it.'

Her use of Rob's favorite expression made him smile. 'Now there's the Mia Rubie I know and—' he stopped, then stammered, 'I'm only surprised that you're able to take off so suddenly from your work, your life in Chicago.'

'It's not ideal,' she said.

Judging by the rapid blinking of her eyes, Luca had struck a nerve. 'I mean, I imagine you're very busy and important.'

'True,' she said, chuckling to herself.

Instantly, Luca was transported back to a time in his life when he'd lived to make this person laugh for a purely selfish reason – simply because he loved the sound so much. He couldn't help but wonder if she was still so ticklish behind her left knee that she laughed until she cried.

'Yes, your father mentioned your very exciting work in – I'm sorry, what is it you do again?'

'Marketing. Strategy. You know the drill, creating a brand and then figuring out how to take over the planet.'

'The planet? I'm afraid that's not a drill I'm familiar with, actually. My target is usually far smaller and more oval.'

He was perhaps a little too pleased with himself when she laughed again, the sweet sound filling up a part of him he hadn't realized was empty. Only she didn't stop and barely squeaked out, 'God, I'm so tired. I don't know why I'm laughing. You're really not that funny.'

So maybe his charm game wasn't up to par. As she wiped away tears, he noticed her eyes were puffy and red. She looked like she needed a solid three days in bed. *Don't go there, Luca.*

'All right, all right,' he said. 'Time to get serious. What can I do for you?'

This time, Mia raised the other eyebrow. 'Pardon?'

'I'm serious, Mia. Your father and I worked together on just about every aspect of this season, from the cars to sponsors to strategy. He felt strongly that this would be our year. I do, too. My car is ready, and I'm ready to help.'

Also, please don't fire me.

Mia leaned back in her chair and drummed her fingers on the desktop. 'In that case, I have one question for you,' she said. 'Why?'

'Why what?'

'Why you? Why are you here, with this team? Why now?' She held his gaze. 'Just why, Luca.'

Her directness awed him. Because that was indeed the million-dollar question – five million dollars, to be exact, which was the salary he and Rob had agreed upon that fateful night in England. It was less than what he'd earned with his former team, and most drivers would've balked at such a lowball offer. His agent had almost dropped him. But after fourteen years as a professional race car driver, he had plenty of money. What he didn't have was a world championship. The car he'd been driving for two years at that point had been amazing, but in his gut, he'd known that what Rob was serving up would be better – world championship better. For him, that was priceless.

'Why not me? I, too, am very important, not to mention impressive,' Luca said, mimicking her earlier statement and knowing full well it wasn't what Mia wanted to hear. But he didn't have the answer she was looking for – and with Rob gone, he never would. 'Look, I don't know why your father wanted me back at Rubie Racing. But there are few people in this world that I respect as much as your dad. Coming back to drive for him just felt right. I don't know how else to explain it.'

'Then you talked about everything that happened?' She bit her lip and shifted her gaze to the ceiling. 'Between us?'

Holy hell. He hated how sad she looked. When she brought her gaze back to him, he shook his head. 'We did not. He asked if we could put the past behind us while also letting me know that he'd only accept one answer to his question. So, we moved forward with the understanding that it was water under the bridge.'

Her teeth released her lip, and her mouth fell open. She clearly wasn't buying what he was selling. Luca couldn't blame her – he hadn't bought it at first either. Part of him now regretted never asking Rob the tough questions that had been on the tip of his tongue dozens of times, find out what had caused him to forgive and seemingly forget. But everything had gone so smoothly last season, and they'd worked so well together, especially over the past few months. He'd convinced himself the topic would come up when and if the timing was ever right, which would be when Rob wanted to talk about it. As fate would have it, that conversation was never meant to be.

Although he wasn't sure if he and Mia could avoid talking about their past, it wasn't going to happen on her first day, and definitely not before his first espresso. 'Well, I know I could use some caffeine. Can I bring you something, boss? A cappuccino, perhaps?'

To his relief, she pushed herself up from the chair and gave him a slight smile. 'If you're referring to that monstrosity of an espresso machine out there, then yes. As long as it's a double and you show me how to work it. We have a lot to do, and one thing is for certain. I'm paying you far too much to fetch my coffee all day.'

And then she laughed, really laughed, as she followed him out the door.

Chapter 10

'I'm sorry, you are again?' Jordan's smug assistant asked Mia when she stopped by his office and found that he was, yet again, not around.

Although her first week as team principal was over in a blink, Mia had managed to at least say hello to all three hundred-some employees of Rubie Racing, save one. Her twin had somehow dodged her every single day. She'd 'just missed him' when she'd checked in on his car, and then he'd been out for lunch, at a meeting, and perhaps her favorite, at the dentist when she'd dropped by his office. His assistant had taken down her name each time and asked the reason for her visit. Each time.

Which was the déjà vu scenario Mia found herself in late Friday afternoon.

Mia was not having it. 'Mia, Jordan's sister and, oh yeah, your boss. Technically. You should probably commit my name to memory, although I'm pretty sure you already have. But. Hello.' As she waved exuberantly, she decided she'd taken one too many trips to Luca's espresso machine that day. 'I'm Mia, and you're Olivia. Let's now consider ourselves formally introduced, although we met the other day. And the day before that. And the day before that.'

'Yes, of course. Hello.'

Mia watched Olivia misspell her name as 'Maya' on her notepad for the fourth time in as many days. She was starting to feel like she was at Starbucks.

'As you're aware, Mr Rubie is grieving right now,' Olivia said softly when she finally looked up. 'I'd suggest a little patience.'

Mia found herself unable to do anything but stare and blink repeatedly at the woman before her. 'Yes, I'm aware. We shared the same father. Mother, too, for that matter.'

'Of course. I'm sorry for your loss, too,' Olivia said. 'And the reason you'd like to see Mr Rubie?'

Inspiration struck. 'Well, as we've already noted, I've stopped by a few times to discuss a couple of items for the upcoming season. But you can let Mr Rubie know I went ahead and made those decisions without his input. Please tell him that the car color is being changed to a gorgeous shade of lilac based on feedback from one of our sponsors and our marketing department.' She paused to smile and shrug her shoulders. 'Oh, you know what? Never mind. The rest is just a bunch of minor details. No need to bother Mr Rubie with them.'

With Olivia's mouth open wide enough to catch flies, Mia turned on her four-inch heels and left, calling over her shoulder, 'Really, he needn't worry about getting back to me. I know he's incredibly busy. And sad.'

Not five minutes later, Jordan barged into her office.

'You're hilarious,' he said.

'While that is indeed true, I'm not sure what it has to do with anything at the moment,' Mia said, contemplating how many of the files stacked on her dad's desk would fit into her satchel with her laptop. She had a long weekend ahead of her.

'You'd better be joking then,' he said.

'About the shade of purple for the car and helmet, or the ties you'll need your stylist to special order? I mean, I know I'm more comfortable if everything matches. I'll have the exact Pantone color sent to your assistant. Who's very pleasant, by the way.'

'You have no right to make these kinds of decisions, Mia. None.'

As tempted as she was to correct him on that, or see how long this might play out, she lacked the time and the energy. 'Oh, for Pete's sake! Cool it, hotshot. No one's getting a Barney-themed car.'

His childhood nickname had the disarming effect she'd hoped for, and he flopped down in a chair in front of the desk.

'Your teeth look nice,' she said. 'Very clean. I assume your membership in the no-cavity club is secure for another six months?'

He responded with a goofy smile, which relaxed into his

familiar scowl more quickly than she would've liked. But even his trademark pout couldn't hide that Jordan looked as worn out as she felt. She hadn't seen him since he left the reading of the will in a huff, although she knew Barb, apparently unable to turn off taking care of either Rubie twin, had dropped off plates of food at his house. He was eating at least.

'So, that must've been some letter Dad wrote you to make the prodigal daughter come home and take her place in the family empire,' Jordan said.

'What can I say? He kind of made it difficult to argue with him this time around.'

As nice as it was to have the only living member of her immediate family sitting in front of her, making any sort of conversation, she wasn't going to tell Jordan any details about her letter. And as curious as she was, she wasn't going to ask Jordan about his. But they were siblings, the last of the Rubies, and there was a decision only the two of them could make.

'Speaking of Dad, his ashes are ready to be picked up.' Mia swallowed her feelings rather than show them to her brother. 'We'll need to decide what to do with them.'

Jordan leaned forward and rested his elbows on his knees. 'Oh.'

Mia had expected more of a response than that, even though she hadn't a clue where their father's final resting place should be. He'd left no direction, which was surprising since he seemed to have left a detailed plan for every other element of his afterlife.

'Mom's in their bedroom. Why don't we just keep them together in there for now.' A corner of Jordan's mouth raised in sad smile. 'Let them catch up.'

They sat in silence for a minute before Jordan moved to get up. 'Is that it?'

Mia shook her head, then took a deep breath. That wasn't why she'd been stalking him around the building for days. She felt bad asking him on the heels of a rare, nice moment, but there was one more thing she needed to know.

'So, Jordan. Are you doing this?'

'What do you mean?'

Mia couldn't believe he was going to force her to spell out that his inheritance hinged on his leaving the Rubie Racing team. Not that he was a poor man without those millions — she'd reviewed his contract, and his compensation package and bonus structure were more than generous. Sure, he might make more with another team, but he'd have to find one willing to overlook the fact that he hadn't won a race or stood on the podium in years, let alone his attitude.

'Come on, Jordan. I was in the room when Cliff read the will. Are you driving for the team or are you racing away with your share of Dad's estate?'

His face turned an intense shade of red, and he began stabbing through the air at her with his finger. 'This is Rubie Racing, and I am Jordan Rubie. My spot on the team is my legacy, and neither you nor Luca nor anyone else can take it away from me. Are we clear?'

As much as angry exchanges with her brother always made

her shake inside, she kept her voice even and calm. 'Crystal,' she said, then pointed her own finger at him when he moved to get up. 'But know this: no more skulking around the building. As of this moment, I expect you to start acting like a member of this team. That means you show up at meetings with Brian and Luca. I don't expect you to sing Kumbaya, but it wouldn't kill you to hum along once in a while.'

His scowl deepened.

She added, 'If we're both doing this, and apparently we are, then we're in it to win it. Are we clear?'

He managed a slight nod before he got up and made an icy retreat out the door. It was as close to a yes as she was going to get. Alone, she inhaled deeply and exhaled a deep cleansing breath before glancing around the office. She'd hardly made a dent in the two tall stacks of files on her father's cluttered desk and seriously considered relegating the rest of them to the trash can. But making decisions without the full scope of data wasn't her MO.

It hadn't been her father's either, shouted the right side of her brain, which wanted to go home, have a glass of wine, and binge a baking show with Barb. Given that he'd already made most of the decisions for the season, and she had discovered nothing useful so far, she could justify skipping looking through every file. It's not like she was taking the time to click through every folder on his computer.

Wait, should she be?

The left side of her brain, never one to miss out on a little light reading for the sake of the common good, had somehow found two cymbals and was clashing them together loudly inside her skull.

Argh, she thought, cracking open the top file and flipping through the papers tucked inside.

One hour and seven useless files later, Brian stuck his head in the door. 'Go home.'

'While that's a lovely idea, these files won't review themselves,' she said, 'as much as I wish they would.'

'Trust me when I say they're not important. Your father had a strange habit of printing out everything and anything, and then filing it away in folders he never opened again. Have you gotten to the one full of emails yet?'

Mia gave him a look of pure disbelief. 'Why on earth would someone print out emails? There are folders right in your inbox.'

'You're asking me? Open any cabinet in this place and you'll find stacks of file folders, just like those, dating back years. At the end of every season, he hid that year's stack away. And before you ask why they're stacked and not hanging neatly, don't. Although I suspect it's why he couldn't keep an assistant. Drove them all mad. Literally and figuratively.'

Mia swiveled her chair around and opened two doors to discover exactly what Brian had described. She suddenly wasn't sure if she felt sorrier for herself and the few hours she'd already wasted, or for the many trees whose lives had been so needlessly sacrificed.

'Seriously, we could have an amazing bonfire,' he said. 'You bring the marshmallows, and I'll find some sort of metal rod in the garage to roast them on.'

'Well, OK then.' The revelation was all the tension that had been building in her back all week needed to reach her neck and shoulders. While working non-stop was a welcome distraction from her grief, it had added to the physical weight she felt from her father's death.

Eleven days had passed since she left Chicago, which made twelve days since her last workout. Her body was in exercise withdrawal. There was a barre studio near her dad's house, but spending dawn to dusk at the Rubie Racing complex had left her with just enough energy to eat one of Barb's home-cooked dinners each night and veg in front of the television. Her tote bag of workout clothes had done nothing more than ride shotgun to and from the complex every day.

'You look weird,' Brian said, snapping his fingers and releasing her from her thoughts. 'Earth to Mia? What's happening in that head of yours?'

'Yes? Oh. I'm leaving. It's barre time.'

'While I don't think booze is the solution to your troubles, I'm willing to take one for the team,' Luca said, his face wearing the same look of concern as Brian's. 'I'm sure we can find a bottle of something around here.'

Luca had been popping in all week, especially in the mornings when there were few others milling around. She'd found herself looking forward to his rap on the door, engaging in mindless chit-chat, and cracking up over silly haikus he'd started writing. This morning's was an ode to what she'd come to realize was his favorite beverage: Espresso is good. I drink it more than I should. But less than I could.

It was better than yesterday's, which featured a goat and boat that, for whatever reason, floated in a moat.

'A haiku doesn't typically rhyme,' she'd finally told him.

'But do I get extra credit for rhyming?' he'd asked hopefully.

'Maybe,' she'd said, feeling like a traitor to her eighteen-year-old self, along with the broken heart she'd nursed for longer than she liked to admit, for the borderline flirty banter. But as much as she'd long envisioned not giving Luca the time of day if they ever saw each other again, she simply didn't have the energy.

'Not bar, barre,' she said, as if repeating the homonyms aloud would help clear up the confusion written across both of their faces.

She tossed a few things in her satchel. If she left right now, she could make the last class of the evening. Not that it would be the same without Star complaining and moaning next to her.

'It's… never mind,' she said, breezing past them. 'Sorry, Brian, the campfire songs will have to wait for another day.'

Chapter 11

As Luca neared Mia's office, he heard something he rarely heard at Rubie Racing – shouting.

'Why don't I think it's a good idea?' Brian yelled. 'We're days from loading a multi-million-dollar car into an airplane and flying it over a very big ocean to Spain. If that's not reason enough for you, I'm not sure where to start.'

'Don't bother explaining, I get it,' Mia fired back. 'But to be clear, I wasn't asking for your permission. This was more me being courteous and letting you know the situation.'

Permission for what? Luca's heart sank as he stopped short of the room and his brain flashed to the contract Mia had shuffled out of his sight her first day in the office. Was she firing him? Had he broken his long-standing protocol of coming in on a Saturday – one of his final Saturdays of the off-season, no less – only to be fired?

'We can't afford to have you stuck in Chicago, Mia. Whatever you need to do there isn't anywhere near as important as what we need you for here. Not to mention that you'll be driving that four-door excuse for a car into a snowstorm.'

Luca couldn't stop himself from stepping through the doorway, even though it meant copping to eavesdropping on their conversation. 'Hold on, are you telling me that thing in the parking lot belongs to you? I assumed someone had abandoned it.'

Mia groaned. 'Not you, too. What the hell is so wrong with my car?'

'I don't know,' Luca said. 'Besides everything? It's a sedan? It's the color of sand? It's boxy?'

'Boxy? You drive a freaking Range Rover. And I will have you both know that my sedan was voted "car of the year" three years in a row.'

'By whom?' Luca asked.

'Seriously, who?' Brian chimed in.

Mia shot daggers at them both before shifting her focus solely to Brian. 'Look, I just want to pick up some of my stuff. I'm fully aware of the schedule, but this is my last chance for even a quick trip back. And before you say it, I know I could send a messenger or Barb, but I'm not keen on letting anyone dig through my things. If you'll recall, I left in a bit of a hurry, and I'm not sure what's where. I had no clue I was about to take leave from life as I knew it.'

That silenced everyone. Luca had dealt with the craziness of the past week and a half with his old tried-and-true trick of putting his feelings about Rob's death in a box and placing it on the highest shelf in the darkest corner of his mind. He planned to open the box at some point in the future, when he had time to process it all. He assumed Brian was using a similar method in order to push through his grief.

But Mia had lost her father, not her boss. And as much as she'd thrown herself into all things Rubie Racing, that level of sorrow wasn't as easily packed away as theirs.

When Brian spoke again, his tone was much softer. 'I can't imagine what you've gone through, Mia, and I think I speak for Luca and everyone else in this organization when I say how grateful we are that you've stepped up the way you have – not to mention, impressed as hell. However, you can buy whatever you need here. Look around. You own an Apex racing team. You can afford to treat yourself to a whole new wardrobe.'

'A new car even,' Luca mumbled.

'Trust me, I've spent plenty.' She gestured to her jeans and sweater, which Luca took as an invitation to admire more than her outfit. 'And enough about my car.'

'Luca, help. Please. Talk some sense into her.'

Wait, what? Luca's gaze shifted from Mia's sweater to Brian.

'I'll take her,' he said, as surprised as anyone when the words came out of his mouth.

Brian's eyes nearly rolled all the way to the back of his head. 'Seriously, man. This is simply not a priority right now, especially not on dicey roads. Think of the team. Both of you.'

Luca put his hands up. 'Mia's right. This may be the last break we have for a while, and at least I can get us there and back safely – and quickly.'

'So now you're doubting my driving skills?' Mia asked.

'Sweetheart, no one in this room has ever questioned your abilities behind the wheel,' Luca said. 'But I think we can all agree that my vehicle is the better choice on a snowy winter's day.'

While he waited for her answer, Luca considered all he was signing himself up for. Namely, a good ten hours alone with Mia. Maybe not the wisest move given that after watching her zip around the building the past week, charming everyone from the head engineer to the cafeteria server in a way that came as naturally to her as it had Rob, he was already like a moth drawn to a flame.

Please say yes.

'Fine, but with one condition,' she said. 'If your concern is sincerely about my car, which I would like to point out has some of the top safety ratings in the industry, then I'm driving.'

'And I would like to go on the record as saying this is a bad idea,' Brian said.

'Seriously? What exactly?' Mia asked.

'All of it.' Brian began walking toward his office, waving goodbye over his shoulder. 'But I will gladly stay here and hold down the fort while you two gallivant across the Midwest. Enjoy. I hope it sleets.'

Luca checked his watch. 'It's eight o'clock. If we leave here by nine, we'll be there early this afternoon, and then home again this evening.'

Mia nodded. 'I can be ready in fifteen minutes if you can.'

'Deal,' he said, digging his keys out of his pocket and

placing them into her hand. Given that his SUV had keyless entry along with every other bell and whistle, the gesture was purely symbolic. 'And we'll take turns driving. You can even have the first shift.'

Luca should've known Mia wouldn't yield the wheel. An hour and a half in, the snow began to fall heavily, and he pointed out a rest area on the navigation system for a swap point. But she drove past it saying, 'That rest area? Right there? Oh, sorry, I missed the exit. The next one maybe.'

The problem was, Luca hated being a passenger. He couldn't remember the last time he was one, and didn't know what to do with his hands, his feet... his eyes. Especially since those kept wandering in Mia's direction – to see how hard it was snowing on her side of the car. Not for any other reason.

'Since when did you become so fidgety?' Mia asked, turning on the satellite radio system.

'I don't know, maybe since I became a virtual prisoner in my own car?' he said.

Luca was running out of ways to distract himself. After examining the contents of the glove compartment and perusing the owner's manual, he contemplated climbing into the backseat and trying out the video screens in the back of his and Mia's headrests. He doubted that they'd ever been turned on.

He tried to only half listen to the disturbing show Mia had found about police using forensic evidence to solve violent crimes and cold cases. 'If you're not going to let me drive, I should at least be able to choose what we listen to,' he said, reaching for the touchscreen. 'After all, this is my car.'

Mia slapped his hand away. 'Driver controls the radio. It's a rule.'

'You Rubies and your rules. God help us all,' he said. 'And keep two hands on the wheel, please. Ten and two.'

'Any more comments about my driving and you're never getting your turn,' she grinned.

One episode rolled into another, and Luca was thankful he could only hear about the gruesome scenes. Who kills someone and saves their victim's foot in a cooler? Or dissolves a body in a barrel of acid? He made a mental note to always question slabs of freshly poured cement.

When they finally passed a salt truck, Luca wasn't sure if he should count it as a good sign or a bad sign. They were more than halfway there – with Mia still refusing to turn over the wheel – so there was no sense in turning back. He watched as she deliberately maneuvered the car on the slick roads, masterfully following the tracks the car in front of them had made on the snow-covered highway. He'd bet she would still be one hell of a race car driver.

'What are you staring at?' she asked.

He shrugged a shoulder. 'You. You were right. You are different than you used to be.'

'I would hope so,' she said. 'I was a teenager when we knew each other before. Now, I'm a fully formed adult.'

As his eyes widened, a blush crept up her cheeks and he couldn't help but laugh. The theme music began playing again, alerting them to the beginning of a new episode.

Luca groaned. 'Have you had your fill of murder yet?'

She reached out and turned off the radio without taking her eyes off of the increasingly slippery road. 'You're lucky I heard that last episode on my way to work a few weeks ago. If you're creeped out now, try hearing about a murder in a subway car full of strangers. Spoiler alert: The husband did it. Big surprise.'

'Why would you want to listen to that twice? What has happened to you?'

She shrugged. 'The talking keeps me more focused than music. Plus, I don't know, I like knowing that people who do bad stuff don't always get away with it.'

'We kind of did.' Luca hadn't meant to say the quiet part out loud, but it was out there now.

Her grip tightened on the steering wheel. 'It's hardly the same, but someone did get hurt, if you'll recall. All because we were young and dumb.'

'Yes, I believe if you look in the dictionary, you'd find those exact words for the definition of young love,' he said.

She kept her eyes focused straight ahead. 'If you say so.'

'I do,' he said.

After spending so much time with Mia the past week, Luca couldn't help but wonder what would've happened with the two of them if that night had played out differently. If they would've beaten the odds and stayed together; what that might've looked like. The women he'd dated since were like Julia Sullivan in more ways than he liked to admit, but then race car drivers could hardly throw a rock without hitting a model or an equally beautiful woman hanging around on race weekends. It's not like his bedroom had a revolving door, even if most exited nearly as quickly as they entered. He was OK with that. He'd learned a long time ago that sex and friendship didn't mix. For that matter, neither did sex and love. His relationship with Mia had taught him that.

Luca had banished from his brain the night that ended everything with Mia a long time ago. He would've assumed she had, too, except the tension coming from the driver's seat seemed to be about more than the slick roads.

'Do you ever talk to him? Scott?' he asked.

Mia was quiet for so long that he wasn't sure if she was going to answer. 'No. He wasn't at the funeral either.'

Before Luca could say anything else, she took one hand off the steering and tapped the touchscreen, which he took as a sign that the conversation was over. A blood-curdling scream surrounded them in seconds, so clear that the woman could've been being murdered in the backseat.

His deep sigh was equal part frustration, resignation, and regret for upgrading the sound system. 'Let me guess... he gouges out his wife's eyes and strings them on a necklace.'

'That's the spirit,' she said. 'You're close, only think smaller and more dangly.'

At least his groan was rewarded with a laugh.

Turns out Brian had been right to say they shouldn't go, although neither of them was likely to admit it to him anytime soon. The snow was so heavy as they rounded Lake Michigan that even murder became too distracting for Mia. He attempted to occupy them with snow-themed haikus until they watched a car slide off the road into a ditch. That stretch of the journey was always the worst, she assured him, and Chicago would be fine. The city was cold, but huge snowstorms were rare. Those didn't hit more than once every five years or so.

'That's good to know,' he said. 'When was the last big storm?'

'Six years ago? Maybe five. It was horrible. People had to abandon their cars on Lake Shore Drive, the snow hit the city so fast. Some guy left this door open by accident and his SUV filled up with snow.'

'Hmm,' Luca said. 'One more question: What do you think the odds are of us ending up on your murder show as Brian's victims?'

'Pretty high. And you know what would make a great pair of earrings?'

Even her giggle couldn't stop him from cringing at that image.

Chapter 12

Mia was glad she'd remembered to grab the clicker to her building's underground garage. By the time they made it to downtown Chicago, the snow was really falling. With a few inches already on the ground, finding a parking spot on the street would be next to impossible. Not that Luca would want his baby parked out in the open. And not that she could blame him.

As much as she hated to admit it, his Range Rover beat her car of the year, hands down. It wasn't even a contest, especially given their harrowing drive from Michigan. Which is why she tucked the key fob in her handbag instead of placing it in the hand he extended.

'I'll just hold on to this for you,' she said, heading to the elevator. Once they were inside, she pressed the button for the top floor and exhaled a deep sigh of relief. 'Well, that was fun.'

'Yes, what a lovely experience, Mia. I can't wait for the second act after our brief intermission.'

They exited the elevator in front of her door. As much as her car shouted, 'Mia Rubie, average person on board,' her condo screamed, 'a wealthy racing team heiress lives here.' For that reason, only a small and select group of people had ever passed through the front door.

When she'd accepted her position in Chicago after graduate school, her dad had insisted on flying in and helping her find a place to live. Dreams of a quaint vintage unit with loads of character fell by the wayside when the first two her real estate agent had shown them failed to pass his muster. (Or, quite possibly, current building codes.) Before she knew it, he'd raised her maximum more than slightly, and soon they were looking at properties she could hardly afford the taxes on, let alone the mortgage. But she hadn't resisted when her dad had plunked down a million dollars for a penthouse because she would've had to have been crazy to turn down the panoramic views of Lake Michigan and downtown.

'Here we are,' Mia said, dropping her handbag on a bench in the entry before leading him into the large open space that the living room, kitchen, and dining area shared. 'Usually there's a lake out there, not a blur of bright white.'

Luca's eyebrows furrowed as he took in the room. 'Nice digs. Although not what I would've expected to be your taste.' From an end table, he picked up a weathered wooden seagull with beady black eyes that Star claimed came alive at night and watched Mia sleep. 'It kind of reminds me a little of your dad's house, to be honest.'

Unfortunately, Mia also hadn't put her foot down when her

dad had insisted on sending in his interior designer, which is when she really should have. What had been proposed as a cozy mix of country French and shabby chic had instead resulted in an eclectic floral design theme that screamed old cat lady.

'That might be because he gifted me the services of his decorator,' she said. 'I'd just started my job so I didn't have a lot of time to spend with her, and next thing I knew, it was all said and done. I've been trying to figure out a way to redo it without hurting his feelings.'

Oof. A familiar pang of sadness hit her when she realized his feelings were no longer a factor – in any of her decisions. With the exception, of course, of the one that was taking her away from this very space and had turned her into a *persona non gratis* at the company she'd devoted her entire professional life to.

What she'd come to recognize as sympathy washed over Luca's face as he sat down on the floral sofa, looking as uncomfortable as she knew it to be. The cushions were supposed to be goose-down, but she'd long suspected that they might've been stuffed with entire geese. When she turned around to make her way toward the kitchen, she heard him mutter, 'At least the car is starting to make more sense.'

After dumping the cup of coffee she'd abandoned in her rush to get out the door and to her dad that fateful morning, Mia loaded and started the dishwasher. She opened the refrigerator to find a couple of lonely yogurts, milk, and cottage cheese past their expiration dates, and a crisper drawer filled with rotting vegetables.

'I don't know about you, but I prefer my salads less slimy,' said Luca, his head peeking over her shoulder. 'Also, I'm starving. Let's grab lunch before we hit the road again.'

'I agree with you on all counts,' she said, making quick work of sorting out what went in the trash and the recycling. 'We can get rid of this on our way out.'

Her favorite snow boots and insulated winter coat were in the closet right where she'd left them. If the years of living in Chicago had taught her anything, it was that the wind whipping off the Great Lake was brutal for even a born and bred Michigander. She couldn't help but notice Luca's smirk as she donned mittens and a wool hat and wrapped a long scarf around her neck, mouth, and nose, but the joke would soon be on him. He was going to freeze his ass off in his leather driving jacket and loafers.

He tapped on her forehead. 'Mia, are you in there?'

She moved the scarf away from her mouth. 'Tell me what you're hungry for because we're not stopping until we get there.'

'Not pizza.'

She'd already guessed that Chicago's famous deep-dish pizza wouldn't be on his list — as delicious as a couple pounds of cheese baked into a heavy pie was, it didn't really complement a race car driver's pre-season diet. Protein and vegetables would be more his speed.

'Noted. Follow me.'

Fifteen minutes later, they walked into her favorite steakhouse. An Italian one, at that. She handed her winter garb to the host and asked for a seat near a fireplace when she saw how reluctantly Luca gave up his coat.

'Nicely done,' said Luca with a wink. 'You've hit my two favorite food groups.'

The server brought over a basket of bread and read the specials, but Mia shook her head when she mentioned wine. 'While that sounds lovely, we need to head to Michigan later this afternoon.'

'Oh, I seriously doubt that,' the server said, sliding the wine list onto the table. 'That storm out there is just getting started. We're supposed to get eight inches in the next three hours. We may close early, and we haven't done that since the last big storm. Remember that one—'

'—five or six years ago?' Luca asked.

The server nodded as he skimmed the wine list and pointed at something before Mia could object. 'Given that I just learned about that storm, we'll have a bottle, please,' he told her with a smile.

As soon as she walked away, they both attacked the bread. 'A bottle of wine? At lunch? Really?' Mia asked.

'You told her wine sounded lovely, and I concurred,' he said. 'This bread is still warm. Do you think anyone would notice if I used a couple of pieces to warm my hands?'

'Sit on them. Your hands, not the bread.' She'd tell him after lunch about the extra pair of mittens and earmuffs that lived in her handbag.

They sat in a comfortable silence for a few minutes, as Luca warmed his hands with his bottom and Mia inhaled more than her share of the bread. By the time he shook his hands out and reached for the basket, a single piece remained.

'I think you're enjoying this a bit too much,' he said.

She would've agreed, but her mouth was too full of focaccia to speak. But he was right, and his observation and the bread were both a little tough to swallow.

If someone had told her a month ago that she'd be having a relaxing lunch with Luca Toscano, she would've laughed in their face. The two of them falling into a strange groove of teasing and joking around? She would've been rolling around on the floor laughing, begging them to stop so she could catch her breath.

But then Mia from a month ago didn't know what was in store for her, or how easy being around Luca again would be. She'd never imagined that he'd be one of those people she could go years without seeing and then feel like no time had passed. Not that she was planning to pick up exactly where they left off.

She wasn't. She couldn't. Not only would she be a traitor to her broken-hearted eighteen-year-old self, but her thirty-three-year-old self knew better than to repeat past mistakes – especially when said mistake was now her employee.

'This will not go over well with our home base,' Mia said once their wineglasses were filled with a healthy pour of the red Luca had chosen. 'Speaking of... who's going to make the call to Brian?'

Just as Luca opened his mouth, Mia belted out, 'Not it!'

He burst out laughing. 'Is this how the owner of an Apex

team delegates tasks? Interesting. I would personally vote that neither of us calls.'

Mia watched as he pulled out his phone and typed a quick text message, then set it face up between them. After the server took their order and delivered another breadbasket, which Luca claimed for his side of the table, they sipped their wine and stared at the screen. It finally lit up with six words: *I told you this would happen.*

'Well, that's taken care of,' Luca said, putting his phone away and swirling the wine around in his glass. 'Now, tell me about your life, you know, before you were dragged back into the world you left behind.'

'You want me to cover the last fifteen years in one bottle of wine?'

'I'm sure they have more.'

Mia pointed to the breadbasket, and Luca tossed her a roll. She chewed slowly to give herself time to consider her answer, decide how much she was willing to let her guard down.

Obviously wise to her procrastination tactics, Luca threw her a softball question. 'Let's start with why you chose Chicago.'

'A job. When I came to interview, I loved the city's energy and the lake.' She omitted that she'd also been drawn to the anonymity such a big city offered, and that she'd chosen the large public university she'd attended for the same reason. 'And it was driving distance to Dad. I didn't want to depend on flights if something bad ever happened and I needed to be there.'

Of course, what was that old saying about the best laid

plans? The five-hour drive from Chicago to metro Detroit had turned out to be four hours too long.

As if he could read her mind, Luca said, 'You couldn't have known things would go the way they did, Mia. Jordan lives nearby and didn't even make it to the hospital in time, even though Barb drove over to his house and dragged him out of bed.'

'Are you telling me that my father died alone?' She'd assumed that Barb or Jordan had been in the room when their dad passed away. As much as she wished someone had told her earlier, she also wished she could've remained in the dark.

'I'm sorry, Mia. I thought you knew.'

She shook her head and blinked away tears. Imagining her father leaving this life with no one he loved by his side, holding his hand, was almost too much to bear. 'Well, I guess that's karma for you.'

Half-eaten bread roll in hand, Luca chewed and swallowed the bite he'd just taken. 'Karma? How do you figure?'

'I rejected the very thing he loved most in the world, Luca. And I refused to look back.'

'I don't know if I'd call that karma,' Luca said, refilling both of their glasses. 'Sounds more like Rubie stubbornness.'

She took a large gulp of wine before continuing. 'When I left Detroit, after us, and the crash, and everything that happened afterward, it was pretty clear I needed to settle down. The straighten up and fly right lecture Dad gave me still echoes in my head every now and again.'

'I know the lecture of which you speak, in case you weren't aware,' Luca said.

Mia shook her head because she wasn't, of course. 'But here's the thing, he didn't need to lecture me. As disappointed as he was in me, I was a thousand times more disappointed in myself. So, I did straighten up. Fly right. But to do that, I had to become someone else, someone not fueled by that obsessive genetic need for adrenaline. So, I became the woman whose penthouse looks like it belongs to an eighty-year-old cat-loving heiress, only without a freaking cat. A woman who drives a very functional car with four doors and no frills. Did you know you have to special order the base model? I actually paid extra to not have all the bells and whistles.'

Luca put his hand over hers on the linen tablecloth. 'We all change, Mia. Hopefully, we become a better version of ourselves. From what I've seen the past week, you certainly have. Even if the new and improved Mia has the most hideous sofa that I've ever seen in my entire life. And you've clearly made something of your life. You have a job you love – your dad told me that much – and you have friends. Well, the one friend at least.'

'Damn! Star! I forgot to call and tell her I was going to be in town. I *had* one friend.' Her eyes welled with tears again, and she wiped them away with the back of her hand before remembering the napkin in her lap. 'I do love the life I built for myself here. I'll miss it.'

Not that she'd hardly given that life, her job, a second thought since her phone call to Sarah.

'I wish I could say I don't regret any of it, but I do, now, looking back. Do you know my dad sent me an email before every race, offering to fly me wherever in the world they were going to be, and I never said yes? Not once. I guess I thought we had... more time. I don't know how the years slipped by.'

'Your father loved you, and yes, he missed you, but I think he understood. Otherwise, he would've given up, and he wouldn't have given you the space and time you needed.'

'Just think, if he hadn't died, I'd still have that time and space,' she said. 'But I'd probably be none the wiser on every level.'

Their steaks arrived, and Luca attacked his New York strip. 'Also, for what it's worth, I think you would've made a great cat mom.'

Mia looked down at her filet, trying not to give him the satisfaction of a laugh, and picked up her fork and steak knife.

'Now what would you like to know about me?' Luca asked between bites. 'Ask me anything.'

She nearly choked on her first bite of steak. 'You? Nothing, thank you very much.'

Mia already knew more than she wanted to about Luca's fifteen years of goings on. Even from the outside peeking in occasionally, she hadn't been able to escape the news of his good years, or of his not so good ones. Ditto for the string of women on his arm.

'Ouch,' he said, and actually looked hurt. His brows furrowed as he put down his silverware and folded his arms in front of his chest. 'I haven't exactly been a degenerate, Mia.'

'True, I'll give you that. But from what I've read in the tabloids, you haven't exactly been a saint either.'

Maybe it was unfair to judge him by the company he'd kept, especially since she hadn't exactly been living in a convent.

'What can I say, except don't believe everything you read,' Luca said. 'Unless you come to the source, that is. Come on, Mia. Aren't you the least bit curious? I'm an open book, I swear.'

Mia couldn't help but wonder how many women had read that book in braille. 'OK, fine. Are you getting married?'

It was his turn to almost choke. 'I'm sorry, did you say married?' He gulped down some wine and dotted his now-watering eyes. 'To whom?'

Was he actually going to make her say the name out loud? Given the perplexed look on his face, apparently, he was.

'Julia Sullivan,' Mia said, rolling her eyes. When that didn't appear to ease his confusion, she added, 'The model.'

Stunned replaced confusion on his emotional billboard. 'Are you serious? Good god, you are.' He looked straight at her. 'No. We stopped seeing each other months ago. And even when we were together, the answer would've still been no. Never. At least, not to her.'

Although she didn't care – *she didn't* – the breath she didn't realize she'd been holding escaped her body like a deflating balloon. It must've been the wine, because she had no desire to explore any other reason for having to bite her lip to keep from smiling.

They focused on their meals for a few minutes. It wasn't until Mia finally pushed her plate aside that she broke the silence. 'I have one more question. Are you still happy you came back to Rubie Racing? Even though it's me, and not my dad, bossing you around for the season?'

Luca sliced his last bit of steak into two even halves and then savored each piece as if he was finishing his last meal on earth. After a sip of wine, he leaned back in his chair and folded his arms across his chest.

'Now that's an easy question to answer. Yes. Your dad got me more excited about racing, more hopeful, than I'd been in a long time. I'll be honest, I hadn't even realized anything was missing. For lack of a better phrase, he got my motor running again. And now, even with the change in management, that feeling hasn't changed. I'm glad to be here.'

'Are you trying to tell me I get your motor running, Luca?' One hand shot up to cover her mouth while the other pushed her wineglass away. 'Rewind. Delete that. And I'm cut off.'

This time, it was definitely the wine, or perhaps the fire, because she refused to admit that the way his hazel eyes crinkled as he grinned was what made her heart melt – just like it used to so long ago.

'Already forgotten,' he said. 'And there's no way I'm finishing this bottle by myself.'

As they shared the rest of the wine, they chatted about the team and the long list of to-dos waiting for them back in Detroit. Just as their server had predicted, the snow was falling thickly when they left the restaurant, leaving the city quiet and still. It was so beautiful and fluffy that Mia fought a sudden urge to lie down and make a snow angel, cold be damned.

When she suggested they take the long way back to her condo, Luca shoved his hands in his pockets. His unenthusiastic nod changed its tune when she pulled the extra items out of her handbag. He ducked his head so she could slide the earmuffs she received in her office's last holiday gift exchange in place.

'How do I look?'

'If anyone can pull off panda earmuffs, it's you,' Mia said, handing him the matching mittens with bear faces covering the fingers to their tips. 'Don't forget these two guys.'

They trudged across the snow-covered sidewalks, joking and laughing as a million snowflakes danced around them, until they reached Lake Michigan. Staring out at the water, so darkened from the lake effect storm, Mia felt like she was balancing on the edge of the world.

Maybe she was. Her world, at least.

Mia wasn't sure how long they stood like that, side by side, in the falling snow. Or how she sensed when he'd stopped staring at the water and turned his gaze toward her.

All she knew was that when Luca put his hands on her shoulders, it wasn't to help steady her. He was going to kiss her and, when he lowered his face to hers, she kissed him back.

Chapter 13

When Luca saw Mia staring at the icy waves of Lake Michigan, lost in thought, her cheeks rosy from the wine and the cold, he couldn't think of anything but kissing her.

And when she leaned into him, it was all over. With one kiss, a dam burst and a tidal wave of pure bliss washed over him – like the first time he sat in his car each season and Christmas morning all rolled into one. But better, so much better. Even if he'd been blindfolded, his lips would've known hers from that first touch. And in that instant they remembered, he couldn't fathom how he'd ever forgotten how soft her lips were and how sweet they tasted. Like Mia.

After so much time, he wasn't sure if he was lost in their kiss or if he'd actually been found.

How quickly their passion ignited – from zero to a thousand in a matter of seconds – also came rushing back. When Mia abruptly broke away, Luca gasped like the boy he'd been when they last kissed. In answer to his questioning look, she pulled off one of her mittens with her teeth, shoved it in her pocket, and moved her bare hand to his nape. Her warm fingers played on the back of his neck, then worked their way under his hat, into his hair. This time, when his lips came back to hers, they were somehow closer, deeper than before.

The heat they were creating was no match for the storm. Although he was hard-pressed to think of a better way to ride out the weather, they needed to get to Mia's before they were frozen in place like a hero and heroine in some erotic fairytale. Mittened hand in mittened hand, they walked back to her condo, neither of them saying aloud what might happen next. Even when, once inside, they brushed the snow off each other and began peeling away the layers.

Foreplay in the Midwest, he laughed to himself as he followed Mia to the fireplace, then watched as she sparked another fire with ease.

'You know what's the weirdest thing about this, Luca?' she asked over her shoulder when the kindling and logs were fully engulfed in flames.

He tossed a few pillows from her floral nightmare of a sofa onto the rug behind where she knelt, then laid down on his side. 'No, I can't say I have any idea, Mia. Tell me.'

Within seconds, she stretched out next to him. 'That this doesn't feel weird.'

Humming his agreement, he tucked a lock of hair behind her ear as an excuse to slide the silky blonde waves through his fingers. 'But you know what would be weird? If you still weren't sensitive right here,' he said, rolling toward her and bringing his mouth to her neck. His tongue landed on a spot about a thumb's distance under her right ear and, within seconds, Mia began to squirm.

'Or here.' Luca shifted down to lift her sweater, then freed her breast and licked her nipple until she was gasping his name. He moved up again to give her a long teasing kiss before removing her sweater, then working his lips down her body so he could unbutton her jeans. Once he tugged them off, he reversed course, planting tiny kisses up her legs. 'And we certainly can't forget to check here.'

Her groan as he licked the inside of her thigh proved to them both that whatever this was, it was anything and everything but weird. By the time he reached the core of her and eased the fabric covering her aside, Mia was already shaking.

'Luca,' she gasped, her back arching. 'Please.'

Suddenly, he found himself at her mercy instead of her being at his. Any plans he had of prolonging this, of reacquainting himself with every inch of her body, went out the window and were lost in the snowstorm as he focused on only her. Even though he was about to explode.

But when she reached for him, he shook his head and growled, 'No, no, I insist.'

Within seconds of putting his mouth on her, she was screaming his name. But his tongue kept at it until every last vibration had been squeezed out of her and the hands tugging on his hair went limp along with the rest of her body. Only then did he make quick work of removing his own clothes and finally freeing himself. Once he'd sheathed himself with a condom, he fully covered her body with his and nudged against her entrance.

But first, Luca brushed a thumb across her flushed cheek and captured her lips in a kiss that was, hands down, the most passionate of his life.

'I can't believe you remembered all of that,' Mia whispered.

He smiled against her lips. 'You were the first and only person I've ever truly made love to. How could I possibly forget?'

Hours later, Luca woke up alone, warmed only by the few sparks remaining of the fire, the memory of Mia's body pressed against his, and a pastel blanket that appeared to have been knitted for a person half his size. He'd fallen asleep so quickly that he had no recollection of any pillow talk, let alone her covering him up and leaving. Murmurings drifted into the living room, and he got up and wandered toward their source – under Mia's closed bedroom door – but couldn't catch more than a word here and there. Not enough for him to know who she was talking to, or about what, although he did have a solid guess as to both.

Through the windows, he could see that the snow had finally stopped falling, leaving the night and the lake so dark that he couldn't tell where the sky ended and the water began. He robbed the guest room bed of its comforter, fed the fire, and, while he waited for Mia to rejoin him, said a quick prayer for snowplows and salt trucks, knowing there'd be hell to pay back in Detroit if the roads weren't clear by morning.

When Luca opened his eyes again hours later, it was to the sound of Mia stacking bags and suitcases near the door. As he stretched, she appeared over him, not looking nearly as relaxed as he felt. If anything, she appeared downright tense.

'There's a pot of coffee on the kitchen counter. It's not the fancy stuff you're used to, but it's caffeine. Feel free to grab a shower. Towels are in the linen closet in the hall. I'll be ready in a half hour.'

Before he could respond with 'good morning,' 'there's no rush' (even though there most definitely was), or 'why don't you lie back down here for a couple of minutes,' she was gone. It wasn't how he'd imagined, or hoped, they'd begin the day. As he listened to her pack, he realized why he'd made his rule about sex and love. It raised the potential of the morning after feeling like a sock in the gut.

Not that he was in love with Mia again. Hell, he wasn't sure if they were even friends.

With a sigh, Luca rooted around for his boxer shorts.

Exactly thirty minutes later, she readily relinquished his key fob. Once she'd directed him out of the city and they were on the highway, she reclined the passenger seat and closed her eyes. No talk of murder. No talking at all.

Even though he'd once flown nonstop from London to Sidney, this was proving to be the longest trip of his life. His fingers tapped out reasons for her silence on the steering wheel. His top choice: that he'd worn her out, which he smugly told himself three orgasms were bound to do. Her being sad about officially leaving Chicago behind was also in the realm of possibilities. But then, so was his last choice: She regretted it all.

And that would be unfortunate because he was having a hard time mustering an ounce of regret. If Mia woke up right now and asked him to climb into the backseat with her, he'd do it again in a heartbeat. Instead, she slept, and he relived the day before, racking his brain for miscues but coming up blank no matter how many times he rehashed it.

She'd wanted him as much as he'd wanted her. Luca was sure of it. That's how it had always been between them, since the first time he saw her, after a qualifying session during a grand prix weekend in Italy.

At eighteen, Luca was sitting on top of the world. He was in pole position – his fifth time starting first on the grid in a race that season. He was the defending champion in an Apex feeder series and one win away from clinching the title again, with four races left in the season.

A handful of Apex teams were watching him and had been for a couple of years. His agent expected him to receive multiple offers to be an Apex reserve driver. Although that meant he'd only be a backup to the team's two main drivers, in case they weren't able to drive, he'd still be able to get behind the wheel of an Apex car during practice sessions and at pre-season testing, as well as get time in their simulators.

He didn't say out loud which team he was leaning toward, not even to Wyn, who wouldn't shut up about his top choice.

But after living internationally since childhood, he was eager to honor his Italian roots. Drive the storied red car. Finally make his father proud, even though the guy hadn't lived in the boot since he'd left Italy for college in England.

Rubie Racing wasn't even on Luca's short list. It was a newer team, and American. U.S. teams weren't known to dominate in Apex. The same for American drivers. But Rob had been a unicorn in that regard, and he was well-liked and respected by just about everyone. So when Rob walked in the team garage that day and extended his hand, Luca was happy to shake it.

But not as happy as he was when he locked eyes with the girl standing with Rob.

'This is my daughter, Mia,' Rob said. 'She's driving this division next year so, unfortunately, you won't have the opportunity to experience her kicking your butt.'

He knew who Mia was, of course. The second unicorn of the Rubie family – the teenage girl who raced cars, who liked to go fast, and who was also the cutest thing he'd ever seen in a racing suit – was on every young driver's radar.

'That's a pity,' was all he managed to say as he extended his hand toward her. 'Luca Toscano.'

Although Mia rolled her eyes as she gripped it, he couldn't help but notice the color creeping up in her cheeks. So, he didn't let go.

After an awkward amount of time, Rob cleared his throat. Luca released her grasp, gave the man standing in front of him a sheepish grin, and began a conversation that would forever reroute his plans. Mia watching the two of them all the while.

He would later tell people that he sensed there was something different about Rob and his racing team right away. That he liked how Rob laid it on the line instead of sending smoke signals or coded messages through his agent.

While that was true, it wasn't the whole truth. Perhaps he didn't even fully admit to himself why he made a snap decision to ditch the prospect of Italy for Detroit, and a guaranteed winning ride for a car that was, at best, a gamble.

But deep down, he always knew that his path changed the moment he saw Mia. Even at sixteen, she'd had his number. Apparently, she still did. It was a good thing the roads were slick because, otherwise, he would've taken out his frustration about the current silent-treatment situation on the gas pedal.

It wasn't until they pulled into the parking lot of Rubie Racing that Mia opened her eyes again. The tired 'thank you' she muttered after he helped transfer her belongings to her car were the last words she'd spoken to him.

Until now.

'Earth to Luca? Hello...'

He emerged from his thoughts to find Jordan, Brian, and Mia focused on him, and without a clue why. He tried to remember what they'd been talking about around Mia's conference table, but came up blank. 'I'm sorry. I blanked out there for a minute. You were saying?'

Mia frowned deeper than he thought her face capable of and began speaking slowly. 'I was saying that given recent events, we should consider a larger press conference before testing in Barcelona. Hit the ground running, unless you and Jordan think it would be too distracting with everything else.'

'We talk to the press at every race, so I have no issue with that,' Luca said. 'What you're proposing will probably be more anxiety-producing for public relations and marketing, but then that's your field of expertise, not mine. That aside, I think we can all agree that what the racing world wants from Rubie Racing right now, regardless of whether they're saying it out loud, is you.'

Jordan threw his hands in the air in what appeared to be an obvious attempt to over-exaggerate his exasperation. 'You can't seriously think that we should put Mia out there, front and center, after what could best be described as a one-week crash course.'

'Excuse me? One week? Lest you forget, I'm a Rubie, too, and the one Dad entrusted to carry on the family legacy.'

Yikes. Luca had never seen Mia like this, and he wasn't sure if he was scared or turned on or both. Only his emotions weren't top of mind at the moment – he needed to brace himself for the top to blow off the pressure cooker seated next to him. But Jordan simply pushed back his chair and started to get up.

'Oh, no, you don't.' Mia pointed at him. 'Sit down.'

To Luca's amazement, Jordan did as he was told. But he didn't say another word, not even when Mia gave him homework. Yes, she even called it that, going as far as writing her brother's assignment on a piece of paper that she slid across the table before dismissing him from the meeting. When he left the room, she looked from Brian to Luca, as if she were challenging either of them to open their mouths.

'Anyone else feel like giving me lip today?' she asked.

Luca glanced over at Brian, and they both shook their heads.

'Nope, I'm good,' Brian said.

'Same here,' Luca chimed in.

'Glad to hear it,' she said, grabbing her notebook full of notes and ideas. 'Now, I'm going to go break this news to our friends in marketing and PR.'

'I can come with you, help soften the blow.' Luca knew it was a ridiculous proposition but, at this point, he couldn't have cared less. She'd been dodging him for nearly two days, and enough was enough. He grabbed his empty coffee cup off the table. 'Just let me refill.'

'Not necessary,' she said, already walking out.

Brian also moved to leave, but when he reached the door, he hesitated and shut it instead. He turned to look Luca straight in the eye. 'Soften the blow? Have you developed some "in" with marketing that I'm totally unaware of?'

Luca shrugged.

'OK then, would you care to share what's going on here with the rest of the class?'

'I'm not sure what you mean,' Luca said, even though he had a pretty good hunch.

'Well, then. Let me be a bit clearer. Last week, we were all practically braiding each other's hair like a bunch of adolescent girls at summer camp, which, all things considered, was pretty damn amazing. Then you and Mia drive off together into a blizzard and when you reappear twenty-four hours later, things are icy as hell. So, again. What's going on?'

Luca's brain quickly processed his options, a benefit of working in a field that required lightning-fast reactions. No way was he spilling about him and Mia sleeping together, and he doubted Brian would want to hear about that anyway. But he wasn't going to outright lie to his team manager, especially considering he was a horrible liar. The middle of the road was where he needed to be right now. Vague. Light on the details.

'The drive was a bit treacherous going around the bottom of Lake Michigan, so we had a decent lunch when we realized we were going to be stuck there. Everything seemed fine, but she woke up quiet.'

Brian raised an eyebrow. 'Alone?'

Luca feigned annoyance but was secretly grateful his answer was truthful, even if her abandoning him in front of the fireplace still stung. 'Yes, Brian. Alone.'

Naked and alone.

'I know your history, Luca. Not just with women in general – with Mia. Just so you're aware, it was discussed when you came back to the team.'

'That's interesting, given that it was never discussed with me,' he said. 'Regardless, that was a long time ago. We were teenagers. And like I said, I'm not sure what's gotten into her.'

Except for him, of course.

The look Brian gave him screamed that he wasn't entirely buying what Luca was selling, but he left without another word. It was the first time Luca had found himself alone in Rob's office — Mia's office — since his boss' unexpected death. Even though Rob had been gone for two weeks, it still looked like he'd just stepped out. Luca spied a pair of running shoes shoved under the desk and the partially open closet door revealed Rob's spare team jacket, a sport coat, and the dress shirt and tie he'd kept on hand for unexpected meetings.

The only evidence that Mia now inhabited the space was the leather tote bag next to the desk, the puffy blue winter coat and fur-lined snow boots near the door, and the purple day planner open on the tabletop. All were packed up at the end of each day. If she walked out and never came back, there wouldn't be a trace of her.

But he couldn't forget. Not again. She'd already been banished for too long to that high shelf in the darkest corner of his mind, stuffed with all his memories of her into a box he'd never needed to label. After their night together in Chicago, the lid on the box had blown clear off and those memories had flooded over him again. Their first kiss, in Belgium, after her inaugural climb to the top of the podium. When she found out that he'd never seen *Star Wars* and forced him to binge every film on a flight to Japan. How much she loved daisies.

Luca took in the room once again. The three-sixty brought him back to the table. To Mia's planner, which was rarely out of her reach. Before he could stop himself, he flipped through the pages, finally landing on her daily schedule.

A grin found his face for the first time since he'd fallen asleep in Chicago. He bounded from the office before anyone, except him, was any the wiser.

Chapter 14

Mia gripped the ballet barre and shifted into a perfect figure seven pose, with her back flat and her butt sticking out into the middle of the studio. Her muscles began to relax for the first time all day, and she closed her eyes and breathed deeply into the stretch. When she opened them again, a large pair of feet squeezed into hot pink socks came into focus below her.

'Pardon me, but is this space taken?'

She filled her lungs with air once more and then exhaled a loud sigh before abandoning her pose to stand up and face the person she'd been actively trying to avoid. How in the hell had he tracked her here?

'I thought Italians took more notice of their footwear,' she said, pointing toward the floor.

Luca lifted his left foot to show her the rubber spots dotting the bottom of the sock. 'Apparently, these grippies are the key to my success,' he said, lowering his foot back to the floor. 'While this particular shade of pink wouldn't be my first choice, it has proven to be quite the conversation starter.'

'I'm afraid you won't be able to do much talking for the next hour.' She gestured to the open section of barre space next to her. 'But please, make yourself at home.'

She sat down and leaned against the wall, willing herself to look as relaxed as she'd felt only moments earlier. Luca set his water bottle down beside hers and went in search of the weights, yoga strap, and small exercise ball her stretch of barre had already been stocked with. He returned with the heaviest dumbbells and smugly placed them next to the pale pink, two-pound pair she preferred for the high-repetition strength training set sandwiched in the middle of class.

When the instructor began class with a marching warmup, Mia heard Luca chuckling beside her. A glance in the mirror revealed him lifting his knees in unison with the ten other women in the class, and twice as many eyes watching his well-toned legs move up and down to eighties Madonna. Her eyes included.

While men hadn't been an infrequent sight at the barre classes she'd taken in Chicago, they'd typically been your average sort of guy dragged in by a wife or girlfriend. They didn't look like Luca did in a pair of shorts and a T-shirt. He was all muscle, without an inch to pinch anywhere. And she would know – she'd tried the other night. A memory she clearly didn't need to think about now, or maybe ever.

Nothing's changed, she reminded herself for the millionth time since she peeled herself away from Luca's sleeping body to make an emergency call to Star. After Mia had convinced her best friend that she couldn't come over and see for herself the naked race car driver in the living room, they'd decided that the two of them having sex had been inevitable. Their steamy past had been bound to catch up with them, and now that it was out of the way, they could get down to business – just not business-business. Plus, grief had weakened her defenses. That had been one huge, guilt-laden pill to swallow. Mere weeks after her dad had died, she'd gone to bed with Luca. And now, here she was, gawking at his defined calf muscles.

Her brain was grateful when, a couple of minutes later, the class dropped into a high plank and could only focus on lifting her belly button up to the ceiling and keeping her eyes fixed on the floor. But after the first minute ticked by, she noticed that Luca was no longer laughing.

This is going to be good, Mia thought as they dropped down to their forearms at the minute mark and began lifting their legs one at a time to challenge their stability. She may have kept hers up for an extra second or two and leisurely flexed and pointed her airborne foot. When the instructor gave everyone the option to drop to their knees, Luca actually grunted, but didn't release his plank. His face was beet red when he was finally able to sit back into child's pose, and then lifted his head and shot Mia a look of disbelief when, mere seconds later, they moved onto abdominal exercises. Little did he know that was only the first set of three.

When they stood up and shifted to the barre, it was Mia's

turn to chuckle. With a lime green ball squeezed between his parallel thighs and his heels lifted high, Luca struggled to repeat the small up-and-down movement. His hands gripped the barre so tightly that his knuckles were turning as white as they'd been on the steering wheel on the drive home from Chicago, when she'd pretended to be asleep. But his form was annoyingly perfect.

'If you don't mind, I'm trying to focus here,' he whispered. 'I would appreciate it if you would stop leering at me.'

'Not so cocky now, I see,' she said, just as the instructor told the class to gyrate their hips back and forth with their knees bent. Luca's eyes widened as she followed along to 'tilt, release, tilt, release, tilt, release.'

He winked and matched his rhythm to hers. 'Oh, I wouldn't say that.'

Feeling her cheeks go up in flames, she looked away and decided it was probably best to focus on her own workout. Her timing couldn't have been more perfect, given that the next exercise involved them balancing on tippy-toes while shifting their bodies in time to 'up an inch, down an inch.'

As she remembered how she'd demonstrated that very move the other night, there was a solid chance she may actually spontaneously combust and end up as nothing more than a pile of goo.

Not surprisingly, Luca received plenty of attention even without her keeping a close eye on how his body was positioned. The instructor seemed to have her hands on every part of him over the course of the next forty minutes, correcting his stance and repositioning him, even though his alignment was textbook. By the fifth time, Mia fought a growing urge to swat the woman's hands away — not that who touched Luca's body was anything to her.

They ended class back in another high plank. Mia loved how much stronger her body felt after a good workout. Holding the plank for a full ten seconds after Luca collapsed was just the frosting on the cake. Before she could razz him, the lights lowered for *savasana* and everyone flipped onto their backs to end class in a still quiet. The instructor made a beeline to Luca, grabbed him by the ankles and helped stretch his legs, then gave his calves a quick massage.

'Oh, for Pete's sake, hands off, lady,' Mia muttered between clenched teeth. With any chance of relaxation out the window, she squeezed her eyes closed and waited impatiently for the room to brighten. When she opened them, she found Luca on his side, facing her, his shirt creeping up just enough to reveal a hint of his perfectly sculpted six-pack.

'Color me impressed,' he yawned. 'Maybe tomorrow we see who can lift the most weight with their necks.'

Before Mia could find any words to respond, Ms Hands-on was back to ask how Luca enjoyed his first class. Mia took advantage of him being distracted by putting her props away and sneaking out of the studio. Boots and coat on, she was ten steps out the door when a deep voice yelled her name.

She turned around to find Luca sprinting across the parking lot toward her, pink socks and all.

'Luca, what?'

'Where are you off to in such a hurry? I wanted to see if we could talk.' He rubbed his bare biceps with his hands and smiled.

'I was actually heading home to work on some ideas marketing came up with about the launch.' *Liar*. Her brain was more fried than the rice she'd been fantasizing about all afternoon, and the only things she planned to manage that night were chopsticks and the remote control.

'Can you wait while I go grab my things?' he asked.

Before she could respond, Ms Hands-on appeared at Luca's side and poked his arm with a glittery, well-manicured nail. 'Hey, sorry to interrupt, but I'm going to need those socks back. Plus, I have some suggestions for your practice, if you have a sec.'

'Oh, you don't need to worry about me absconding with these,' he said, gesturing toward his feet. 'I'll be right back in.'

She glided back to the studio, no doubt with her abdominal muscles completely engaged. Luca turned his attention back to Mia, but before he could open his mouth, she cut him off.

'I'll catch up with you later, Luca. But thanks, I guess, for showing up uninvited to my workout and inserting yourself into the only space still free of all this racing madness. I really do appreciate it.'

And scene, Mia thought, walking to her car while searching her phone for the number of her favorite Chinese restaurant.

Barb looked up from a crossword when Mia walked into

the living room thirty minutes later and held up a bag. 'Almond boneless chicken for two.'

'Well, I hope you worked out enough for the both of us then,' Barb said, following her into the kitchen.

After her move to Chicago, Mia had discovered that the roots of her favorite dish were more Michigan than China, and that it couldn't be found on a menu outside of the metro Detroit area. After that, her one requirement on visits home had been a stop at the Chinese restaurant her dad had taken her and Jordan to since they were kids.

'God help me, but almond boneless chicken is my one true weakness,' she said out loud for no reason.

Barb raised an eyebrow. 'Sure, if you say so.'

'If you're thinking what I think you're thinking, it's not like that,' Mia said, the serving spoon she'd grabbed out of the drawer hovering in midair. 'We're friends. Actually, not even that. I'm his boss.'

'I was actually going to say brownies, but apparently you've gone in an entirely different direction,' Barb said.

'Nope, I was talking about brownies, too,' Mia said.

Judging by the look Barb gave her, she clearly wasn't buying it. Mia set the utensils on the counter and then grabbed a flavored fizzy water from the fridge. She poured the can's contents into a glass Barb handed her.

'Luca was at my workout class tonight. He just showed up.'

Barb took two plates out of the cabinet. 'That's odd, and it doesn't sound like Luca. Did something happen between the two of you?'

Mia shrugged. 'Maybe. Kind of.'

Definitely.

Not that she was about to tell the only mother figure in her life about her one-night stand, which is what it had been. Or that afterward, when Luca had tucked her into his chest and spooned her, she hadn't been able to think of another place in the world where she'd rather be.

Barb's 'hmm' let Mia know that what she'd left unsaid spoke volumes.

'It doesn't matter.' Mia pulled the traditional Chinese food takeout boxes out of the bag. 'It was a mistake.'

She finally got up the nerve to look Barb in the eye, expecting to see a face painted in disapproval. But Barb only shook her head and smiled.

'Not everything is exactly one thing or another, Mia. I know how that brain of yours works. Before you start beating yourself up, maybe consider that some things happen because they're what you need in a certain moment in time.'

Chimes from the front doorbell ricocheted through the main floor, interrupting their conversation. Barb headed out of the room, calling out behind her, 'I wonder who that could be? I certainly wasn't expecting anyone.'

Mia set about splitting up the thick slices of breaded and fried boneless chicken, placing them on top of what was now a bed of warm, wilted lettuce, even though she never ate it and didn't understand why it was there. She slathered the chicken with gravy and dished a big spoonful of fried rice onto each plate.

'They only gave us one egg roll,' she shouted. 'Do you want to split it?'

But instead of Barb, a deep voice too familiar that evening replied, 'Either that or I get the whole thing. I can't eat Chinese food without an egg roll.'

Mia looked up to find Luca standing in the doorway. 'First my workout and now my kitchen? You're having a real issue with my personal space tonight, Luca.'

'Am I?' he asked, sitting at the island and sliding one of the plates in front of him. He glanced down and frowned. 'What the hell is that? Please tell me this isn't what you consider post-workout fuel.'

'*That* is Barb's,' she said. 'And what I put in my body is really none of your business.'

She cringed as his eyes became as round as the plate she tried to pull away from him.

'I think it's probably best that I don't respond to that,' he said, winning their game of tug of war. 'Now, tell me, what exactly is... this?'

'First, tell me what you did with Barb. Do I need to check to make sure she's not unconscious in the front closet?'

'She said something about being tired and heading to her room.' He smiled and pointed his fork at the chicken. 'So, what's with the gravy?'

Mia shook her head and gave him the brief history of almond boneless chicken, emphasizing that it wasn't a dish to be enjoyed cold or leftover, which was the only reason she wasn't going to delay her dinner any longer.

They ate in silence. When Luca finished, one of his hands went right to his stomach. 'That's going to hurt on my run tomorrow.'

'I hate to break it to you, but that's going to hurt in about fifteen minutes,' Mia said. 'It's best to consider it carb loading.'

'If you consider whatever that was a carb, we definitely need to talk,' he laughed.

Mia pushed both fortune cookies toward him and gestured for him to choose one. When he put his hands up to object, she shoved them closer. 'You have to pick so I can take the one that's left. It's a rule.'

With zero deliberation, he grabbed the one to his left and cracked it open. 'Do you always let someone else decide your fortune?'

'I've never thought about it that way. It's more that I let fate choose my fortune for me.'

Although in this scenario, Luca had a starring role as fate. Best not to dwell on that or share that she'd saved her fortunes since she was a girl, and often came across them in random drawers and handbags.

Luca scanned his tiny slip of paper, shrugged, then moved to stick it in his pocket.

Mia grabbed his arm. 'No, no. You have to read it out loud. It's a rule.'

'You have a lot of rules about Chinese food,' he sighed. 'Fine, but you go first.'

Mia cracked open the remaining cookie, brushing the

fragments aside as soon as the fortune was in her fingers. 'It's a good one: Your determination will bring you much success.'

'In bed?' he asked, then laughed when she made a face. 'Yes, even foreigners know about adding "in bed" to the end of fortunes. Especially ones who have been persuaded to come to the United States by a certain racing family.'

'Ha ha,' she deadpanned. 'Your turn.'

'Mine is a good one, too. I mean, I hate it when a fortune cookie tells you that you're about to get hit by a bus or lose money in a pyramid scheme.' He rolled his eyes, then read, 'You are talented in many ways… in bed.'

'I wouldn't touch that one with a ten-foot pole,' Mia groaned, getting up to load their plates into the dishwasher. *Even if it was true.*

'That would be awkward, actually, with both us wielding ten-foot—'

'Stop, stop, stop.' She took her time tidying the kitchen, knowing full well she was stalling the inevitable conversation that had led Luca to track her down at the barre studio. She could feel his eyes on her as she rinsed out the to-go containers for recycling, then wiped down the countertops.

Luca pointed to a spot on the island in front of him. 'There's a bit of gravy here. Might want to get that now so Barb doesn't have to blowtorch it off tomorrow or scrap these countertops for new ones altogether.'

The thought of new countertops gave Mia a sudden pause, and she glanced around the kitchen. Her dad had renovated the space a decade ago, and the heavy dark wood and thick granite countertops were surely more his taste than Barb's. It was basically a man cave with shiny appliances. But this house belonged to Barb now, and she had every right to rip it all out and get rid of the wealthy aristocrat vibe her father's decorator had created. Start over. Change the countertops and anything else. Everything else.

She suddenly felt more attached to the oak cabinets than she had any right to.

'I think I've had enough change to last awhile,' she said to herself, putting all the strength she could muster into scrubbing the gravy spot, which was already beginning to congeal. She feared for her digestive system.

'Mia?'

She looked up to find Luca watching her. 'I'm sorry, but did you say something?'

'I think you got it,' he motioned toward where she was scrubbing.

'Got what?'

'The gravy. It's gone.'

Her heart raced as he slowly rounded the island toward her. But when he reached her, it was to take the dishcloth from her hand, rinse it out in the sink, and drape it neatly over the faucet. Just how Barb preferred.

'Believe it or not, my intent tonight wasn't to torture you, or me, for that matter. Between those planks and whatever the hell that concoction was—'

'Almond boneless chicken. And it's a delicacy!'

Luca nodded as his hand went to his stomach again. 'Right.

All I'll say is my body is a finely tuned machine and I feel like I just accidentally put chocolate pudding instead of gasoline in the tank.'

'I'd say that's totally normal, given the circumstances.'

'Is that supposed to make me feel better? Because it doesn't.' He hopped up to sit on the counter across from where she stood. 'Look, I think we should talk. About what happened in Chicago.'

'Yes, that was one hell of a snowstorm,' Mia said.

Luca's hazel eyes sparked. 'I was referring to what happened indoors.'

He didn't need to elaborate – their fireside activities were forever etched in her brain.

'No more beating around the bush then,' she said, hoisting herself onto the island. Mia couldn't ignore him forever, she knew that, but as long as she didn't talk to him, see him, or hear his name, she hardly thought about him at all. Still, they needed a better strategy for the long-term. Their best course of action was to admit they'd made a mistake, agree not to repeat it, and move on. Surely, he'd come to the same conclusion. 'I say we blame the wine and forget it ever happened.'

'Vino or no vino, it was out of line, and I owe you an apology,' Luca said. 'And as much as I probably deserve the silent treatment, I'd like to call a truce. For the good of the team.'

Sacrificing things for Rubie Racing was becoming an annoying trend in her life as of late. 'Fine. No more cold shoulder. But to be clear, this' – she gestured with her hand between the two of them – 'isn't happening.'

He nodded. 'Got it. It was the definition of bad timing, and I'm sorry. I mean, your dad just died and you've just taken over leading the team. You're right, we probably shouldn't go there. At least not right now. But I'd like us to be friends.'

Right now? Friends?

When Mia didn't respond, Luca repeated the word already echoing around in her head. 'Friends?'

'In a million years, I never thought I'd be sitting face-to-face with Luca Toscano, talking about being friends. Do you honestly think that's possible?'

'Sure, why not?' he asked.

'Where do I start?'

He folded his arms in front of his chest and sighed. 'You'll have to tell me, Mia.'

When Luca had left without saying goodbye all of those years ago, she'd spent months pinballing around the grief scale. But when she'd finally landed on anger and fantasized about telling him off, he'd never looked sad. She'd also never imagined enjoying spending time with him again, or traveling around the globe together for eight months.

But friends?

'I'll tell you what, you can be a "reserve" friend,' she said, emphasizing the word 'reserve' with air quotes.

Luca snorted. 'Like a reserve driver?'

'Exactly.'

'And this works how? Please, enlighten me.'

As genius as this brainstorm was, Mia was going to have

to wing the details. 'Much like a reserve driver is part of the team but not involved in races, unless they're called up, a reserve friend is, um, you know, there. Waiting.'

'Waiting... to be called up as a friend?' he asked. At least confusion had overtaken the wounded look clouding his hazel eyes.

'To have earned the right to be a friend,' Mia said, continuing to make this up as she went along. 'To show he's actually deserving of the role.'

'Right,' he said. 'You do know that some drivers spend their whole lives as reserve drivers.'

She shrugged. 'That's their choice though, right?'

At that, Luca shook his head. 'Talk about going full circle with the Rubie family. But what the hell, I'm game. Given what a stickler you are about eating Chinese food, I assume there are some rules I should know about?'

'Of course.' She closed her eyes and began tapping her finger to her lips, only to open them and find Luca watching her mouth and swallowing hard. 'First and foremost, no kissing. I mean, that should go without saying, considering I'm your boss now. Beyond that, what did you do as a reserve driver?'

He leveled her with a stare she felt in her uterus. 'If kissing isn't allowed, I don't think you want me repeating anything else I was doing back then. As I'm sure you recall.'

How could she forget? 'Do not go there unless you're looking for some of that leftover gravy to end up in your espresso tomorrow.'

Luca faked a gagging noise. 'Point taken.'

'Second, no stalking me around town and barging into my home and stealing my Chinese food.'

'Stalking and stealing are pretty strong allegations, Mia,' Luca said. 'Although you probably shouldn't leave your planner out in the open. Just saying. You know, wandering eyes and all.'

She shook her head in mock disgust. Mystery solved. 'Point taken.'

Unsure of what else to add, Mia was relieved when Luca hopped down from the countertop and extended his hand. 'This may not be the best time to bring this up, but we could really use a reserve driver. But for now, you have your reserve friend.'

Chapter 15

Thanks to Luca, strolling through the Barcelona airport didn't go unnoticed. Only instead of a few photographers here and there, or a nudge or two between fans, every other person had their mobile phone out and pointed at them. To his credit, Luca appeared completely at ease, almost animated, as he led them through the concourse while chatting with Brian. They walked directly out the door to find a massive SUV waiting, and only after Luca had opened the door so she could climb inside did he acknowledge their onlookers with a quick wave and thumbs up.

'Now that wasn't so bad,' he said, once they were all buckled in and on their way.

'Speak for yourself,' Mia said. 'Smartphones hadn't been invented the last time I found myself in a crowd of fans. I think our picture just posted to about a thousand social media feeds.'

'What can I say? People can't get enough of racing team managers,' Brian piped in from the front seat. 'The paparazzi follow me everywhere.'

Without a word, Luca pulled his phone from his pocket, pointed it at Brian, and snapped a photo.

After a week of working twelve-hour days to make sure they, the team, and the turbo pumpkin were ready for testing in Spain, and being awake for more hours than her tired brain could count, Mia dissolved into a crying-laughing jag. Which only made Luca howl and then her laugh more.

Some reserve friend he'd turned out to be.

Brian milked his joke for all it was worth for the remainder of the day, pretending to shield his face with his hands whenever he saw a mobile phone in their vicinity. By the time they finished dinner and headed back to their hotel, the trio was beyond slap happy. Mia's abdominal muscles felt like she'd done a dozen barre classes in a row from laughing so much.

'See you both bright and early,' Brian said when the elevator door opened on his floor and he stepped out, leaving Mia and Luca to ride up to their floors alone.

She leaned against one of the wall panels and yawned loudly. 'I don't think I've ever been so tired.'

'Hmm. Could it be that you stayed awake the entire flight over with your nose in an e-book, instead of trying to catch just a few winks of sleep?'

'I have a hard time sleeping on planes.' She was surprised he'd noticed, considering he'd been sound asleep whenever she'd stolen a glance his way. 'You appeared to have no issue with that.'

'If there's one thing I do very well in bed, or really anywhere with the slightest bit of an incline,' he backed out of the elevator with a wink, 'it's sleep. G'night, Mia.'

'Goodnight' was all she managed to choke out as the doors slid closed.

If the man thought flirty innuendos were enough to make her regret the stupidest idea that she'd ever come up with, he was right — at least when her defenses were down from exhaustion. Thankfully, she lacked enough energy to pry the doors open.

Overall, the last week with Luca had gone far better than Mia had expected. Cordially. She could do months of cordial. With her ex-boyfriend at arm's-length, she could put on a happy face — at least that part came naturally — and live out her dad's final wishes. She could travel the world with the Rubie Racing team, make multimillion dollar decisions, even deal with her brother. She could stay calm, collected, and in control. She could do this for one season.

Just as soon as she got some sleep.

Since Mia had taken over her dad's hotel bookings, she was spending the team's nearly two weeks in Spain in the royal suite. When she'd checked in, she'd envisioned ending her days on the terrace, taking in the view of Barcelona with a relaxing glass of wine. Instead, she barely made it to the leather sofa before collapsing.

Only to her frustration, she found herself staring at the ceiling instead of the back of her eyelids. She grabbed her phone and sent a quick text to Star.

Mia: *I didn't know it was possible, but I think I'm too tired to sleep.*

Star: *So go find that sexy race car driver and do something else.*

Mia: *Please. Stop. How many times do I have to tell you that was a one-off?*

Star: *I'd guess as many times as you need to say it to convince yourself.*

Mia woke up smack dab in the middle of the king-sized bed. A hazy memory emerged of stumbling into the bedroom and out of her shoes and jeans in the middle of the night. Her head pounded like she'd drunk a pitcher of sangria instead of a small glass, and she climbed out of bed in search of water and ibuprofen.

Curse you, jet lag.

The fully stocked kitchen, which she'd deemed ridiculous not fifteen hours ago, was now the answer to her prayers. Especially the uber-fancy espresso machine calling her name.

Two tiny cups later, Mia's headache felt less like a woodpecker and more like a persistent yet pesky hummingbird mining for nectar. Still, she almost didn't register that the light knock wasn't inside her brain. She opened the door to find Luca mid-knock, looking straight out of the centerfold of a race car driver magazine.

And she still wasn't wearing any pants.

'Something tells me you're not ready to head downstairs for the meeting,' Luca said, the struggle to keep his gaze above her waist more than obvious.

After what seemed like every media outlet on the planet

had shown an interest in the direction of Rubie Racing following her dad's death, Mia had scheduled a breakfast meeting with the public relations team to make sure everyone was on the same page before that afternoon's press conference. She'd thought kick-starting the day bright and early would help her adjust to the time zone change.

Of course, she'd also imagined she'd be wearing pants.

When tugging at her shirt proved to be a futile attempt at covering her legs, Mia sprinted to the shower, yelling over her shoulder, 'I'll be ready in ten!' And then, 'Espresso!'

Hours later, Mia found herself sitting in front of a sea of reporters, with an actual sea – the Mediterranean – stretching to the horizon behind her.

Dressed head to toe in Rubie Racing attire, the team easily fielded the questions they'd anticipated about the season's cars. She asked Brian to give an overview of the new design and engine modifications, and then Luca and Jordan each provided their own sound bites. Questions about her father's death and its impact on the team and the season went to her and Jordan. They both kept their answers as straightforward as possible, although both of their voices cracked more than once.

Once the reporters seemed to accept that Rubie Racing was managing to forge on without their fearless leader, Mia added, 'Look, I realize you all wish my dad was the one sitting here, answering your questions, not me. I know many of you have spent your careers covering him as a driver and a team owner. But for reasons we'll now never know, this is what he wanted, and I'm determined to honor his wishes and continue my family's legacy with my brother.'

The somber mood that had hovered over the entire news conference now covered the room like a thick blanket. A few sniffs filled the silence. Even Jordan seemed affected by the gravity of their father not being there for the start of the season – for the first time in his own career. When he shifted in the chair next to her, she noticed his pout was absent of even a trace of scowl and his eyes were attempting to blink away tears.

No one anticipated that the fresh-faced reporter, who Mia had noticed flipping through notes and scribbling furiously at different points, would raise her hand when everyone else seemed ready to wrap things up.

Mia smiled. 'Sure, we can take another question or two.'

The reporter beamed as if her day had just been made and, in an American accent, said, 'Thank you. I saw some photos that seem to hint at you and Luca being involved. Is this true?'

Mia's smile didn't waver. 'I'm sorry. I'm unclear about which photos you're referring to.'

The reporter held up her phone and began blindly swiping through them. 'Here's one of the two of you at lunch in Chicago, another of you together at the airport, and one from early this morning. You appear to be freshly showered.'

Mia squinted. 'Actually, I believe that last one is of a small dog. Some sort of terrier maybe?' Laughter filled the room. 'Although I'd prefer to not publicly comment on my private relationships, I will say that Luca is a valued member of the Rubie Racing team and a longtime friend.'

The reporter shifted her focus to Luca. 'That would've been fast, I guess, with Julia Sullivan spotted here in the hotel, too.'

Mia's jet-lagged brain searched for a perfectly rational reason for Luca's supermodel ex-girlfriend to be randomly wandering around the same luxury hotel in Spain that the racing team was staying in. But she was damned if she could think of one.

She shouldn't care what her reserve friend was up to during his personal time. Only she did, damn it. He'd told her they'd broken up. If the reporter didn't nudge Luca for an answer soon, she might have to.

'Luca?' the reporter asked.

'Yes?'

'Do you have a comment?' she prodded.

'Have you asked a question?' he responded.

Mia could feel Luca's tense up beside her. For the first time in her life, she was grateful for being gifted her dad's permagrin over her mom's pout. That smile didn't waver.

'Are you and Julia Sullivan together?'

Mia leaned in slightly, as if she'd hear whatever Luca spoke into the microphone before the rest of the room.

'No, we are not,' Luca said. 'Our relationship has been over for quite a while, actually.'

'Then her visit to Spain is?'

'I don't have the slightest—'

'To see me,' Jordan piped in from her other side.

Mia's eyes widened as Luca leaned toward her, covered his microphone, and whispered, 'Now there's a match made somewhere slightly south of heaven.'

She could see he was struggling not to laugh. He gulped from the glass of water in front of him. Pinched the bridge of his nose. Bit his bottom lip. All the while, Jordan wore the same expression as the fabled cat who'd swallowed the proverbial canary.

'Interesting,' the reporter said, writing in her notebook.

From the end of the table, Brian tapped his microphone. 'Excuse me, but what publication are you with?'

When her pen stilled, she looked up and smiled. 'Madison Davis, the411.com.'

The mention of the popular and controversial gossip website elicited gasps from around the room. The people seated closest to Madison leaned away, and Mia immediately regretted every celebrity article she'd ever clicked on that led her to the digital tabloid.

'Well, if there are no more questions about Rubie Racing,' Mia said, stressing the latter two words, 'then I suppose we'll wrap this up.'

But Madison clearly didn't get the message because she started speaking again. 'About fifteen years ago, you were all on a Rubie Racing team for a twenty-four-hour race in Daytona. A lot of rumors swirled around about what exactly happened that night, but we all know the result – a crash that totaled the sports car and ended the career of your team's top driver,

Scott Carrington. Now, Mia, that race had been your and your brother's debut with your father's team and, as it turns out, your only race. And Luca, you'd been moved up from reserve driver for that race, which was a big deal. But then you were gone soon after, with Jordan taking your place as reserve driver.'

The entire room seemed to be holding a collective breath, Mia included. Under the table, Luca's knee knocked hers.

'I think we're done here,' Brian said, getting up.

Madison ignored him and charged on. 'It seems that this was an off-limits topic for Rob Rubie but, well, he's no longer here, sadly. So, my question is twofold, really. What happened that night? And, Mia, why on earth would your father leave you in charge of a team that he didn't even trust you to drive for?'

Calm. Stay calm.

Brian's voice boomed out through the room, even without the assistance of his microphone. 'And now I know we're done. Thank you for coming, everyone.'

Chapter 16

'What the hell was that?' Mia shouted as soon as the elevator doors closed.

Luca had escorted her from the conference room, casually strolling to the elevator bank and then nonchalantly pushing the button for Mia's floor, even though his heart had been pounding out of his chest. It was a level of panic he hadn't felt since he was twenty years old, when he'd been on top of the world in one second and had nearly lost everything the next.

'I wish the fuck I knew,' he said, resting his head on the panel above the control panel.

Once they were in her suite, Mia headed directly into the bedroom and climbed under the covers, shoes and all. Luca followed, grabbing a bottle of *orujo* from the fully stocked bar on his way. Climbing into bed next to her, he poured a splash into a glass and tossed it back, then refilled it for Mia.

'Drink this,' he said, nudging her with his foot. 'Then we talk.'

She sat up, grabbed the glass, and downed the amber liquid in a single gulp. Her eyes widened. 'OK, what the hell was *that*?'

'I believe the locals call it "firewater."' He refilled the glass again. 'Not the smoothest liquor I've ever had, but given the circumstances, it will do.'

Mia grabbed the glass and took another dose before lying back down. Luca followed her lead, then set the bottle and glass on the nightstand. He watched as she tucked a lock of hair behind her right ear.

'I don't know what it says about me that the people in my life think shots of booze are all it takes to calm me down,' she said.

'Is it helping?'

She shook her head. 'Nope. This is still a disaster.'

'Maybe,' he shrugged a shoulder, 'or maybe not.'

'Maybe *not*? You're definitely cut off, Luca.'

'It was all bound to come out at some point, don't you think?'

'No, I don't think. It happened before camera phones and social media. Before random crap went viral.'

He shook his head, amazed that Mia didn't see the situation for what it clearly had been – a master cover-up job. 'I don't know how your dad managed to keep it all under the radar back then, not that either of us was important enough at that point to merit a scandal. But that's all this is. Granted, the timing is hardly ideal, but whomever leaked it planned for maximum impact.'

'If this was my brother's doing, I may be tempted to pull a Cain and Abel,' Mia said.

'I don't know who else it could be.' Not to mention, his teammate had seemed a little too smug when the press conference veered off course. 'But for the record, I, for one, am a little relieved to have one less skeleton in my closet to keep track of.'

'You always were annoyingly positive,' she said.

'Think about it, Mia. We've both been caught in the marbles over this for years. In different ways, of course. But now, for better or worse, we can move on.'

Her eyes widened. 'Caught in the marbles?'

'Yes, Mia, marbles. Those tiny pieces of rubber that settle on the track? Have you been away from racing for so long that you've forgotten the lingo?'

As she shook her head, a single tear trickled down her cheek and onto the pillowcase. He reached over and pushed her ever-errant lock of hair back behind her ear, then inched down until he was lying on his side facing her.

'And Julia?' she sniffed. 'Are you upset that she's apparently switched teammates? I saw photos of the two of you, Luca. Happy. Holding hands. The race car driver and the supermodel. It's a legitimate fairy tale come true in the Rubie family.'

'Trust me when I say that being with Julia was no fairy tale, and there will be no happy ending. At least not with this race car driver, and probably not for your brother, either.'

What he couldn't say out loud, given his current status as

reserve friend, was that he felt far more for Mia than he ever had for Julia. There was no comparison. It was practically killing him to lie next to her and not take her in his arms and soothe her the best way he knew how.

Mia's eyes drooped and she drifted off to sleep. It was nearly two o'clock in the afternoon, and they were due at the track for a final check on the cars before testing began tomorrow. He texted his team as well as Brian to say he'd be late, but at this point, they'd need a helicopter to get there at all.

Getting her away from the press conference had been a spur-of-the-moment decision. Maybe the booze wasn't his best idea, but it had been the first thing he thought of to take off the edge.

OK, the second thing.

Luca must've drifted off, too, because a light rap on the door had him jumping to his feet, his heart racing again. He opened the door to find Brian standing in the hallway, arms crossed in front of his chest and not looking the least bit happy.

'What the hell was that?!'

Luca shook his head. 'Apparently, that's the catchphrase of the day.'

He stepped aside so Brian could pass through, then followed him into the living room area, stopping to shut the bedroom door on the way. Mia hadn't moved – a little *orujo*, too much emotion, and leftover jet lag proved to be her kryptonite.

Brian perched awkwardly on the arm of the sofa. 'This is not what we need right now.'

'You think? How bad is this for Mia?'

Brian gave up his balancing act and slid down onto a sofa cushion. 'There were some tweets from the press conference, and that reporter with too many questions had an article up on the internet within minutes. It's full of holes and assumptions.'

Luca paced around the room. 'Since when do we let reporters from gossip rags in?'

'Not a clue, but I plan to find out,' Brian said. 'The PR folks are trying to do damage control, but it's like dealing with a tsunami when you didn't know there was an earthquake. No one knew this was coming. Well, next to no one.'

'Come on, Brian. Obviously, we didn't know. It was a long time ago. Another lifetime.'

'If there's a saving grace, it's that the other teams are pissed. You know how it is. The owners are a tight group, and they took Rob's final request to support Mia as they had him very seriously.' Brian glanced at the closed bedroom door and lowered his voice. 'But here's the thing – no one really knows what happened. Hell, I don't even know the full story. It was gossip Rob managed to bury long ago, to protect Mia, I assume, and no one dared to resurrect it. Until now.'

Luca never faulted Rob for sweeping the incident under the rug. If anything, he was grateful. Even if he had intended to only save Mia's reputation, by default, he had saved Luca's career. At the time, Luca had been more than willing to move on with his life and toward his dream of being an Apex driver.

Even though it had also meant moving on from Mia.

A quick internet search on his phone led Luca to multiple racing sites. The damn article had gone viral. *Great*.

The reporter didn't know everything about that night, but she knew enough. Brian, though — he deserved to know everything. So, Luca told him about how he had fallen for Mia. Hard. Right from the beginning. How her devil-may-care attitude had awakened something inside of him. How, for the first time in his life, he'd been driven by a passion for something other than racing and winning. How all of that had led to him — and Mia — being reckless, impulsive, and, ultimately, foolish.

When Mia and Jordan turned eighteen, Rob made a huge announcement: Rubie Racing would enter a twenty-four-hour sports car race during the off-season. And that team would consist of four drivers: Scott, Luca, Jordan, and Mia. Since Scott had been Rubie Racing's number one driver for years, Rob had charged him with guiding Luca, which he was already doing for Apex, along with his son and daughter.

It was Luca's second season as a reserve driver for Rubie Racing, which meant that he and Mia had been sneaking around behind everyone's backs for a year, since she'd turned seventeen. He had wanted to come clean, especially to his boss. He hadn't thought them dating was a big deal. But Mia had been adamant that her dad might fire him and end his career. Considering Rob had the power to do just that, and more, Luca had continued pretending Mia was nothing more to him than the sister he never had, a best friend with breasts.

And then stripping her clothes off whenever and wherever they were alone.

'OK, young love, first love, crazy love, I got it,' Brian interrupted. 'Are you writing a teen romance, or are you getting somewhere with this?'

'You asked,' Luca sighed. 'But, OK, to the race then.'

He could still feel the excitement of that race day. It seemed like every driver in the world had descended on Daytona, Florida, and they weren't there for the sunshine. Many were driving on a team regardless of the kind of cars they were behind the wheels of during their regular seasons.

Although Rob never said it aloud, the race had been a big deal to him, too. It was Rubie Racing's first foray into sports cars, and his children were making their debut in the big leagues, along with Luca.

They were a team of four dividing up twenty-four consecutive hours of driving around the storied three-and-a-half-mile track near the Atlantic Ocean. But it was no day at the beach – they'd be switching on and off according to a timed schedule Rob had determined based on Scott's years of experience and everyone's strengths and weaknesses. They had to follow the rules of the race, too, including that no driver could be behind the wheel for more than four hours of a six-hour period. Teamwork was key.

Scott drove first – a smart choice that also allowed Rob not to play favorites. Luca was second, Jordan next, and then Mia before they repeated. Once a driving shift was over and they'd debriefed the engineer on duty, they were free for a couple of hours.

Luca stayed in the pits for Mia's three-hour shift. Watching her drive, masterfully weaving through the mass of cars on the track, had his blood pulsing through his veins faster than when he drove himself. When she finally got out of the car, he could see that she was as amped up as he was. She muttered a few sentences to the engineer before brushing him off, hopping on a scooter, and giving Luca a look.

That look.

Most Rubie Racing team members could be found in the team motorhome between shifts, or in their assigned garage. Everyone, from the mechanics to the engineers, did their best to catch some sleep while they could. Imagine thirty people either milling around, sleeping, or trying to wake up at any given time. Not really ideal for two teenagers looking to be alone.

'We ended up in the backseat of some random unlocked SUV,' Luca told Brian, who cringed. 'I know, not my finest moment. Neither was, uh, finishing to find you have an audience, and it's the girl's father.'

'Oh, Christ, Luca,' Brian said.

'No walkie-talkies with us, and no mobile either, so we didn't know that Scott had realized he wasn't feeling well soon after he took over for Mia, and that Rob was frantically trying to find us to get one of us in the car.'

'Jordan?'

'He wasn't around either, not that it mattered. He'd driven a full shift before Mia, right, so his six hours weren't up. It had to be me or Mia.'

Brian shook his head, and Luca knew it was because he

realized what was still coming. The story didn't end with his pants down in the back seat of a Ford Explorer. That was the part that people didn't know.

'It was probably right around then that Scott hit the wall,' Luca said. 'And everything changed.'

Mia's eyes had popped open when the door clicked shut, and she'd laid awake in the bedroom eavesdropping on Brian and Luca's conversation. Clutching the covers, cringing as Luca spilled all of the sordid details of that day, hearing his version for the first time. It matched perfectly with what had been replaying on an endless loop all these years in her own head.

Not that her brain could've exaggerated her father's rage when he'd flung open the SUV's door and yanked Luca off of her and out of the vehicle. How she'd scrambled to pull up her racing suit to cover herself. How her father had shoved Luca away from the car, yelling, 'You. Get the hell out of here. Now.'

How chaos had begotten chaos. How things had gotten worse, so much worse.

She remembered standing in front of her father, waiting for him to yell at her like he had Luca. To say something. Anything.

But he couldn't even look at her.

'Dad,' she started, as his phone rang.

He turned away to answer it, and when he turned back around, the look of devastation on his face told her all she needed to know. She grabbed his arm and led him to the two scooters she and Luca had ditched a few aisles over. They arrived back at the track to find Scott had been freed from the car and was being attended to in an ambulance. Mia tried to keep back, to slink quietly away, but her father made sure she stayed present in every way.

For hours, she was at her dad's side. She saw exactly what he wanted her to see — the consequences of her actions. The wrecker hauling the smashed and contorted remains of the team's beautiful teal sports car to their garage. Scott being airlifted to the hospital, with Mia knowing full well how dire the prognosis was when a driver was taken by helicopter instead of ambulance or treated at the onsite medical facilities. She and her dad waiting at the hospital. Scott waking up after surgery and giving his boss a groggy and strained thumbs up.

Scott would live another day.

Mia wasn't so sure she'd be as lucky. In all those hours she spent next to him, her dad didn't glance her way once.

It wasn't until they made it back to their hotel suite that her father finally turned toward her. She expected to experience the same rage he'd unleashed on Luca. But instead of anger, his eyes were filled with disappointment.

'I know these past few years have been tough, and I'm partly to blame for today's events because I've chosen to look the other way too many damn times, Mia,' he said. 'But no more. What happened today will not be repeated. This lesson is done. Finished. You will straighten up and fly right. Am I understood?'

She nodded.

And then he put the final nail in the coffin of her wild and carefree youth. 'As for Luca, he's no longer a part of our team, and no longer a part of our life. You will see him again over my dead body, and we won't discuss him or this again. Agreed?'

She nodded and retreated to her room, where she bawled for hours. Somehow, in the course of a day, she'd lost her father's respect along with her best friend and her boyfriend. She awoke a few hours later to find an airline ticket had been slipped under her door. She was going home. Alone.

Mia holed up in her bedroom for weeks, hiding in her bed during the day and emerging only under the cover of darkness when the rest of the house was quiet. She couldn't eat or sleep. She was filled with shame, yet she missed Luca. Her dad had made good on his promise. Luca was gone from her life.

She couldn't stop picturing the smashed car or Scott in the hospital. And she certainly couldn't quell the wheels spinning in her brain, round and round, trying to figure out how, why this had all happened.

Then, one day, those wheels stopped turning, and she realized the common denominator behind all of their pain, heartache, and grief.

It was her.

She was the reason Scott almost died. She was responsible for a race car being destroyed. She was why Luca lost his ride with Rubie Racing.

She had nobody to blame but herself. So, on that day, she

put the brakes on the Mia Rubie everyone knew but no longer loved. Including herself.

All of her racing gear and trophies were packed away and hidden in the basement crawl space. When her father finally ducked into her room to make peace and invite her to a team meeting, she refused. And when he kept asking, she kept saying no. She reneged on her ride for a second year in the feeder series, and her dad found out through the grapevine.

Her father wanted her to straighten up and fly right. He got his wish. In spades.

Mia applied to colleges, thankful that she'd let Barb convince her to take the college admission tests even though she had no intention of ever going. She chose Michigan's largest public university after visiting and loving being a small fish in a big pond. Schoolwork became a priority for the first time in her life, not just something crammed in between practices and races, and she realized she was good at it. Smart even. She found she had a head for marketing, and decided to go on to graduate school. With two degrees in hand, she accepted the job in Chicago – an even bigger pond to swim around in unnoticed.

Eventually, Mia stopped thinking about how right it felt to sit in a race car, to have adrenaline pulsating through her body. To be in control of the uncontrollable. To live in the eye of a storm of your own making.

She became content with being on the outside looking in, because it meant that everybody on the inside stayed safe.

Until her dad died and her carefully crafted life went to hell in a handbasket.

Her phone beeped from somewhere in the room. Spotting her bag near the door, she crept over and brought it back into bed with her. It was a text message from Barb, and while it didn't mention the interview, the news was clearly out in the universe.

Barb: *Just checking in to see if you're OK. LOL. Barb*

LOL? Odd.

Mia: *Does feeling completely humiliated count as OK? Embarrassed? Thinking not. Have had better days... months... years.*

Barb: *Here if you need to chat. LOL. Barb*

Mia: *Not sure what you've heard across the pond, but this really isn't a reason to laugh out loud. At least for me it isn't.*

Barb: *What?! I'm confused. LOL. Barb*

Mia: *LOL is short for laugh out loud.*

Barb: *Oh, for Pete's sake. I thought it meant lots of love. Methinks I have some apologizing to do. LOL. I got it right that time. Lots of love! Barb*

Mia: *Now I actually am laughing out loud. Thank you. But maybe I should just come home.*

Barb: *Nonsense. Things will get better, but you need to stop hiding in your bed. Lots of love! Barb*

Mia tossed her phone on the bed and sat up. Luca and Brian were still talking and, even with their voices lowered, she could hear that they were trying to formulate a plan for getting through the next few days. With or without her, should she pull a vanishing act.

Her dad's face, awash with disappointment, flashed before her eyes again. But not after that night from hell — it was years later, when she'd told him she was moving to Chicago.

'But what about racing, Mia? It was always your dream, what you're meant —'

She'd held up her hand and cut him off mid-sentence. 'No. That's ancient history now. I don't want to hear about racing, Apex, race cars, race car drivers, or anything else associated with Rubie Racing. It's like you once said, Dad, "It's done. Finished."'

With a shake of his head, he'd walked away with his tail between his legs. It was only the second time in her life she'd ever seen her dad look defeated.

But now, because of something she'd overheard Brian say to Luca, Mia realized there might be another side to her dad's story. One she'd always been too focused on her own grief, her own shortcomings, to see.

Her dad had been trying to protect her reputation and the future racing career she'd wanted so badly, one that, at that time, involved few women. The thought made Mia want to throw up. Although, to be fair, that could've also been due to the firewater Luca had poured down her throat earlier.

Yes, her dad had been angry and shocked. Honestly, who could blame the man for reacting like he had after catching his daughter in the literal act. It was a miracle that he hadn't washed his eyes out with bleach. But maybe he'd done the next best thing by washing away the whole incident and keeping her reputation intact.

If only her dad was here to help her deal with this new load of dirty laundry. Mia grabbed her phone and dialed the one person who could help her figure this out.

Star answered on the first ring. 'The three Ds, *mija*.'

'Hello?'

'No time for niceties. You're calling for my advice about this nonsense from when you were a teenager. I'm giving it. My three Ds. What are they?'

'Distract, deflect, divert. How did you—'

'That's my girl. I set a search alert on your name. I have to jump into a meeting, but call me back tomorrow so we can talk about why you're still not sleeping with the hot Italian driver. And don't try to deny you don't want to. I saw how you were looking at him in those photos.'

Star clicked off without saying goodbye. Know-it-all.

Chapter 17

The woman who greeted Mia at the meeting for team principals looked vaguely familiar, but it was her Brazilian accent that gave her away.

'Hello, stranger. I wanted to tell you how sorry I am about your dad.'

Mia smiled. 'As I live and breathe, Cat Carvalho.'

A lifetime had passed since they were girls playing together at racetracks around the world. Once upon a time, with Mia's tenacity and Cat's sass, the two had been a force to be reckoned with among the pack of drivers' kids.

Cat's father had raced alongside Mia's and then started his own racing team, too. Although Cat never followed in his footsteps behind the wheel, she'd worked alongside him for years in the family business. Mia vaguely recalled her dad telling her last year that Cat had been named team principal of Carvalho Motorsport, which explains why they were both at the same meeting before testing officially began at the Circuit de Barcelona-Catalunya.

Seeing a friendly face was such a welcome surprise that Mia couldn't help but embrace her childhood friend. 'You do still go by "Cat"?'

'Is my hair still a wreck of curls that you're dying to tug on?'

Mia nodded. 'Actually, yes.'

'For the record, hair pulling is no longer appropriate at our age,' Cat said.

'Then I'd suggest you don't do anything to persuade me,' Mia laughed.

The only two women in a sea of men, they grabbed seats next to each other. Even though Mia had wanted nothing more than to stay in her bed and hide for the second time in her life from the world of racing, she'd forced herself to be there. It was the least she could do for her dad, given the lengths she now knew he'd gone to in making sure she'd have a place in Apex. Not that she expected anyone to point at her and yell, 'Shame! Shame! Shame!' but it was a relief when almost everyone gave her a friendly 'nice to see you' or a shoulder squeeze when they walked by.

Much of the meeting went over Mia's head. She had some catching up to do before she felt ready to contribute to discussions about rules and regulations, spending limits, and media coverage. Cat, on the other hand, engaged the room often. By the time they wrapped up, Mia was in awe – and not just of Cat. Any doubt she'd had about the inability of the racing world's brain trust to take a woman seriously had been a serious misjudgment on her part.

The room cleared within minutes, with everyone anxious to check on their teams and ensure they were ready to begin the six days of rigorous testing on the cars they'd been working on for the upcoming season – work that had begun before that last season even started. This would be the first time they'd see how the cars born from months and months of time, talent, and sweat, and, certainly not least, money would perform on the track. It was hard to believe that teams couldn't drive their multi-million-dollar investments any time they wanted, like on tracks near their headquarters during the off-season, but there were rules against it. And in Apex, you didn't break the rules. Period.

Instead, Rubie Racing and every other team waited as patiently as possible for pre-season testing and, in the meantime, clocked hundreds of hours in wind tunnels costing millions of dollars. The massive fans created an environment where air rushed by scale models of the cars, simulating how the design would perform aerodynamically in the real world – even though on tracks, the effect is reversed, and cars would speed through the air.

Mia was more concerned about facing the Rubie Racing crew than the speed of their car. She'd skipped the team dinner last night after looking online to see exactly what had been written about her and found articles like 'Racing princess has checkered past,' 'Is Mia Rubie finished before the season starts?' and 'Teenage love ended with a crash.' All had cringe-worthy details that, while not entirely accurate, weren't too far off.

The comments were worse – so much worse. Spoiler alert: She'd been a teenage Jezebel and, apparently, an extremely flexible and adventurous one at that.

'Don't worry about all that garbage from yesterday,' Cat said as they readied to leave, as if she were reading thought bubbles floating over Mia's head.

'No offense, but it's kind of hard not to.'

'Not true. I know it's been a while, but you're now living in an alternate universe. The team principals may throw shade at each other or poach a driver every now and again, but when it comes down to it, we have each other's backs. Plus, what was that, fifteen years ago? And you were what, eighteen? Tell me another story. I'm bored.'

For the first time in a day and a half, Mia found a reason to laugh. 'Thanks.'

Then Cat leaned in and, with in a low voice, said, 'By the way, Luca Toscano? Not too shabby,' and sailed through the door.

Knowing she couldn't avoid her team forever, Mia took a deep breath, gathered her things, and walked out to find another familiar face waiting for her.

'Brian, I told you I'd be there,' she said to her team manager. 'An escort isn't necessary.'

'I thought we could walk and talk,' he said, handing her a coffee. 'I need to catch you up on some things.'

'Considering how much I was able to contribute in there, I'm not sure how much help I'll be.'

Brian frowned. 'Knock it off, Mia.'

She rolled her eyes in return. 'I'm so pissed at my dad for being dead. I'd really like him to be around right about now.'

Watching Cat in the meeting had made her wonder what it would've been like to climb the Apex ropes with her dad by her side. Mia's stomach ached with sudden regret.

'Just so you know, I'm not ignoring that — and I would love for him to be here, too — but we're going to have to deal with that later and move on,' Brian said. 'Because believe it or not, we have bigger fish to fry at the moment. Sorry.'

Seems that, suddenly, everyone wasn't happy with the schedule they'd set for their two drivers during testing. Mia had little doubt about the identity of the 'everyone' Brian was referring to, especially considering Luca was set to drive first. It made the most sense since they'd decided to fly his RR1 across the pond for testing, for no reason other than his car had been ready to go first.

Both RR1s were identical, engine-wise, but the chassis had been modified to fit each driver. Design engineers had been working with both Luca and Jordan for months, beginning with the cockpit layout and how it fit each of them before the frame was even finished. The seat, steering wheel, headrest — basically, anything the driver could touch or feel — had been set up for maximum comfort and to precise measurements. Not surprisingly, Jordan's pickiness had tested the patience of his design engineer.

'Jordan now wants to drive first, and my bet is that Luca would've just gone along with him in an effort to not rock an already rocky boat,' Brian said.

Mia groaned. 'I feel a huge "but" coming on.'

'But Jordan's claiming that the schedule favors – sorry, but I'm going to have to quote your brother here,' Brian raised his hands and made air quotes, '"whoever's sleeping with the boss."'

'Oh, geez,' Mia said. 'Why does he have to be like this? Also, to be clear, absolutely nothing is going on with Luca and me.'

Not counting their night together in Chicago, which she wasn't.

'Yes, I got the whole "we're just friends" spiel from Luca,' Brian said. 'You're both very convincing. Wherever will you keep your Academy Award? I hear Kate Winslet's is in her bathroom.'

Mia stopped walking and narrowed her gaze at him. 'Let's focus on the task at hand, shall we? Who do you think should drive first? Luca or Jordan?'

'Neither,' he said.

'We didn't exactly fly a car and eighty people across the world to teach a grown man a lesson,' she said, knowing from experience that trying would be a colossal waste of time. 'One of our drivers needs to be in that car, on the track, pronto.'

'Yes, ma'am,' Brian laughed. 'Only I think that the driver should be you.'

'Have you been drinking?' Not that she would blame him if he had been – she was more likely to pull up a barstool and join him. 'I haven't been in a race car in fifteen years and in case you've forgotten everything that hit the fan yesterday, it didn't go well.'

'I think you're the one with memory issues because, by all accounts, you drove pretty damn well that day. So, let's get a few things straight: It wasn't your first and only time in a car. You weren't the one who crashed. And before you tell me you might as well have been, stop.'

Mia opened her mouth to tell him he was still bananas, that the drivers needed time in the car as much as the team needed data, but Brian spoke first.

'Look, it's not a perfect plan, but it's not horrible either. We both know you can do this, and I'd like to shut down any talk of you not knowing your ass from an Apex car right now. I can think of a few certain someones I'd like to see eat their words.' Brian paused and gave her a broad smile. 'Not to mention, I'd love to see you drive.'

'Again, it's been *fifteen years* since I've driven any race car. I'm afraid you're the one who's going to be eating your words.'

Truth be told, Mia was terrified. And, to her dismay, every synapse in her body was already firing at the thought of being behind the wheel of one of the most powerful cars on the planet.

But even with her heart pounding, she suddenly realized what Brian was truly offering. 'I think I just got hit in the head with a D or three.'

The look he shot her was one of pure confusion. 'I don't know what that means, and I don't think I want to. But I am surprised that you don't look like you're about to send me packing.'

'Absolutely not. In fact, I don't say this often enough, but Brian, you're a freaking genius.'

Luca had never known Brian to come up with such a hare-brained idea and didn't have a clue how he had managed to sell it to Mia. But as a result of Jordan throwing what could best be described as a hissy fit over who would drive first on day one of testing, neither of them were.

Instead, Brian had walked into the team's trackside garage with Mia, asked for everyone's attention, and said, 'Good news, we have our reserve driver!'

Everyone had looked around for Jordan and Luca, who were also looking around before locking gazes with each other. Their confusion had only deepened when Brian said, 'Let's get Mia ready for day one,' and clapped, like he'd just said something sane.

Not that the team didn't need a new reserve driver, given that theirs had hightailed it out of town right after Rob's funeral. Luca hadn't blamed the kid for looking out for his own best interest. He was at the beginning of his career. He'd performed well enough in the feeder series that Rubie Racing hadn't been the only team vying for his attention, and he'd made it clear to Brian that Rob had been the deciding factor before he cleared out.

But Mia? It was madness, not to mention dangerous.

When Brian walked by with Mia minutes later, he only said, 'This isn't up for discussion.'

Not one to sulk in a corner, Luca headed to the team's

motorhome to brood in private. He was careful to keep his chin up as he made his way through the paddock area that stretched behind the trackside garages. The press would soon be all over Mia's time in the car, and the last thing he needed was random video of him stomping around and slamming doors a few hours before she got behind the wheel.

As they'd found out during yesterday's press conference, there was always someone lurking. He'd never noticed anyone taking their picture at the Italian steakhouse in Chicago – and was glad that whoever it was hadn't followed them to the lake and captured their kiss. Considering how many people were now obsessively speculating about what went down between Mia and him fifteen years ago, that would've been a total fiasco.

Of course, Rubie Racing's home away from home would be at the far end of the paddock. As he walked past the other team's motorhomes, he couldn't help but notice that a few had upgraded their command centers. Even he had a hard time believing that the massive multistory buildings were assembled and unassembled for each race like carnival rides, or that they could be folded down flat and shipped from track to track throughout the season.

Why in the hell hadn't he grabbed one of the team scooters? He would've been there already. At least most of the other teams were gathered in their garages, so his odds of running into anyone were low.

'I said, what's occurin'?' a voice bellowed from behind him.

Luca turned around, and Wyn came into focus. He backtracked a few feet and put on the happiest face he could muster. It wasn't good enough.

'Alright, how's it going, alright?' Wyn asked.

'Alright,' he said. After living with Wyn and spending time with his family, Luca was well-versed in Welsh lingo – although right now he wished the guy could just say a simple 'hello' and be done with it.

Wyn shook his head and opened his arms wide. 'Looks like someone needs a *cwtch*.'

'Hug me and you'll be trying to figure out how to drive a race car with only legs,' Luca said.

Wyn put his hands up and backed away. '*Och*, wouldn't be the first.'

Luca cringed. Loss of limb was no joke in their field of work. Racetracks were full of former drivers with missing appendages and odd shuffles to their gait. 'Sorry, sorry,' Luca said. 'I've had better days.'

'Not driving today, then?'

'Nope, not today,' he said, deciding it was best not to elaborate. The clock was already ticking on the entire track knowing that Mia was in the RR1, and he certainly wasn't going to be the one to shove that cat out of the bag. As much as he trusted Wyn, this was big news. Huge news. As in, run back to the Carvalho garage and tell everyone you see along the way kind of news.

Luca made a quick escape with a fake excuse about a meeting and promised to catch up with Wyn over the next couple of days. Judging by the look his friend gave him, it would be sooner than later. Wyn clearly wasn't buying the cool act Luca was desperately trying to sell.

It was a miracle when he finally made it to the motorhome without breaking into a full-on sprint. Except for staff members in charge of feeding the team and keeping the lights on, the first floor was nearly empty. Seems word of what was happening in the garage had traveled fast to the remainder of the team, and they'd all wanted to see it go down firsthand.

By the time he flopped down on a sofa in a private room on the second floor and pulled out his phone, he'd convinced himself that it didn't matter if he'd heard from Mia or not. Which was good, because he hadn't. He shouldn't have been surprised. She'd bailed on the team dinner the night before and hadn't answered the door when he'd stopped by afterward to check on her. She'd never even looked his way in the garage.

And then there was the fact that he was a reserve friend – not that he'd gained any clarity about what the hell that meant since the night she'd bestowed the title upon him. Luca closed his eyes and focused on his breathing, willing himself to mentally swat away whatever thoughts and images popped into his head. But it was fruitless. They were all of Mia.

Two hours later, he was back in the team's garage, watching as Mia slipped into one of Jordan's spare racing suits. The two were nearly the same height and build, and it was hard to say who that had bothered more during their teen years. (His bet: Jordan.) The crew in charge of resetting the car for each driver couldn't have been more pleased as they busied themselves making far fewer adjustments than they'd anticipated when Brian dropped his bombshell on everyone. Their biggest challenge was locating a green light to mount on the rear of the car, which warned others on the track that Mia didn't have the required special license that Apex drivers can spend years securing.

'This is bullshit,' Jordan muttered from behind him.

'Wise words from a man who has only himself to blame,' Luca said loud enough for only Jordan to hear.

When he'd rejoined Rubie Racing and found Jordan's personality as challenging as it had been in their youth, he'd made a vow to never engage his teammate, even when provoked, out of respect for Rob. And he'd kept to it, even though there'd been loads of provoking over the past two years.

But now, the gloves were coming off.

Not that he didn't agree with Jordan, for the first time ever. Mia had no business climbing into the RR1. To his knowledge, she hadn't driven a race car or been behind the wheel of anything fast since that fateful day fifteen years ago. Her four-door sedan certainly didn't count. That sand-colored nightmare wasn't capable of going more than two hundred miles per hour in a straight line. It didn't have a paddle shifter behind the steering wheel and eight gears for forward motion. It couldn't go from zero to sixty miles per hour in three seconds.

Luca willed Mia to glance his way. Just once.

But she didn't. Not once.

He wasn't close enough to eavesdrop on what she, Brian, and a few members of the team were chatting about. He studied their mouths and perhaps it was wishful thinking since he couldn't actually read lips, but he could swear he saw Brian say, 'Go out slow, take her around once, and pull her back in. This is all for show.'

Not that her doing a single lap would put either him or Jordan in the driver's seat that day. Given their late start due to the adjustments to the car, day one would belong solely to Mia. A short drive wouldn't do the team much good either. The more laps the car completed during the six days of testing, the more data they acquired and the more tweaks they could make before the first race in Australia.

He should walk over there. Insert himself into the conversation. After all, it was his car.

Her car.

But his brain couldn't quite convince his legs to move. And so there he stood, on the periphery of all that was happening. Watching, waiting, and more than likely, misreading lips.

Brian finally broke away from the group surrounding Mia and strolled his way. 'You pissed about something?'

'Where would you like me to start?' Luca asked.

'Look, I'll explain more later, but I need you to trust me on this,' Brian said. 'OK?'

He regularly trusted Brian with his life. Only this was Mia's life they were talking about.

'You don't have to stay. I understand if you want to leave, and I'm sure Mia will as well.'

There was his out, not that there was a chance in hell Luca was going to take it. 'No, I'll stay. Tell me what you need me to do, where you need me to be.'

At that, his manager grinned. 'How do you feel about being in Mia's ear?'

Luca considered for half a second being the one communicating with Mia over the radio, every word of their exchanges recorded for racing posterity, then nodded. 'Fine. But I do think it's a bit unorthodox.'

'Oh, buddy, we've blasted right by unorthodox,' Brian laughed, shaking his head.

No one was better suited to helping Mia make her way around the Circuit de Catalunya than he was. Between a career's worth of testing, practices, and races, he'd looped the nearly five-kilometer track hundreds of times and knew each of its sixteen corners like the back of his hand.

Before Brian walked away, leaving Luca on the sidelines again, he leaned in. 'Seriously, though, trust me on this one.'

It seemed like forever before Mia was prepped and in the car on pit lane. As much as he hated to admit it, she looked good in his turbo pumpkin.

Luca was set up only a few feet away in one of the coveted spots at pit wall, in front of a row of computer screens next to pit lane. Beside him, the team's engineers were waiting with bated breath to see how the car performed. Not only would cameras follow Mia around the track, the on-board computer system would transmit the car's technical information back to the team in real time. If anything went wrong, they would know before Mia and could alert her.

After the pit crew performed their last-minute checks and stepped back, Brian nodded to Luca.

'Are you ready, Mia?' Luca said over the radio.

Her head jerked toward the pit wall, and her gaze locked with his. After a few seconds, she nodded, and then turned to face straight ahead.

'Then get out there.'

If Mia had any hesitation about being back in a race car after so many years, it didn't show. As soon as the crew's designated 'lollipop man' held up the stick with the round sign signaling her to go, she eased smoothly into pit lane, gathered speed as she approached the exit, and then accelerated as she entered the track.

'Take these first few laps easy, and I'll walk you through the circuit,' Luca said, even though he knew she'd gone over the map several times before getting behind the wheel. Still, most drivers studied courses for weeks before driving around them at top speed, spending time in a simulator, reviewing past races, and strategizing how they'll approach every curve and straightaway. At least this was testing and not a race, so the focus was on the performance of the car instead of the driver. Not that this made the situation any less dangerous; she would still be traveling at close to a hundred and sixty miles an hour – speeds an average person never came close to.

'I appreciate the refresher,' Mia said over the radio. 'It's been a while.'

Refresher? But of course, teenage Mia had raced at Catalunya, although it had been at least sixteen years since she'd driven the course. For the first ten laps, Luca took Mia through the three sectors the circuit was divided into, each slightly less harrowing than the next. All the while, he kept a close eye on the computers to see that she was shifting through all eight gears and braking accordingly.

Damn if she wasn't almost textbook perfect. And he wasn't the only one who noticed. The Rubie Racing team was abuzz around him as they watched her conquer the track from the wall of screens, too.

When Mia rounded the New Holland curve – the final one on the course that led to the front straightaway and, during races, the finish line – for the tenth time, Luca decided she was ready to be cut loose.

'You got this?' he asked.

'Yep.'

'Go do it then.'

And she did just that, rounding the course over and over again, taking corners a little quicker and picking up speed on straightaways, each go-around.

After the novelty of having her on the track wore off – Luca was right, her presence hadn't gone unnoticed by anyone – other teams began sending their cars out. She handled sharing the road with ease. To the delight of Rubie Racing team members, the RR1 more than held its own.

Mia came through pit lane when requested for one tweak or another, or for the pit crew to change tires, from soft to softest, from medium to hard, and then back to soft again, in mere seconds. When she'd completed just over a hundred and fifty clean and trouble-free laps, Brian tapped on Luca's shoulder and motioned for him to call her in for good.

'OK, Mia, the day is done. Bring her home,' he said.

'On my way,' she said.

A minute later, she pulled neatly in front of the team's garage, stopping the car precisely when the lollipop man flipped his sign to 'stop.'

The team gathered around the car and cheered. Mia sat motionless for a minute before removing her helmet and the steering wheel and handing both to a pit crew member.

Brian helped her climb out, and Luca caught her eye as she jumped off the car. He couldn't help but flash back to the last time he'd watched her drive, how proud he'd been at the end of her stint at the wheel, and how badly he'd wanted to walk over and grab her, not caring who saw.

Oh, hell, he thought, tossing the headset he was still holding onto a nearby chair and cutting the distance between the two of them in seconds. She turned toward him just as he reached out to pull her in for a *cwtch* that, as it turns out, he really did need.

Chapter 18

Shampooing and slowly rinsing her hair for a third time was bringing Mia no closer to solving the mystery of how a thirty-three-year-old woman who'd spent her adult life trying to avoid anything fast ended up zooming around a racetrack for hours on end.

And loving every single second of it.

The race cars she'd driven as a teen couldn't hold a candle to an Apex car. The turbo pumpkin was quicker and more complex in every way. Within seconds, that feeling of being exactly where she belonged came flooding back. If she hadn't believed in out-of-body experiences before, she was fully bought in now.

As much as she'd wanted to say no to Brian's plan, it was far more brilliant than anything she'd been able to come up with in the past twenty-four hours. That was exactly nothing. But Brian had managed to throw a bullseye and nail Star's three damn Ds on his first try — distracting, deflecting, and diverting in a single shot. It was either beginner's luck or her dad had been right all along. The man was some sort of genius.

The never-ending shower was also doing nothing to quell the energy that had begun pulsating through every fiber of her being the moment her body and mind connected about what was about to happen. The feeling had accelerated each hour she spent behind the wheel. Every single cell was wide awake, lit up, and flashing; a state of hyper-awareness that showed no signs of shutting down.

And then there was Luca. Damn him and his deep voice in her ear all day. And that bear hug. If she could take any wisdom from her eighteen-year-old self, it was that she needed to stay as far away from him as possible, or she was liable to pin him to the nearest mattress. If past experience proved correct, that energy always needed to go somewhere.

When Mia finally turned off the water, she heard someone knocking. Loudly. She grabbed an oversized hotel robe from the bedroom closet on her way to the door, knowing who she'd see through the peephole. Luca, wearing his team uniform and a look of dread.

She tightened the belt on her robe and opened the door. 'Hey,' she said, tucking a strand of wet hair behind her ear.

'Can we talk?' When she didn't respond, he added, 'Please, Mia. We agreed to be friends, um, reserve friends, remember? No more silent treatment.'

She stepped aside and let him in. 'Fine, but give me a minute.'

Once Mia was in the bedroom with the door shut, she

slipped into the uniform of her previous life – her yoga pants and well-worn college sweatshirt. It was hard to believe she'd led that life just one month ago, when her ex-boyfriend was firmly in the past, not in the next room, wanting to know why she wasn't talking to him. Which was rich considering how long she'd waited to hear from him all those years ago.

Suddenly, the pent-up energy from her hours in the car found an outlet. 'Why didn't you call me?' she shouted.

'I texted you ten minutes ago. Check your phone.'

She opened the door and leaned against the doorframe. 'No. Fifteen years ago, when we went from a thousand to zero in about five seconds. Why didn't you call me then?'

Mia's heart raced as she waited for him to respond. She wasn't sure why she suddenly needed to know what she'd convinced herself didn't matter, but after the last few days of their past spilling out for the world to see, she did. And she needed to hear it from him.

Luca took a deep breath and looked her straight in the eye. 'Your dad told me that if I walked away, he'd recommend me to another team. That he'd never say the real reason it hadn't worked out. But if I hung around, he'd make sure I never drove a race car again. I believe his words were, "Good luck even finding a carny who'll let you ride around in circles in the mini race cars." Either I chose to have nothing or to still have it all.'

Ouch.

'Just so I'm clear, I was slotted in the nothing category. Having it all didn't include me. Us.'

Luca ran his fingers through his hair. 'You were eighteen, and I was twenty. Things were just beginning to happen for me. I couldn't give up everything I'd been working toward since I was nine years old, Mia.'

'I get it. I do. Maybe more than anyone else. Except I did give it all up. Walk away.'

Mia had forced herself not to look back. Until today, she hadn't realized what an enormous sacrifice she'd made by altering the course of her life so drastically.

'It surprised me when I didn't see you around the next season, or the season after that. I didn't expect you to quit racing, Mia. I never would've asked you to do that.'

He was right. She'd made that decision all on her own, and every single one after that.

'True. Even so, you left, and you didn't even say goodbye. After everything. I didn't even know where you'd gone for months. I waited for you to call, write, send a carrier pigeon. Anything.' But she never heard a peep from him, not even after she contacted him against her father's express wishes. 'I tried to get in touch with you. Did you get my message?'

That stopped him in his tracks, and his gaze shifted to his shoes. 'I did. I know I sound like a jackass, but it was easier to pack that part of my life in a box, hide it away, and move on. I wish I could say that if I could go back and do things differently, I would.'

'But?' she prodded.

He sighed. 'But... if we're being honest here, that's probably not true.'

'Makes sense. I mean, things have worked out pretty well for you, right? You've driven for some of the best teams, spent a good amount of time on the podium, dated plenty of beautiful women. Hell, you even eventually made up *with my dad*.' Something dawned on her. 'Even yesterday, no one thought any worse of you. She directed those questions at me. The headlines were all about me, my apparent lack of morals. Not yours.' Maybe it was wrong to blame him for society's misogynistic attitudes, but she was on a roll. 'You know, maybe you were the smart one, realizing we were just two horny teenagers. It's not like we really knew each other. I mean, I didn't know myself very well at that point.'

'Mia—'

Every synapse was firing now, and Mia didn't let him get a word in edgewise. 'Here's another question I always wanted to ask. Why don't you have an Italian accent, Luca? You're Italian, but your accent isn't. Even back in the day, I could never put my finger on what it was.'

From his puzzled look, she gathered he was having a hard time keeping up with her. She couldn't really blame him.

'I don't know, maybe because I never actually lived in Italy. Because of my dad's job, we moved around a lot. My nanny was British, and my mother always enrolled me in British schools. Between all of that and spending more time with my nanny and then at the track with kids from all over Europe than with my parents, I guess I never picked up their accent. Or anyone's.' He looked like he was coming to a realization about himself. 'Sometimes I feel like I'm from nowhere.'

'I feel like I don't know anything about you.'

'Like I've told you before, you can ask me whatever you want, Mia,' he said.

Their lunch in Chicago seemed like a distant memory, given how much had happened in the last couple of weeks. The last two days. She shook her head.

'I can't fix the past, Mia.'

And neither could she. Her brain kept spinning a million miles an hour, in a million different directions, and she was powerless to stop it. 'I hurt my dad; I disappointed him.'

'Sorry? I have to be honest, I'm struggling to follow your train of thought,' he said. 'But please pull the emergency brake before you go completely off the tracks. You have a second chance here. We have a second chance to know each other again, as adults. I'm an open book, I swear. No one cares what happened years ago. That's ancient history. It will die down in a few days – it's already dying down.'

'Nothing feels ancient right now, and it's only dying down because Brian gave them something else to talk about, something they couldn't ignore.' She began pacing the room. 'Do you know the worst part, Luca? My dad and I never talked about it, any of it. Everything changed that day – for me, you, Scott – and he didn't bring it up again. I never brought it up. Now, it's too late.'

Their conversations after she first left for college became so stilted that she'd skipped the first holiday home to avoid the awkwardness. Once they'd removed the one thing they had in common, they'd struggled to find anything to talk about. Years passed before her dad had sprinkled race cars and Rubie Racing into their conversations and she hadn't changed the subject.

'What can I say? Race car drivers are more focused on what's ahead of them than behind them,' Luca said. 'I bet he thought this would come up again down the road, and the two of you would sort it out then. I mean, he'd planned for the alternative.'

Mia gulped.

Luca ran his hands through his hair. 'I'm sorry.'

'It's not your fault,' she said.

His voice broke. 'Oh, I think I bear some responsibility. I'm the one who left. I loved you, and I never looked back. Not once. Do you want to know something I put in that box that I stashed away? When I got your message, I listened to it once and deleted it. Because I knew if I didn't, I wouldn't be able to keep moving forward. I would've listened to it every damn day until I broke down and called you.'

They both sat in silence until Mia realized what she needed to do, finally. She got up, crossed the room, and opened the door.

'What's happening here, Mia?' Luca asked.

'Something that should've happened years ago. We're breaking up. It's called closure.'

With a shake of his head, Luca left.

Mia plopped down on the sofa, closed her eyes, and focused on breathing deeply. She willed her body and mind to relax with each breath, and waited for the sense of peace and resolution she'd hoped finding closure would bring. But her brain continued to whirl and pick up speed, like a tornado on a steady diet of mobile homes and livestock. It refused to let go of how willingly Luca had taken the exit ramp her dad had offered. Finally knowing that piece of the puzzle hurt like hell.

Closure, apparently, was overrated.

This time, when she heard the rap on the door, Mia knew Luca wouldn't be on the other side. She turned the knob to find Brian standing in front of her.

'Am I interrupting something?' he asked.

'Nope, I was just relaxing,' she said.

He gave her a puzzled look. 'No offense, but I think you're doing it wrong.'

'Thanks, I guess. What's up?'

'I ran into Luca in the lobby, and we're headed for an early dinner with the engineers. We have numbers on the car's performance today to go over.' He hesitated before throwing his hands in the air and adding, 'Look, I don't know what's going on, well, with anyone on this damn team right now, but I'll be perfectly honest, I don't care. Sorry if that sounds harsh, but we have a lot to accomplish and even more to do back in Detroit before the season starts.'

'Fine,' she sighed. 'Give me fifteen minutes.'

'Take as long as you need. I'll be at the hotel bar having a *cerveza*. Which, for the record, is how one relaxes.'

When Mia made it to the lobby, she found Brian, Luca, and a few other members of the Rubie Racing team gathered at the far end of the bar, their eyes glued to the televisions mounted above the shelves of brightly colored bottles of liquor. She stopped in her tracks when she noticed the turbo pumpkin flying across multiple screens, followed by the sport's two most famous British commentators reporting trackside.

'And that, gentlemen, is how it's done,' Brian said, raising his glass for those around him to clink with theirs.

'Wait,' she interrupted, stepping up to the bar. 'What are they saying?'

Luca shushed everyone and bent an ear toward the television. He listened intently to the commentators until the commercial break, then turned to her. 'They said you drove like the racing heiress you are and if you handle the team as well as that car, Rubie Racing is in good hands for the season.'

The men around him nodded in agreement, to her surprise. One lifted his bottle and shouted, 'Cheers! To the boss!' To which the others responded with, 'Hear! Hear!'

She had little doubt that if they were a few more beers in, she would've been treated to a raucous rendition of 'For She's a Jolly Good Fellow.'

As if she weren't already feeling a little emotional, a photo of her flashed on the screen alongside one of her father. They were both clad in Rubie Racing gear and standing next to a race car, and they both shared the same look of self-satisfaction. Their small crowd quieted at the sight of the man who was never far from their thoughts, especially this week when they were testing the car that he'd poured his heart and soul into.

'Check out those matching smug grins,' Brian said, then added quietly, 'I never realized how much you resembled your father.'

'That's understandable. How many times did you see us side by side in the last fifteen years?' Mia looked around to find everyone's eyes were anywhere but on her.

Luca cleared his throat. 'Is Jordan joining us?'

'That would be a solid no,' Brian said. 'He was, ah, busy and, amazingly, still somewhat grumpy.'

'Why is that surprising? My brother is always grumpy.' A few seconds passed before Mia grasped what Brian was inferring. 'Oh, wait. Gross.'

Everyone laughed. Luca tossed a wad of bills on the bar as Brian reminded the crew to call it an early night and escorted their group toward the entrance of their hotel, a thick file folder in his hand.

Three hours later, they'd all had their fill of paella and data. The team's head engineer agreed that the car had performed as well on the track as they thought it would on paper. His praise for her driving and ability to take direction at top speed was borderline uncomfortable, particularly when he emphasized how proud her father would've been.

Guilt, always lurking close by these days, pulled up a chair.

Once they plotted out what they hoped to run the car through the next day, when Jordan took his turn in the driver's seat, they called it a night.

It wasn't until Brian stepped out of the elevator and left her alone with Luca that awkwardness settled around them for the first time that evening. Floor after floor passed in silence. When she opened her mouth to say something, anything, the door opened on his floor.

'Sleep well, Mia,' he said quietly as he moved past her.

'You, too, Luca.'

He looked back and gave her a slight smile as the elevator door closed between them.

Chapter 19

'So that may have been the craziest pre-season testing I've ever been through, from beginning to end,' Brian said to Luca about halfway over the Atlantic Ocean. They were digging into their second meal of the flight, using eating as a way to stay awake until they were on the ground in Detroit.

Luca grunted. For the first time he could recall in his career, he wasn't itching to head to Australia to launch the season. He needed more space to get his head on straight and refocus. Mend his heart, if possible. A few nights in his own bed certainly wouldn't hurt either.

Brian leaned in, as if any of the Rubie Racing employees seated around them on the private jet were eavesdropping, and asked in a lowered voice, 'I've been wondering, do you think we should ask Mia to give Jordan some pointers?'

That was all it took for Luca to spray his steak with red wine.

*

His teammate had disappeared after the second day of testing. Jordan climbed into the RR1 full of piss and vinegar and when he climbed out hours later, he was minus the vinegar. Sure, he drove well and put the car through its paces. He knew what he was doing behind the wheel. Even a legacy driver needed skill and talent to avoid getting killed or, worse, killing someone else at racing speed.

But Jordan was unable to beat Mia's best time, no matter how hard he tried.

And oh, how he tried.

Even Luca cringed each time another lap came up short, and he was hardly ever in the guy's corner.

Jordan's fastest lap of the morning was three-tenths of a second behind Mia's. To a layperson, a second or two is barely a blip. But in the world of auto racing, a few seconds may as well be a few hours when they separated your car from the one ahead of you. In this instance, Jordan was following a ghost car with his sister at the wheel. And she was simultaneously haunting him from the day before and, Luca suspected, a couple of decades earlier.

To Jordan's credit, he refused to give up, even pressing to take Luca's afternoon shift in the car. He was a bear no one wanted to poke, which was obvious when Mia and Brian left the decision up to Luca.

'Data is data,' Mia said, with Brian nodding next to her.

'Fine by me,' Luca said. No way was he going to pick up a stick and jab Jordan either. Although he was itching to get behind the wheel after the winter break and see how the turbo pumpkin performed for himself, he was equally curious to see how this played out.

Unfortunately, a few more hours in the car didn't help his teammate any. When Brian finally told Jordan to call it a day, everyone in the garage seemed to steel themselves for his return.

Jordan didn't disappoint. The gloves came off with his helmet. He immediately spouted off at the team members he thought had done a 'piss-poor' job readjusting the car to fit him following Mia's drive the day before, berated the engineer for the lack of engine performance, and then screamed at Brian for slacking off on the job when Rubie Racing needed him most. It was a page right out of the Jordan Rubie playbook: blame everyone but himself. The only people he didn't give a piece of his mind to were Luca and Mia, although the daggers he shot at each of them as he stormed out of the garage spoke volumes.

It probably didn't help that Mia looked straight at her brother when he moved past her and said flatly, 'Man, I wish I still had my little pink dress. We could reenact my favorite awards banquet ever.'

With that remark, any hope of Jordan showing up for the third day went out the door with him. But no one thought he'd skip town altogether, with three more days of testing still on the agenda after a two-day gap to examine data and tweak the car. A snapshot of him at the airport early the next morning, with Julia trailing unhappily behind him, appeared on a racing fan website under the headline, 'When your twin wins.'

Luca almost felt bad for Julia. Almost.

As much as he hated to admit it, the whole scene with Jordan had him slightly anxious when he climbed into the turbo pumpkin the next day. Even though Luca knew the point of testing was to get the car ready to take on the season, not which team member ran the hottest lap. Still, he was more than relieved – a little ecstatic, maybe – when Brian radioed his lap time, and Mia's ghost car was solidly in his rearview mirror.

If only he could do the same with the woman herself.

While closure appeared to have left Mia cool and collected, it'd had the opposite effect on Luca. In what seemed like an instant, she'd overwhelmed him. Although if he was being completely honest with himself, the feeling had been building since he first saw her again. She was right, what she'd told him that night behind the scenes of Rob's afterlife party. The Mia he'd once known didn't exist anymore – she'd changed. Of course she had. Only not in the way she thought.

Teenage Mia had been a whirlwind of energy who struck without warning or remorse. But at some point over the years, she'd manage to somehow not only harness that power but also stand in the center of it. No wonder the lid on his box of Mia memories had blown clean off and disappeared into the stratosphere. She was the smart, gorgeous, irresistible eye of the storm.

As much as Luca had wanted her before couldn't compare with how much he wanted her now.

And he couldn't have her.

While the team's engineers spent testing's two days off-track to focus on the car's inner workings, he decided to hole up and do the same. His body needed attention after an entire afternoon in the car. Recovery took longer than it did at the beginning of his career, and a good massage and stretching helped. When he searched out his favorite online yoga class, he spotted one for barre, too, and decided a little planking certainly couldn't hurt.

As it turned out, planking had an added benefit of engaging his mind along with his abs. Combined with concentration exercises and juggling sessions with Wyn – who raised an eyebrow but didn't question his sudden obsession with the game they'd played since adolescence to improve their focus and reflexes – Luca felt physically and mentally ready to face the final push of testing. Both the hours in the car... and out of it, with Mia.

With Jordan gone, Luca would drive in the mornings with Mia taking the afternoon shift. Even if her stint in the car on the first day had been intended as a one-off, the schedule made sense. As much as he loved being behind the wheel, three full days in his turbo pumpkin would be too much.

But first, he needed to face the other drivers at their debrief.

Luca normally looked forward to these meetings with the Apex powers that be and his peers every race weekend. But then he usually wasn't dealing with a teammate who'd been fined for pulling a vanishing act, and a dead owner who'd left the team to his daughter, a woman the world had just learned was his ex-girlfriend and better behind the wheel than half of the guys in the room.

Showing up seconds before the meeting began seemed like his best option, and the hush that fell over the room when he entered proved he was right. He smiled and nodded at Wyn and others he'd raced against for more than half his life as he made his way toward an empty seat up front, only to plop down and discover it was next to Henri.

'*Bonjour*,' he said, appearing equally surprised.

Before Luca could return a hello, the meeting started. Perfect timing, especially given that half of them, himself included, needed to get back to their garages and into their cars as soon as they were finished.

They were a strange group, drivers. Beyond loyal, even knowing full well that they could take each other out with the smallest of mistakes. It wasn't a shock when Wyn stood up and addressed the group once the official business was over.

'I'd like to remind everyone that this is a family, regardless of how we feel about each other when we're out on the track,' he said. 'Luca, you're our brother. Whatever's going on with your team right now, we're all behind you.'

He had no choice but to stand up. 'I appreciate your support. We place our careers and our lives in the hands of our team principals. My trust in Rob was strong enough to carry me through what's happening now. But it's nice to know that you all have my back. Which is what most you will be seeing this season on the track.'

Next to him, Henri snorted. *Arrogant bastard*.

The remainder of testing flew by. He'd driven many amazing cars during his career, but none could compare to the RR1. It felt different, right, like every part of it had been purpose built for his body, his intuitive handling of a race car, his style. It was damn near a religious experience.

He wondered if Mia felt the same way. But with each of them in the RR1 at opposite times, sponsor schmoozing, and photo and media sessions, their interactions had been limited. He wasn't avoiding her, he told himself, after two days had passed with little interaction. Not after he'd lectured her about giving him the cold shoulder. He was simply letting her have the space she'd wanted.

And she was taking it. On the final day, she swapped their drives, taking his morning shift in the car and leaving him the final testing slot. When he brought the turbo pumpkin back into pit lane, the team cheered. Mia included.

Not that there was much time for celebration. Team members immediately began breaking down the garage to ship the car and everything they'd dragged with them to Spain back to Detroit. As he looked around at the twenty tons of equipment needing to be packed up, he was glad his only job was to drive a car around in circles.

That's when he noticed that Mia was gone. She flew out that night, as it turns out, instead of with him, Brian, and the rest of the team as scheduled the next morning. Which was absolutely fine, although even a reserve friend might've said goodbye.

*

Next to him on the plane, Brian nudged his arm and took a swig from the beer he'd been nursing since dinner. 'You're welcome, by the way.'

'For?' Luca asked, motioning to his favorite flight attendant for another glass of wine because, why not?

'Redirecting the attention away from you and Mia and everything else. It was definitely a gamble, but it sure paid off in the end. In spades. Man, can she drive.'

'That she can. I take it you'd never seen her in action before.' Luca took a sip. 'She's, ah, something else.'

'Look, I'm saying this as a friend, not your team manager.' Brian lowered his voice. 'I don't know exactly what's on your mind, but considering that you're suddenly acting like a moody teenage boy with a crush on his teacher, I think I have a pretty good idea. The two of you? Don't. Between Rob dying, which I still don't think any of us has fully grasped, her especially, her new role with the team, and leaving her life in Chicago behind without expecting to, she has too many cars on the track right now without—'

Luca looked around to find headphones in the ears of the staff members within listening range. 'Me taking her for a ride? I understand what you're saying. I do. Trust me, I have no intention of leaving the friend lane.' This may be the most personal conversation he'd ever had with another guy. 'But being around her has stirred up... things.'

'Do I want to ask about these things?' Brian suddenly looked as uncomfortable as Luca felt.

Luca shrugged. 'Things I perhaps moved past faster than

she did. Or maybe never dealt with at all. I don't know. It's hard to believe now that Rob told me to forget about her, and I did. I didn't think twice about it.'

'You were a kid,' Brian said. 'And that was a lot of shit to hit the fan. I mean, *a lot*.'

'Maybe he was testing me. To see how I felt about her?'

Brian shook his head. 'Absolutely not. First of all, that wasn't Rob's MO. He said what he wanted to say. Second, he caught you having *sex* with his *daughter*. In that moment at least, he wanted you gone. Maybe dead. Can you blame him?'

'Not at all,' Luca said. 'I guess the real mystery, then, is why he wanted me back.'

'That I can't tell you. Like I said before, he only shared that you and Mia had been involved, but it was all in the past.'

'And that's where it needs to stay,' Luca said, trying to convince himself as much as Brian. 'Also, yes, I do need to thank you. It seemed like a harebrained idea at the time, but I don't think Mia could've taken another couple of days of muck being dredged up.'

The negative headlines had started to fade once the press caught sight of her masterful driving. The process had sped up when Jordan had failed to best her at what he considered his own game. Mia had remained in the news for the remainder of testing, but for all the right reasons.

'PR wasn't happy when I sprung the whole Mia-in-the-car thing on them, but at least it took them off damage control,'

Brian said, handing his finally empty beer bottle to a passing flight attendant and reclining his chair flat. 'Now, if you don't mind, I'm going to take advantage of a little shut-eye. And before you say it, I know it's a mistake. But I'm exhausted and the next few weeks aren't going to include much time for beauty sleep.'

Luca grabbed his computer tablet and browsed the articles recapping testing for the twelve teams signed on for the season. Rubie Racing was being rated up top with the big budget teams. Damn if he didn't wish Rob was here to see that, considering how frustratingly close Rubie Racing had come last year and how much effort his boss had put into working out the bugs for this season. Rob's instincts had been spot on.

That is, for everyone except Jordan.

Maybe he should feel worse for his teammate than he did, especially since his lackluster performance at testing in a car two others managed to successfully pilot was bound to give rise to the background noise already buzzing throughout the racing industry. If his last name didn't match his team name, would he still have a ride? Not likely. Jordan had won one race in his career and hadn't stood on the other two levels of the podium in three years.

As dysfunctional as their father–son relationship had always seemed, Rob had never hinted at tossing his son aside for another driver. Plenty of guys would've killed for a chance to sign on with Rubie Racing, to be one of the legendary Rob Rubie's protégés. Hell, Luca had been one of those guys.

Twice. But Jordan had taken little interest in seeking or heeding his father's advice. Or anyone's, for that matter. And it showed.

Although Jordan was a solid top-ten finisher, adding points toward the championship for the team, he had never committed to growing as a driver. He was quick to point a finger of blame at anyone except himself. His tantrum during testing was par for the course.

Luca had realized long ago that his natural talent and a fast car weren't enough to get him a world championship. That took work, hard work and lots of it, to one day be remembered among the racing greats. Maybe that's why the sacrifices he made for the sake of his career — living away from his family since his teenage years, having little to no privacy, not having a normal life — never felt like sacrifices to him.

His thoughts drifted again to Mia. When she walked away from racing, she'd thrown so much away. He'd never considered that she might have sacrificed her passion, her dreams, because of him. He'd given up nothing professionally and never thought twice about it.

Until now.

Chapter 20

Mia dragged her luggage up the stairs to find her childhood bedroom just as she'd left it, except for the fresh towels in her en suite and clean sheets on the bed. She fought the urge to collapse onto it, even though she knew the best remedy for jet lag was to fight through and stay awake until at least eight o'clock. But that bit of logic was about to go out the window given the several flight delays that had brought her back into Detroit just before the team jet, which had left a half day later. She'd only wanted some time to herself to process her hours in the turbo pumpkin and decompress. So much for her best laid plans.

She was sorting laundry when Barb stuck her head in the doorway.

'I'll grab those for you,' Barb said, heading toward the growing piles of lights and darks.

'You certainly will not. It's bad enough that I'm treating your home as a bed and breakfast. My dirty clothes are off limits. Stand back, lady!'

Barb put her hands up. 'Fine, fine, do your own laundry. See if I care. But find me in the kitchen when you're settled, so I can at least feed you the decent meal included in your package here at Barb's B & B.'

Mia watched as the woman who'd dedicated years of her life to caring for this house, her dad, Jordan, and especially her, backed out of the room like she'd stumbled onto a bank robbery.

No doubt, Barb had landed in the Rubie family's life at precisely the right time. When Patricia Rubie exited this world, those she'd left behind weren't exactly keeping it together. At all. They'd been caged birds for months, as all three went from limiting their time on the road to staying home altogether as her condition went from bad to worse to unbelievably horrible. And when they were again free, they weren't. Mia began running wilder than she ever had before, and Jordan's innate sullenness turned to anger after the loss of his greatest ally. Powerless for the first time in his life, their dad threw himself into something he could control – running what was then still a young racing team. He put in long hours during the off-season and pretty much packed up and left town for the rest of the year.

When Barb moved in a couple months after their mom died, she slowly brought the house under control. Not just by putting things in order – she made sure everyone ate and slept and breathed in and out. She kept their bodies alive until their spirits followed.

Since her father passed, Mia had finally begun to understand how he justified turning his kids and the keys to his house over to Barb. But at the time, she'd felt abandoned. First by her mother, and then by her father. Always assertive behind the wheel, her driving had turned borderline aggressive, like she had nothing to lose.

She hadn't. At least she hadn't thought she did. Until Luca.

Barb had been there again during those weeks Mia spent hiding in her room after Luca vanished from the face of her earth. The kitchen had been stocked with her favorite foods; her sheets changed during the rare moment Mia wasn't tucked under them; her most comfortable clothes quickly washed and ready for wear. When Mia had finally reentered the world, Barb had been the one she confided in about going away to school. It had been Barb who drove her to visit colleges and then encouraged her to tell her dad her plans.

Most importantly, she'd let Mia cry over Luca and never asked any questions.

Until today.

After Mia showered off at least a dozen hours' worth of airport and airplane grime and started the first of what would be many loads of laundry, she found Barb ladling chicken, mushroom, and wild rice soup into two bowls. The hearty concoction was Mia's favorite, along with the loaf of thick, crusty sourdough still warm to the touch.

'Oh, how is Frank?' she asked. Francisco, as Barb's sourdough starter was formally known, had come into the Rubie house along with her, and Mia had been fascinated with the bubbly mixture that lived in their refrigerator. When she moved to Chicago, Barb had sent along part of her old friend to help start Mia on her new life. It hadn't ended well.

'Better than little Frankie, that's for sure,' Barb said dryly, softly blowing on her first spoonful of soup. 'There's enough for Luca. Will he be around later?'

Mia attempted a nonchalant shrug of her shoulders. 'No, he flew back with the team. I decided to come home early.'

Barb slid the loaf of bread closer to Mia. Damn that woman for knowing carbs were her kryptonite.

'Things got weird after the whole story of our secret teenage love affair was broadcast to the world. I kind of unloaded on him? I honestly don't recall exactly what I said. Anyway, it doesn't matter. Whatever was between us is in the past, and that's where it's going to stay.'

'You don't say.'

'Us trying to be friends is crazy enough.' Mia tore off a chunk of bread and began sopping up the broth with it.

Barb followed suit. 'Well, it was fun having him around again. Nice kid, that one.' She nodded a tad too casually.

Mia scooted her chair back and headed to the stockpot on the stove for a refill.

'Don't fill up on soup,' Barb warned, scraping the bottom of her bowl. 'I made brownies, too.'

'Bread and back-up chocolate? Someone pulled out the big guns today. I'm half afraid Star's about to jump out of the broom closet.'

'Don't think I didn't consider it.'

To be safe, Mia opened the closet door. Only instead of

her best friend, she discovered several bottles of her favorite Côtes du Rhône nestled among the cleaning supplies. 'Vino, too, Barb? What exactly did you think I needed to spill?'

'Fine, fine. I already knew things were weird with the two of you. I received a report from the front, you might say.'

Mia raised an eyebrow, grabbed one of the bottles from the closet, and shoved it toward the woman who was more concerned than nosey. After a half bottle of the rich red, which paired perfectly with the dark chocolate brownies, the events of Spain poured out of her. How the disastrous press conference had led to her getting behind the wheel again, which had driven her to realize that in walking away from Rubie Racing so many years ago, she'd hurt herself as much as her father. How she'd gone off on Luca.

'I mean, it just ended. Like that.' She tried to snap her fingers but somehow failed. Stupid jet lag. 'You were there, you remember. That was it, nothing for years. Until now. He meant more to me than racing. Racing meant more to him than I did.'

'If only the world was so black and white,' Barb said. 'You were young, Mia. You both were. Don't you think people deserve second chances?'

Mia steered clear of that question. 'He broke my heart to the point that I didn't think it would ever heal. There's no way I can risk getting hurt like that again.'

'That was a lifetime ago. And you know what? You've changed. And so has he.'

'What exactly are you proposing?'

'A new perspective, one that better suits the smart and strong woman sitting in front of me.' Barb took a sip from the glass of wine she'd been nursing. 'Some shades of gray, perhaps?'

'Hmm. I don't know, I think I prefer red,' Mia said, tipping the last of the bottle into her glass. 'And after that, bed.'

The next morning, Luca sat down, slid her regular espresso order across the conference table, and proceeded to rehash testing like the awkwardness between the two of them in Spain had been a figment of her imagination. And Mia played along because, once again, she could handle cordial Luca.

The remainder of her day was spent in meetings with team members about fine-tuning the cars before the first race of the season. Even though everyone was overwhelmingly pleased with the RR1's performance during testing, a host of tweaks and slight modifications were put on the table and discussed and debated at length.

The race to the season opener was on.

More than once, Mia sent up a thank you to her dad for putting together such a stellar crew. Otherwise, she'd likely be freaking out that in a few short weeks, both cars needed to be disassembled, crated, and shipped to Melbourne along with every computer, tool, and part they might need during the Australian Grand Prix. Or that Luca's car was still on its way back from Spain and wouldn't be reassembled for a couple more days.

Noticeably still absent was her brother, who hadn't been

spotted since leaving testing in a huff. As his sister, she didn't care to expend the energy required to deal with him or whatever Jordan was stewing over, and she couldn't have cared less if he showed up at work or not. If she was being perfectly honest, she preferred not to have him there. But as his boss, she had to suck it up and figure out how to get him to play nice with everyone else on the team or her dad would haunt her from beyond.

At four o'clock, she shut down her computer, grabbed her keys, and gritted her teeth.

Julia answered when she knocked on the door of Jordan's lake house in the Irish Hills, a once kitschy tourist area west of the complex. It appeared her brother owned the entire lake, a fact she would've known if she'd ever been in his home. She'd gotten his address from his file in human resources.

'May I help you?' the supermodel asked, tossing her hair back in a straight-from-the-movies mean-girl kind of way.

Oh please.

Beautiful women didn't intimidate Mia. She'd grown up with a former Miss Universe for Pete's sake. Her mother had literally been the queen of all supermodels. Of course, this particular one did know Luca in the biblical sense, a thought she banished to the back of her brain for the time being.

'Julia, I presume.' Mia forced her natural grin wider. 'It's nice to meet you. I'm Mia, Jordan's sister. Is he in?'

'I'm not sure if he's receiving visitors at the moment,' Julia said, her fake smile rivaling Mia's.

'Oh, I'm sure he'll want to see me.' Mia squeezed past

the woman attempting to block the door to find herself in an entryway leading to an open first floor that, at first glance, appeared as uncomfortable as her condo in Chicago.

The modern decor was straight out of the pages of a magazine and contrasted sharply with the pine trees and small frozen lake visible through the floor-to-ceiling windows. Jordan was sitting on a smooth white leather sofa facing a gray marble fireplace, where a roaring fire was charged with providing the only warmth in the colorless, cool space. It was a tall order.

The two glasses of white wine on the glass coffee table made her think she'd interrupted something until she noticed only one had been touched. Plus, the scowl on her twin's face didn't appear fresh, nor did it scream romance.

'Mia, what a pleasant surprise,' he said, the tone of his voice giving away that he found her visit neither pleasant nor a surprise.

He didn't invite her to sit down, so Mia perched on the arm of the sofa. Julia, now in full-on hostess mode, appeared with a third glass and a half-full bottle of Chardonnay. As tempting as an alcohol lubricant was for this conversation, Mia shook her head. Julia shrugged, refilled the empty glass on the coffee table, and drained a good portion of it as soon as she sat down next to Jordan.

Mia had strategized on the drive over how best to approach the situation. Considering how well bringing up the stipulations of their dad's will had gone over before, she hoped flattery might get her somewhere. Especially since there's no way she'd bring up such a sensitive subject in front of Julia. What little Mia knew about the woman she didn't like.

'I noticed you weren't at the complex today,' Mia said. 'We have a lot to do and could certainly use your years of expertise.'

Jordan smirked. 'Oh, I'm sure.'

She envisioned Jordan's car sitting in the building virtually untouched while the hours until it was shipped to Australia ticked away. Although the engineers could follow the data and duplicate some of the changes they'd already made during testing to Luca's car, Jordan needed to sit down and debrief his race engineer on those long hours he'd spent in the driver's seat in Spain.

'I'm serious. You've been in a Rubie Racing car for longer than anyone else in the history of the team. Only you know what feels right, and what feels off. Only you can affect the change needed to make sure your car is the best it can be for you this season.'

He rolled his eyes. Beside him, Julia finished off her glass of wine and refilled.

Mia sighed thinking of Detroit's best automotive minds twiddling their thumbs instead of at work on Jordan's RR1. 'You're the one in the car, Jordan. Not the engineers, not the mechanics, and not me.'

'But you wish you were, don't you?'

She shook her head. 'No. You're the Rubie sibling who's earned a place on this team, on the track. Not me.'

Mia took a deep breath and prepared herself to do something that she hadn't done in her whole life without being forced to – apologize to her brother. And not just because she needed him back in the car, although that would've been reason enough. Her pink dress comment had crossed a line, and she'd regretted it almost immediately. Regardless of how he treated her, she'd always tried to not lower herself to his level. In that moment, she'd failed miserably.

'I didn't consider the impact me getting in the car in Spain would have on you,' she said. 'I was only thinking of myself and how it would help me. I'm sorry.'

When Jordan responded with silence, she stood up and went over to the windows. The lake was frozen over and most of the trees had dropped their needles for the winter, but the view reminded her of where their mom had taken them in northern Michigan when their dad hit the circuit without his family and the three of them needed a literal change of scenery.

Mia looked at her brother and glimpsed the boy who'd spend hours on the dock, pole in hand, until he caught enough for their mom to fry up for dinner. 'Do you catch many fish here?'

Julia burst out laughing as if it was the most absurd thing she'd ever heard. But Jordan said quietly, 'I put a dock in but, you know how it is, I'm rarely around during the summer. Racing season and all.'

She gave him a half smile. 'I still wish I knew mom's secret recipe. I've tried to figure out the spices she used in the batter, but I can never get it quite right.'

'Me neither.'

Their mom's ability to fry fish had become legendary, probably because her efforts in the kitchen were otherwise lackluster. But she'd never written the ingredients down and they had no idea that the summer they spent at the lake before she was diagnosed with breast cancer would be their last. Her recipe had died along with her before the next summer had rolled around.

'Paprika maybe?' Mia asked.

When Jordan shook his head and looked away, a wave of sadness like she hadn't experienced in years washed over her.

'Well, I should leave. I'll see you tomorrow?' She didn't wait for him to answer before adding, 'Julia, it was lovely to meet you finally. Enjoy your evening.'

To her surprise, Julia lifted her nearly empty wineglass and said, 'Likewise. Be sure to tell Luca I said hello, will you?'

'You got it,' she said, not glancing back as she walked toward the door.

Mia was able to fulfill Julia's request not two hours later, when an oversized pair of feet in tie-dye socks appeared in her sight line as she stretched at the ballet barre. She blew out a deep breath before standing up to face Luca.

'What, they were out of pink?' she said.

'Those were loaners,' he said, lifting his foot to show off the green and purple design. 'These babies are all mine.'

Once her pre-class stretching routine was complete, she plopped down on the floor next to him. 'Your ex-girlfriend extends her best wishes, by the way.'

His eyes narrowed. 'Excuse me?'

'Julia.' She said it as if this were the most natural line of conversation in the world the two of them could be having. 'I saw her at Jordan's house earlier. She wanted me to tell you hi. So, hi.'

The puzzled look on his face remained. 'Like I said, excuse me? And also, your brother's house? I always assumed he hung upside down in a cave somewhere.'

Mia hadn't told anyone that she'd decided to pay her brother a visit and attempt to smooth things over. She'd been afraid they'd try to talk her out of it, and possibly succeed, even though she'd known it was what she needed to do.

If anyone understood her history with Jordan, it was Luca. She took a chance and told him the truth. 'I had to go talk to him. My brother isn't perfect, by any means, but he didn't deserve his sister kicking him while he was down.'

Luca cringed. 'Pink dress?'

She nodded.

He shrugged a shoulder. 'You're right, it was a low blow. Good for you for being the bigger person. How'd it go?'

'About as good as can be expected.' She leaned back against the wall. 'I hope it was enough. The team can't survive losing another member this season. Even Jordan. It would throw us into chaos. We're barely keeping it together, and you know it.'

'I think you're doing a great—'

She immediately put a hand in front of his face to silence him. 'I'm doing my best. But we can't lose Jordan right now, not when we're without a reserve driver. It can't happen. This won't work without him. Trust me.'

She failed to mention that, thanks to her dad's will, what Jordan stood to gain was massive whether he stayed with Rubie Racing and helped take the team to a championship season or chose to leave of his own volition. Those details were no one's business outside of the family – even though this particular tidbit of information would be helpful to Brian. It was up to Jordan to divulge his dad's final ultimatum. Especially given that only one of the options her dad had spelled out left Jordan's pride intact, which was the main reason she expected to see him bright and early the next morning.

Just as Luca opened his mouth again, the music began to pulse, signaling the beginning of class. Mia turned to face the mirror and follow the instructor. After a second, Luca stopped staring at her and did as well. For the next fifty minutes, she did her best to avoid looking at him, but couldn't help noticing how much he'd improved. And she wasn't the only one – Ms Hands-on was visibly disappointed about the limited number of corrections he required to his form.

The class ended in child's pose, and Mia usually enjoyed sinking her upper body deep between her knees and giving her back and shoulders a good stretch. She lasted seconds before whispering to Luca, 'OK, what gives?'

Luca turned toward her and raised an eyebrow, as if he had no idea what she could be talking about.

'Not two weeks ago, you were stumbling around here like

some idiot in training for the clumsiest clown competition' – OK, that may have been an exaggeration – 'and now you look like you could qualify for the barre Olympics.'

He laughed, low and quiet, then sat up and began gathering his weights and accoutrements to put away. 'I have no idea what you're talking about.'

It was her turn to raise an eyebrow. 'I call bullshit.'

'Fine, I found some videos online while we were in Spain,' he admitted. 'They've been a great stress reliever. I'll send you a link.'

The thought of Luca working on his core in front of his computer, clad in his tie-dyed socks, stretched a smile across her face. And even though she'd just caught the live show, the image refused to leave her brain.

'Earth to Mia…'

Her eyes focused to find Luca's face mere inches from hers, within kissing distance. Now another vision implanted itself in her brain, along with the accompanying sensation of his soft lips pressed to hers. She shook her head before she could picture her hands in his hair – or elsewhere on his body.

'Sorry, I guess I zoned out there for a minute. You were saying?'

'I need to head out, but I'll see you tomorrow?' he asked.

She followed him out the door of the studio. 'Oh, yes. Of course.'

He screeched to a halt, and she nearly ran into him. 'You're OK, Mia?'

'Yes, fine. A-OK.'

She wondered where he was off to in such a hurry, then reminded herself that he had his own life. It's not like they were going to have an almond boneless chicken party every time they did a barre class together. Not that she couldn't stop on the way home for carryout. Her stomach grumbled in either hunger or protest – it was hard to say – and she heard Luca laugh softly beside her as he put his coat on.

'I know what you're thinking, Mia, and I would strongly advise against you stopping for that chicken and gravy concoction. Trust me, your body will thank you later.'

He was out the door before she could think of a witty comeback.

'Is he your boyfriend?' Ms Hands-on asked from behind the desk. 'I'm sorry. It's none of my business. Never mind.'

Except she thought it was, or she wouldn't have asked.

'No, we're not together. He's not exactly the boyfriend-type, if you know what I mean.'

Her 'hmm' screamed 'we'll see about that.'

'Trust me on this one,' Mia said, wanting to exit this conversation and quickly. She decided to simply stop engaging and get out. But when she glanced back at the desk on her way to the door to say goodbye, Ms Hands-on was tossing her a look that said she didn't trust Mia at all.

That's all it took for Mia to fish her phone out of her bag and hit speed dial for her favorite restaurant.

Chapter 21

The Rubie Racing team emitted a collective sigh of relief when Luca's turbo pumpkin landed back in the building. Apparently, the thought of something, anything happening to Rob's car had put them all on edge.

Luca dreamt that the plane had gone down and his precious turbo pumpkin started racing around the bottom of the ocean with a hammerhead shark behind the wheel. He couldn't help but text Mia and Brian about it when he woke up.

Mia's response: *Your subconscious couldn't have chosen a more aerodynamic fish?*

'I'll have you know the hammerhead is one of the most respected sharks in the ocean,' he told her when he marched into her office and thrust her morning espresso across her desk. 'The Hawaiians believe they watch over their families. It would be an honor to have an *aumakua* driving my car. An *honor*.'

He may have done some googling.

'I believe technically that's my car,' she grinned. 'But point taken.'

Thankfully, with the team frantically trying to put everything in place for the season, their interactions were limited to quick moments. Which was good, since his new plan was to plank his way to self-control when necessary.

Which is how Jordan, who never visited his or anyone's office found him. Who'd shown up at the complex the day before like he hadn't behaved like a miserable s.o.b. in Spain. Who was now standing over him, watching with Luca as the timer on his phone slowly ticked down the seconds before he could end the plank.

When it finally reached zero, Luca nonchalantly got up, took a seat at his desk, and pointed to his side chair. 'What can I do for you?'

To his further amazement, Jordan sat down. 'I was thinking we should set up a couple of meetings to talk about our overall strategy as drivers for the season. Once the season begins, it's too much of a shitshow to think long-term.'

Who was this person and what had he done with Jordan Rubie? Although he was suspicious of the sudden Mr Hyde-Dr Jekyll personality change, Luca nodded slowly, not wanting to spook the magical creature in front of him. 'Sure, that sounds great, and you're right on about tackling this now before we lose our lives to the circuit. Thoughts on who we should circle in on this conversation?'

'I'd assume Mia, unless that makes you uncomfortable. Your call.'

Ah, there was a hint of Mr Hyde. 'Not at all,' Luca said, ignoring the insinuation. 'Why don't you have your assistant set something up? Shouldn't be difficult to nail down a time. I think we're all here twenty-four-seven until we head to the Land Down Under.'

'Will do,' Jordan said, not moving from the chair.

'Is there something else?'

He cleared his throat and began talking as if he were reading from a script. 'As I'm sure you're aware from my sister about the stipulations of our father's will, I thought I'd let you know that I'm determined to see this season through and help move the team forward.'

Luca didn't have a clue what Jordan was talking about, but the stiffness in his teammate's posture and voice betrayed the casualness he was working overtime to convey. Something was up. Way up.

He played along. 'That's good to hear.'

'We'll get 'em this year,' Jordan said flatly as he got to his feet.

'We certainly will.' Luca had never been so relieved to see someone leave in his entire life. 'Thank you for stopping by, Jordan.'

'My door is always open to you as well.' Jordan paused before he crossed the threshold, turned, and rapped on the doorframe with his fist before adding, 'No hard feelings about Julia.'

'Not a one.' Luca shook his head and chuckled. 'I'm completely serious. Good luck to you both.'

The smug smile on Jordan's face transitioned into his infamous scowl before he whipped back around.

Five minutes later, Luca was still half wondering if he'd blacked out mid-plank and imagined the whole encounter. But a meeting invite popped into his inbox from Jordan's assistant. When he replied to Olivia's email, he was tempted to ask what on earth she did all day, every day. With Rubie Racing team members dedicated to marketing, PR, and travel, and every other minutiae of the business, Luca had never been able to figure out Jordan's need for his own assistant. He'd always managed just fine on his own. Even Rob had done without one for the last year of his life, although that was mostly because his lack of organization drove them all away. The empty desk now gathered dust and doughnuts.

The days until the season started were a blur of debriefings and meetings, including an awkward strategy session with Mia and Jordan, along with twice-a-day workouts. Mia joined him for more barre classes, although he continued to head out as soon as he could get his coat on.

On his final Friday night at home, she asked if he had a hot date as he stripped off another pair of tie-dye socks in shades of orange, which Mia pointed out matched his turbo pumpkin. As if he hadn't realized that. They'd been an early birthday present to himself — likely the only one he'd receive. Luca couldn't remember the last time anyone celebrated his birthday, including him. Its timing was bad for a race car driver, right as the season was about to begin. He likened it to having a summer birthday as a kid, and never getting to bring in a treat for the class. This year, it was the day before he flew to Australia, so even more inconvenient.

But Mia wouldn't remember something as mundane as his birthday. She was just making more small talk – they were perfecting the art of small talk – and if he had a hot date, it would only be with her.

'My only plans are with my bed and myself.' He cringed as soon as the words left his mouth.

Her eyes widened. 'All right. I wouldn't want to keep you then, from that.'

He winked. 'It is our last weekend together. I'm flying to Aussie bright and early Monday morning, so I want to make the most of what little time we have left.'

'I forgot you were going in with your team,' she said. 'I guess I'll see you there, unless you're planning to be in over the weekend.'

The temptation to ditch his plans to pack and shop for the season was suddenly strong. Maybe Jordan's assistant hired herself out for minor tasks.

Don't go down this road again. Even if the view takes your breath away, it's a dead end.

He reluctantly shook his head. 'Nope, with my car buttoned-up and in transport, I'm down to personal prep. Laundry, shopping… you know all of those glamorous things that race car drivers do behind the scenes. At least the ones without a personal assistant.'

He was babbling, but couldn't seem to stop. Luca Toscano doesn't babble, he told himself. Only, apparently, he did.

'But if you want to grab a bite to eat, let me know,' he said, unable to stop himself from extending an olive branch and hoping like hell she'd grab it, and maybe him, in the process.

'Sure,' Mia smiled. 'Maybe I'll do that.'

But as the weekend went by, she didn't. Which was totally fine.

Aside from his workouts, he focused on getting organized, so the next eight months on the road didn't devolve into chaos. He stocked up on his favorite exercise nutrition and hydration – Rubie Racing would ship food and water to every race, not chancing unsettled stomachs from foreign fare. Although he'd have team and sponsor gear waiting for him, he readied a full set of clothes as well as backup clothes for the next trip, just in case a hiccup kept him from dealing with laundry and repacking. Stranger things had happened while traveling the circuit.

He also spent some solid time just enjoying his loft. Baking focaccia. Watching as, with spring nearing, more ships and freighters made their way up and down the Detroit River, destined for ports along the Great Lakes and beyond. Like him, crew members were away from home for months at a time. Although he had a feeling their quarters were significantly more cramped and less luxurious than the hotel rooms he'd be booked in.

When his phone rang early Sunday morning, he was pleasantly surprised to hear Barb's voice on the other end of the line. 'A little bird told me you were heading out tomorrow,' she said. 'Come over for a home-cooked meal tonight so I can wish you good luck.'

It was his stomach that wouldn't let him say no. Not any other part of his body.

'Only if I can bring something,' he said.

'Of course, bring yourself and be here at five,' she laughed. 'We'll see you then.'

Which is how he ended up in the suburbs, sitting around the formal dining table with Barb, Cliff, and Mia. With a birthday cake in front of him.

'This wasn't necessary. Really, it's not a big deal.' Luca watched as Barb worked her way through lighting the many, many candles in the chocolate frosting. His breath caught in his throat, and he hoped he'd be able to summon enough air to blow them all out.

'Nonsense,' Barb said. 'Everyone should have a birthday cake on their birthday.'

The doorbell rang, and Mia jumped up to answer it. She ushered Brian into the dining room just as Barb lit the thirty-sixth candle.

'Whoa! I hope someone has the fire extinguisher handy,' his team manager joked, taking a seat at the table.

After a rousing rendition of 'Happy Birthday to You,' they told him to make a wish.

'What'd you wish for?' Mia asked from beside him as Barb cut the cake and began passing slices around the table.

He winked. 'I'd tell you, but then it wouldn't come true.'

'Superstitious much?'

His jaw dropped open in disbelief at her question. 'Of course I am, Mia. I'm a race car driver. We're quirky as hell about a lot of things, including wishes.' *And especially this particular wish, even if it was a shot in the dark.* 'Also, I won't get into who the little bird is chirping about trips and birthdays. But thank you.'

'You're welcome,' she said. 'And wish or no wish, we all know you're going to be world champ—'

'What did I say?' he asked, his hand going over her mouth. Although he could feel her smile against his palm, he didn't take his hand away until he heard a muffled 'sorry.' The word felt like so much like a kiss that he decided to consider it an unexpected birthday gift.

Luca dug into the homemade layer cake with gusto, thankful he'd been doubling up on his workouts. Not to mention he'd be planking later at home, or maybe next to his car in the driveway in ten minutes if Mia didn't quit licking the frosting off her fork.

When the little hand on his watch reached eight, Luca pushed his chair back and thanked Barb for the unexpected celebration. He informed Mia that he and Brian would have a Vegemite sandwich waiting for her in Melbourne, which evoked fake, exaggerated gagging from everyone. Barb hugged him and wished him good luck for the race and the season, which damn near did him in for some reason.

Then Cliff pushed back his chair, stood up, and offered to walk him out, which was odd. He knew Rob's best friend, of course, but the two weren't what anyone would consider close acquaintances. It had been a surprise to see him there tonight. When the door closed behind them, Cliff reached into his jacket pocket and pulled out a folded white envelope, which he placed in Luca's hand.

'Not sure if you know about the letters Rob left for various people in his life, but there was one for you, too,' he said.

Luca shook his head.

'The note at the funeral about Mia taking over Rubie Racing was just the tip of the iceberg. At the reading of the will, Jordan and Mia each received letters, as you'd expect, as well as Barb. And I got one, too. But there were a couple more letters tucked in the file folder with the others, including one for you, with instructions to give it to you at a time I saw fit.'

'And this is that time?' Luca asked. 'Now? Today?'

'What can I say? It was burning a hole in my pocket.' He stopped to clear his throat. 'But in all seriousness, yes. Even though I have no idea what it says, something says your birthday is the perfect time. I don't think I need to tell you how Rob felt about you. You were like another son to him.'

The gravity of Cliff's remark wasn't lost on Luca, who choked up for the second time that night. Damn, he was getting sentimental in his old age. 'He left a hole, that's for sure. I hope I can do him proud – wherever he is.'

'I know you will.' Cliff reached out and grabbed Luca's shoulder, giving it a squeeze. 'No doubt at all. Happy birthday, Luca. Make the most of your new year.'

It wasn't until Luca climbed into his SUV that he took a closer look at the envelope. His name was written on the front in that neat script he would've recognized anywhere.

He fought the urge to rip the envelope open and read the letter right there in the driveway. Instead, the letter rode shotgun back into the city, with Luca guarding it protectively, as if it might somehow fall off the seat or leap out the closed window. Once parked in his spot, he carried his unexpected message from Rob from the beyond up to his loft, where he plopped down on the leather couch.

With the lights of both Detroit and Windsor, Ontario, illuminating the cold, dark water of the Detroit River outside his window, he read:

Dear Luca,

Of all the questions you now wish you had asked me, I'll assume top on your list is why I brought you back into the Rubie Racing family after so many years. My answer is simple: You belonged here.

Out of anger and anguish, I set into motion a series of events that changed paths and lives. The 'what ifs' haunted me for years. I've started working to rectify these consequences but may have to die before everyone is back on the right track. Hopefully, that's not the case.

I'm proud of the driver and man you have become. Take good care of my daughter.

Love, your friend,
Rob Rubie

So now he knew why he had unexpectedly found himself sitting across from Rob in an out-of-the-way pub in England.

Why Rob had included him in Rubie Racing's quest for a world championship. Why Rob had welcomed him back with open arms.

He read it over a few more times, fixating on the words 'proud' and 'love.' Fatherly words. Foreign words, for him at least.

But 'Take good care of my daughter' was the line for the ages. Rob apparently hadn't expected that his daughter may not want Luca to care for her. Luca wondered if, somewhere, that was causing Rob as much anguish as it was him.

Mia.

He wondered what was in her letter, and if she knew about his. After one more read, he placed his letter back in the envelope and slid it between the pages of one of his favorite books, 'The Art of Racing in the Rain,' which lived on the coffee table.

Luca yawned and looked around his space. For the first time in his career as a driver, he had mixed feelings about leaving for the season. It's not that he was any less excited than normal about getting behind the wheel for the next eight months. He was going to miss his off-season life. Even though he'd be back for a few days or weeks here and there, it wouldn't feel the same as these solid months with his head landing on the same spot every night had.

He wandered into his bedroom, set the alarm, and fell fast asleep thinking about his first birthday wish in years – and hoping like hell it would somehow come true.

Chapter 22

Mia's amnesia about the complete craziness of a race week proved temporary. As soon as her plane landed in Melbourne on Tuesday morning, she hit the ground running. Even though she'd been traveling for a full twenty-four hours and had left for the airport from a last-minute sponsor meeting. Even though her internal clock was struggling to reset itself to local time. Even though the race was five days away.

The Rubie Racing team had been descending on Down Under in waves, beginning with the group responsible for greeting and reassembling the two RR1s, setting up the garage with all those supplies they'd shipped over, and assembling the team motorhome in the paddock area. The rest of Rob's well-oiled machine had been trickling in – Brian, the drivers, engineers, and other key players from public relations on the team plane, and everyone else flying commercial. Only a few people were left holding down the fort in Detroit, which Mia knew as the team member bringing up the rear.

'Nice of you to join us,' Jordan said when she walked

into the garage for the team meeting with two minutes to spare.

She rewarded her brother's snark with the sweetest smile a person who'd just spent a full day traversing the earth's circumference in a metal tube and was in desperate need of a shower could muster. A quick stop at the hotel to dump her bags had barely included enough time to change into Rubie Racing attire and throw her hair into a ponytail.

Mia's plan to stand in the back was foiled when Brian motioned her to the front of the room. As soon as she made her way through the one-hundred-and-fifty team members crowded into the workspace and came to stand beside him, the room quieted within seconds.

'And here we all are again.' He immediately caught himself and visibly gulped in air to suppress an emotional struggle she could tell he hadn't anticipated. 'Well, not *all* of us.'

Without thinking twice, Mia stepped in to save him. 'Actually, Brian, I'm pretty sure my dad's here. There's not a chance in heaven, or hell, that he'd let us fly solo the first race of the season.'

'Too true.' Brian laughed, and the rest of the group joined him. He dipped his head toward her, silently asking her to continue. Even though she hadn't planned on speaking, she suddenly knew just what to say.

'I'll be honest. I'm not sure what my father usually said to get you revved up at the beginning of a season, but I'm sure it was something masterful and memorable. He had a way with words, especially when it involved Rubie Racing.

Dad was fortunate enough to live his dream until the day he died. In large part, that was thanks to all of you. Whether you knew it or not, when you joined this team, you also signed on as a member of Rob Rubie's family. And like every decision he made, he chose his team carefully and deliberately. This couldn't have been more evident as I've gotten to know each of you better. I could've stumbled and muddled my way through this sudden and unexpected turn of events, but not one of you would've let that happen. So, I want to personally thank you for that, for welcoming me back to Rubie Racing.'

She paused and looked around the room, her eyes locking briefly with Luca's before she added, 'I'd like to say that my dad couldn't be prouder. But we all know that would be a lie because there was one thing he wanted more than anything. Let's go out there and honor his memory with a world championship.'

'Hear! Hear!' Brian said.

The room erupted in a round of applause and 'woo-hoos,' which caused heat to rise in Mia's cheeks. She took a step back, and Brian proceeded to go over the schedule for the remainder of the week: three practice sessions spread across Friday and Saturday morning, qualifying on Saturday afternoon, and then the Australian Grand Prix on Sunday. There was a lot of ground to cover before those fifty-eight laps.

The just over three-mile racetrack, with its sixteen turns on roads normally open to the public around Albert Park Lake, was known to be fast and technical. A driver's dream.

Rubie Racing had performed well there last year, with Luca taking a podium spot in his first race with the team and Jordan adding points with an eighth-place finish. Even a repeat of that performance would be a great way to launch the season.

Mia hadn't heard from Luca since his surprise birthday dinner in Detroit. When she exited the garage, she spotted him just outside the door signing autographs. Her dad had been a firm believer in giving back to fans for the support they gave the team, so she wasn't surprised to see Luca engaging with a teen boy who'd cornered him and answering questions while he made his way through a stack of photos.

But when the kid began pulling hats and shirts out of his backpack, Luca signed only a few before waving him off. Then he turned to find her watching the entire scene.

'What'd he need so many pictures signed for?' she asked. 'Do you think he's taking them to sick kids in a hospital or something?'

He responded with a deep belly laugh. 'Not likely, unless a sick child buys an autographed picture of me first on eBay and pays for hand delivery. I don't always do sellers a favor, but he was polite enough and there was no one waiting. And why not? We all have to make a living somehow.'

'You mean not everyone is lucky enough to get paid to drive a fancy car real fast?'

'No, and thank God,' he said. 'With a little more competition, I might find myself without a ride.'

That was doubtful. Plenty of teams would give anything to have Luca on their roster and were likely to pay him a lot more than Rubie Racing was. The thought made her stomach drop.

'Nice speech in there, by the way,' he said. 'Your rallying cry is similar to your dad's. I'm sure the team found that comforting. I know I did.'

'That's quite a compliment. I never would've realized, having never taken the opportunity to hear one firsthand. And on that high note, I'm going back to the hotel for a much-needed shower and maybe a nap.'

Luca ran his hand slowly through his hair and gave her a pained look before heading to a nearby orange scooter adorned with the team logo. 'Well, then, I guess I'll see you tonight, Mia.'

'Tonight?'

'At the sponsor dinner? Seven o'clock? You haven't forgotten?'

'Of course not,' she lied. Not only had the dinner completely slipped her mind, she wasn't sure of the current time at that moment.

'Might be best to stay up until then,' he added, turning the ignition key and zooming off.

As much as she was looking forward to being near-comatose until the next morning, skipping the sponsor dinner wasn't an option. Sponsorships could make or break an Apex team, especially mid-sized ones like Rubie Racing. Her dad had mastered the art of wooing sponsors, keeping the team competitive over the years. Without the two hundred million dollars their sponsors brought to the table, Rubie Racing would be toast. Every team member knew it, which is why they all put on their Sunday best every race week to make small talk and break bread with the folks who wrote those big checks.

So far, none of the sponsors her father had secured for the season had bailed on their long-term contracts. Such a move would've appeared callous so soon after his death, but it was always a possibility going forward. Inadvertently, Mia had done her part to keep them happy with that spur-of-the-moment spin around Catalunya. The RR1, plastered with sponsor logos, had flashed across millions of television screens worldwide and gone viral on social media. She had been big news, and by default, they had been, too.

It'd be a total win—win if not for the fact that she needed to appear and look coherent in... how many hours? She glanced at her phone again, then headed back to the hotel.

Eight hours later, her feet ached, her brain hurt, and she was having a hard time articulating simple sentences like, 'Hello, I'm Mia Rubie. It's nice to meet you.' She muddled through the cocktail hour, careful not to over-imbibe for fear of falling over right where she stood. During dinner, she managed to eat without dribbling the main course on herself or the long-term sponsor seated next to her.

As soon as the dessert dishes were cleared, Luca stood up across the table and said his goodbyes. Mia felt a flash of envy until he stopped in back of her chair and offered to share a car back to the hotel.

She was the epitome of dazed and confused, but apparently

very entertaining, judging by the number of low chuckles coming from Luca's side of the backseat.

'Why is me asking if you've ever held a koala bear so funny? They're cute,' she slurred. 'I love their little paws and how they look like they're ready to give you a hug. Wait, have you hugged one?'

When Luca nodded, she was jealous. But not of Luca, she realized. She envied the koala.

She must've drifted off because minutes later, Luca woke her up with a quiet, 'Mia, we're here. Come on, it's time to get out of the car.'

She vaguely registered walking through the lobby and into the elevator. Once the doors slid closed, she was glad to have Luca there to hold her up because she'd been more steady after a St Patrick's Day bar crawl. Without his arm around her, she was in danger of sliding to the floor. When she turned into him, his other arm wrapped around her, too.

'Is this how the koala bear hugged you?' she whispered. His chest shook beneath her cheek. 'Is there a picture?'

Although Mia insisted that she could make it to her room on her own, she immediately destroyed her case when she swayed on her way out of the elevator, stumbled, and took a stunned Luca down to the floor with her. As she mumbled her apologies, he shook it off, picked her up, and carried her to her door, across the threshold, and into the bedroom.

She was more than half asleep when he pulled off her shoes, tucked her in, and called the front desk to schedule a wake-up call. But she fully registered the kiss. Light, on her cheek.

'Luca,' she said, rolling onto her side.

He knelt down, bringing his face level with hers. 'Go to sleep, Mia.'

'Thank you for taking care of me.'

'Always.'

And with that, he was gone, and she completely faded away.

'Well, if it isn't sleeping beauty,' Brian teased at breakfast the next morning.

Mia was glad to see she wasn't the last to arrive in the team's motorhome, even though she had rolled over and fallen back asleep after her wake-up call. Her first of three wake-up calls as it turned out, thanks to Luca's foresight.

'You'd think I'd never traveled between time zones before.' She dug into the buffet of eggs, bacon, and potatoes, all of which had been flown in from Michigan, along with everything else needed to feed the Rubie Racing team three hearty square meals a day for more than a week. 'I'm not sure why my butt was so squarely kicked yesterday.'

The pounding in her head wasn't anything a little coffee wouldn't fix. Her eyes scanned the room until they landed on a familiar espresso machine.

Brian followed her gaze. 'Having an Italian on the team definitely has its benefits.' His eyes widened before he added, 'You know, because of the coffee.'

'Yes, exactly, the coffee,' she said, setting her plate on a table and crossing the room, drawn equally to a double shot of espresso as to the person manning the machine. Luca turned just as she reached him and placed a cup into her hands.

'I had a feeling you'd be in need of a double this morning.' He turned back around and started on his own drink. 'Are you feeling better? Or at least, not like you're about to topple over and take some unsuspecting good Samaritan down with you?'

A vision of her tripping as she walked out of the elevator popped into her mind. 'Oh, I'd forgotten about that. And you—'

'Came along for the ride. No worries, didn't even leave a bruise.'

'Still, sorry, but thank you for this.' She raised her cup. 'And for making sure I got to bed safely last night, and up on time this morning.'

'Was the second wake-up call the charm? Or the third?'

'Third. How'd you know?'

'Lucky guess,' he said. 'You should really consider talking to your dad's sleep schedule person. She's a miracle worker. Or, at the very least, packing that e-reader in your checked luggage.'

When they returned to the table where she'd left her food, they found Brian chatting with Jordan, who appeared to be straining to not roll his eyes at the sight of the two of them together.

'Good morning,' she said. 'Sleep well?'

'Not a lot of sleep,' her brother grinned. 'But it's all good.'

Now everyone at the table was straining to not roll their eyes. Julia had been at the sponsor dinner with her brother the night before, but Mia had always found herself on the opposite side of the room. The jury was still out on exactly who'd been avoiding who.

Talk shifted to the day's schedule, which proved to be a more palatable topic. Luca and Jordan would spend the rest of the morning with their crews, ensuring their cars would be ready for the practice sessions beginning the next day. Brian would flit between the two of them, and Mia would attend a debriefing on the race. Then, after lunch, there was a press conference at the track's media center – her first since the debacle in Spain. The team's PR gurus had encouraged Mia to sit this one out, 'if she wanted.'

'I'm going,' she'd insisted. 'I can't avoid reporters forever, so why start now?'

Plus, her dad had established a format for race week press conferences that the team was sticking to: driver, driver, picture, picture, questions, and out. He'd never sat up front with the drivers, so she didn't plan to either. She and Brian would be there on an as-needed basis only.

Still, when Mia saw the tabloid reporter who'd done too much digging into her past lurking outside the room, she wanted to turn around. Instead, she plastered on that famous Rubie grin and walked right on by.

But a half hour later, when the press conference was over and she and Brian were ready to leave, she heard, 'Hi, Mia.'

Ms Overly Ambitious Reporter stood before her. 'I was

wondering if you could spare a few minutes to chat with me,' Madison said.

Brian shook his head and tapped on the face of his watch, as if their tight schedule was the only reason Mia wouldn't honor Madison's request.

'As you can imagine, we have our hands full today,' Mia smiled. 'But if you email the team's PR rep, maybe she can try to find something on my calendar later in the season.'

Fool me once, shame on you. Fool me twice, shame on me.

'All right, I'll do that then.' Madison returned an equally unflappable smile, leaving no doubts that this wasn't the last they'd see of her.

'Nicely done,' Brian said. 'I'm impressed.'

'What can I say? I'm impressive as hell these days.'

Chapter 23

Joseph Linwood: It's certainly a beautiful day here in Melbourne as we begin another Apex season at Albert Park. I'm Joseph Linwood, back again with Nigel Rose for Horizon Sports.

Nigel Rose: Yes, indeed, Joseph. As always, I'm happy to be here with you to cover what really is one of the greatest spectacles in sport.

Joseph Linwood: We have few new faces on the grid today as well as the expected team changes for three drivers. But we're also noticeably missing one person.

Nigel Rose: Yes, Rob Rubie, the owner and team principal of Rubie Racing, passed away unexpectedly in the off-season. Before the race begins, drivers, team members, and fans will take a moment of silence to remember Rob. You also may have noticed the square black decal with his initials on all of the cars. It's a fitting tribute for a man who did so much for the sport, both as a driver and as a team owner, for many decades.

Joseph Linwood: You were lucky enough to race with Rob, weren't you Nigel?

Nigel Rose: I don't know if lucky is the word I'd use. He gave me many a sound beating in those few years that I was on the track with him, at the end of his career and the beginning of mine. He was a fine driver, and no one will forget how close he was to becoming world champion. Of course, Rob took it all in stride and kept moving forward. As was his way.

Joseph Linwood: Now upon his death, we learned that his daughter, Mia Rubie, would be taking over team leadership. Although we've seen little of her since she was a talented up-and-coming driver, she's all anyone can talk about these days after a turn in the car during pre-season testing in Spain.

Nigel Rose: She certainly gave us all quite a surprise when she hopped in the car. She doesn't just look like her dad; she drives like him, too. Not sure I would've wanted to be a fly on the wall at the family dinner table that night, although we might have more insight about what led her brother and Rubie Racing driver Jordan Rubie to fly home after his turn in the car the next day.

Joseph Linwood: That bit of theater earned Jordan a five thousand dollar fine. Of course, we have Luca Toscano, one of the most experienced drivers on the track, in the other Rubie Racing car. In my opinion, Toscano has never looked stronger and the fact that he's starting on the front row today proves it. OK, let's pause for that moment of silence...

Nigel Rose: Drivers are in their cars! Our defending world champion, Henri Aveline, has the season's first pole position, and you can bet Toscano will be fighting to reach him as soon as he can from the second position. I know this is only the formation lap, but I have to say, Joseph, that's a fine-looking field this season with twenty-four cars in the hunt.

Joseph Linwood: Here come the leaders around the final turn and yes, there's the green flag! We're racing again in Australia!

Nigel Rose: That's a nice, clean start, but I think everyone is holding their breath as they clear these first few corners. The first laps of the season are always tricky as drivers get back into the groove and find their pace after months away.

Joseph Linwood: It appears Jordan Rubie is seeing some trouble. He's dropped three places to fourteenth.

Nigel Rose: That's the trouble with qualifying poorly, Joseph. It's riskier to start with more cars in front of you. So much can go wrong.

Joseph Linwood: Apparently, it's an issue with his tires, according to his radio transmission. He's, well, very unhappy with how the car is handling. Looks like he's driving in for an early pit stop. That's unfortunate.

Nigel Rose: Very unfortunate. Hard to come back from a start like that. Ask me how I know.

Fifty-four laps later

Nigel Rose: It's taken him most of the race to close the gap, but Toscano has been gaining over a second a lap and finally has Aveline in his crosshairs.

Joseph Linwood: There's certainly no love lost between those two former teammates.

Nigel Rose: I can't say I mind. They've provided us with some of the best racing we've seen the past few years, and today promises to be no exception. If Toscano can keep up this pace, he should be able to overtake Aveline in the next lap or two.

Joseph Linwood: Let's hope he can then hold off the Frenchman for the final three laps. Oh, dear, looks like they're both going to have to get by Toscano's teammate first.

Nigel Rose: Rubie has been bringing up the rear all day. No one on his team seems to be able to figure out what the issue is with his car, but his radio transmissions have been, shall we say, colorful. An unfortunate start to the season, his first without his father.

Joseph Linwood: Wait, what's this? Rubie moved over for Aveline to pass, but he appears to not be giving his teammate the same courtesy.

Nigel Rose: He moved right back into the middle of the track in front of Toscano. Not sure what's happening here, but he's a lap down and should get out of the way of his teammate. Toscano should be thankful drivers aren't fined for using foul language over the radio.

Joseph Linwood: It's a real shame. He's by Rubie now, but those few seconds just cost us a great finish and Toscano a shot at the win.

Dripping with anger and champagne, Luca made a beeline to the garage from the podium, where he'd stood one infuriating step below Henri. This was hardly the first time in his career a teammate had screwed him over, but he was going to make damn sure it would be the last.

Considering that the long walk through the paddock did nothing to temper his rage, it was probably good that Jordan was nowhere in sight. As always, his eyes quickly found Mia and, despite her being deep in discussion with her brother's race engineer, he marched up to her.

But before Luca could get a word out, Mia grabbed his hand and pulled him toward an empty meeting room. 'Not here,' she said over her shoulder.

Once she shut the door and turned to face him, the fierce wind left his sails. There was as much sadness in her eyes as anger. It damn near broke what was left of his heart.

The reality of the situation hit Luca so hard that he had to catch his breath. He and Jordan had never been teammates in the traditional sense of the word, but they'd managed to play nice enough last season. There were only two new variables in the equation: Rob's death and, of course, Mia.

Now Luca wasn't sure what galled him more – that Jordan had done this to Mia, or that he'd been caught in the crossfire. It might be a tie, which was almost as bad as losing in his book.

'He's testing you,' Luca said. 'This isn't about me. This is all about you.'

'You don't think I know that? It's always been about me. You remember that season he and I drove in the Apex starter series. He was miserable and did his best to make sure I was miserable, too.'

It hadn't worked. Luca had made it his personal mission to be the yang to Jordan's yin that season. Thinking about his pursuit of her happiness combined with Mia beating her brother at literally every turn made Luca smile for the first time since his teammate robbed him of the win. 'But he didn't succeed. You weren't miserable, if you'll remember.'

If Mia recalled the exuberant efforts of her secret teenage boyfriend to soothe her ego, she didn't let on. Instead, she rubbed her temples and sighed. 'I wish I knew why he was like this. I mean, we were never best friends but now, it's like he hates me. Sabotaging your win? It's unhinged. I don't know what to say, except I'm sorry.'

'It's not your fault, Mia. But, please, please tell me that he doesn't get away with this.' Luca wasn't sure what he'd do if Jordan skated on such egregious behavior, considering his first thoughts after climbing out of the turbo pumpkin were murder and finding an online video on how to pour cement.

'Hardly. I didn't think the expression "so angry you could cry" was a thing but, apparently, it is.'

Luca's brows furrowed. 'Hmm. I'm pretty sure it's *spit*. As in, so angry you could *spit*.

'Really? Gross. I'm not doing that.' Her finger tapped at her lips, and Luca couldn't seem to pull his gaze away. 'Wait, what's cry then?'

'Happy. So happy you could cry.'

'Well, I'm not doing that either.' Her nose wrinkled. 'Who cries when they're happy? I mean, besides the criminally insane.'

Luca was more than willing to help her discover happy tears, but before he could offer, there was a quick knock on the door. It opened wide enough for Brian to stick his head into the room. When he saw Luca and Mia, his body followed.

His team manager had stood below the podium as Luca accepted his second-place trophy, smiled and waved to the fans, and then sprayed every ounce of champagne the magnum bottle held on Henri. He knew Brian had been concerned, but Luca had never been one to spout off to the media or act like anything other than the professional he was.

'Where's your brother?' Brian asked Mia.

'Oh, he was out of here in a hot second – fastest thing he did all day,' Mia said.

'Did he say anything?' Luca asked. 'Did you?'

'No and no,' Mia said. 'I wasn't going to have an epic throwdown with my brother in the middle of the garage. Not that he doesn't have it coming to him, and not that everyone isn't aware of what he did. You should've seen his own team and engineer cringe when they realized what he was up to.'

'I've scheduled a meeting for tonight, here,' Brian said. 'I've asked both of your race engineers to be present.'

'That's fantastic,' Luca said. 'I'll be there. My engineer will be there. One question: Will Jordan?'

'He will if he knows what's good for him,' Mia said.

Whether that was the case, at six o'clock sharp, a clearly disgruntled Jordan sat across the table from Luca, acting as if he were the one who'd been wronged instead of the perpetrator. Beside him, his engineer looked as if he'd rather be anywhere else, doing anything else, with anyone else. Luca's own engineer sat quietly next to him, clearly annoyed.

When Mia and Brian arrived together, Luca couldn't help but wonder who'd play the good cop and who'd be stuck in the role of bad cop. Before he could fully contemplate, Mia grinned.

'Jordan, thank you for joining us. I was hoping you could tell us what happened out there today. We had a solid chance at a win, and perhaps hearing your side of the story will ease the frustration the team is experiencing.'

'I was obviously having tire and setup issues,' he said. 'I had no grip. Didn't you listen to my radio transmissions?'

'Yes, we've reviewed everything. We looked at the tires we took off when you decided, on your own, to pit early. We talked to your team and ran some diagnostics of your car before they started disassembling it for transport.' She slid a spreadsheet across the table to her brother. 'We found no issues with your tires or the setup of your car.'

Jordan flipped through the sheets but barely glanced at the information on the pages. 'I don't know what to tell you, Mia. I know my car. Do you think I'd pit off schedule for no reason?'

That's what Luca couldn't figure out – why Jordan had pitted early on purpose. It certainly hadn't done him any favors, considering his poor performance in qualifying had caused him to start in the middle of the pack. He hadn't a chance in hell of placing in the top half of the field after blowing his single pit stop strategy.

'Just to be sure, we also ran the same diagnostics on Luca's car, and they were identical,' she said, then looked around the table. 'Kudos to both of your engineers for that, by the way.'

'I'm not sure what you're trying to say, sis.'

'I'll be clearer then. I'm saying the issue wasn't with your car.'

At that, Jordan jumped up, put his hands on the table, and leaned toward his sister. 'Are you saying it's me?'

To Mia's credit, she wasn't the least bit cowed. 'I'm not sure there's any other explanation for what happened at the end of the race. You're about to be lapped. Our competitor floats by you, but your teammate doesn't. Your engineer instructs you to let Luca pass. You don't.'

'Then my *sister* tells me to get out of the way—'

At that, Mia was on her feet, too. 'Correction: Your *team principal* told you to move aside.'

Luca suddenly wished he'd opted to listen to the race recordings instead of going for a post-race five-mile run to cool down.

'Sit down, Jordan.' He did as Mia instructed for the second time that day, only she remained standing. 'This is a team. The world is watching. Dad is watching. I'm going to go on the record right here and say that whatever happened out there today ends now.' She paused to point her index finger up in the air and then straight down to touch the table. 'Now.'

A meat cleaver couldn't have cut the air in the room at that point. Everyone at the table looked expectantly at Jordan, but he only moved to push his chair back.

Mia wasn't finished. 'This incident will not be repeated. And just so there's no confusion about all that encompasses, I'll spell it out for you. You will not block your teammate. You will not blame others or your car.'

Before Jordan could make a break for it, she added, 'Before you can ask about the consequences, let's just say they won't serve you well, Jordan. And I think you know what I mean.'

As he watched Jordan leave, Luca made a mental note to avoid Mia's bad side. Not that her bad cop act wasn't something he'd like to see again in another setting. He turned to Brian, 'Tell me, were you supposed to be the good cop or the mute cop? Because you really have the latter nailed.'

'What can I say?' Brian laughed nervously. 'She keeps stealing all my lines.'

When they left the meeting room, breakdown was in full swing. The next race wasn't for two weeks in South Africa, but much of this equipment was being shipped ahead to China for the third race. An identical kit was already on its way to the southern tip of Africa via ship. But with the two-week break, the cars would head home for more improvements.

So would Luca.

While packing up that night, his agent's name flashed across the screen of his phone. Considering that Alex Griffin only dealt with high-level professional athletes, he sounded surprised to catch Luca on the first try.

'I was sorry to see that kerfuffle on the track today,' Alex said. 'What a boner move.'

'Not what one would expect from a teammate,' Luca said.

'Well, it didn't go unnoticed, which is why I'm calling,' he said, getting to the point, as always. It was one of the many things Luca appreciated about his agent. 'Catalina Carvalho reached out to me tonight. She was curious about your long-term plans with Rubie Racing.'

'That's a bit bold,' he said. But not surprising. The Brazilian team had approached him before, three years ago, when they signed Wyn. For no particular reason he could put his finger on, Carvalho Motorsport hadn't interested him.

'She wondered if the new management coupled with Jordan's antics today might have you thinking it's time for a change. And she wanted to put it out there that she and her father would be happy to sit down with you when the time is right.'

Luca considered what to tell his agent. On one hand, he hadn't thought of leaving Rubie Racing, even after Rob's untimely demise. But on the other hand, if Jordan didn't shape up, he might be tempted to cut and run. 'Tell them that I appreciate their interest, and I'll reach out if that time comes.'

'OK,' Alex said. 'You have my number.'

A half an hour later, in bed, Luca allowed himself to consider leaving Rubie Racing. The money would be better with a bigger team like Carvalho Motorsport and he'd be teammates with Wyn, who Luca not only liked but also respected. And then there was Jordan. On a normal day, the thought of not having to deal with that particular Rubie twin again was a plus. Today, it was the biggest plus in the history of pluses.

But there were minuses, too, and the biggest one had to do with the other Rubie twin. It far outweighed all of the pluses combined, even if he didn't have a clue if he and Mia would ever be anything but reserve friends. Or if he'd ever figure out what that was exactly.

Not to mention, his role at Rubie Racing was atypical. He was more involved with the inner workings of the team than he'd been with any other team during his career. He was more than a driver, and he liked being a part of the big picture planning. A lot. The RR1 was damn near perfect, and if he didn't win the world championship this season, he was certain he would the next. If he could just hold on.

And then there was Rob's letter, and his final request. How could he take care of Mia if he was driving for Carvalho Motorsport? Not that Luca had any idea what that meant, and he fell asleep thinking that Mia was doing a fine job taking care of herself.

Chapter 24

Before the second race, Mia discovered the sheet of stickers in her childhood desk. In an attempt to put an end to the seemingly endless fights about what belonged to which Rubie twin, their mother had ordered them each a set of stickers personalized with 'Property of Mia' and 'Property of Jordan' and told them to have at it. That experiment had lasted exactly one hour, having been called off when Jordan had tagged all of the pop and snacks, while Mia, always thinking big picture, had placed a sticker on the swinging door to the kitchen and laid claim to everything inside.

Eight-year-old Mia had adorned the remaining stickers with drawings of colorful race cars and then, apparently, put them in a desk drawer and forgotten they ever existed.

Although her brother had cleaned up his act since what she and Brian now referred to as the 'Debacle Down Under,' Mia was sorely tempted to do a little decorating at the Ruby Racing complex. The sheet of stickers went in her work bag for the next time Jordan tested her patience.

As it turned out, it was Luca.

He'd come in behind Henri again in South Africa and was convinced there was an issue with his car. No other team had reported their cars bouncing on the straightaways at top speed, and Luca was sore in every sense of the word. But after fifteen minutes of listening to him rant in her office, she'd sweetly reminded him it was *her car*, not his, and he was lucky she was letting him drive it.

Not that she didn't feel bad that the bouncing had caused another loss, or his neck and back to hurt, which he clearly wasn't exaggerating based on how he winced when his head whipped around when she emphasized *her car*.

'I need a massage,' he said, rubbing his neck. 'Since it's *your* car, maybe *you* could treat me to an emergency sports massage. By a professional, of course.'

'Of course,' she gulped, thinking it ironic that she was paying someone to rub their hands all over Luca's body when, at one time, she'd happily done it for free. 'Only the best for our star driver.'

While Luca was gone that afternoon, Mia tracked down his engineering team. They were easy to find, since the turbo pumpkin had just returned and they were going over it with a fine-tooth comb.

After asking about the bouncing, which they were also puzzled about, she pulled the sheet of stickers from the file folder she was carrying. 'I have another question. Would there be an issue with sticking one of these inside the cockpit for the next race? Someplace where the driver would only see it if he were sitting in the car?'

The three men and one woman looked at each other as they wordlessly debated what was a legitimate question, given that any added weight to the car could have an impact on its performance. They all rubbed the sheet between their thumbs and index fingers to gauge the thickness of the paper, and then they peered into the cockpit and pointed at a couple of areas. After a round of shrugs, Luca's race engineer delivered the verdict — yes, but they would need to think about where exactly to stick it.

Since Mia had felt silly enough asking, she waited until the next race to see where they had landed on the sticker's placement. But once the busyness and enduring jet lag of race week took over, she nearly forgot about her attempt to literally stick it to Luca.

Until she heard him burst out laughing over the radio at the start line.

Everyone else probably assumed he was just overjoyed about qualifying in the prime front row spot, but Mia knew it had nothing to do with pole position. When Brian glanced her way and shook his head with the slightest of knowing grins, she just shrugged.

And when he stood at the top of the podium, no one could think about anything besides savoring the glory of the season's first win for Rubie Racing. Including Mia.

But on the long flight home to Detroit, the sticker greeted her from the accordion door of the plane's restroom in the middle of the night. She appeared to be the only one awake when she walked back through the cabin to her seat, although she could've sworn there was a smug look of satisfaction on Luca's sleeping face.

Their first morning back at the complex, Mia waited in her office until she heard a loud groan and knew what Luca had found stuck front and center to his beloved espresso machine.

He peeked in her office, his hazel eyes narrowed. 'Is the race champion allowed to have a cup? Or will I need to ask the owner's permission every morning?'

'As long as you get my order, feel free to proceed as normal,' she said.

Her phone pinged early the next morning.

Luca: *One shot or two?*

Mia: *Two*

Luca: *Got it*

Mia: *Oops, hit send too soon. Two shot caramel macchiato. Extra hot. Upside down*

She may as well make it interesting. Even if she hadn't a clue what upside down meant — and had once rolled her eyes at Star when a hipster in line ahead of them at Starbucks tagged that on to his painfully long order.

The days went on with the sticker going back and forth and her coffee order steadily increasing in difficulty. How well Luca played barista was nearly as amazing as how sticky the aging sticker remained after being stuck to one thing and then carefully peeled off and stuck to another.

But when she left the office late one night and found the sticker on her car, Mia was so mortified that she removed it on the spot. The day before, she'd heard some team members joking around in the cafeteria about the strange sedan that had appeared in the parking lot, and she'd laughed along as if she hadn't a clue who would drive something so hideous.

At least she'd discovered a benefit to being the first person in and the last person out. No one knew that the sedan belonged to the woman who also owned two of its polar opposite.

The next morning, she connected her phone wirelessly to the entertainment system of her dad's SUV and smiled when a bloodcurdling scream bounced off the walls. She eased the pang of guilt that surfaced when she drove past her steadfast sedan, but told herself this was a one-time thing. It wasn't good for an electric vehicle to sit for too long without being run and, technically, it was a company car.

'I can't believe you're downgrading from your beloved car of the year,' Mia heard when she peeled her hands off the heated steering wheel and stepped out into the crisp morning air that felt more like winter than late spring.

She turned to find Luca post-run, the skin on his legs red from what appeared to be an obsessive need to run in shorts regardless of the weather.

'Like everything in my life these days, it's temporary,' she said. But as the words left her mouth, they rang far hollower than they would've a month ago. 'Although, maybe it's time to let some things go.'

Maybe.

When they readied to fly off for the next race, the sticker remained in Luca's possession. Brian shook his head in disbelief at Mia when he saw Luca climb into this car before the first practice and affix it to the exact same spot in the cockpit.

'What?' Luca said. 'The bouncing disappeared with no explanation for why it had appeared in the first place, and only one thing changed.'

'Don't tell me you think it's that small sticker,' Brian groaned.

Luca shrugged. 'Who am I to question the wisdom of the universe? As far as I'm concerned, this little guy will ride shotgun all season.'

'I sure as hell wouldn't jinx it,' Mia said. 'If Luca gets another win, I might have to lock the rest of the sheet in my dad's safe.'

Or even if he didn't. Because truth be told, finding and hiding that sticker had become the highlight of her day. Not that it had anything to do with the man who pulled out of the garage or who, three days later, stood atop the podium again. Not one thing.

Chapter 25

'Pretty fancy, *mija*,' Star said as she boarded Rubie Racing's private jet and looked around. 'This is yours, too?'

Before she could answer, a low voice piped in from behind Mia's right ear. 'Yes, yes, this plane belongs to Mia. Everything belongs to Mia. If ever you're in doubt, just look for the sticker.'

Star and Mia both turned around to find Luca pointing toward the best seat on the plane, the one on the aisle in the front row with plenty of legroom that everyone always fought over. There, stuck to the headrest, was one of the 'Property of Mia' stickers.

'Why, thank you, Luca. It's so nice to sit in my rightful place without having to arm wrestle for it.' Mia carefully removed the sticker and held it up to his face. 'I'll be saving this for another time.'

'Oh, I bet you will,' Star said under her breath as she tossed her stuff on the seat next to Mia's.

Laughter erupted from the row behind them. 'This is going

to be fun,' Brian said, sticking his hand toward her friend. 'Brian Smith, team manager.'

Star shook it. 'Estrella Martinez, best friend and keeper of so many secrets that they're weighing me down. But you can call me Star.'

'Don't make me regret letting you tag along,' Mia said.

'Ha, you begged me.' She turned toward Brian and Luca and mouthed, 'begged.'

Which was true. After their blurry tour of Asia, she'd found herself missing her best friend. Knowing Star was long overdue for a vacation, she'd pitched a free trip to the Spanish Grand Prix. Complete with a ride in the team jet.

Only she hadn't considered what might happen when her old, sane world collided with this new, adrenaline-laced one. The thought of the lines between the two blurring even more than they already had gave her a such a shudder that she unbuckled to grab a sweatshirt from the bag under her seat before takeoff.

'Let's see what Mia is reading,' Star said from beside her.

Mia whipped around to see her e-reader open and her friend scrolling through its library.

Luca spoke up from behind them. 'I'll wager fifty dollars that it's something to do with murder or dismemberment.'

Star laughed. 'And I will happily take that fifty dollars off you. Sorry, buddy, murder is podcast fodder only, although I can't tell you the twisted logic behind that. But I will bet you one hundred dollars that her current selection features a laird and a tartan-clad damsel in distress.'

Her weakness for historical romance usually stayed hidden, thanks to modern technology. Mia shuddered again, this time at the thought of Star reading one of the novel's steamy passages out loud. Hopefully, admitting her friend was right would save them all from that torture. 'Fine, winner, winner, chicken dinner.'

Her best friend beamed as she raised a hand above her head and her reserve friend slapped a crisp hundred-dollar bill into it.

'I have to say, that bit of information was worth every penny,' Luca said.

She huffed defensively. 'I enjoy the historical perspective this particular genre of literature offers.'

'You enjoy men in kilts,' Star said. 'Tell me I'm wrong.'

She wasn't wrong.

'Just so you know, I own a kilt.' It may have been her imagination, but his voice sounded deeper and huskier than usual.

'Interesting,' Star said, elbowing Mia, who suddenly found herself feeling very warm and shoved the sweatshirt back under her seat.

The chitchat and laughter between the two front rows continued until the cabin lights were lowered for the kind of shut-eye encouragement typically reserved only for the five and under set. When they were awakened with breakfast trays, it started back up again. By the time they landed in Barcelona and made their way to the hotel, Star had been declared an honorary Rubie Racing member. There was even a brief ceremony, with Luca presenting her with a team jacket. Mia was forced to use her sticker to remind everyone whose friend Star was.

'This life suits you,' Star said later, when they were relaxing in their suite after a sponsor dinner, pajamas on and wine open. 'Don't even try to pretend like you're not loving every second.'

'Not every second.'

'Liar. You've got that weird hyper-aware-ninja thing going on. When you transformed into Neo from *The Matrix* during a project, I always knew we were golden.' Star paused. 'All right, down to the nitty-gritty. What's the deal with Luca? And don't get all cagey. It's a legit question given what I've seen already.'

Mia had been careful about how often she mentioned him during their conversations, since she could always sense Star's ears perking up on the other end of the line. It had been difficult, considering she spent the majority of her days with him and Brian. But mostly him, between their ongoing plank challenge – she was winning, of course – and, as much as she hated to admit it, how much she enjoyed hanging out with him.

'There's no deal. We're together all the time by circumstance.'

'Liar,' Star said again, this time with more emphasis.

'Look, I tried to ignore him, but that clearly isn't an option if I want this team to be successful. And I do.'

'You ignore your brother.'

That wasn't exactly true… or untrue. Even after all these

months, her interactions with Jordan were limited. She was beginning to suspect that Julia rarely let him out of her sight, but regardless, he didn't go above and beyond the call of duty for the team. He was basically showing up and driving. Nothing more. At least he was driving well enough to place in the top ten and earn points for the team.

When Mia didn't respond, Star pressed on. 'So, you're telling me nothing has happened since the two of you slept together in Chicago?'

'For the record, I regret telling you about that. But yes, that's correct. Like I've told you before, we're reserve friends. That's it.' Her phone vibrated on the table. 'Speaking of.'

Mia couldn't help but grin at the expected text from Luca, and sent off a quick reply. She looked up from her phone to see Star grinning like the cat who ate not only the canary but all of its feathered friends and neighbors, too.

Star yawned. 'Sorry, but I'm going to have to call this as I see it, which is clearly BS.'

'No, this is good. Don't you see? This is healthy for me. I have everything under control. It's normal – new normal.'

'Oh, *mija*.' Star shot up with a serious look on her face. 'Just in case you need to hear someone to say it, it's OK if you have feelings for him. Love him maybe. Even after everything and so many years.'

'Thanks, but I don't...' Her phone buzzed again from her lap, and she paused without thinking to read Luca's goodnight message.

Star cleared her throat to catch Mia's attention again. 'Luca is clearly more than a reserve friend to you — whatever the hell that is.'

'I don't have those kinds of feelings for him. *I don't.*'

'Fine, if you say so, but at least give the poor guy a promotion,' Star said through another yawn. Within seconds, her breathing deepened as her body lost the fight to jet lag.

Mia glanced at the clock. Another hour and she could crash, too, according to the sleep schedule that had changed her life. She tossed a blanket over her friend, then scrolled through the string of messages between her and Luca. Sure, there were a lot of them, but nothing in their banter suggested anything but friendship.

She woke up early to find Star crashed out in her bed, having crawled in at some point during the night. She picked up her phone to send a quick message to Luca before jumping in the shower.

'I hear you tapping over there. Who in the hell are you texting this early in the morning?' Star's voice was muffled by the pillow her face was buried in until she heard Mia's answer and rolled over. 'That was actually a rhetorical question. I'd already assumed it was the same person you were texting with before I passed out last night.'

Mia interrupted. 'And if you hadn't fallen asleep mid-conversation, I would've told you that he always texts me when we're on the road, to make sure I get back to my room. It's a safety thing, Star.'

'Suppose I buy that. Why the need for the morning message?' She was sitting up now.

'How else would we know who's responsible for making the day's first espressos?'

In a moment of guilt after asking Luca to make her a low foam cappuccino heated to exactly one-hundred-and-ninety-five degrees, and then arriving in the office to find him standing next to five mugs with a liquid thermometer, she'd offered to take turns on daily coffee duty.

'Of course. I mean, God forbid you'd both accidentally make coffee one day, although' – she singsonged the end of the word – 'that's right out of one of those second-chance romance novels I'm beginning to understand why you love so much. Anyway' – more singsonging – 'I assume you make enough for the whole team then? Everyone texts in their order and then the two of you, well, whoever is up first, gets to work?'

'You're missing the point. Also, you're a smart-ass.'

'I bet your boyfriend looks hot in a barista apron.'

'He's not my boyfriend, and he doesn't wear an apron.'

'But now you're thinking about it.' Star managed to laugh and yawn at the same time.

'Am not.'

'Liar. Even I'm thinking about it. Is he bare-assed in yours?'

'Well, he is now.' Mia threw off the covers and headed toward the en suite. 'I'm getting in the shower. This train leaves the station in forty-five minutes. You'd best be ready, missy.'

Star wasn't one to be star-struck. Mia had once watched her approach a movie star working out on a treadmill at their gym, only to tell him that his time was up and he needed to move it along like everyone else.

But then she'd never experienced all of the wonders of an Apex paddock.

'I know you're living in an alternate universe, but you do realize that these aren't "motorhomes," right? At least not the Midwest's definition of one.' She was standing in front of a new three-story monstrosity in Henri's team's signature red, mouth agape. 'Next thing, you're going to show me a yacht and call it a pontoon boat. I mean, these are insane.'

Seems that competition hadn't been limited to the racetrack while she was away from the racing world. The compounds that teams carted around to the European races had become shiny palaces with plenty of wow factor. Mia was glad she had nothing to do with putting them up and then breaking them down after every race.

'Don't be too impressed. You haven't seen ours yet.'

As other teams had become obsessed with bigger and more luxurious motorhomes, her dad had chosen to stay the course and direct as much money as possible into his cars and staff. At this point, Rubie Racing's motorhome was being kept together with duct tape. That might be a slight exaggeration, given that it was still two stories and had space for the team to meet and eat, and for the drivers to relax and mentally prepare themselves for races away from prying eyes.

Star stopped next to Mia in front of the smallest motorhome on the lot and shrugged. 'It's cute at least.'

'True, but between you and me? I kind of wish we had an observation deck.'

'You're the boss now. Get one.'

'Why bother?' Mia asked. 'I won't be around next year to enjoy it.'

'Pfft, keep telling yourself that and maybe you'll believe it,' Star said under her breath.

Mia chose to ignore that comment, even if the first half of the season was moving by far too quickly for her liking.

They'd gone over the schedule on the way to the track from the hotel, so Star was aware that Mia was basically dumping her off, then heading to meetings after a quick breakfast. The first couple of days at the racetrack weren't all that exciting. She offered to rent Star a cabana on a beach somewhere, but her friend insisted on seeing the inner workings of race week.

'I can go anywhere with these?' Star gestured at her credentials with the quadruple shot of espresso she'd texted Luca for while Mia was in the shower.

Mia made a mental note to not leave her phone unattended again as she gathered her belongings and stood up. 'The very fact that you're asking this, and drinking that, makes me nervous. Are you sure you wouldn't like a nice spa day? A paella cooking class? My treat.'

'Go. Do your important team principal stuff. I promise I won't get into any trouble. I'm going to take a walk and get my bearings. I'll be right here when you get back.'

That did nothing to ease Mia's fears about what mischief Star might get into. 'Don't make me regret this.'

When Mia returned to the motorhome three hours later, she shouldn't have been surprised to find Star dressed head to toe in Rubie Racing garb, regaling Luca and Brian with some story that had them both doubled over with laughter.

Their happiness seemed contagious until she got close enough to hear Star saying, 'She literally pushed him off the Vespa in the middle of Santorini. Said he was driving it wrong and made him walk two miles back to their hotel in a bathing suit and flip-flops.'

Mia shook her head. 'Oh, no. No, no, no. Sorry, kids. Story hour is over.'

'But I was just getting to the good part,' Star said.

'There's a better part?' Luca winked at Mia.

'Personally, I'd like to know how exactly someone drives a scooter "wrong,"' Brian said.

'He was going so slow that we were wobbling all over the place. It was ridiculous.' She didn't add that she'd already been pissed because her ex-boyfriend had told her that he should drive because he was the man, so him refusing to take any of her helpful advice had been the final straw. She could still picture his face in the side mirror when she sped away, perfectly balanced. 'Obviously, I had to break up with him.'

'Obviously,' Brian laughed. 'Please, Star, tell us more.'

Star looked at her and said, 'Please?'

When Mia rolled her eyes, Star shared how they'd run into said ex a year later as he was cycling on the Chicago lakefront path, and he'd taken one look at the two of them running toward him, caught his tire on some sand, and wobbled.

'He tipped over! Lucky for him, it was to the beach side of the bike path,' Star said.

'Don't forget to mention how you pointed and laughed while I at least attempted to help him up,' Mia said.

'I like this girl,' Brian said.

Luca leaned back in this chair, stretched his legs out in front of him, and folded his arms across his chest. 'Me, too. Maybe we can get a drink later and you can tell me more about the Chicago version of Mia. I have so many questions.'

Given that a drunken Star was even more loose-lipped, Mia squinted at her friend. 'You'll be sticking with me for the rest of the week.'

Luca raised an eyebrow at Star, who returned a wink and whispered, 'She can't watch me all the time.'

Even if Mia couldn't imagine why any aspect about her life in Chicago would be of interest to Luca, she was lucky that Star didn't want to be anywhere but in the thick of things as the days wore on. She was fascinated by what went on behind the scenes to get ready for Sunday's race, from reassembling the cars from their flight to getting them ready for practice and qualifying to the sponsor dinners and press conference. She even managed to joke around with Jordan.

The wheels in Mia's head went into overdrive when she overheard Star drilling one of the engineers on the different types of tires and the rules for using them during race weekend after dinner the night before race day.

'Don't think I don't know what's going in that brain of yours,' she said when they were back in Mia's suite. 'You know that there's no way I could leave my family for months out of the year. Not to mention, move to Detroit.'

Star and her five siblings were so close that they all crowded into their parents' house every Sunday for dinner. Mia had been given an open invitation and felt so welcome that she'd never hesitated to drop in.

'It's just a thought, and it's probably selfish on my part,' Mia said softly. 'It's just been so nice having you here. And you already haven't followed the path you thought you would.'

She didn't have to spell out that at thirty-seven, Star was the only Martinez sibling who wasn't married with kids. Star had heard it enough already. They both had — their lives as single women were a frequent topic at those Sunday dinners. This hadn't been Star's plan, Mia knew. She wanted marriage and a family. Things simply hadn't worked out that way.

'This is your life, Mia, not mine,' Star sighed. 'And that's just how it is.'

'When you think about it, everything up to now has just been foreplay,' Star said race morning.

'Just wait,' Mia said with a wink.

Brian snorted in the middle of swallowing his coffee. 'I think some of that may have come out of my nose.'

The three of them were in the motorhome, having taken a helicopter to the track from Barcelona. Although it was only twelve miles, they hadn't wanted to get caught in a traffic jam, with tens of thousands of fans pouring into the small town of Montmelo for the race. Star being able to see the racetrack in all its glory from the sky had been an added benefit.

Star refused a ticket to the exclusive club above the pits and garages, and all of the luxuries that went along with it. Instead, she donned the same team apparel as Mia and promised to keep out of everyone's way.

'Where's Luca?' Star asked. 'I mean, it's kind of crappy that I had to make my own coffee on my last day.'

'Drivers are a little particular about their race-day routines, so unless he's made you a coffee before every race of his career, there's not a chance in hell he's going to start now.' Mia had picked up on a few of Luca's quirks over the past couple of months but kept her teasing about them to a minimum. 'He's around, and so is Jordan. You'll see them both soon enough.'

'I still can't believe we have to wait until three o'clock.' She moaned. 'This is turning out to be the worst foreplay ever.'

Next to her, Brian took a deep breath and pushed his chair back. 'No worries. The climax of the day will be here before you know it.'

Star moaned again, purely for effect.

There were a handful of other races that day before the Spanish Grand Prix, along with paddock tours and a driver parade, which Mia normally missed in the rush of race day. But that day, she found herself being dragged to where the drivers were ready to launch.

'You know they're not going to toss candy to the crowd, right?' she asked Star.

'Oh, *mija*. They are the candy.'

Looking at the twenty-four Apex drivers who had been loaded onto a specially designed semitrailer so they could wave their way around the track, Mia couldn't argue with her. A quick scan of the group for Luca found him engaged in conversation with Wyn. Pride swelled in her chest seeing him in the colors of her family team, which was ridiculous because he was in Rubie Racing attire most of the time. But when those hazel eyes found hers watching him and his whole face smiled like they were the only two people in the world, another emotion took up residence.

Oh, no. Star was right. Luca had outgrown his role as reserve friend, even if Mia couldn't — wouldn't — put her finger on what her feelings for him were exactly. She only knew that over the past few months, what at first had seemed surreal had become very, very real. Mia smiled back at the face she looked forward to seeing every day and ignored her best friend gloating next to her.

In what seemed like a flash, she and Star were making their way to where the cars lined up on the track to begin the race.

Luca had placed third in qualifying, which gave him the third-best starting position on the starting grid. He'd clearly been disappointed to be starting off the front row, even though he was still likely to find himself on the podium. Jordan was starting further back, in ninth, and it was unlikely that he'd place among the top three. They stopped by his car on their way to Luca's, and Star once again managed to coax a smile from Jordan as well as, by some miracle, Julia.

They finally found their way through the throngs of sponsors, team members, and celebrities to Luca, who was chatting with his race engineer next to his car.

'Can I give you a hug?' Star asked. When he shot her a puzzled look, she added, 'I hear you're weird about shit on race day.'

'I swear, I didn't say anything,' Mia said. 'I don't even know your weird shit.'

Luca turned to Star. 'I'll tell you what. I can't give you a hug, because if I win, you'll be forced to fly in for the rest of the races this season or I'll have to blame you for any losses. But I will give Mia a hug, since she has to be here on account of, you know, owning the team.'

Before Mia could object, Luca wrapped his arms around her and gave her a tight squeeze. She could hear Star beside her say, 'Uh. Yeah. OK.'

'Be safe out there,' she breathed into his ear before he let go.

Back in the garage, Mia set Star up with a set of headphones so she could hear the conversations with the drivers while she watched the race on monitors with the rest of the team.

'You made sure her microphone is turned off?' Brian asked when Mia took what had become her standard spot beside him at pit wall. The wall of computers were next to pit lane, where the cars would come in when directed for tire changes and quick fixes for minor, non-race ending mishaps on the track.

'Better than that, I had it completely disconnected,' Mia said.

The race itself was largely uneventful, although Luca did manage to move up to the second position thanks to an ill-timed pit stop for the driver who'd qualified in that spot on the starting grid. Unfortunately, that wasn't Henri, who continued to maintain his pole position throughout the race.

Mia gritted her teeth when a blur of red crossed the finish line, followed by a blur of orange only seconds later.

As it turned out, Jordan was the surprise of the race, turning his ninth-place start into a fourth-place finish. Mere seconds off the podium. Whether he connected this breakthrough to his listening to team instructions remained to be seen.

'Nice job, hotshot,' Mia said when her brother made his way back to the garage.

Before he could respond, Star catapulted herself at him and screamed. Mia watched in awe as Jordan opened his mouth wide and laughed, and she realized that it was the first time all season she'd heard anything resembling joy come out of her brother's mouth.

Star leaving was tougher than Mia anticipated. She had been so busy with her new life that she didn't realize how much she missed her old one until it was standing in front of her saying goodbye. She made Star promise to come to another race, even if it was only for the weekend.

'I hate to admit it, but you're where you belong, *mija*,' Star said as they hugged goodbye.

They both turned to find Luca sprinting into the garage, peeling off his champagne-soaked racing suit as he made his way toward them.

'And you, can I have that hug now or will you make me your scapegoat for all the bad things that happen from here on out?' Star asked.

He laughed and pulled her in. Mia couldn't hear what Star whispered in his ear, but whatever she told him, and his response, took long enough for Star to pat him on the back several times.

And with that, she was gone.

A couple of hours later, after all of the driver debriefs and media interviews were finished, Brian walked by Luca and Mia, stopped, took a few steps backward, and howled.

'What?' Luca said.

Brian pointed at his back, still laughing. Mia turned Luca around to find some familiar artwork between his shoulder blades. She pulled off the 'Property of Mia' sticker and held it up for him to see.

'She sure has my number,' Luca said quietly.

'Don't flatter yourself,' she said. 'The woman has everyone's number.'

Chapter 26

Joseph Linwood: I have to say, Nigel, not only do we have an absolutely stunning day on the French Riviera, this is shaping up to be one of the more exciting races I've seen on the streets of Monaco in quite some time.

Nigel Rose: I can tell you, Joseph, this isn't an easy course. It's slow. It's twisty. It's narrow. The smallest of mistakes can ruin even the most accomplished driver's day. Precision is the name of the game.

Joseph Linwood: Although it doesn't appear that any of those challenges are having an impact on Luca Toscano's drive.

Nigel Rose: Considering he started from the third row, it's nothing short of miraculous. I remember once or twice trying to pass here where it wasn't wise, which, honestly, accounts for most of this street course. But his level of determination and control is without equal in today's race.

Joseph Linwood: Oh, no! It appears his teammate's day suddenly isn't going quite as well.

Nigel Rose: Wyn Thomas bumped wheels with Jordan

Rubie and sent him into the barrier, and it looks like Rubie's right rear tire has been punctured.

Joseph Linwood: This certainly puts a damper on Rubie's day. We'll have to see if can he make it back to pit lane before that tire shreds completely.

Nigel Rose: Well, he doesn't have too much further to go, and he's doing a good job of taking it slow and staying out of the other drivers' way. I can hardly believe it, but he's going to make it back around and hopefully finish the race. In the meantime, officials have ruled this to be a racing incident and I have to agree, this is one of those unfortunate things that can happen at top speed.

Joseph Linwood: At one point, I would've been concerned about his reaction but I dare say we're seeing a new side to Jordan Rubie. Not sure what happened inside Rubie Racing after that disastrous first race but there's definitely been a change in his demeanor, for lack of a better word.

Nigel: His drive last week in Spain was the most inspired we'd seen from him in years. Ah, yes, he's made it to his waiting pit team and, under the conditions, that was a speedy pit stop.

Nigel Rose: New tires on and he's good as new.

Joseph Linwood: But wait, he's nearly hit another car coming out of the pits. I'm not sure what's happened there, but that will definitely cost him. And there it is, a five-second time penalty for an unsafe release by his pit crew.

Nigel Rose: I doubt he can finish in the points now. This isn't Rubie's day.

Joseph Linwood: But it may be Toscano's. We're fifty laps in and he's now managed to pick off two of the four drivers who started ahead of him.

Nigel Rose: And there's another one! He's gone from fifth to second place with less than a third of the race to go. Only Henri Aveline is left. More often than not, whoever has pole in this race finishes first, but I'm not so sure that's the result we'll see today.

Joseph Linwood: If only Rob Rubie were here to see this.

Nigel Rose: I'm not certain I'd count Rob Rubie out. He never missed a race in Monaco. I doubt he'd start with this one.

This was happening. Impossible to pass, my ass.

But that red car was in his crosshairs. Again. And this time, Luca wasn't letting him get away.

His brain had stopped registering where he was on the course. The famous corners and landmarks were nothing more than a blur. It was only when they sped through the tunnel that he focused on anything other than the task at hand.

Brian's voice replaced his race engineer's in his ear. 'Six to go. Three seconds back. You're a little quicker every lap. You can do this.'

That's all he needed to hear to push the turbo pumpkin right up behind Henri. But Henri was making his car wide on the corners, staying smack dab in the middle of the track. Limiting Luca's chances to pass.

Brian again. 'Two laps to go.'

And then the Grand Hotel Hairpin, the hairpin of all hairpins that has haunted drivers' dreams for decades, became Henri's nightmare. He took the U-shaped curve slightly wide, a split-second mistake that gave Luca a better line, a chance for momentum through the tunnel. Side by side, they shot out into the bright light, and then Luca got it.

The pass.

The lead.

Brian. 'Final lap.'

Henri was behind him, trying to pass at every opportunity. But it was Luca's turn to make his car wide. His lead to defend.

When the checkered flag waved, he screamed into the radio like he'd never won a race before, or even this race. Twice in a row.

'P1. P1. P1. Well done.'

Mia.

Luca celebrated his second win in Monaco with the entire Rubie Racing team at one of the principality's most opulent restaurants.

'I'm surprised you were able to book a party this size at the last minute,' Mia said from beside him.

'It probably helped that I made the reservation eleven months ago,' he said, raising his glass and not putting it down until she did the same.

'A little cocky, wouldn't you say?'

He winked. 'Always.'

This is how it was meant to be, he thought as the team partied around them. With one notable exception: Rob.

It was hard to say who'd been more excited about Luca's victory in Monaco last year, but his money was on Rob. Taking the top podium in Monaco wasn't the same as being crowned world champion, but it was damn close. The race was the most watched, the most star-studded, and quite possibly the most prestigious of all the races in the world. But for Luca, that win had been bittersweet. Henri had been taken out in a crash, giving him an easy win. This year was a battle. Luca deserved every ounce of champagne he'd sprayed on the crowd, his team, Brian, and especially Henri.

'It was nice of your parents to come,' Mia said.

'Well, they do have a home here,' he said. 'It wasn't exactly out of the way.'

Few people in the world knew how distant his relationship with his parents was. Mia was one of those people. Or, at least, she had been, which he assumed was why she hadn't questioned why he wasn't staying at their apartment, hadn't asked if they wanted to watch the race in the garage with the team, or wondered why they weren't at his celebration dinner.

He and his father weren't exactly close. Even in those early days, when his love of racing and natural inclination had magically intersected, his dad had never been one of the fathers hanging around the track, wrenching on the karts they trailered in. No, Giovanni Toscano's support of his only child was always largely financial.

Not every driver was so fortunate to be handed a blank check to pursue a very expensive dream. But Luca's parents had done just that, even when it had involved leaving their thirteen-year-old son behind in the UK when they'd needed to move back to the European mainland for his father's job. Luca had lived with a host family near the track until he and Wyn had been recruited for the same driver development program. After that, they'd lived mostly on their own near the team's facility, save the chaperone his parents had hired to keep an eye on the two fifteen-year-olds and take them to and from the track.

He'd called his parents to share the news about Rob's death. They'd known his boss, of course, from those early days of his career and then last season. They never understood why he'd signed with Rubie Racing the first time, and were completely confounded when he'd announced his plans for a second go-around with 'that American team.'

'What do you have against the Italian team?' his father had asked. As if a seat in the most famous red car in the world wasn't the be-all and end-all of every race car driver. Let alone an Italian. While there'd been whisperings over the years about having an Italian driver join the storied Italian team, Henri had been the chosen one the last time a spot opened up. He certainly wasn't going anywhere anytime soon, not with a world championship under his belt, and the odds of them choosing Luca to be his teammate down the road were slim, for myriad reasons.

Once he'd settled back in at Rubie Racing, Luca hadn't given any of that a second thought. Except for when Henri beat him to the finish line. Then, he quite literally saw red.

Monaco had long been the race he could expect to see his parents at, and not just because they used the principality as a tax haven. They typically hosted a party on a yacht so his father could entertain clients while catching the occasional glimpse of his son racing the streets of Monaco. A twofer, as they say.

But this year, they'd watched the race from a terrace near the finish line and had been waiting for him when he'd arrived back in the garage, soaked in champagne and trophy in hand. His father had given him a hearty handshake, and his mother had kissed his cheek. It was the most pleased he'd seen them in years.

Mia leaned toward him and bumped his shoulder with hers. 'Hey, they showed up. It was a good day. It *is* a good day.'

To his surprise, Mia had greeted his parents with a smile and, while he debriefed his race engineer, chatted with them for a few minutes. They'd met briefly when she was a teenager, but had never spoken more than a handful of words.

'Did you have an enjoyable conversation with them?' Luca asked.

'Very pleasant, actually,' she said.

He raised an eyebrow, and she leaned into him.

'OK, plain ol' pleasant, but that's not the point.'

Mia was right. He should be happy that his parents had been there. And he was. But seeing them had made Luca realize that it was the approval of the woman sitting next to him that he wanted – along with the rest of her.

Chapter 27

Everyone was downright giddy, and a little hungover, on the flight home from Monaco.

Luca's win deserved some of the credit, especially for the latter. But the win was only the tip of the iceberg.

They were heading to Detroit for nearly two weeks, and everyone had been given a rare two-day pass that would begin as soon as the plane touched down. The next race, the Grand Prix of Montreal, was in neighboring Canada and the same time zone.

Their season was going amazingly well. Rubie Racing was still in the hunt for the championship, thanks in large part to Luca's steady stream of podium spots. But Jordan deserved credit for his top ten finishes, too; Monaco aside. After the five-second penalty had been added to his time for the pit stop incident, he'd come in sixteenth.

For the first time in as long as she could remember, Mia felt contented. Even if they were headed back to Europe after Canada and cramming in five races before Apex's summer break at the beginning of August. It would be a blurry six weeks, but what about the past few months hadn't been?

In the next seat, Luca smiled in his sleep. Dreaming of his victory, no doubt.

Her dad had once told her that winning the Monaco Grand Prix was the crowning achievement of his career, and not just because he'd received a trophy from an actual prince, although that element had played out in many a bedtime story in the Rubie household.

She closed her eyes and pictured him at the end of her bed. 'And then the handsome driver was crowned the king of racing and ruled all of the racetracks in the whole world.'

'Does that make me a princess?' she always asked.

She could still feel the goodnight kiss he pressed to her forehead. 'It makes you whatever you want to be, daughter of mine.'

Two-day pass or not, Mia was planted in her desk chair within hours of landing in Detroit. Her plan was to stay upright and busy until dinnertime, stuff herself with one of Barb's home-cooked meals, then turn in at her normal bedtime and be back on schedule the next day.

As it turned out, jetlag and a champagne hangover were a bad mix. The office was pitch black when she heard, 'Come on, Mia, time to wake up. Let's go home.' She launched out of her chair like a rocket, jammed her head into Luca's chin, and screamed bloody murder.

'Hey, hey, it's me,' he said, grabbing her by the elbows to steady the two of them.

'You scared the hell out of me.' That was why she was breathing heavily and her heart was suddenly beating out of her chest. 'What are you doing here?'

'Barb was concerned.' His hands slid up to her shoulders and kneaded them until they relaxed. 'You didn't show up for dinner, and you weren't answering her calls or texts.'

Mia grabbed her phone from her tote bag to find it was still on airplane mode. As soon as it reconnected to cell service, a rapid-fire buzz of new messages filled the otherwise silent office.

Luca grinned sheepishly. 'I may have been a bit concerned, too.'

'It's nine-thirty? No wonder I'm starving,' she said, hitting send on a quick text to Barb to let her know that she was, indeed, alive. And hungry. 'Thank you for coming to rescue me.'

'Never a problem,' he said, then pointed to her computer screen, which was filled from top to bottom with the letter Y from her falling asleep on the keyboard. 'Should I be worried here?'

'You caught me. I was searching for the meaning of life. In shorthand. Through osmosis.'

'I'm sorry I interrupted then.' He pulled her chair back and helped her up. 'But since I did, let's go. I'm starving, too, and Barb offered to pay for this rescue mission in pulled pork and macaroni and cheese.'

'And you harass me about my almond boneless chicken? That sounds like a gut bomb.'

But an hour and a half later, she was next to Luca at the

kitchen island and in front of an equally clean plate, clutching her stomach and cursing Barb and her mad cooking skills. The brownie chaser certainly hadn't helped matters.

'As delicious as that was, I feel like I should run home.' Luca clutched his gut.

'I promise to make something lighter for you kids tomorrow,' Barb said, loading the dishwasher. 'Can't have them letting out your racing suit in the middle of the season.'

Mia shot Barb a look.

'What?' Barb asked a little too innocently. 'It's just as easy to cook for four as it is for three.'

'Four?'

'I thought you might like to see Cliff,' she said.

'That would be nice,' Luca said through a yawn.

Mia checked the time. How was it after eleven? Luca was fading and still faced a forty-minute drive back to the city. 'Hey, I know how much you enjoy sleeping in your own bed, but I'm sure there's a bed comfortable enough for you here.'

Barb cleared her throat and made a hasty exit toward the doorway. 'I'll take that as my cue to leave. Sleep tight, you two.'

Mia called after her, 'Oh my God, Barb. That's not what I meant.' She then turned to Luca and stressed, 'Seriously, that's not what I meant.'

'I know, I know.' He yawned again. 'I got the reserve friend memo ages ago. No need to resend.'

'About that,' she said. 'In honor of your search and rescue mission tonight, you're being promoted.'

This time, he paused mid-yawn. A goofy grin spread across his face. 'You don't say. I assume some sort of job title and description will follow shortly?'

'Yes, be sure to keep an eye on your inbox.'

Mia leaned over, intending to plant an innocent kiss on his cheek. Only at the exact same moment, Luca turned his head to say something. Regardless of what they each intended to do, their lips locked, and stayed locked.

Because, honestly, even if he didn't taste like fudge brownies, she couldn't have pried her lips off his if she'd tried. Or kept her fingers from combing through his silky locks, then drifting to the back of his neck to find the warm, soft spot she knew existed just beneath the collar of his shirt.

This may not have been the promotion Mia had planned for her reserve friend, but as their kiss deepened and her body sighed into his, she realized it was one she truly wanted to give him.

Because in that one kiss, what she'd known all along hit her full force. He was it for her.

Mia pulled away and looked at Luca. She allowed herself to study his face, to fully take in the man he had become. With her fingers, she traced the creases forming in the corners of his eyes, the result of so many years of life she hadn't been a part of, and knew she didn't want to miss whatever moment brought the next line, or the one after that.

Her breath caught at the realization.

His gaze narrowed, and he leaned forward, resting his forehead on hers. 'Please, Mia.'

With a slight nod, she exhaled and burst out crying.

Of all the tears Mia had shed since her dad died, these were the most confusing. They weren't tears of sadness, or anger, or any emotion in between. They were hopeful and grateful and something so big that it filled her heart until it overflowed. Apparently, her tear ducts were now her body's default release valve.

Luca pulled her close. 'Hey, it's OK.'

'Actually,' she whispered in his ear between sobs, 'it's more than OK.'

Chapter 28

It had been years since Luca had woken up fully clothed next to an equally swathed woman. Sixteen years, to be exact.

Coincidentally, it had been the same woman and the same bed.

Only this time, he didn't have to sneak quietly out of her bedroom, sneakers in hand, hoping no one had noticed his car still parked in the driveway at four o'clock in the morning. He simply rolled over and molded his body around the curves of a still-sleeping Mia. She stirred slightly but, to his relief, only burrowed deeper into him, found his hand with hers, and pulled his arm tightly across her before dozing off again.

The sobbing that had overtaken her in the kitchen had continued upstairs in her bedroom. When she'd hesitated at the doorway, he'd taken her hand and led her to the bed, lifted the covers, and then climbed in after her. Then he'd wrapped his arms around her and let her cry.

Eventually, she'd gone into her bathroom, emerging a few

minutes later in flannel pajamas, with her face washed, and her hair on top of her head in a messy bun. 'I left a toothbrush on the vanity for you,' she'd told him before climbing back in bed.

He'd taken his turn, stripping down to his boxers and T-shirt, and joined her. They'd both passed out within seconds.

But this morning, he was *fully* awake.

He pulled Mia closer and kissed the back of her neck until she stirred again. She turned to face him and yawned through a 'good morning.'

'It is a very good morning indeed,' he said, brushing her cheek with his thumb before moving his lips softly to hers. He pulled back and smiled down at her, then shifted his body to fit with hers and kissed her more deeply. He couldn't remember anything ever feeling so right outside of a race car.

But when his hand found the top button of her pajamas, she caught his fingers and whispered, 'Maybe not so fast?'

'Not exactly what a race car driver ever expects to hear from a team owner,' he said, lacing her fingers into his and praying she wasn't having second thoughts about last night's kiss or the one they were midway through this morning. Although he wanted nothing more than to persuade Mia otherwise, he also wanted to be sure that she didn't do anything she regretted. In truth, she could've asked him to wait until their wedding night and he would've agreed, as long as he was able to stay in her sphere.

With a slight groan, he eased onto his side, then pulled

her to face him. 'Do you want to talk about last night? You can tell me anything. I'm not going anywhere.'

Much to his relief, Mia leaned in for a soft, lingering kiss. 'I was overwhelmed, in a good way.'

Luca understood. She'd been overwhelming him for months – years, if he was honest with himself. 'Happy tears?'

She nodded, her eyes glassy again. 'More than happy.'

'Hmm, I like the sound of that,' he said, rubbing her low back under her pajama top. 'I know this is complicated with you owning the team, but I can't hide how I feel for you. I don't want to keep this – us – under wraps again.'

His body sighed with relief when Mia kissed him again. 'I don't think I could if I tried.'

'We're in it to win it?'

Her breath caught at the mention of her father's favorite catchphrase. 'Go ahead and try to get me the hell out of the way.'

They laid there, wrapped up in each other, for what seemed like hours. His mind spun with all of the things he wanted to do with her, show her. Since she'd put the kibosh on any involving her childhood bed, his mind grasped onto another idea.

'What do you say about spending the day together?' Sensing she was about to protest, he added, 'You did give the entire Rubie Racing team the day off.'

She snuggled up to him. 'I did.'

'And we're pretty much the epitome of Rubie Racing, are we not?' He waited for her to nod. 'Then, by powers vested in you, we're free for another twenty-four hours.'

'You make a solid point,' she said. 'What exactly did you have in mind?'

'I'll tell you what, put some clothes on and you'll find out,' he said.

'Not exactly what one expects to hear from a race car driver in bed,' she said, her Rubie grin a little wider than normal as she tossed off the covers.

When Luca heard the shower turn on, he found his clothes on the floor and made his way down to the kitchen. The nineteen-year-old in him couldn't help but look for Rob around every corner, regardless of how unrealistic that now was. Still, as he scavenged the cabinets for a coffee mug, he jumped a foot when Barb cleared her throat behind him.

He suddenly felt a bit sheepish for a thirty-six-year-old man who had done nothing more the night before than spoon a fully dressed thirty-three-year-old woman.

Barb walked past him to the cabinet directly over the coffee maker and pulled out a couple of mugs. 'I noticed your car in the driveway when I woke up earlier, so I made a full pot today – assuming you'd no longer feel the need to tiptoe out of the house under the cover of darkness.'

He laughed and filled the mug she handed to him, passing it back to her before filling the second one for himself. 'So, we weren't as secretive as we'd hoped back then, I guess?'

She scoffed. 'Teenage boys are rarely as quiet as they think they are.'

His eyes widened at the thought of anyone overhearing his and Mia's youthful indiscretions. Barb struggled to swallow her coffee and not spray it across the kitchen.

'That's not what I meant,' she laughed. 'You weren't quiet getting in and out. Well, that's no better. I heard nothing, I saw nothing, and I'm changing the subject right now. Will the two of you be having breakfast this morning?'

Luca nodded at both the new topic of conversation and the prospect of more of Barb's home cooking. His stomach rumbled, even though it hadn't fully digested the feast from the night before. 'I hadn't considered, but yes, if I can help.'

'One race car driver special coming up,' she said, then pointed to a chair at the island. 'Sit. I work better alone.'

Luca was on his second cup of coffee when Mia wandered in, hair wet, and gave a perplexed look at the scene before her.

Barb turned from the stovetop, where she was sautéing vegetables for scrambled eggs. 'Breakfast is just about ready,' she said, giving the two of them a knowing grin. 'And before you come up with some silly excuse, you're an adult, and what you do in your room is none of my business.'

When she took the chair next to his, he whispered, 'We're busted now and, as it turns out, back in the day, too.'

To his amusement, Mia blushed.

'What?' she whispered when she caught him staring.

He leaned in and kissed her softly. 'Nothing.'

Barb cleared her throat and slid a plate in front of each of them. 'Like I said, what happens in your room is none of my business. What happens here in my kitchen is another story.'

'Noted,' Luca laughed, and dug in.

As they drove to his loft in downtown Detroit, Luca came to a stunning realization. This would, essentially, be his and Mia's first date.

All of the sneaking around they'd done years ago didn't count. So, during a quick pit stop at his loft so he could shower and change his clothes, he began to formulate a plan. This date was too long in the making to not be perfect.

When Luca came out of his bedroom, he found Mia sitting in his favorite leather chair next to the window, legs tucked under her, watching a freighter make its way down the Detroit River. On her lap was his copy of 'The Art of Racing in the Rain,' and in it, unbeknownst to her, Rob's letter.

She registered his presence without looking up. 'Where do you think that ship is going?'

'It could be stopping in Detroit, just further downriver, or it might be heading to Toledo.'

Her eyes followed the freighter as it inched along. 'I like your view.'

'Me, too,' he said, his gaze not leaving her.

As he weighed whether to tell her to flip through the pages and find the envelope with her father's telltale script on the front, she got up and put the novel back where she'd found it on the coffee table.

'Are you ready?' he asked.

'This isn't it? For whatever reason, I thought this may have been a ploy to get me' – she tilted her head in the direction he'd just come from – 'back in bed.'

As amazing of an idea as that sounded, Luca had something else mind, for the next several hours at least. 'Look at you, putting the cart before the horse. That hopefully comes at the end of a date, not before.'

'A date?'

'Yes, indeed. Our first date, by my records.'

He crossed his arms as he watched the wheels turning in her head.

'Luca, we were together for two years—'

'But we never went out on an actual date. We somehow skipped that part by sneaking around, but sneaking around does not a date make.'

'I've seen you almost every day for months. We eat lunch and dinner together.'

He shook his head. 'No, again, because if that counted, Brian would be the most persistent third wheel in history.'

Mia tapped her index finger on her lower lip. 'You bring me coffee?'

He grabbed her finger and directed it to his own lips, grinning as he kissed it. 'You're really reaching here, Mia. That was to keep you happy and caffeinated, and just maybe so I could see you every morning.'

They headed out without Mia conceding. A half an hour later, they were standing in front of an unassuming white, two-story home with bright blue trim and doors and a sign reading 'Hitsville U.S.A.' The Motown Museum had long been on his list of things to do while he was in Detroit, and given the playlists he'd spied on her phone, he had a sneaking suspicion she was a fan of Motown music.

'Damn, the sign says it's closed for a special event,' she said, the disappointment in her voice impossible to miss.

Luca shrugged a shoulder. 'I'd say a first date seventeen years in the making qualifies as a special event, don't you?'

She laughed. 'You didn't.'

Oh, but he had. Or at least, he'd set the ball in motion with a nine-one-one text to his agent before jumping in the shower. He'd find out later how much this surprise was costing him. Based on how Mia was looking at him, whatever the price of admission, it had been worth it.

That feeling was confirmed over and over again during their private tour, but especially in the music recording studio. Where, in the amazingly small space where more than a hundred hit songs were born, Mia sang along to 'Signed, Sealed, Delivered, I'm Yours.'

Truer words were never spoken.

When their guide turned to point out the instruments that were part of the exhibit, he couldn't help but cup the back of her head with his hand, pull her to him, and kiss her soundly.

The day moved on with more greatest hits – only they were his. They crisscrossed the city as he showed her what had become his favorite haunts in his adopted home. The renowned Diego Rivera murals at the Detroit Institute of Arts. The nearby record shop, where music was pressed onto vinyl records at the small processing plant in the back. His favorite coffee shop, where they stood outside the small walk-up window in an alley and chatted with the barista while Mia sampled the house espresso blend.

They ended up at a corner pie shop, walking out with three slices because neither of them could make a decision, and then headed to the island park in the middle of the Detroit River to eat them. They found a bench with a view of both the United States and Canada and the bridge that connected them.

'My dad used to bring us out here once in a while,' Mia said, licking the last of the salted maple pie off her fork in a way that was probably illegal in a handful of countries. 'I thought it was so cool, being able to look across the river and see another country.'

While he still possessed a modicum of self-control, he held out his hand for her fork, which she gave a final swipe of her tongue, and then grabbed the now empty cartons to toss into a nearby garbage can. When he came back, he pulled her to her feet and led her to the paved road around the island.

'Having Canada outside my window was one of the reasons I bought my place,' he said. 'Well, that and being able to watch the river itself. I've felt more at peace here than anywhere else I've lived, and I think it's the water. This may sound strange, but it soothes me in a way.'

They walked for a bit, hand in hand, until Luca spied a telltale skid mark on the pavement and directed Mia's attention to it.

'Remnants of the Detroit Grand Prix?' she asked.

He nodded. The U.S. racing series most like Apex had raced on the island for years but had shifted to the streets of downtown Detroit. Soon they were walking the former track, following a map Mia pulled up on her phone. It took far more time to do a lap on foot than in a car, but the nearly two-and-a-half miles gave them a chance to talk about how to manage telling the team they were together.

'Are you worried about telling Brian?' she asked.

Although months had passed since his conversation with Brian, Luca wasn't sure how the news would go over with him now. 'Worried? No. Terrified? Maybe.' He squeezed her hand. 'I'm kidding, but he did warn me off pursuing anything with you at the start.'

She didn't seem surprised that Brian had suspected something had happened between the two of them when they'd been stranded in Chicago during the snowstorm. But his unsolicited advice to Luca after testing in Spain – that Mia needed space and more time to grieve her father – seemed to give her pause.

'Are you mad?' he asked.

'At Brian? No, of course not.' She shook her head and laughed. 'I mean, do I wish he'd trusted that I would've put you in your place on my own? Sure. But he was just looking out for me.' She stopped and pulled him back to her. 'But would you have made a move? Back then?'

'Maybe, but it would have been a mistake,' he said. 'Neither one of us was ready, and we really didn't know each other. Not like we do now.'

When they finally crossed the finish line and made their way to the massive fountain that winning drivers had once plunged into as part of post-race celebrations, Luca felt like they were ready. Mia grabbed her phone from her back pocket. Within seconds, Brian's face filled the screen, his mouth already moving.

'I knew you couldn't last two full days without' – his head jerked from left to right, as if craning his neck would allow him to see outside of the phone and around Mia – 'wait, where are you? Is that the fountain on Belle Isle?'

Luca found himself pulled into full view of the camera, out-grinning Mia for once. 'As a matter of fact, yes. *We* are.'

Brian's groan morphed into something between a sigh and a laugh. 'I guess it was inevitable. I mean, let's just say your poker faces need some work.'

After Mia told Brian she'd talk to HR about the best way forward, they invited him to join them for dinner at the Rubie family's go-to Italian restaurant. He only shook his head.

'I have a feeling I'll have plenty of opportunities to feel like a third wheel coming up,' he said. 'You kids go have fun.'

Luca led Mia to the sofa later that night, claiming people on first dates didn't jump right into bed. Even though that was absolutely where he wanted this first date to end up.

When she climbed on his lap and took off her shirt and bra, he realized she had plans of her own – and he was more than happy to let her take control. For a few minutes at least.

She undid his jeans just as he was about to pop the button.

'Is this OK? Are you sure you wouldn't rather work on that diabolical two-sided puzzle on your dining table?'

He answered her by capturing her breast in his mouth. After he used his tongue to lavish her nipple with attention, she pulled away before he could make sure her other breast wasn't neglected.

'No, no. First, I get to see what I can remember about you.'

As it turned out, Mia remembered everything, just as he had. She started with his earlobes and kissed her way down, as if she was following a long-hidden treasure map with Xs marked everywhere. When she was finally on her knees in front of him, he was shaking.

'As much as I love what you're doing here, I have to warn you that this will be over before it starts if you stay the course,' he panted.

The woman grinned like an evil temptress. 'You know what? I'm willing to take the risk.'

After one swipe of her tongue, Luca realized he wasn't. Within seconds, he pulled her up, her pants off, and eased her onto his lap. 'Is this OK,' he asked. 'I have a clean bill of health.'

'Ditto, and I'm on the pill,' she said, lowering onto him.

His last conscious thought was that he was finally home.

Afterward, Luca carried Mia to bed and prepared to do it all over again, only with him in the driver's seat. But she climbed on top of him again and put her hands on his chest.

She nipped at his lip as she rocked against him, then

stopped. 'Now that I have your attention, let's set a few ground rules. Obviously, no public displays of affection.'

'Obviously,' he said, taking a moment for her to appreciate that there were no rules about private ones. 'Also, remember, I'm a superstitious guy, and I have a firm no-sex rule for the night before races.'

Her eyes widened. 'What about the morning of?'

'Sorry, but no.'

'Hmm,' Mia said. 'I bet I could persuade you.'

Although she was likely right, Luca shook his head. 'I already added my one new quirk to this season, thanks to you and your obsession with laying claim to all things Rubie Racing.' He flipped her onto her back. 'And I do mean all things. Nicely done, by the way.'

Mia's attempt at a pout was a massive fail. 'As much as I stand by the sentiment of the sticker, there's no reason for it to continue weighing you down.'

Even though his engineering team had determined the cause of his car's bumpiness races ago, Luca refused to stop placing the Property of Mia sticker in the cockpit each race weekend. Little did she know that part of his ritual included kissing his fingers, then transferring the kiss to the sticker.

'Weigh me down? Is that what you think that sticker does?' He cupped her face in his hands and feathered a kiss on her lips. 'It grounds me, in the best way. And so do you.'

Chapter 29

Once upon a time, drivers slept at the racetrack. Those RVs had been none too shabby, but Luca much preferred experiencing the cities of the world even if it was just from his hotel window. Montreal was no exception.

But then there was tonight when, upon the advice of his agent, he was meeting with Catalina Carvalho.

'You pay me good money for my guidance, Luca,' Alex had said. 'You might try listening to it every once in a while.'

Still, he felt like a number one schmuck, especially since he and Cat were meeting at the hotel, in his room, in an attempt to avoid the legions of fans already roaming the streets of Old Montreal four days before the Canadian Grand Prix. Thank God he was booked in a suite.

How had Alex managed to talk him into this?

'Just hear her out,' he'd said. 'There's no harm in listening.' And the kicker: 'I know you're happy with Rubie Racing, but if things turn south again with Jordan, who do you think they're more apt to release? The guy with the last name Rubie or Toscano?'

The truth was, he'd never put Mia in that position. So, he agreed.

While Jordan hadn't pulled any more stunts since the first race, he still wasn't a teammate in any sense of the word and that incident had done nothing to shake his years-old distrust of the guy. When he and Mia had sought him out in his office to personally share that they were together again before they told the rest of the team, he'd offered a halfhearted congratulations.

It's not that Luca expected Jordan to help him on the track, even if they did drive for the same team. Once they were in their cars, they were autonomous, ready for battle with every other car in the field, even the one that looked exactly like the one they were driving. But they didn't sabotage each other either, which had clearly been Jordan's intent in Australia.

Cat arrived right on schedule, and Luca cut to the chase as he showed her to the sofa. 'I hope you don't mind if we keep this short. Beauty sleep and all.'

'Of course,' she said, and laid it on the line. Carvalho Motorsport wanted him for the next season, and they were willing to pay whatever they needed to get him into their car. The initial number she threw out was twice what he was earning with Rubie Racing. When he frowned at the realization, she must've thought he was playing hardball and tacked on another million.

'Your driving is exceptional, Luca, and I know you're

looking to close out your career on a high note. My father and I want to help you hit it.' Then Cat leaned in, as if they were in a crowded room and she wanted to make sure no one overheard them. 'Plus, with all of the turmoil at Rubie Racing, I can't imagine you want to stick around for much longer. Word in the pits is that it's a real mess.'

'Really? I hadn't heard that.'

She nodded. 'Your team manager is ready to walk if things don't improve. I mean, taking orders from a newbie can't be easy, or fun, at his level.'

And just like that, Luca had Cat Carvalho's number. She didn't know squat, but she sure wanted to.

His eyes narrowed. This meeting may have been a bad idea, but things were getting interesting. 'I'm not sure I'd describe Mia as a *newbie*...'

'Oh, I hope you don't think I'm talking poorly about Mia! I've known her since we were little girls, and I think the world of her.' Cat placed her hand over her heart for effect. 'And I know you two have a history. That can't make things any easier either, I assume.'

Hmm. Obviously, word hadn't reached her that they were back together, but Luca wasn't about to correct her. He was too curious about what reason she pulled out next.

'I know Jordan isn't happy, and he's her brother.'

'Oh?' He feigned surprise, as if his teammate's unhappiness was news to anyone in the racing world, or anyone who'd ever met him, for that matter. The man's scowl was legendary. People might write songs about it one day.

She stumbled, then rambled, 'I mean, it's obvious, right? Really, I can't imagine what would've possessed Rob to make such a ridiculous decision. There are rumors it won't hold up in court, especially given the hoops Jordan has to jump through to not even get near what his sister got.'

At that revelation, Luca sat up straight. 'There's been talk of it going to that?' he asked.

'Oh, I don't know.' Cat stood up and walked toward the door. 'I'm just sharing what's out there. In the interest of our sport, of course.'

'Of course. Thank you for your insight, and I appreciate the offer. I'll have Alex call you and your father with my decision.'

As if he hadn't already made up his mind. He'd tell Cat himself on the spot, except extending this interaction a second longer was the last thing he wanted. Well, besides for this meeting to have never happened in the first place.

But instead of opening the door, she stopped, her hand on the doorknob. 'I'd appreciate you keeping this to yourself. No reason to get Wyn's hackles up unless a change is definitely in the books.'

With that little nugget to add to the list of things Luca wished he didn't know, she was gone.

Well, damn.

Wyn had made it no secret that he planned to ride out the rest of his career with Carvalho Motorsport. While he couldn't do much for his friend at the moment, he could look out for the best interests of his own team. He was contemplating how to broach the subject without looking like a traitor when there was a loud knock.

'Did you forget something?' Luca opened the door, expecting to find Cat. Instead, Mia glared at him. Something told him that she'd seen Cat leaving his room.

'Yes, I absolutely forgot something, but you can bet I won't make that mistake again,' she said, walking away.

If he lived through this, he was going to kill his agent. Even if the majority of the blame rested squarely on his own shoulders.

Mia was halfway down the hall before he caught up with her. 'Wait, it's not what you think,' he said, grabbing her hand and waffling her fingers with his. 'Come back. Let me explain.'

She jerked her hand away and crossed her arms in front of her chest, which heaved from her breathing. 'Are you seeing Cat, too?'

'Wait, what? No, of course not.' Luca looked up and down the empty hallway, but was still wary. 'I don't think we should have this conversation right here.'

To his relief, Mia followed him back into his room, where she sank down on the sofa and rested her head in her hands. 'I can't believe I trusted you. I'm such a fool.'

No, I'm the fool. 'Mia, please, listen. Nothing is going on with Cat. She wanted to talk to me about driving for Carvalho. Alex set it up, and against my better judgement, I said yes.'

Mia's head lifted and her mouth literally dropped open. She turned on a dime from a mix of sad and angry to straight up furious. 'Oh my God, that's so much worse than if you were sleeping with her.' She took a ponytail holder off her wrist and knotted her hair on top of her head, then immediately ripped it down. 'I can't believe you said yes. I can't believe you're thinking about leaving me. I mean, the team.'

In the name of all that's holy, what had he been thinking? Luca had often wished for the ability to time travel over the past few months and make different decisions. Reversing the current situation would now make the top of the list.

He dropped down to his knees in front of her. 'No, no, no. I said yes to the meeting. Not to her. I swear to God.'

'So, you told her no?'

He cringed. 'Not exactly.'

Mia was ready to launch, but Luca couldn't let that happen. He was afraid that if she walked out his door again, it might be for the last time.

'Not yet, but I am. There's no way I'm leaving Rubie Racing, or you. You have to believe me. I'll tell you anything you want to know. But first,' he grabbed his phone and sent a nine-one-one text, 'we have a bigger issue to deal with.'

Brian was barely inside the door when he took one look at a somewhat distraught Mia in her college sweatshirt tossed over her pajamas, and grinned. 'What's the emergency? Please don't tell me there's already a little Toscano on the way.'

The man had no idea how close they were to that never happening.

It didn't take Luca long to spill everything about his offer from Carvalho Motorsport and his visit from Cat. Their responses were simultaneous.

Brian: 'Are you kidding me? Please tell me you're not thinking about taking it.'

Mia: 'I still can't believe you talked to her behind my back.'

'I'm not going anywhere,' he told Brian before turning toward Mia and adding, 'I'm sorry. Even though it wasn't something I was seriously entertaining, I was uncomfortable bringing it up, given… everything. Regardless, I'm glad I did meet with her. Our conversation was enlightening, to say the least.'

'How so?' Brian asked.

'I think Jordan has been talking to other teams – or at least, he may have approached the Carvalhos.' Luca relayed Cat's comments about Brian and Jordan's unhappiness and the supposed talk among the teams about the state of affairs at Rubie Racing, as well as her offhand remark about Rob's will being contested.

When he shared about the unevenness of how Rob had split up his estate, Mia sprang to her feet and paced the room. 'I won't even get into Cat stabbing me in the back like this. I guess acting as her lookout so she could kiss boys in empty garages doesn't count for much twenty years down the line.'

Brian laughed.

'But the court thing? That isn't going to happen. Dad's will is ironclad, and Jordan knows it. And him leaving… that could happen. In the interesting tidbits that should've been shared department, I have some information for the two of you.'

Luca's mind drifted to the letters Cliff had mentioned, but snapped back to reality at what Mia said next.

'Jordan didn't get anything from Dad's estate,' she paused, 'at least not yet.'

'Nothing? Nada? Holy crap,' Brian muttered and lifted his wrist. 'I mean, even I got this watch.'

She explained that as long as Jordan remained a driver for Rubie Racing, he'd only receive his salary and the bonuses he and their dad had agreed to. Only if he resigned from the team would he collect his millions.

Luca flashed back to the legal documents he'd seen Mia shuffling out of sight her first day in the office. She hadn't been looking to get rid of him after all, and the weight that realization lifted off his shoulders was more bothersome than a relief. He hadn't trusted her a hundred percent either.

'I know this is none of my business, but what's his bonus structure?' Luca asked.

'It's similar to yours, only it's weighted heavier to the team winning the championship, not him alone.' She hesitated, then added, 'And there's also some money for him if you become world champion.'

'I'd have to check, but I don't think I have a reciprocal clause in my contract,' he smirked.

'You don't,' she said. 'I'm sure Dad knew one wasn't necessary.'

Brian snorted. 'While we're in the sharing circle, I'd also like to set the record straight. I have no intention of leaving Rubie Racing.' He turned to Mia. 'Yes, I miss your dad and his tutelage, but I'm not suffering under your leadership. And even if I was, I'd talk to you about it directly, not let you find out through the Apex gossip mill.'

'Well, then, was Cat making things up to sway Luca, or has someone been feeding her false information?' Mia looked at Luca. 'What have you been saying to Wyn?'

Even though the question was legitimate, given how close he and Wyn were, it still stung. 'Nothing. He did ask before the season started if I wanted him to put a word in with the Carvalhos, but I told him no. Plus,' he cringed, 'it appears this move wouldn't serve Wyn well.'

The look on their faces told him he didn't need to spell it out.

'I think we all know who the "someone" telling tales might be,' Brian said.

'Who else could it be besides my brother?' Mia finally sat down and buried her head in her hands again. Luca couldn't help but go over and rub the back of her neck.

As much as he knew Jordan was at the root of this, Luca didn't want to believe his teammate was capable of throwing a hand grenade into his own garage and spraying shrapnel on everything his father had dedicated his life to creating. Even if he was likely the anonymous source Mia's favorite reporter referred to in her reporting about that long-ago night in Daytona and Mia's abandoned racing career, would Jordan really sink that low?

'So, what exactly did you tell Cat, Luca?' Brian asked.

'Nothing yet,' he said. 'I told her my agent would be in touch.'

'Make her wait a bit,' his team manager said. 'You never know. This could get interesting.'

Luca looked at Mia. 'Only if you're comfortable with that.'

She nodded.

After Brian left, Luca checked the clock and realized he had only seven hours before he started his race day routine. He tugged Mia toward him, wrapped his arms around her, and whispered, 'I'm yours. The only reason I've kept my hotel rooms is because I didn't know if I could sleep next to you the night before a race without being tempted.'

'I was coming for a kiss goodnight,' Mia said. With a kiss on the cheek, she was gone, leaving him to get what little rest he could.

Once he was in bed, he couldn't help but grab his phone and send Mia a message.

Luca: *Seriously, I'm not leaving RR. You can't get rid of me that easily*

A bubble appeared as she began typing back right away.

Mia: *Like I would let you out of your contract*

Luca: *I wasn't aware playing hardball was your style*

Mia: *Watch and learn*

He had to admit, the thought of that was a little exciting.

Notre Dame Island was still asleep when Luca arrived at the break of dawn the next morning. He laced up his running shoes and set out to do two laps of the just over two-and-a-half-mile Circuit Gilles Villeneuve. His mind cleared of Mia, Jordan, and Carvalho Motorsport. Instead, he envisioned himself in his turbo pumpkin, masterfully maneuvering each of the fourteen turns for seventy laps.

Winning.

When he made his way through the Senna 'S,' the set of two curves named for racing legend Ayrton Senna, he let his mind wander to another spring race day in Montreal, six years ago. To the crash that had nearly ended his career.

With each step, he made peace with the driver, the accident. Just as he had every year when he visited this track. Neither of them had walked away, but they'd both lived.

Only one of them still drove in Apex.

Although he'd experienced his share of crashes, this one had been the hardest to move past. It didn't help that every season, on this specific race weekend, the footage received plenty of airplay. As broadcasters liked to say, it was spectacular as crashes go. A clip on the internet had logged ten million views and counting.

He'd watched that clip exactly once, saw how they battled, pushed each other. How right before the Senna S, the other driver made the slightest of mistakes, barely touched his left tires to the grass, then lost traction. How he veered unexpectedly to the right, took the nose off Luca's car before smashing into the wall. How his car shot back, flipped over, and landed on top of Luca's.

Watching it hadn't helped fill in any of the blank spaces from those minutes of his life. His brain would forever skip like an old record. Driving along. Indescribable pain. Being pulled from his car. The helicopter. The hospital bed.

But it was time again to push what little memory he had of the accident from his mind and focus on today's grand prix. If he mastered all seventy laps, he'd be in first place for the season. By only a few points, but still, it would be a start. The only problem was, he'd never won on this track. Not before the accident, and not since.

On his second lap, he pushed himself hard. Running through each curve, every straightaway, mentally and physically. No checkered flag waved when he crossed the finish line, but something else caught his eye.

Mia.

'Demons conquered?' she asked when he walked over to her.

'I'd say I'm definitely getting there.' He planted a kiss on her lips.

'I'm kind of mad at you, you know.'

'If it helps, I'm kind of mad at myself.' He kissed her again.

When she kissed him back, there was no mistaking the gentle tap between his shoulder blades.

He reached his hand back as far as it could reach and made sure the 'Property of Mia' sticker adhered to his sweaty shirt. Not that it mattered if it fell off.

He was hers.

Ten hours later, he was on top of the podium and on top of the world. The coveted grand prix trophy was between his hands and hoisted high above his head. Below him, fans cheered alongside Rubie Racing team members. Brian hugged Mia. His whole world celebrated.

At the post-podium press conference with the second- and third-place finishers, a reporter asked, 'After everything this track almost took from you, this win is special, isn't it?'

'Maybe a little,' he grinned. 'But in all honestly, it feels amazing to come out on top at a place where I experienced one of my career lows. Not that I could've done anything to prevent that accident on the Senna S, and not that I blame the driver who took me out. In this sport, sometimes you're just in the wrong place at the wrong time. But sometimes you're in the right place at the right time. Like today.'

'Are you saying this is all just a game of chance?' the reporter followed up.

'I guess that depends on your definition of "chance." I like to think of chance more in terms of opportunity. Today, I had that opportunity, and I took it. I'm thinking that's how I should face every opportunity going forward.'

He spotted Mia at the back of the room and returned that famous Rubie grin.

Chapter 30

A clone. That's what Mia needed. How else could she possibly keep an eye on Jordan, Cat Carvalho, and Luca at the same time? And keep her head in the game?

A quick phone call to Cliff had confirmed her suspicions. If her brother decided to challenge their dad's will, he wouldn't have a leg to stand on. And he knew it. The weasel had broached Cliff within a week of the will's reading and had been solidly shut down.

Which explains why Jordan was sniffing around Carvalho Motorsports, but not why he'd decided to trash the Rubie family name – his own name – in the process. Could he be that mad at their dad? At her? If anything, she should thank him for setting the family loyalty bar so low that it was now almost impossible to limbo under.

And Cat. They weren't best friends, by any means, but Mia felt stabbed in the back all the same. She was certainly second-guessing meeting for the occasional glass of wine. She scanned what she could remember of their conversations, checking for any vulnerabilities she may have shared about the team or Luca.

'It's business not personal,' Brian said to her over and over again, to the point that her head hurt from shaking it so much. 'These types of conversations happen behind the scenes all the time.'

'Jordan willingly jumping into Cat's net is business. Cat tossing him back and setting the hook for Luca is personal. Trust me.'

What she wasn't sure about was what to do with all these nuggets of information. She considered channeling her father, but once again, her brother wouldn't have pulled any of this if he were alive and running the show. She owned this issue alone, even if she hadn't a clue how to solve it.

It wasn't fair to lump Luca in with Cat and Jordan, but she couldn't quell her irritation about him meeting with Cat behind her back — whether or not he had any intention of leaving her or Rubie Racing. That definitely felt one hundred percent personal. She would've bailed on his celebration dinner, except he insisted on picking her up.

But she found it almost impossible to be mad when she opened the door to find Luca wearing a tailored suit coat, a kilt, and a disarming smile. 'Come in, my laird.'

'Considering I'm Italian and I wore this kilt in Wyn's wedding and he's Welsh, not Scottish, that title isn't entirely kosher.' He winked. 'But I'm willing to play fast and loose with the definition if you are. Or, if that makes you uncomfortable, I can take it off.'

She ogled the tartan in shades of turquoise and rust that ended at his knees. 'Not on your life. I'm thinking you might be a little warm wearing that out and about, unless,' she took a deep steadying breath, 'it's a little drafty by chance?'

'I'll let you discover that for yourself later.' He leaned in and gave her a kiss. 'Slight change of plans. Did you know that one of the best restaurants in Montreal is right here in this hotel? And that if you ask nicely, they'll deliver?'

'I suppose that could be a plan, although I doubt there's room for the entire team in here.'

Mia led him into a suite as spacious as the others she'd been staying in all season. Since the team's travel coordinators booked hotel rooms a year in advance, switching them would've been nearly impossible.

Luca leaned against the wall. 'Actually, they're all enjoying the finest Canadian beer and smoked meat the city has to offer as we speak.'

'On your dime, I assume?'

'Possibly.'

'And should I also assume that you just happen to have a menu for this fancy restaurant located right here in the hotel?' Mia asked.

'No, you cannot.' He bit his bottom lip. 'I took the liberty of asking the chef to put together something special for us. What time is it?'

She glanced at her watch. 'Seven-thirty on the dot.'

He pointed to the door, and, like magic, they heard a

knock. 'Then I hope you're hungry, because the first course has arrived.'

Within minutes, the dining table was transformed with linens and formal settings for two, and she and Luca were enjoying their first course: oysters paired with a crisp, white wine. He clinked his glass to hers and, with a smile that made her ovaries clench, said, 'To tonight.'

'Don't you mean, "To today," Mr Top of the Podium? That was quite a show you put on out there.'

'Too true.' His one-shoulder shrug hardly came off as humble. 'But I owe today's win to the efforts of many, present company included. Which is why I hope you know I'm being truthful when I say I had no intention of leaving Rubie Racing when I met with Cat.'

'Then why bother meeting with her?'

He set his wineglass down and grabbed her hand. 'The first time my agent called me about their interest was after Jordan blocked my win in Australia. I didn't exactly tell him I would consider it, but I didn't tell him I wouldn't either. Your brother has always been a challenging teammate, but that race elevated his hostility to a new level. I wasn't sure how easily he would fall back in line without your dad around.'

She nodded because, at the time, she'd had the same fears. And now, thanks to Luca's conversation with Cat the night before, her suspicions had returned in spades.

'I shouldn't have doubted that you'd be able to run this team as well as your father. I keep thinking that I wish he was around to see you handling it like a pro, but I'm even sorrier that the two of you never worked side by side. The Rubies would've been the father-daughter duo to be reckoned with, no doubt there.'

Whenever Mia saw Cat and her father together at the racetrack, she wondered what it would've been like to learn the ropes with her father guiding her. She was rarely jealous of other people, but she was jealous of Cat.

'I wonder what my dad thought when he saw the Carvalhos?'

'Rob was the most optimistic guy I knew. I'd say he never lost hope, Mia.'

She lifted her glass and waited for Luca to do the same. 'To my dad.'

Six more courses followed, and Mia could feel her defenses crumbling with each one. The perfect wine pairings and sprinkling of conversation and laughter didn't hurt. As she scraped the last of the chocolate mousse from the bottom of a small ceramic pot three hours later, Mia couldn't help but groan.

'Good God. I can't remember the last time I felt so satisfied.' She already felt flushed from the wine flight, but her cheeks burned when she realized how that came out.

Luca went completely still and slack-jawed. After what seemed like minutes, yet was likely only a few seconds, he tossed back the last of his sweet red dessert wine and gave the cockiest of nods. 'Challenge accepted.'

Her heart pounded as she watched Luca move in slow motion. He eased his chair back. Ambled over to the door their server had been in and out of all night. Hung the 'do not disturb' sign. Locked the door.

But when he crossed the room back to her, he sank down

onto his knees and rested his head in her lap. Mia's fingers combed through his silky locks until he finally looked up, his face awash with regret and worry.

'Are we OK, Mia?'

'Always,' she said, and meant it.

Luca sighed in relief.

'But I could probably be more than OK,' she said.

'Is that so?' He stood up, pulled her to her feet, and captured her mouth with his. When she licked his lips, he laughed. 'Chocolate mousse?'

'Better.' She sampled him again. 'You.'

Since that night in Detroit, they'd been thoroughly enjoying reacquainting themselves with each other, often racing to revisit those favorite spots they'd never forgotten while also leisurely discovering new ones. But the look Luca gave her before leading her to the bedroom was new. Intense.

When she pulled at his clothes, he took her hands in his. 'Not so fast.'

Mia grinned. 'Not the typical words out of the mouths of race car drivers.'

He undressed her slowly, kissing every inch of skin he uncovered, and then silently invited her to do the same. Mia couldn't help but reach under his kilt to grab a handful of exactly what she'd hoped to find. Nothing but Luca.

'Funny girl,' Luca quipped.

He sprinkled kisses over her face before easing her down onto the bed. Once he settled on top of her, he cradled her face in his hands.

'Open your eyes,' he said, brushing his lips softly over hers until she did what he asked. 'I love you, Mia. I always have, and I always will.'

She gasped as Luca stretched her, filled her in ways she never imagined were physically or emotionally possible. Joined by more than their bodies, they drank each other in. Then, with kisses and whispers of love warm against her skin, he inched her toward a place where they no longer existed separately. Together, they rode a wave that washed over them again and again until they finally crashed as one.

Afterward, Mia studied Luca's face, tracing his cheekbones with her thumbs and allowing herself to believe what had once seemed impossible. For better or for worse, this man was meant for her.

'What are you thinking?' he whispered.

'That I love you, too,' she whispered back.

Chapter 31

By the time they landed in Hungary for their fifth race in seven weeks, Luca wasn't sure which way was up. Thank God the summer break was just over the horizon, when Apex forced teams to take a vacation whether they wanted one or not. The lights would be turned off at every factory and wouldn't come back on for two weeks. During that time, not an engine would be tweaked, not a tweet sent, not a meeting held. There might as well be a 'gone fishing' sign on the door.

Just one more race, and hopefully one more win, to go. Then he and Mia were going off the grid in the Upper Peninsula of Michigan. Cliff had offered them the use of the lodge Rob had left him, and they'd both jumped at the chance to steal away from all of society.

With equal parts luck and skill, he'd kept Henri and his red car at bay. At the Circuit Paul Ricard, he'd landed at the top of the podium again – *Vive la France*! It hadn't been the most exciting race, with the finishing order nearly mirroring the starting grid, but he'd savored the satisfaction of beating his nemesis at his home track. In Austria, he'd come in a disappointing fifth. England and Germany had earned him two more podium finishes, a first and a second, allowing him to eke out a decent lead in the points.

This was in no thanks to the woman lying next to him. He'd officially nicknamed her 'evil temptress' after she'd persuaded him to break his rule of no sex the night before the Austrian Grand Prix.

'But it's not sex,' she'd pouted. 'We're making love.'

After years of being disillusioned about how sex and love didn't mix, he'd been unable to resist. While he couldn't technically blame his season-worst finish on their lovemaking – his car had experienced issues all day – race-eve celibacy had been immediately put back into effect and he'd refused to bend again. In any way.

That hadn't stopped Mia from teasing him about his superstitions. She was merciless; case in point, her current state of nakedness.

She'd climbed into the bed the night before and peeled off her pajamas. 'Budapest is positively steamy. I bet it's all those hot springs under the city. Maybe we should try to squeeze in a trip to the thermal baths before we leave. What do you think?'

Then she'd kicked off the covers.

Evil. Temptress.

Luca was contemplating whether his rule about race-day hanky-panky was as solid when his alarm went off. He stretched, rolled over, and saw immediately why it was. Six o'clock. He kissed a sleeping Mia on the cheek before jumping out of bed and heading to the shower.

Since his morning run on Montreal's Circuit Gilles Villeneuve had kick-started what turned out to be one of the most momentous days of his life, on and off the track, Luca had decided on a new tradition. One that, of course, was not to be jinxed, down to the exact shoes, shorts, shirt, and yes, socks.

'Wait, I think your right sleeve was rolled up just a little that day, or was it the left side? Oh, no! I can't remember.' Mia was sitting up slightly in bed, the sheet barely covering her. How long had she been awake and watching? 'Sorry, should I not have said something?'

'How dare you mock me, woman!' Luca launched himself onto the bed, landing on top of Mia and tickling her where he knew she was the most sensitive. She responded with a nip to his shoulder.

'Maybe you should cross-train instead of run today.' Her body shifted under his into just the right position. 'Start a new tradition. It's not like you've been doing this one forever.'

'I'd think the owner of an Apex team would be more supportive of whatever her top driver felt he needed to do to secure a spot on the podium. Besides, I think I know what your idea of cross-training is, and that's definitely not a sanctioned race morning activity.'

Or was it more of a gray area? While he was contemplating, Mia managed to move his lucky shirt up a notch, and his lucky shorts down just enough. And that was all she wrote.

Once he started a race, there was no stopping until he crossed the finish line.

'You suck,' was all he managed to say twenty minutes later, when they came up for air.

'You can still go for your run,' she laughed. 'Consider it a warmup.'

'Yes, because my body feels so raring to go now,' he growled.

'Don't be mad,' she said, getting up and heading for the shower. 'For what it's worth, I'm sorry. I mean, I hope I didn't derail your whole day for something so, I don't know, mediocre.'

The door to the bathroom clicked shut behind her – but didn't lock. The shower turned on.

'I'll show you mediocre,' he yelled, going in after her.

Maybe Mia wasn't entirely to blame for the morning's escapades, but as Luca waited for the elevator a half hour later, he decided she wasn't entirely guiltless if he missed his opportunity to run the track on his own two feet. On the other hand, if he won today, he had a new, slightly more enjoyable tradition to not jinx after the summer break.

At least a call to the front desk confirmed his car service was still waiting downstairs.

The elevator doors opened to reveal Julia and an entourage of suitcases packed inside. She moved over enough for him to squeeze in beside her, then proceeded to repeatedly jab the close door button. The elevator finally complied and began its descent, leaving them both to stare straight ahead until they reached the main floor.

Luca turned to face her as he walked out. He may have never cared for her like he should have, but he couldn't ignore the situation in front of him. Julia loved the pageantry of race day. Something had to be seriously amiss for her skip out of town early.

'Do you need help, Julia?'

'No, thank you,' she said, her chin literally up in the air. 'I have this under control.'

Out of nowhere, a bellhop appeared and began shifting her luggage onto a cart.

He nodded and searched his mind for something to say, but all he could come up with was, 'OK, then. Good luck to you.' And then he walked away without looking back.

An hour later, his feet were pounding the Hungaroring as he tried to visualize himself speeding around the track in the turbo pumpkin. But the ritual wasn't working; his mind wouldn't clear. Instead, he thought of Julia and how her baggage filled an elevator. Being with Mia had made him realize what a mistake his time with Julia had been, that there was more to a relationship than sex. He doubted Julia's time with Jordan had been anywhere near as enlightening.

He completed a single lap before race officials asked him to clear the track. It was probably for the best, considering the heat coming off the pavement already – the expansive valley the Hungaroring was in provided zero shade or breeze. The race would be a hot one, as usual. Damn thermal springs. Damn July in Budapest.

Thankfully, the rest of the morning and early afternoon

went like clockwork, but he still gave Mia his sternest, most disapproving look when he climbed into his RR1. By the time he was sitting in pole position waiting for the race to begin, he was ready. The lights overhead flashed from red to green, his foot hit the gas pedal, and he was off.

A benefit of starting first was not worrying about the muck the cars behind him trudged through as they jockeyed for position. He looked straight ahead and focused on nothing but the first of the Hungaroring's fourteen turns. When he heard 'yellow, yellow' over the radio thirty-one laps into the race's seventy, he didn't know what had happened in the field behind him. It wasn't until he slowed his speed and tucked behind the safety car that he saw the carnage with his own eyes. Four cars were out, and debris littered meters of the track. He hoped officials wouldn't pause the race and send cars back to pit lane to wait out the track clean-up. For whatever reason, this was one race he was eager to put behind him.

Eleven slow and methodical laps later, Luca pulled into pit lane for a tire change. Even though he had to give up his prime spot behind the safety car, any placement he lost would be made up when he didn't have to pit again before the end of the race. Hopefully, they'd be able to avoid another yellow.

His car's twin pulled in as he pulled out. He hadn't seen bright orange in the wreckage, so he knew Jordan had avoided the crash that, Brian radioed, had taken out both Henri and his teammate. An accident like this could work in Jordan's favor if he played it smart. He could turn his ninth-place start into a podium spot. Wouldn't that be something?

After three minutes back on the track, he got word over the radio that the race was going green after the next lap. He was now planted midway in the pack in the parade behind the safety car. Passing wasn't allowed while the track was under yellow, and he anxiously awaited his opportunity to make his way up to the lead spot again.

'Green means go,' he heard over the radio. The gas pedal hit the floor, and he began picking off the cars in front of him. With ten laps to go, he was back up to a podium spot. Then he noticed Jordan closing in on him.

Every track had its preferred spots for getting around other cars, and the twisty Hungaroring was especially known for being tricky. Even though Jordan was technically close enough to pass him, his teammate was looking for luck, and trying to take Luca's spot in all the wrong places. When they hit the straightaway, Luca pulled away, but his teammate remained determined. Desperate. He'd be impressed if he wasn't so damn annoyed.

It was a fire rarely sparked in Jordan. They were racing each other – not something teammates did every day. At least, not these two teammates. And although Luca was winning, Jordan kept at it like a pesky mosquito desperate to draw blood.

The laps ticked down. Luca needed to pass the car in front of him and pick up another spot. There were points on the line, and he needed them. He could handle second place if the math still worked in his favor.

Jordan continued his battle, too, with each failed attempt

to pass making him more aggressive for the next one. He bullied Luca, as if running the turbo pumpkin off the track was a valid option instead of passing. But he still couldn't get by.

'This is getting annoying,' Luca finally said on the radio. *Dangerously annoying.*

'Yes, we can see that,' his engineer radioed back.

As always, Luca weighed his words carefully. 'This won't end well.'

Jordan's car slammed into his. All drivers know what to do in those seconds when the world turns in slow motion and reality blurs. Luca instinctively braced as his car spun, flipped, and flew through the air.

As his car fought gravity while G-force pressed every cell in his body into that perfectly molded seat, Luca had two thoughts. The first: He needed more time with Mia. The second: This was bad, very bad.

And then there was a crash, a flash, and everything went dark.

Chapter 32

Nigel Rose: It's always dangerous when a car goes up in the air. No one has control at that point.

Joseph Linwood: I can't imagine what was going through Jordan Rubie's mind, but let's save judgement until we get word that these drivers are OK. Although one thing is for certain, Rubie Racing just threw away a lot of points.

Nigel Rose: This has certainly been a day for aggressive racing between teammates with dire consequences. Will certainly make for an interesting and unexpected podium.

Joseph Linwood: Quite. We're getting word that both drivers are moving, which is a good sign. But they're not climbing out of their cars on their own.

Nigel Rose: From the replay, it looks as if Rubie missed a breaking point in his quest for a podium spot and Luca Toscano simply had nowhere to go. It doesn't take much for these cars to go airborne. Especially when your car runs into the rear end of another.

Joseph Linwood: I hope some of these drivers learn a

valuable lesson today. You don't make a lot of friends when you take your teammate out.

Mia pushed open the door to the hospital room. Even with the lights off and the blinds closed, she could see the figure in the bed shift slightly. At least Jordan was alive, so she could kill him herself.

She walked over to the foot of the bed, crossed her arms, and stared down at her brother. His left leg was partially in a cast, his right arm was in a sling, and his left hand played host to a thick IV line.

'What do you want?' Jordan grimaced, his eyes fixed on a spot on the ceiling.

'What do I want? I want to know what the hell is wrong with you. I want to know why you would do something so incredibly stupid. I want to know what you could've possibly been thinking.'

She reached up and brushed away a tear from her cheek. When had her hands started shaking?

Silence blanketed the room. Mia shoved a chair next to his bed and sat down.

'How's Luca?' Jordan finally asked.

'Alive, too. Other than that, I don't know yet.'

'Don't tell me you came here first.' His eyes widened in surprise, but stayed fixed on the ceiling.

'Yes.'

The same way her heart had known that Luca was OK, it had also known that Jordan wasn't – in any capacity. Maybe it was a twin thing. Maybe it was their parents. She'd almost felt her their hands on her back, pushing her toward his hospital room.

A nurse appeared to check Jordan's IV, then assess his pain level. When he rated it at six out of ten, she nodded and left the room.

Mia's brain flashed back to a different hospital room, a similarly uncomfortable chair, and another too silent family member; to those many weeks their mother had spent in the hospital with Mia at her bedside. Waiting… for their mother's death, for the wisdom she needed to get through the rest of her days without a mom. But no wisdom had been imparted. There had been little conversation at all. The lack of words at the end of her mother's life still haunted her.

Even though Jordan would live to see another day, Mia wanted answers from him. 'Why do you hate me so much? I don't hate you, Jordan. I don't understand you, but you're still my brother.'

He didn't respond, so she pressed on.

'I know you talked to Cat and tipped off that tabloid reporter.' Actually, she hadn't been one hundred percent sure of the latter until that moment, when Jordan didn't object to the accusation. 'Is wanting me to fail enough reason to destroy the team? Everything Dad worked for? Mom?'

'Why do you even care, Mia? I mean, you bolted out of town years ago and never looked back. I know you always secretly blamed *Mom*' – his voice broke – 'for deserting the family, but when it comes down to it, she didn't have a choice. You did.'

'Blamed Mom?' she paused as her voice began to break, too. 'Why would I have blamed Mom for dying? I mean, sure, I hated that she left us but –'

Oh.

'Is that your beef with Dad dying? Do you blame him for dying, because by doing so, he brought me back into the fold? I have to say I'm surprised you even noticed I was gone.'

'It was kind of hard not to, working with Dad every day,' he said.

Of all the people who'd been affected when Mia had walked away from racing all those years ago, Jordan was the one person she'd never considered. She'd always assumed he'd been glad she'd left. She never imagined he'd suffered collateral damage when her life crashed.

And now the roles had been reversed.

'You know, Dad never gave up hope that his brilliant daughter would return. It was sad as hell. I drove in your shadow for years, and it made me hate every second of it.'

She shook her head, realizing that the pink dress comment at pre-season testing had only been the tip of the iceberg when it came to causing her brother misery. 'And then Spain happened. What about now?'

His gaze shifted from the ceiling to her. 'Your shadow is impossible to avoid when you're in the same room.'

In that moment, Mia knew that Rubie Racing wasn't big enough for both of them. Neither of them would thrive. And not only did the team belong to her, she now belonged to the team in a way Jordan never would. She was also scared for her brother, what he might do next.

'I think we both know what needs to happen.'

'You're going to fire me.' He said it like a statement of fact.

Mia thought back to her last conversation with Cliff, about how he'd shared that she'd have a good chance of gaining the millions that Jordan stood to inherit if he chose not to honor the terms of their dad's will. But even if firing Jordan would help boost Rubie Racing's bottom line, she would never be able to live with herself. Not when there was another way to set him free.

'No, Jordan, I won't do that. But you're leaving the team. You've become a danger to not only yourself but to every other driver on the track. If today's race is any indication, I'm afraid of what your end goal is. I won't lose another family member, at least not on my watch.'

'I'm what?' he asked, a puzzled expression on his face momentarily unmasking the emotional pain that had joined the physical pain.

'Leaving. I'll expect your resignation within three days. Given your responsibility for today's accident, I know you'll want to do the right thing and pay to fix both cars. But other than that, you're under no obligation to direct your inheritance to anything related to Rubie Racing.'

She watched his face as it registered the realization of what she was offering.

'Marketing and public relations will call you after the break to handle the optics. Until then, try to focus on your healing.'

Jordan responded with a single nod, then closed his eyes. Knowing that was the only reaction she was likely to get, Mia got up and walked to the door. When her hand gripped the handle, she realized the gravity of this moment. She was leaving her twin brother alone, in immeasurable pain on myriad levels.

Mia shook her head and gave one last look back at the bed. 'You know, you're the only Rubie I have left. It didn't have to be like this. It doesn't have to be like this.' She turned to leave, not expecting a response.

'Mia,' Jordan said. 'If it makes you feel any better, it's not an exclusive club. I pretty much hate everyone.'

Even though nothing was broken, the doctors had told Luca he was damn lucky. Considering that every inch of his body was either bruised, sore, or both, he had to agree. And based on what his concussed brain registered when the medical crew pulled him from the wreckage, he'd fared far better than Jordan.

Luca was still assessing his body, part by part, bit by bit, when the door to his hospital room opened. He didn't need to look up to know who it was.

'How's your brother?' he asked.

'Gone.'

Luca gasped as he struggled to launch his body out of bed at her.

She waved her arms to stop him. 'Sorry, sorry! Gone from the *team*. Not gone-gone. Although, he may as well be.'

When her voice cracked, he slowly shifted over on the bed to make room for her to slide in next to him. She took one look at his spectacularly bruised arms, and burst into tears.

'Come here,' he said, patting the sheet. 'Lay with me.'

'That's what got us into this mess,' she sobbed, once they were side by side. 'I'm sorry.'

'For what? What did you do? Please, tell me.' He didn't have a clue why she was apologizing, but then his head was pounding and his brain wasn't in any shape for playing guessing games.

'For jinxing you this morning with my evil temptress ways.' She sniffed and wiped away her tears with his hospital gown. 'I knew better, but I went ahead and did it anyway.'

'Do you see now that this isn't all fun and games?' He poked her in the arm with his index finger and gave her a shaky grin when she gasped. 'I'm kidding Mia. You in no way caused today's crash. Responsibility for that rests solely with your brother.'

'Are you sure?'

'Absolutely. I mean, you saw the crash, right?'

She nodded and started sobbing again.

Luca winced at the thought of Mia having to watch both him and Jordan being freed from their cars and flown away from the track, knowing full well that it's never good news when a driver is taken offsite. Pain be damned, he wrapped his arm around her and pulled her closer.

Once she contained her sniffling, she asked what the doctors said.

'I have a concussion and a lot of bruises but, amazingly, nothing's broken. I'll be plenty sore for a few days though. But really, I'm more worried about you.'

'Me? I'm not the one who was just smashed into a wall going a gazillion miles an hour and then loaded into a helicopter and flown away.'

And there it was. He kissed her temple. 'I'm OK, Mia. I'm going to be OK.'

'Don't try to act like a concussion isn't serious. You're not fooling anyone.'

She was right, of course. Concussions weren't just a concern for football players. Race car drivers experienced plenty of serious knocks to the head, what with driving around at top speed in an open cockpit and occasionally crashing into things and each other. Adding the halo hadn't been popular – mostly because it looks like a thong mounted on top of the car – but it did offer a measure of protection during crashes and against flying objects.

Not that there was much a halo could do when one teammate decided to ram another in the ass end.

This wasn't the first punch on Luca's dance card, although he'd suffered only one other concussion in his career. That had come during his 'spectacular' Montreal crash. No surprise there.

Even though his head was pounding, Luca knew he was fortunate. Like all drivers, he tried not to focus too much on crashes – they were part of the job, and obsessing wouldn't be productive the next time he climbed in his car and pressed down on the gas pedal. But this crash was different. When he'd hit the wall, what he stood to lose had flashed before his eyes.

Mia.

He knew what he wanted to do. What he needed to do. He pressed his lips to her temple again and breathed her in, then turned her face toward his.

'Marry me.'

Tears appeared again, and she didn't attempt to blink them away. 'Yes.'

His heart thumped in his chest, as if it had been holding its next beat until she answered. 'Well, that was easier than I expected.' He sealed the deal with a kiss. 'I promise you a better proposal later with a speech and flowers and a ring and everything.'

'I don't need the works, Luca,' she said softly. 'I just need you. When you and Jordan crashed, I thought I was watching my family disappear. And I realized that my family is you. I love you. Always have, always will.'

'I love you, too.' They sat there in silence, wrapped together. 'What now, fiancée?'

'We get married? Live happily ever after?'

'I'll cast my vote for eloping,' he smiled. 'But I meant with the season. Where do we go from here?'

'What season? It's over.'

It was hard to believe he could experience such a high and such a low in the span of minutes, but Mia was right. 'With summer break, I'll be cleared before the next race. But if Jordan is out, we're short a driver.'

Even if Jordan wasn't leaving the team, he couldn't drive with a broken ankle. Apex required teams to start each race with two cars. Two cars needed two drivers. Rubie Racing was down to just one.

'We have no reserve driver,' Mia said, stating the obvious. 'I knew that would bite us in the ass.'

A throat cleared from the doorway. 'Actually, we do. And I wasn't eavesdropping. Except... I was.' Brian crossed the room and looked down at them lying together on the bed. 'Congratulations, by the way.'

'Thanks, mate.' Luca grinned at the man he now considered as much his friend as his team manager. 'But please, tell us more about this mystery driver you have in your back pocket.'

Brian flashed open his hands toward Mia and shouted, 'Ta-dah!'

'Do you have a brain injury, too?' Mia shook her head. 'The last time I checked, I was the team principal, not a reserve driver. I have the business cards to prove it.'

'While your business cards are indeed correct, you're still listed as a reserve driver from testing at Catalunya. Surely you remember that? When you flew around the track like you were born to it? Oh, that's right, you were.'

Luca felt Mia stiffen next to him. 'Apex will never accept that,' she said. 'There are rules. There has to be an alternative.'

'I just saw Jordan, and even if you changed your mind and refused to accept his *resignation*, I'll go out on a limb and say that we don't want that. Not to mention that he's going to take more time to heal than we have left in the season. His ankle took a nasty break.'

Luca thought about how close he was to being world champion. How Rubie Racing still had a chance to take the championship title as a team. The zero points they'd earned from crashing out of today's race were about all they could afford to spare. He could bring home the podium spots he needed to seal his deal for the season. But he was nowhere without them having a second car on the track.

'We need you, Mia,' he said. 'I need you.'

Brian pulled a chair to the side of the bed and plopped down. 'Luca's right. Without you, we basically flush this season and all of our hard work – all of your dad's hard work – down the toilet.'

They both stared at her.

She sighed. 'Let's say I agree, hypothetically speaking. You still haven't answered the question about Apex letting this slide. I've been in a race car a handful of times in the last fifteen years, and that wasn't with a full field of cars around me. Not to mention, we're heading into the summer break. How am I supposed to prepare for this when we can't work or even be at the complex? And before you suggest we do anything on the sly, the answer is no. I've heard the rumors about Apex spying on teams to ensure they're shut down, and that's not even what scares me the most. My dad would come back to haunt us in a hot second if we didn't adhere to the rules of the break.'

Rob had embraced the summer break with pure zeal. The

other principals he'd worked for accepted but resented the forced time off every year. Even though he was a complete workaholic, Rob had been the first person out the door and missing in action for the duration.

In the north woods of Michigan, where he and Mia had planned to spend their break, mostly naked.

Damn.

'Our vacation, Mia. I'm sorry. They said I should be able to fly home in a couple of days, but I doubt a ten-hour drive on top of that would be recommended.'

'It's OK,' she said, kissing his cheek and locking her eyes with his. 'We have plenty of time for vacations. A whole lifetime, remember?'

Brian cleared his throat. 'Look, I'd love nothing more than to leave the two of you alone – seriously, nothing more – but time's a ticking and we need to clear this up in the next twenty-four hours, before we can't even talk about it. So, here's what I'm thinking. Mia, you and I will head out now and lobby Apex. As far as getting you prepped is concerned, the simulator is, sadly, off limits. It's at the complex and on the list of forbidden fruits. But... how do you feel about video games?'

Chapter 33

Three days later, Mia found herself sitting in a 'gaming chair' eerily similar to the seat in the cockpit of an Apex car and surrounded by three sixty-inch television screens. A steering wheel was mounted in front of her, and three pedals and a shifter completed the setup. It seemed too close for comfort to the simulator locked up a few miles away at the complex.

Brian noticed her frown and paused in his attempt to set up the latest video gaming system with a huff and an eye roll. 'What now?'

'Are you sure this is legal? I mean, it feels pretty legit.'

'For the fifth time, it's a toy, Mia. Not a simulator. I ordered all of these things online. They sell them to everyone, including children. In fact, you're probably the oldest person in the country about to play this game right now.'

As if on cue, Barb poked her head into the den they'd taken over in her house. 'You kids need a snack?'

'Juice box, please,' Luca called out from the sofa.

Barb's head whipped in his direction, and her hands

immediately settled on her hips. She was not pleased. 'What are you doing in here? You know you're not supposed to be looking at screens when you're recovering from a concussion. I don't want to even think about what those monstrosities would do to your brain. Out. Out right now, before Brian figures out how to turn it on.'

Since they flew back from Budapest the day before, Barb had been fussing over Luca like a mama bird caring for a chick that had taken a ten-story tumble out of the nest and whacked its head on every ledge before landing on the sidewalk below. She'd insisted he recuperate at her house, and Mia hadn't had to do much to convince him that it would be better than them camping out in his loft.

They'd arrived to find a 'Congratulations!' sign taped to the front door and flowers and bridal magazines on her nightstand.

'I bet if you do what she says that you'll get that juice box, and maybe a brownie, too,' Mia whispered to him.

'But my head feels fine,' he pouted, slowly hoisting his body up anyway, since Barb clearly wasn't budging until he did. As he walked by Mia, he bent down and kissed her forehead. 'No one else has driven on these tracks. I wanted to help you.'

'I've got it covered,' Brian said, checking his watch before returning his attention to fiddling with the cables. 'Mia has a playdate arriving momentarily, if I can figure out how to hook this damn thing up. I swear you'd think a master's in engineering would offer some benefit here, but I'm thinking a ten-year-old could've gotten this done in half the time.'

'Playdate? You've got to be kidding,' Mia said. 'I mean, I only have one controller.'

'Nope, not joking.'

Luca shrugged as he padded after Barb out of the room. Mia couldn't imagine who was about to walk through the door. They'd opted to not tell anyone on the Rubie Racing team the exact plan for the remainder of the season – just that the show would go on. With summer break starting as soon as the cars and supplies were packed up, they wouldn't have been able to do anything but worry for two weeks. And they had enough of that on their plates, knowing that postvacation, they'd have mere days to put two wrecked cars back together. They all knew the seriousness of the situation.

Knowing that she'd left her brother alone in a hospital room in a foreign country made her inexplicably sad. According to his doctor, Jordan would have to spend at least a few more days in the hospital, and Cliff had flown out that morning to be there with him. Mia was relieved – their goodbye when Luca was released was short, awkward, and just plain awful.

The doorbell rang, and from the enthusiasm of the voices trickling in from the hall, whoever had arrived was no stranger. She was about to go see for herself when a face she hadn't laid eyes on in fifteen years appeared.

'Hello, Mia.'

Her lungs clenched at the sight of Scott Carrington, the driver whose crash had weighed heavily on her conscience for most of her adult life. But her last memory of him – in his hospital bed, giving her dad a thumbs up – didn't jibe with the man who now stood before her.

'Scott, hi,' she said, feeling a bit foolish in her gaming chair. She stood up and gave him a hug. 'What a nice surprise.'

Before Scott hit the wall in Daytona and everything went south for Mia, they had known each other well. She was a girl of eleven when Scott had signed on with Rubie Racing, and Rob had treated him like he did every other person on the team, as if he were a member of the family. Her performance in the role of annoying little sister had been award-winning, although Scott had never seemed to mind answering her endless questions about racing, race cars, and eventually boys. When he met and married a woman from southeast Michigan, Mia had served as a junior bridesmaid. It had been one of the few times in her adolescent years that she hadn't fought putting on a frilly dress.

'It's been a long time – too long,' he said. 'I'm sorry about your dad. Em and I were hiking in the Andes with the kids when it happened, and we didn't get word until the day of the funeral. What a shock. I was thinking of you all, and I heard it was one heck of a party. No surprise there though, especially since your dad planned it himself. The man could turn anything into a celebration.'

Scott's absence at the funeral hadn't gone unnoticed, but Mia had heard he and Emily had moved West after he retired from Apex.

'I thought maybe you didn't want to deal with seeing me,' she blurted out.

'Why on earth would you think that?' A look of confusion clouded his face.

She couldn't believe the man she'd worshiped as a child was going to make her say out loud how she'd helped destroy his career. 'Because of Daytona?'

His eyes widened. 'Geez Louise, do you think I blame you for that crash? That I've been carrying a grudge for all these years?'

'Maybe?'

Definitely was more like it. That crash hadn't just changed her life and Luca's, but Scott's as well.

'Well, that's ridiculous. I'm the one who was to blame. I should never have gotten in the car that day. I wasn't feeling right but chalked it up to the heat and lack of sleep from the new baby.'

'But Luca and I weren't where we should've been. If we hadn't snuck off, you would've been out of the car before you hit the wall.'

'That's a little hard to say for certain, don't you think?' He put his hand on her shoulder and gave it a squeeze.

After years of playing her own judge, jury, and executioner, Mia could only return a weak nod. 'You stopped racing, though.'

'My days in Apex were already numbered, and your dad and I had talked about what my role might be when the day came. I'd always hoped that would entail molding you into an Apex driver, to be honest. And we are.'

Of all the revelations of the past few months, this one

struck Mia the dumbest. Scott didn't hate her or even blame her. He was even willing to help her.

'I'm sorry you've dwelled on this because I haven't. But then we race car drivers have to learn to put our crashes behind us, don't we? If you keep them in the middle of the road, you have to keep dodging them.'

Maybe if Mia had kept driving, she would've done just that – moved past the crash instead of letting the wreckage block her path. In a few weeks, after so many years, she'd have a chance to put Scott's theory to the test.

'You know, for a guy of, what, forty-eight, you're pretty wise,' she said.

A snort from the floor reminded Mia that Brian was still in the room. 'Let's save the wisdom for the game, shall we? It's actually ready to go, so I'll leave you both to it. Let's play some racing!'

Since Scott was already aware of the situation at hand, the two of them got straight down to business. The game's options seemed endless, but she managed to pull up the Spa-Francorchamps circuit. The Belgian Grand Prix would be the first of the nine races she'd drive to complete the season, given that the Apex gods had approved her as Rubie Racing's second driver during an emergency meeting at the eleventh hour before the summer break. After a brief learning curve with the racing wheel controller, pedals, and shifter, she was making her way around one of the world's most beloved and tricky tracks in an imaginary turbo pumpkin.

Scott pulled up an ottoman and stared at the screen in

amazement. 'Man, this is so realistic it's freaking me out. Video games sure have come a long way since the days of Pac-Man. No wonder my kid hardly ever comes out of his room.'

He began pointing out the nuances only a driver who'd completed Spa's nearly four-and-a-half-mile laps year in and year out could know. Mia absorbed his insight like a sponge.

After a couple tries at driving the track solo, she restarted the game and added a full field of drivers. She wouldn't be racing alone in a few short weeks, as appealing as that sounded at the moment. The game filled in her competitors with actual drivers. Among them: Luca, Henri, and Wyn. And Jordan.

'In the interest of time, I say we jump right into the race,' she said.

There'd be time to do a full race weekend, with practice and qualifying, later. Maybe. Right now, she wanted to take advantage of her time with Scott. They had a lot of virtual ground to cover.

The rest of the afternoon flew by, with Barb popping in occasionally with drinks and snacks, and to bust Luca for trying to sneak back to his spot on the couch. Before they knew it, they'd managed to hop from Belgium to Germany, then Singapore. But there were still a lot of races left on the itinerary.

'I don't think we're going to get through all the tracks,' Mia said when Barb gave them a fifteen-minute warning for dinner. Her eyes were beginning to burn from staring at the screen for hours on end.

'Sure we will.' Scott stood up and stretched, his back

cracking. 'Although I'm going to need something a little more posture-friendly to sit on than this ottoman.'

'Don't you have to be going soon?'

He shook his head and grinned. 'No ma'am. I'm here for as long as you need me.'

That ended up being five more days, with Scott receiving the royal treatment at Barb's B & B. They played the racing game day and night, with Scott upgraded to the leather lounger from her dad's study. Only Barb's cooking managed to tear them away.

Brian joined them and a still-sulking Luca for most mealtimes. They languished at the table, reminiscing about the old days of Rubie Racing. Stories about her dad, shared by the people who loved and respected him most, made her laugh and cry and miss him more than ever, even though the tears were more happy than sad.

'My heart is full,' she told Luca as she cuddled up to him late one night.

On the final day of Scott's visit, both Luca's doctor and Barb cleared him for limited activity.

'You have thirty minutes, mister,' Barb called out as Luca headed into the study.

He plopped down on the couch. 'OK, what do you need?'

Mia turned and gave Scott a sly grin. They'd finished the track overviews on day four and had since been playing a game of their own creation. Mia closed her eyes as Scott picked a track, opening them only when the race was about to begin, not knowing where in the world she was supposed to be.

Much to Luca's chagrin, Mia was managing to beat the virtual version of him soundly in every race. In the pink race car she'd stayed up too late designing a few nights before, her first kart on steroids, she ruled the remainder of the imaginary season. She hoped to manage half as well in real life and that, if she did, the man she planned to spend the rest of her life with would take it better than most members of the opposite sex had in the past.

At least Luca took his on-screen butt-kicking in stride. 'Look at you go!' he laughed. 'But don't get too used to seeing me in your rearview mirror.'

Scott high-fived Mia. 'I don't know if I'd count on that, buddy.'

It wasn't until right before Scott left, when they were cleaning up the mess only endless hours of video game playing could wreak on a room, did he bring up Jordan.

'Any news on your brother?'

She shook her head. 'Cliff flew over and brought him home, and Barb's been checking in on him. His ankle and shoulder were broken in the crash, but they weren't career-ending injuries. He'll race again.' She paused, realizing the gravity of what she was about to say, considering that Scott's Daytona crash had resulted in one concussion too many, and he'd chose to end his career than risk another. 'If he can. If he wants to.'

'He was always a tough one to figure out, that guy,' Scott said. 'I tried to help him as much as I could, but he had a chip on his shoulder the size of Lake Superior. Never seemed too keen on letting anyone too close.'

'Nothing's changed.' Mia sighed. 'I should probably feel worse about how everything has gone down since Dad died, but after all these years, it's hard to feel anything when it comes to my brother.'

'Sometimes, things take a while to fall into place the way they're supposed to. You and Luca. You and me. Honestly, if your dad's death wasn't so unexpected, I'd think he was some sort of master puppeteer.'

Those same thought had crossed her mind once or twice. Jordan was the only loose thread in the tapestry of the past few months.

'You never know what's down the line for you and your brother,' he said.

Except she did have a good idea. And it looked pretty much the same.

As if sensing her skepticism, he added, 'Time changes people, Mia. Look at you.'

'Me? How have I changed?'

'Really? You don't see it? Mia, you were the kid sister I never had, and I always loved you, but like all kid sisters, you were kind of a... pain in the ass.' Scott paused when he saw tears welling up in her eyes. 'Hey, listen. You were talented, you were smart, and you were confident. Amazing traits for a driver. But you also only saw the world in black and white. Maybe the purpose of all of this — my accident, your experiencing a life outside of the track that career drivers never do, your dad's death — was what you needed to learn how to see shades of gray.'

'I may have heard that somewhere before,' she mumbled.

Mia inhaled a deep breath and thought of the years when she'd equated the intensity it took to be a race car driver with being 'bad.' Back then, it hadn't seemed possible for her to be involved in the sport and be 'good,' or in control. She'd seen it as an all-or-nothing choice and had chosen nothing. But not anymore. She almost hated to think what would've happened if a different decision hadn't been forced upon her — and changed the life she'd so carefully curated.

As much as she'd loved Chicago, Star, and her job, Mia realized that there was probably no going back for her. Not now. 'I'm actually trying to see all of the colors,' she said.

'And you deserve a rainbow.' Scott shook his head. 'Man, have I gotten sappy. But seriously, Mia, I can't wait to see you out there. Give 'em hell, kid.'

The next day, Mia and Luca escaped to his loft. Although Barb seemed reluctant to let either of them out of her sight, they thought she could use some peace and quiet after more than a week of nonstop company. Not to mention that they hadn't been alone since before the Hungarian Grand Prix, the accident, and their hospital engagement.

Mia was also in desperate need of a screen break after six straight days of playing the racing video game, and she didn't trust herself to stay away if she remained in the same house. The addiction was real.

'I know this isn't exactly the summer break we'd planned,' Luca said after he'd thoroughly tucked her in for the night. 'But we can make the most of the next few days. What would you like to do?'

'I don't need anything more than this,' Mia said, resting her head on his bare chest. And she meant it.

Luca slid out of bed and reappeared moments later, an envelope in his hand. Even without seeing her father's neat script on the front, she knew what it was.

'When?' was all she asked as she rubbed her fingers over the name of the man she was going to marry, written by the man whose death had inadvertently brought them together.

He settled back into bed next to her. 'On my birthday. Cliff gave it to me when he walked me out that night. He told me that you all got them, too.'

Mia's own letter was tucked in her childhood jewelry box back at Barb's. She took it out and read it each time she was home, but had never mentioned its existence to Luca. The thought made her feel guilty now that she was holding his letter.

'This isn't an I-show-you-mine you-show-me-yours situation, Mia,' Luca said softly. Given the number of people who'd read her thoughts lately, her poker face might need some work. 'I thought you should read it. I want you to.'

She opened the envelope and drank in her father's message to Luca, then immediately started over again. More enlightenment from beyond the earthly plane. Her father hoping to set things right. She hoped somewhere, somehow, he could see that he had.

'What do you think he meant when he said, "take good care of my daughter?"'

They weren't together on Luca's birthday, she remembered,

but their friendship had been growing and evolving and had continued to flourish and blossom in the months after. Had he seen her father's words as some sort of afterlife directive?

'Well, since you're clearly capable of taking care of yourself, I think he wanted to give me – us – his blessing in case *this* ever happened,' he said. 'I also like to think that he knew we belonged together. This seems strange to talk about in bed with my fiancée, but it was obvious that your dad was never impressed with Julia. At all.'

'He wasn't mean to her?' Mia had a hard time believing that.

'No, of course not. He was more… disapproving. It's hard to describe. Only once did he say anything, though, over a beer. "I have a hard time believing that woman is enough for you," he said. He was right, of course; she wasn't – in any capacity. But I do believe being with Julia made it easier for me to realize what was so amazing about you and me these past months.'

'What's that?' she asked, not wanting to extend any part of this conversation about his supermodel ex, but curious all the same.

'We're not just two puzzle pieces that snap together perfectly, Mia,' he said, pulling her close to prove it. 'We're so much more than that. We're the whole damn beautiful puzzle.'

Chapter 34

Joseph Linwood: Top of mind for everyone as we regroup after the summer break is what's happened at Rubie Racing. Jordan Rubie, who was injured in that nasty crash with his teammate Luca Toscano in Budapest, is out, and not just for the remainder of the season. He's apparently out as a driver for Rubie Racing altogether.

Nigel Rose: The team isn't releasing any details, so it's anyone's guess as to what exactly went down that resulted in Rubie resigning from his own family's team.

Joseph Linwood: And that's not even the biggest news for Apex's only American team. His sister, Mia Rubie, team owner and principal, is now the team's second driver, making her the first female Apex driver in more than twenty years. She's also dating Luca Toscano, and if you'll recall, there was a lot of fuss at the beginning of the season about their involvement years ago. All of this is, shall we say, a little too reality show-like?

Nigel Rose: I knew Rob Rubie well, and I have to say, I

don't think he'd bat an eye. If anything, he'd be pleased as punch to have his daughter in a Rubie Racing car. He wasn't much for caring what other teams thought about his decisions and, in doing so, he broke down a lot of barriers in this sport. Brian Smith was Apex's first Black team manager, and anyone who saw Mia drive as a teenager could've guessed Rob had big dreams for her.

Joseph Linwood: I am surprised at the exception Apex made to allow her to drive. But then what she lacks in hours, she certainly appears to make up for in talent.

Nigel Rose: From what we've learned, that decision had the support of almost every team owner. I believe only the Carvalhos raised an objection.

Joseph Linwood: That's interesting but not surprising considering the struggles they're having this season.

Nigel Rose: I will say, Mia Rubie couldn't have chosen a more storied track to launch her Apex driving career. Not only is Spa legendary, but it was also one of Rob Rubie's favorite circuits.

Joseph Linwood: And for what perhaps is a first, there's no rain in the forecast. We're looking at a beautiful and dry race weekend in Belgium.

Nigel Rose: Fasten your seatbelt, Joseph. We're in for an interesting few months indeed.

Mia's senses were teetering on overload, and the race didn't start for another ten minutes. The risk of her brain shorting out on the first lap was definitely within the realm of possibility.

If only her dad were here. He'd always known how to calm her down and pump her up. First, he'd take her by the shoulders, look her straight in the eyes, and make her take a deep inhale. Then he'd pull her in for a hug, tell her he loved her, and ask, 'Are you in it to win it?'

When she graduated from karts to race cars, her response shifted from a sharp nod to the sassy, 'Well, I'm sure as hell not getting the hell out of the way.'

And a family mantra was born.

'You ready for this?' asked Brian, who made up some cockamamie excuse about checking her RR1 one final time as a reason for being with her on the starting grid and not at pit wall. He could've told her that he needed to take her temperature rectally, and she would've still been glad to have him there.

'Are you kidding me? She was born ready, mate.' Luca swooped in to plant a kiss on her lips.

She pushed him back. 'What are you doing here, mister? As your team principal, I command you to get your ass back to your car.'

'Come on, Mia. You know I can't start a race without a hug from you.' His eyes narrowed, but his grin widened. 'Sabotaging this pre-race ritual had better not be part of your winning strategy.'

Since Star's appearance in Spain, Luca had insisted on repeating their hug on every starting grid, and it had become her favorite of his pre-race rituals. Apparently, it was now one of hers. She leaned in, and his arms tightened around her.

Before he let go, she whispered, 'But we're by my car, not yours.'

'Correct me if I'm wrong, but I believe they're both your cars.'

'You're a quick study,' she laughed. 'I may keep you around for a while.'

He winked. 'Just awhile?'

'Maybe a little longer.' She kissed him. 'I love you. I'm so glad you're my teammate. I can't imagine doing this with anyone else.'

From behind them, Brian cleared his throat. 'As much as I hate to break up this lovefest, you both need to get in your cars and do your jobs.'

After another kiss, Luca wove his way back through the cars, teams, and guests still milling about before the drivers got into their cars. After qualifying third, he was in the second row on the starting grid. She'd qualified ninth in the field of twenty-four, and if she held position, she'd gain points for the team. Not too shabby at all.

'It's time,' Brian said. 'Let's do this.'

The team assistant helped Mia climb into what was now her own turbo pumpkin, which looked as good as new following the crash in Hungary. The team had worked around the clock to put both cars back together again with spare parts and components as soon as summer break was over. Points were on the line if the RR1s weren't race ready in time, and points were dollars — millions of dollars.

The only changes from when it was Jordan's car were to

the cockpit, so it fit her body as well as it had Jordan's, and the number. Mia had considered it a sign that she was able to pick twenty-four, her number from her teenage years.

After the prep crew helped her plug in her radio and secure her seatbelts, they gathered the equipment for keeping her car cool and wheeled it back toward the pits. Brian gave her a final nod and a thumbs up, and jogged away.

And then she heard it: 'Drivers, start your engines.'

Mia thought of the last woman to start an Apex race. Her poster had hung directly across from Mia's bed as a girl, because she'd wanted it to be the first thing she saw every morning when she woke up. Mia hoped that somewhere, she, too, was celebrating the retirement of 'gentleman, start your engines' once again, along with a new generation of girls who'd be watching her Apex debut.

'This is for you, Dad,' she whispered as she stepped on the gas and followed the parade of cars onto the track for the formation lap. Her heart hiccupped.

The transition to racing was a blurry line, with the neat rows melding into a swarm of cars jockeying for a better position. She carefully maneuvered through the track's first curves while playing defense. Blocking, blocking, blocking.

Crashing out before the racing really began would be a colossal disappointment.

The space between the cars grew as the laps fell away one by one. She suddenly found herself racing only two cars.

One was Wyn, who was like a pest in his attempts to pass. Not a chance in hell was one of Cat's cars getting by her.

'Be patient. You're faster than he is. Stay the course. He'll drop away in a few laps.'

Trust your engineer, Mia.

Dad.

The RR1 pressed on, a fly swatter to the Wyn-ed gnat that kept sailing through its grid openings, then attacking again. Finally, he dropped back enough to not be a bother.

The yellow car in front of her was her next target. It was her turn to be someone's pain in the ass. She just needed to catch him.

Her mind wandered, wondering about Luca and how his race was going. If he'd be on the podium and extend his lead for the world championship. She couldn't imagine another driver on the track was more concerned about their teammate's race than their own, but then they also weren't responsible for their teams and mile-long to-do lists.

Focus, Mia. Be a driver, not a team principal.

Sitting so low to the ground in the cockpit meant that she felt every slight bump in the road. Vibrations from the powerful engine shook her from head to toe. Her head felt as heavy as a bowling ball thanks to the G-forces.

This was far easier in Barb's den.

From the moment he pressed down the gas pedal to the second he crossed the finish line, Mia didn't cross his mind once. His brain was trained to compartmentalize on the track.

But as soon as the post-podium press conference wrapped up, his heart took over for his over-taxed brain and Mia was all he could think about. He found her in the garage, celebrating with not only her car's team, but his team, Brian, and a multitude of other Rubie Racing employees. From the doorway, he watched until she noticed him, then joined the fan club to offer what was surely the first of many congratulations on a job well done.

Mia had bettered her starting position, finishing eighth, earning points for the team by staying in the top ten in her first race. Impressive, to say the least.

His efforts mirrored hers. Thanks to his crash and that big fat DNF in Budapest, he entered the race still leading in points for the season but with a very small cushion between him and Henri. Standing on the bottom level of the podium didn't help his quest, but there were eight races left. Plenty of time to widen his lead.

What he didn't expect was being asked if having his girlfriend-slash-boss on the track with him had been a distraction. He stared at the reporter — Mia's favorite, who'd managed to still get into the Apex post-race press conferences — in disbelief. 'Mia Rubie could never be a distraction. And for the record, she's not my girlfriend. She's my fiancée.'

Sure, Luca had wondered what it would be like to have Mia racing alongside him, but any strangeness about Mia taking over as the team's second driver evaporated like raindrops on August asphalt. Her years of thinking strategically made her methodical when it came to accomplishing tasks, and she checked item after item off of her to do list.

It was something to see.

Win over Jordan's team? Check. Although this may have

been her easiest task, considering how her brother had treated the guys who catered to him and his car. Let's just say no tears were shed when they found out Jordan wasn't returning.

Clean practice? Check. To Luca's amazement, Mia had even managed to handle the media feeding frenzy created with one simple press release from Rubie Racing's PR team the second summer break was over.

Awe-inspiring finish? Check.

Other familiar faces soon joined the celebration. Star dressed from head to toe in her Rubie Racing gear. Cliff and Barb, who couldn't stop crying, although that didn't appear to be the reason the two of them were holding hands. Scott, along with his wife, who flew halfway across the world to watch Mia's Apex debut.

'We decided we had to be here,' Scott told them, although he'd stayed out of the spotlight to give Mia her due. 'Well done, kid. I am surprised you could focus without a bowl of sour cream and onion potato chips within arm's reach of your steering wheel.'

Once everyone went back to work – the cars and equipment weren't going to magically pack and ship themselves to Italy – he and Mia made their way to their hotel to get ready for an impromptu dinner with their surprise guests. In the elevator, Mia gave him a heated look, the likes of which he hadn't seen since she was a teenager.

'Really?' Luca asked.

But he certainly didn't argue when she pulled him into their suite and pounced on him as soon as the door clicked shut behind them. Within seconds, she removed her clothes and his and was guiding him home. Adrenaline was a strange and fantastic beast.

'I have to say, those barre classes have really paid off,' he said, once she let him up for air, her body still straddling his. 'Do you feel better?'

'I'll let you know in a minute.' She rolled off him onto the floor, panting as she caught her breath.

'Well, we have exactly one hour before we need to be out the door,' he said.

She cocked one eye open and asked, 'A whole hour, eh?' Then she was on top of him again.

Finally, a teammate he could get along with, and it was the one he was supposed to have all along. All those years ago, Rob had been preparing his daughter to be an Apex driver. Although there'd been a handful of female drivers throughout the years, none were very successful. Rob had thought his daughter was different. And if today was any indication, he was right.

His mind went to those early days with Rubie Racing. His boss had been overjoyed when he and Mia became such close friends. But would he have been as excited to know they were secretly involved? Given how Rob reacted when he found the two of them together, he'd always assumed the answer was no.

Until Rob's letter.

After they finally managed to shower and dress, Luca turned to Mia. 'Back then, did you know your dad wanted you to race in Apex?'

'It was always a given.'

'You were the natural heir to the throne,' Luca said. 'I mean, your brother is better than average, but he doesn't have your talent.'

'Do you think he was watching today? Jordan?'

He'd wondered the same thing, and had come to the conclusion that his former teammate had likely sat and stewed but watched his sister's first Apex race, nonetheless. 'I doubt he could help himself, Mia. You're something to see, and you're even harder to ignore. Especially for Jordan.'

Over the next few weeks, Luca wondered if the other Rubie twin was still watching. If Jordan wasn't, he was the only one. Even as Luca gained more points and looked certain to earn his first world championship, all eyes were trained on the other orange RR1 and the woman behind its wheel.

And he loved every second of it.

Even when he discovered her side of the bed cold in the middle of the night because she was parked in front of the television, racing Scott in real time. And especially when she woke him up with some random racing question and they stayed awake talking for hours, which inevitably led to other activities.

He was one lucky son of a bitch.

Chapter 35

Jordan was sitting at the end of his dock when Mia, Barb, and Cliff arrived at his house on their dad's birthday. October had served up a beaut of a Sunday, and Mia was glad the racing calendar cooperated with a weekend off so they could spend this first birthday without him together. The leaves on the trees were beginning to change, and the palette of autumn colors reflected on the still water along with the puffy clouds.

Without a second thought, Mia grabbed her mobile phone to capture the tranquil scene before her, with Jordan – leaning back on his hands, legs dangling off the dock and his face lifted upward – front and center.

When Barb had shared Jordan's idea of spreading not only their dad's ashes but their mom's, too, Mia had reluctantly agreed. Patricia Rubie had waited patiently for her husband until his urn had finally joined hers in their bedroom. But Barb rarely darkened that doorway, and Rob and Trish deserved a better final resting place than a forgotten space.

But dumping them in a lake? Mia had cringed at the thought.

Until now.

This place was the definition of quiet and solitude. A peace that two people who'd spent so much time in the public eye, and too much time apart, in life and then in death, deserved for all eternity.

Her brother slowly got to his feet, revealing a walking cast on his left leg, and stuck his hands in his pockets before extending a sheepish hello. Her own greeting was equally contrite. Bits and pieces of their last meeting in his hospital room still haunted her in those rare moments that she let herself dwell on them.

Barb reached him first for a quick hug, then grabbed both of their hands when Mia caught up. 'Are you two ready for this?'

They both nodded as Cliff cleared his throat and set a bag holding the two urns on the dock.

'I, uh, have something I'd like to read,' Jordan said quietly. 'I hope that's OK.'

'Of course,' she smiled. She couldn't help but study him as he unfolded a piece of paper from his back pocket, but couldn't figure out what was different.

'It's a poem by E.E. Cummings. It always makes me think of them.' He paused before launching into 'I carry your heart with me.'

The tears that began streaming down Mia's face gathered speed with each verse until she was full-on messy crying. When Cliff put his arms around her and pulled her into him, she sobbed harder. When Jordan finished, she sniffed, 'Mom loved that poem, so much that she had the first line engraved inside dad's wedding ring.'

And then they were all crying.

Cliff reached down and took the lids off both urns, then handed her and Jordan each one. They knelt down on the dock and slowly poured out the contents, the ashes of their parents first mixing in the air before settling atop the water and swirling into one mass that slowly drifted away. Together.

A sudden breeze gently pushed the pair further out into the lake. As if it were a cue to give the Rubie family some privacy, Barb hugged each of them before joining hands with Cliff and walking back up to the house to prepare brunch.

'I'm not sure how long it's going to take for that not to be weird,' Jordan said after they were out of earshot.

Mia welcomed the opportunity to laugh. 'It's *so* weird, right?'

The two stood on the dock, side by side, and watched their parents' journey in silence.

Jordan stretched his arms behind him. 'Convenient that Dad's birthday coincided with an off-week,' he said.

His statement caught her off guard for one reason: It lacked his usual sarcasm. And that's when she realized what else was different about him. His scowl was missing, too. Their mother's legendary pout remained, but his entire demeanor was different.

'It's nice when that happens,' he added.

Mia nodded. She was reluctant to engage in racing talk for

the same reason she'd asked Luca to stay behind – it felt like rubbing salt in an open wound. But Jordan kept on.

'I've been watching the races. I'm not sure why. I didn't plan to.' Jordan laughed. *Laughed*. 'What's going on out there? You're a better driver than that.'

Her head jerked toward him. 'What?'

He shrugged and shook his head. 'Don't get me wrong, you're driving fine. As well as I ever did. But we both know what you're capable of, Mia. What's holding you back?'

'I'm sorry, but are you still on painkillers or something?' She stared at her brother in disbelief. 'I mean, what's happening here?'

'Trust me when I say that I can't believe we're having this conversation, but not only did we just toss what's left of our parents into a lake, I've had a lot of time on my hands to think. More than I've had in my entire life.' He paused and looked at her. Really looked at her. 'Do you want to know what I hated most when we were kids? That I had to try so damn hard, and you just... were. You didn't even have to try. Hell, you didn't even have to *think*. It was infuriating to see you zipping along in that pink kart like it was an extension of you.'

Mia remembered that feeling of being one with her kart. Even as a child, she knew it was special. That she was special.

'Luca drives the same way. Also infuriating, FYI.' And then he chuckled. *Chuckled*. 'I let it get to me. I love racing, but I misplaced my joy for the sport years ago.'

Her lifelong reluctance of revealing too much to Jordan,

of choosing her words carefully, was hard to move past. But she decided to risk the very real possibility of getting hurt because something was off with her driving. She'd felt it in Belgium, and even though she was improving with each race, that off-feeling refused to budge.

'I never thought I would say this, but you're right, Jordan. Being in the car doesn't feel like it used to. Even those days at pre-season testing were different.'

Of course, their dad had been gone only a month at that point and Mia had still been figuring out what it meant to be team principal. Now, she was balancing all that role entailed on top of her duties as a driver.

'You're the only one who can figure this out, Mia, but I can tell you this: It's you, not the car. And I know that because it was always me, all those years. I blamed everyone and everything when I had a bad race, but when it came down to it, the car was doing its job. But I wasn't.'

While she weighed Jordan's raw honesty, she glanced at the lake, to where their parents... were. She gasped and grabbed Jordan's hand.

'They're gone. They're really gone.'

To her surprise, Jordan draped an arm around her shoulders. 'Oh, Mia. There's no way Dad is out of here until you find your way to the top of a podium. But I would say it's a sign that it's time to eat.'

Chapter 36

It hit Mia in Japan, as she was going over her mental pre-race checklists for her dual role as team principal and driver. At four o'clock in the morning.

This was. Too. Damn. Much.

Jordan had hit the nail on the head when he said that she'd always driven without thinking. These days, thinking was all she did.

Unfortunately, Luca was sound asleep. Waking a sleeping race car driver at the beginning of a grand prix week seemed like a bad idea, even if she was on the cusp of a major self-realization. Not that she, also a driver, could manage to catch some Zs or any other letter. She laid in the dark, brainstorming for an hour before she hatched a plan that had any legs. Then she felt around the nightstand for her phone and began tapping out text message after text message.

Just as Mia hit send on the last message, Luca shifted onto his elbows next to her in the dark. 'Can I ask who you've been bothering in the middle of the night?'

'I'll tell you in the morning,' she said, tossing her phone to the floor.

'Come here, then,' he yawned as he pulled her toward him and snuck his hand up her pajama top.

And then she was reminded what happens when you wake a sleeping race car driver. Twice.

Neither she nor Luca heard the first knock, or the second or third. At least, that's what Mia assumed when they woke up to someone pounding on the door.

Her phone lit up on the floor, revealing a lock screen lined with missed messages. As she made a frantic grab for it, she remembered her middle-of-the-night moment of genius.

'You want to explain this?' Brian asked when Mia finally opened the door, shoving his phone screen in her face. 'You'd better have been drunk texting because this shit is not funny.'

She gave him the Rubiest grin she could muster on only a handful of hours of sleep. 'Congratulations, you've been semi-promoted,' she yawned. 'We'll work out the contract details later, but here's a little piece of advice my boss would be very angry that I told you. You can pretty much name your price if you let me go back to sleep.'

'Who's doing my job?'

'Later,' she said, shutting the door. 'But if it makes you feel better, I've called in backup and almost everything has been taken care of. And we'll muddle through what hasn't been.'

'I don't feel better, just so you—'

'Let him in, I'm up.' Luca stumbled out of the bedroom, still shoving what the Good Lord had so graciously endowed him with into his boxer shorts. 'And I'd really like to know what's going on.'

Brian pushed into the room at Luca's invitation, his hands on both sides of this head like blinders. 'Dude, more clothes. And then make some of your fancy coffee. I have a feeling we're going to need it.'

Middle-of-the-night ideas had about a fifty percent chance of being solid, at least that had been Mia's previous average. But as the sun rose over Suzuka, she was as confident as she had been hours before. This could work. This would work.

'It was something Jordan said a couple of weeks ago,' she started, once the three of them were all in equal states of dress and drinking coffee around the table. She'd shared very little about that day at the lake with Jordan, spreading their parents' ashes, with anyone but Luca. But now she told Brian about her brother's introspection on his own driving, as well as hers.

'You're driving great, Mia,' Brian said. His amazement echoed Luca's when she shared the story with him. 'You've been in the top ten every race.'

'Yes, but I know I'm capable of more. I never thought it would be my brother to point it out, but I haven't been able to capture that feeling I used to get when I was behind the wheel. I'm just going through the motions out there.'

'Do yourself a favor and never share that thought with the fifteen-plus career drivers who've been finishing behind you,'

Luca said. 'Except Wyn, and only if I'm there to witness it.'

Poor Wyn. They still didn't know his fate after Luca's agent had told Cat what she could do with her and her father's offer.

She pointed to her ever-present planner, now tattered from its travels around the world. 'It comes down to this. Most drivers worry about driving and nothing else.' She rested a hand on Luca's knee as she turned toward him. 'Even you, although you're far more tuned into the inner workings of the team than any other guy on the track.'

He nodded.

'But I'm doing a hundred things. My brain is scrambled. By the time race day arrives, I'm not energized. I'm exhausted. If this is my one shot at driving, I need to really take it. I don't want to be a token second Rubie Racing car out there. I want work at being the best.' She tilted her head toward Luca. 'Even better than this guy.'

Luca leaned over and planted a kiss on her lips. 'I'd like to see you try.'

The best thing about this man was the truthfulness of that statement. Whether they were challenging each other in a plank hold or on the track, he expected her A game and nothing less. He really was a Rubie at heart. She leaned back in for a second kiss. And a third.

Brian cleared his throat. 'OK. OK. Please. You're tired, I get it. But I'm not sure there's an alternative, Mia. You're the team principal. You have business cards that say as much, or so I've been told.'

She never thought she'd grin thinking about that day in Hungary, when Brian had sprung his own harebrained scheme. But she could now see that it had led to so much positive.

'There are details to still work out, if you're willing, Brian.'

He didn't respond right away. But finally, he took a deep breath, reached into his back pocket, and pulled out an envelope that he slapped on the table. Her father's script stared up at the three of them. 'I don't think I have much of a choice.'

Mia stared at the envelope and wondered how many more of these were floating around, influencing the lives of the people her dad had most valued. 'My, my, he proved to be the prolific pen pal, didn't he?'

'The man did love paper,' Brian joked. 'Who knows what else you'll find when you dig through the stacks he left behind in your office?'

She gave him a nudge. 'That would be your office, at least for the rest of the season. Yes, I'm the team principal, technically, so don't go sneaking off and printing your own fancy business cards. But I'm hoping you can take over most of the load for the rest of the season.' Before he could respond, she put a hand over his. 'I know it's a big ask, Brian, and I know your plate is already overflowing with everything you already do as team manager. But there's no one I trust more, who my dad trusted more, than you.'

Even though he didn't say yes, the nudge he returned told her he was in. Mia breathed a huge sigh of relief. 'Are we good for now?'

'Almost,' Brian said. 'I'm almost afraid to ask, but what did you mean by backup?'

It had cost Mia a pretty penny, but when Star walked in the next evening, looking far fresher than a person had any right to after fourteen hours on a plane followed by three hours on a train, Mia nearly wept. As she'd told Brian during their marathon brainstorming sessions, there was no one in the world she trusted more for what needed to be done. The fact that all Star knew about racing she'd gained during a one-week crash course in Spain was nothing more than a minor inconvenience.

'I don't know how you did it, but I'm yours for the next month.'

Mia lunged at Star and wrapped her arms around her. 'Thank you, thank you, thank you,' she whispered. 'But I think I said six weeks.'

'Don't push your luck, *mija*.'

The twelve-hour time difference between Chicago and Suzuka had worked in Mia's favor. Star was in the office when she received the nine-one-one message and rambling justification. After a quick meeting with Sarah, who Mia had also texted and who was more than happy to collect a hefty consulting fee to have her top strategist explore what could be a lucrative new market for the company, Star had booked a nonstop flight and was on her way to Tokyo the next morning.

Holding onto Luca's hotel rooms for the entire season had seemed like a waste of money once they were sharing hers, but the travel department had pointed out that once they were gone, there was no getting them back. Thankfully, Mia had relented.

After giving the sofa a longing look, Star sat down at the table and looked Mia straight in the eye. 'OK, I have three demands. First, food. Second, spill. And then third, tell me what I need to do before I run out of whatever steam I have left. I mean, I'm hyped now, but you know how hard I'm going to crash.'

'Your wish is my command,' Mia said, already feeling freer than she had in weeks.

The reason she didn't feel bad about pulling Star away was the exact reason why she didn't think twice about bringing her to Japan and unleashing her on race week like the second coming of Godzilla. The two were cut from the same cloth when it came to how they worked. The laptop Mia handed Star was surely the same study in organization that her mentor had left behind in Chicago.

Plus, it wasn't as if Mia was checking out entirely. The team was still hers, and that wasn't changing. But she was confident Brian could manage the racing side of her role along with his, and Star could make sure everything else, especially the team's millions of dollars in sponsorships, kept rolling along.

Not surprisingly, Star had spent every waking moment during her flights across the globe absorbing whatever information she could find on Apex, the current season, and all things Rubie Racing.

Once she had her marching orders for the week, Star made a beeline to the sofa and patted the spot next to her. 'It's a big step for you, asking for help. I know another Mia who would've continued pushing through, come hell or high water. But what you've managed to do over the past eight months, how you've opened yourself up to Luca, to this challenge. I'm proud of you.'

'Me, too,' Luca said, walking through the door at the perfect moment and right over to Star to give her a hug. He sat down next to Mia and tugged her toward him. 'But can we be proud of her tomorrow? Drivers have a pretty strict sleep schedule during race week and this one has been giving me trouble.'

Star shot them both a look that screamed 'sleep schedule, my ass' and gathered up all of her new Rubie Racing accoutrements. 'Oh, I bet she has,' she sang under her breath.

Chapter 37

When Luca finally took a comfortable lead in Mexico City, he couldn't have dreamed a more perfect scene. He stood atop the podium with his nemesis on one side and Mia on the other. And then the two of them sprayed Henri's face with champagne together. It was glorious.

He and Mia hardly made it out of the elevator that day.

'I have to say, I'm rather enjoying sleeping with the next world champion,' she said afterward, propped up on her elbows on the dining table of their suite.

'Don't jinx me,' he growled. 'I'm not the world champion yet. I'm only the points leader, nothing more.'

'Oh, sorry, sorry,' she said, and he could tell she meant it. Not only had she learned her lesson about messing with his racing rituals and superstitions in Budapest, she'd developed a few of her own. A lot of her own. Which he teased her mercilessly about.

Him: 'Are you having two eggs, avocado, and sourdough toast for breakfast again?'

Her: 'Yes, I think so.'

Him: 'You have two different socks on, love.'

Her: 'Well, look at that. No sense in changing now.'

Him: 'Let me help you with your jacket. Left arm first.'

Her: 'No, right! Right! Stop it! Drop the jacket. Now.'

And then there was her car chat. Since he usually sat in the first two rows of the starting grid, he would've never known about this ritual if Brian hadn't let it slip. Her team had noticed her lips moving one day before a race began, and once she slipped up and said something, not realizing her radio was on.

'What'd she say?' Luca asked.

'It was a soft, "You there?"' Brian said.

They both nodded, knowing she had been talking to Rob.

'And?

'No, he didn't answer.'

'Are you sure about that?'

'Actually, not at all,' Brian said.

Luca kept mum until they were in New York for the U.S. Grand Prix. And then he only asked that she tell her dad hi when she checked in before the next day's race. She narrowed her eyes before responding, 'Will do. But don't expect him to help you, buddy. You're doing just fine on your own.'

'Some might say the same about you,' he said.

'Oh, yeah?'

'Yeah,' he said. 'Now go to sleep. There's a race tomorrow, and I need my beauty sleep. And so, might I add, do you.'

*

It had taken weeks before Mia realized she could never be her old self in the car again, that the girl she once was – the adrenaline junkie always on the lookout for her next fix – was gone forever. But to her surprise, the driver she was becoming was so much better. Her on-again, off-again, and on-again relationship with racing, not to mention her months as team principal, had given her a unique perspective. She was somehow both out of control and in control at the same time. It was as if teenage Mia and adult Mia had met for afternoon coffee, stayed through happy hour, and decided to become BFFs.

But it was Star who put the last piece of the puzzle in place when she was looking over Mia's car on race morning at Watkins Glen. Of course.

'We need to stop calling this thing the turbo pumpkin. That's Luca's car's name. This girl deserves her own identity, don't you think?' Star did a little tap dance around Mia's RR1 while she contemplated, muttering possibilities like '*caliente* carrot' and 'sweet potato.' 'Got it. I christen thee the supercharged squash. Now, where's that champagne we were saving for after the race?'

The entire garage shouted no in unison.

'I'm kidding. Relax people.'

'I like it. It suits her.' The voice that came from the doorway belonged to Jordan, who had apparently been observing the entire scene from a distance with Barb and Cliff.

Her brother hobbled toward her on crutches, his cast now up to his knee thanks to a setback and a second surgery.

According to Barb, who checked in regularly with both Rubie twins, he had a long road ahead of him.

She heard from him, too, every now and again; brief text messages as the season wore on. The last one had arrived after her first podium finish in Mexico City: *That's more like it.* At some point, Mia hoped to understand what made her brother tick, but for now, she was grateful that he was no longer a ticking time bomb.

When Star shouted 'surprise,' Barb's caginess about the invitation she'd extended weeks ago to the only American race on the schedule suddenly clicked. Leave it to the woman who had not only mastered but further streamlined everything the team threw at her to find time to plan a Rubie family reunion, too.

Now, the entire garage was holding their breath as they watched Mia and Jordan. Without thinking twice, she finished the distance between the two of them and gave her brother a hug.

'It's good to see you,' she said. And she meant it.

The siblings stepped back to find Luca and Brian, mouths agape. Now it was Mia's turn to hold her breath.

Jordan spoke first. 'Hey, guys.' And then he turned to the team, his former team, and gave a sort of humbled half wave. 'Everyone.'

Luca moved first, then Brian, both of them clapping Jordan on the back and asking about his leg. The small talk was awkward but short-lived, given that pit lane was about to open and Mia and Luca needed to drive their cars to the starting grid.

Barb stood at Mia's side as she watched her team make the final preparations. 'I've been meaning to ask what you're planning to do with that thing you call a car that you deserted in my driveway so many months ago.'

'Seriously, what's wrong with my car?' Mia asked, even though she hadn't sat in its driver's seat in months. As much as she'd love to prove a point to certain people, there was no way she could go back to that sedan now. 'I'm going to give it to a charity.'

'Seems a little like donating expired canned goods, but OK,' Barb said, then laughed so hard at her own joke that everyone around her joined in.

Mia zipped up her racing suit. 'Oh, Barb. I miss you. You're all coming out to the grid, right?'

Cliff draped his arms across Barb and Jordan's shoulders. 'What do you think we're here for, kiddo?'

Nigel Rose: Now that was something to see. I can't recall the last time a driver put forth an effort like what we witnessed from Mia Rubie today. That was masterful.

Joseph Linwood: A few more laps, and I think she might've caught her teammate, Luca Toscano. But her second-place finish after a fourth-place start is certainly no cause for disappointment.

Nigel Rose: Exactly right. And I don't think I need to tell anyone who's been involved with the sport as long as we have who she reminds me of.

Joseph Linwood: You most certainly do not. Rob Rubie had a confidence and a style that appears to be genetic. We caught small glimpses of it at the beginning of Jordan Rubie's career, but he never seemed to be able to tap into the Rubie superpower in the way his sister has managed to.

Nigel Rose: No, unfortunately. It was delightful to see him cheering on his sister today. I'm still hopeful that he'll find himself in a car again once he's recovered. Who knows, perhaps Apex wasn't his car. There are certainly options for an accomplished driver like him in another series.

Joseph Linwood: Of course, Rubie Racing has been tight-lipped about their plans for next season. With the world championship basically a done deal for Luca Toscano, it would be a shame to see him leave the sport. Although if I were to choose who I'd personally like to see more of, it would Mia Rubie.

Nigel Rose: You took the words right out of my mouth.

Chapter 38

It was after the second to last race, in Brazil, that Mia found herself on a private rooftop terrace overlooking Sao Paulo, with strings of twinkling lights overhead blending into the starry night and Luca in front of her on bended knee.

'Mia, I didn't think I'd get to propose to you once, yet here I am, doing it twice in a single season.'

His nervous laugh made her heart swoon. As far as she was concerned, she was the lucky one for getting to say yes to the love of her life twice.

'I've spent my whole life wandering, racing from one thing to the next, from one place to the next, like a nomad without a north star. But not anymore. You're my family, my home. You give my life direction. You're where my heart lives. I love you, Mia. Always have and always will. Please, please marry me.'

'Two pleases?' she teased.

'It was the only way to get the haiku to work,' Luca said, sliding a thick platinum band onto her finger. Her breath caught when she glimpsed the massive diamond flanked by bright orange citrines.

'It's us,' he said, rising and pulling her toward him, 'together always in the turbo pumpkin and supercharged squash.'

'It's perfect. You're perfect. We're perfect.' Mia didn't realize she was crying until Luca kissed a tear away. 'I don't want this to end.'

'Isn't that kind of the point of this whole getting married thing?' Another nervous laugh was soft in her ear. 'Not that you've given me an answer.'

She had, of course, all those months ago in his hospital bed. But Mia said it again, as much for him as herself. 'Yes, I'll marry you. As many times as you ask, my answer will never change.'

As they stood there, a shooting star glided across the darkened sky, like a gift from the beyond. If anyone could figure out how to move time and space, it would be her dad.

With her forehead pressed to Luca's, she said, 'I wasn't talking about us, though.'

Mia had avoided any talk about the next season, even when 'silly season' rolled in and then out, when the rumor mill was rife with assumptions and other teams announced their driver lineups. When Brian or anyone tried to bring it up, she flashed a palm in front of their face. She couldn't bring herself to focus on the next season until they got through this one. But now, only one race remained on the schedule. A discussion about the future of Rubie Racing was unavoidable. Things needed to be put in place.

Barring a DNF at the final grand prix in Abu Dhabi, Luca's win earlier that day in the Brazilian Grand Prix guaranteed the world championship was his, although he still wouldn't allow anyone to celebrate and jinx it. Rubie Racing was out of the running for the team championship, although no one could say her efforts since climbing into the car unexpectedly in August were to blame. She'd finished third that day to Luca's first, with Henri — now officially her nemesis, too — between them.

'What is it that you want, Mia? Whatever it is, we can make it happen,' he said. 'I promise.'

She looked up at the sky and took a deep inhale. 'In my letter from Dad, he asked that I give it a year, lead the team through the circuit. And I'm so glad I did. But now—'

Luca's mouth dropped open as he interrupted. 'Wait. Do you want to go back to Chicago and your marketing career?'

'No, my dad was right. This is where I belong — where we both belong. So, don't even think about calling Cat and taking her up on her offer, which was ridiculous, by the way. Far too generous, in my opinion.'

Carvalho Motorsport's attempts to woo Luca away had become nothing more than a passing joke between the two of them.

'Not in a million years,' he said. 'But you still haven't told me what you want, Mia.'

Mia looked down at her ring and rubbed the two orange stones with her thumb. Although he'd kept his eyes on the prize all season, and she'd been unwilling to look toward the future, she'd sensed Luca was ready to climb out of the car for good. The only issue was, she was just getting settled in.

Mia held up her hand so he could see the gemstones sparkle, and then she gave him that famous Rubie smile.

Critics who lament that Apex is nothing more than a very expensive parade had no cause for complaint as day turned to night on the Yas Marina Circuit in Abu Dabi.

After qualifying in sixth position, her worst start in as many races, Mia spent the first twenty laps picking off one car, then another, and then one more. She could normally be happy with third, but the lowest level of the podium wasn't good enough for this race.

The final race of the silliest yet most profound season of her life.

Her focus was now on the red car ahead of her, knowing Henri was more preoccupied with the orange car in front of him. On Luca.

'Watch your back, *mon ami*,' she said softly. 'The enemy of my enemy is much more than my friend.'

It had been a clean, fast race with no crashes or yellows, which meant that she had to rely solely on race strategy. She and her team had decided on two pit stops and changes to medium-soft and soft tire compounds for the dry desert heat. But before she went in for the second tire change, she wanted the red car solidly in her rearview mirror.

Of course, Henri's driving was flawless. But so was hers.
And Henri's car was fast. But so was hers.

Actually, she realized as another lap fell away, hers was a bit faster. If she could get within a second of Henri in one of the two zones where drivers were allowed to activate the system that adjusted the car's rear wing to be more aerodynamic, the power to overtake him would be hers.

She just needed two things: patience and perseverance.

At each of the track's two straightaways, she began checking her dash for the flashing light that would let her know she was within the one-second striking distance. Only then would her thumb be allowed to press the blue button on her steering wheel and boost her speed.

Each lap, she was a little closer.

'One more,' Mia said aloud as her radio came to life with the same message.

She couldn't help but laugh. 'Jinx. You owe me a Coke.'

'You got it,' said Brian, who'd been in her ear all day. 'Later.'

She pushed herself and the RR1 to the limit, taking each corner at the fastest speed possible, braking as late as she could entering curves, then slowly easing up and accelerating as she exited. The dash light flashed as she entered the next straightaway and, with that extra boost, she passed Henri.

Finally.

'Well done,' Brian said.

The only name left on her dance card belonged to the love of her life.

Henri had been significantly closer to Luca than she expected. She'd been too focused on the red car to notice the turbo pumpkin. Unless… Luca had just ducked in for his second pit stop. She wasn't surprised he'd been called in first. But even with a pit crew that could install four new tires in a matter of seconds, he'd lost time on the track.

If only she didn't have to pit again. Suddenly, the wheels on the supercharged squash weren't the only ones turning at rapid speed.

'How many laps are left on these tires?' Mia radioed.

'About as many laps as you have left in the race if you don't hit a single curb or rumble strip.'

'Best case?' she asked.

'You win.'

'Worst case?'

'What do you have to lose?'

She grinned. Brian had posed the same question to her ten months ago, and her answer hadn't changed. Nothing.

At that moment, she entered a straightaway on Luca's tail, saw the flashing blue dash light, and went for it. Her adrenaline got the same boost as her car's acceleration, or maybe it was from the ensuing battle. Luca chased her down on fresh tires, and she pushed every limit.

Then came the marbles. She took a curve a little too wide as she passed a car in the back of the pack and swerved a little too close to the side of the track where those small blobs of rubber from worn tires like to gather. Even more so in the desert heat, it seemed.

'Marbles, Mia,' Brian warned over the radio as she hit the slippery patch.

Suddenly, her dad was in the other ear.

'Trust yourself,' her dad whispered.

Instinctively, she headed straight through the marbles, slowing her speed until her tires felt clear. She avoided getting caught, but at a cost. Her tight lead shrank, and Luca was now closer to catching her with just two laps to go.

As team owner, Mia wondered if she should get out of his way. After all, Luca was bringing home the world championship for Rubie Racing. Not that it mattered whether he was first or second, except for the finish line photo opp.

But as a driver, she wanted the win.

The radio came to life. 'You earned this, Mia. Take it home.'

She did just that, but only after blocking her fiancé from passing her on each and every point of the track where it was possible for him to get by her.

Finally, the checkered flag waved as she crossed the finish line. The race was finished; the season was over. Luca was right behind her. Rubie Racing's RR1s were one and two again, but in an order she much preferred.

It was hard to say who was screaming into the radio at that point – Star had unfortunately learned to work her microphone – but the voice of her dad was clear as a bell: 'I knew you had it in you, daughter of mine.'

Mia's permagrin refused to fade as reporters lobbed questions at Luca, the newly crowned world champion; at her, winner of the Abu Dhabi Grand Prix; and at Henri, who was none too pleased with either of those things.

Mia wasn't surprised to see her least favorite reporter waving her hand in the air. Her animosity toward Madison had long faded; Mia almost felt that their ambitions were now somehow intertwined. She nodded for her to go on and ask her question.

'You've had a quite a year, Mia, to say the least. What are your plans for next season?'

She glanced to Luca and then to Brian and Star, who were watching from the back of the room, before announcing to the racing world the plans the four of them had hammered out over the past week.

'As you likely expected, Rubie Racing will have a change of drivers next year.' She took a deep breath. 'Now that Luca Toscano has won a very well-deserved world championship, he has decided to retire. The good news is that he has accepted a leadership role within Rubie Racing. He will be taking Brian Smith's team manager role, as Brian will be moving up officially to team principal' – a collective gasp filled the room – 'allowing me to continue on next season as a driver.'

The idea had mostly been Luca's. On the night of their second engagement, when she'd finally admitted to him – and to herself – how much she wanted to stay in the car for another season, Luca had told her of his desire to end his driving career on a high note. World champion at the age of thirty-six, he was ready for a change, a new challenge.

Mia knew in an instant what her father would've wanted. He'd said as much himself in his letter to Luca. Luca was family, and he belonged at Rubie Racing.

Always had, always will.

Just as she'd accepted his marriage proposal without hesitation, he'd immediately said yes to the equally huge commitment of helping lead her family's legacy. With one condition – that Brian fill her dad's shoes.

Next to her at the table, Luca was telling the reporter how glad he was that he'd decided to retire before the Abu Dhabi Grand Prix. 'Otherwise, I might've felt I needed to stay on just to prove I could beat my future wife.'

She winked at him. 'And that might've proved embarrassing for you.'

The room erupted in an uncomfortable laughter. Perhaps they all suspected what the two of them did.

That it just might be true.

Epilogue

'You got this, *mija*?'

Before Mia could answer, Jordan spoke up from beside her. 'You bet your ass she does. Tell them to start the music. Let's get this show on the road.'

With a wave of her maid of honor's hand, the string quartet came to life and Star set off down the aisle, leaving the Rubie twins alone in a comfortable silence neither could've imagined a year ago. But just as she was about to launch, her twin reached for her hand and held her back.

'I'm sorry Dad's not here to give you away,' he said, emotion welling up in his eyes.

'Me, too.' She gave his hand a squeeze. 'But at the same time, I'm not sad that you're here with me.'

It was the truth. Deep down, they both knew that this scene – the two of them standing side-by-side in the back of a cavernous great hall in a Scottish castle with Luca waiting for her – likely wouldn't have played out if they hadn't said goodbye to Rob Rubie eighteen months prior. His death had proved to be a pivotal moment in her life, and in Jordan's, too.

As her wedding approached, she'd included both of her parents in small ways. From her satin dress in the softest whisper of pink to the champagne she and Luca would toast their marriage with, Rob and Trish were part of her special day.

When the song's intro repeated for the third time, she tugged him toward the archway. 'That's my cue. Let's go.'

He tugged back, then placed her hand in the crook of his arm. 'For once in your life, slow down, Mia.' Jordan laughed, shaking his head as his brain registered the untraditional wedding march. 'Pink Floyd?'

She nodded.

'It's perfect.'

It really was, because of all the lessons she'd learned since returning to Rubie Racing as team principal and now as a driver, being fearless had brought her the furthest – both on and off the racetrack.

Even though she missed racing Luca and his turbo pumpkin, Mia and her supercharged squash were having a season for the record books. Her teammate was more than holding her own, too. A slate of seasoned drivers had suddenly vied to live in the Midwest after Luca's world championship win, but the team had plucked the top driver from the professional women's series. The move maybe had been meant to further shock the patriarchy and prove there could be more than one unicorn in the racing world.

And even though it was working, Rubie Racing was the furthest thing from Mia's mind as she pulled Jordan down the aisle toward a kilted Luca.

Like with racing, sometimes the start and finish lines are one and the same. Their years-long journey had been full of unexpected twists and turns but had led them to this moment, where they were always meant to be.

Her last grand prix as a single woman had also been the final race before summer break. Luca had woken her up extra early on race day by making slow, passionate love to her, and then had taken her to the Hungaroring, the scene of the second crash to change her life. Without another soul around, they'd taken a scooter to where Luca's car had flipped and he'd dangled upside down, with Jordan's car balanced precariously on top of his. As she'd stood in the exact spot, with Luca's arms around her, she'd been more grateful than she ever thought possible.

Until now.

Mia barely registered Jordan shaking Luca's hand and hugging her before taking his seat. Or Star prying the bouquet of calla lilies from her grip. She only saw Luca, who took her hands in his and then kissed her deeply – far before he was supposed to kiss his bride.

Later that night, as they danced under the stars, Mia realized that this is what happened when two people, two lives, collided in the best way.

'What are smiling about now?' Luca whispered, tugging her close.

'Us,' she said.

Of all the experiences she'd had on the racetrack, Mia had been waiting for a crash to happen. A big crash. It was inevitable that she'd eventually find herself in a crumpled car or against a wall, and she'd been mentally preparing herself for the day.

She never thought her wedding day would be that day. But everything Mia expected to feel – lost in time and space, completely out of control, her fate resting in someone else's hands – she experienced when she looked into her husband's hazel eyes. And she wasn't the least bit frightened.

'You can crash into me whenever you want,' she said.

'I don't know if that's an invitation, a request, or a wedding present, but you're minutes away from it becoming a reality.' Luca's husky laugh tickled her ear and vibrated through her body. 'I love you, Mia.'

'I love you more.'

'It's not a competition.'

'Hmm.' Mia's permagrin widened. 'We shall see about that.'

A Note from the Author

Crash Into Me is a work of fiction. The World Apex Grand Prix Motorsport Series doesn't exist in the real world, so the rules of similar, actual racing series don't apply. If they did, many facets of this book wouldn't be possible. Likewise, racing teams are complex organizations with many more roles and dedicated people filling them than possible on these pages.

Acknowledgements

Special thanks to Sandhya Krishan, for not only introducing me to sports romance, but also for reading every single draft, and to Camille Pagán, for being there from day one. Likewise, Patti Smith, Jodi Helmer, and Lauren Faulkenberry, your insight and enthusiasm as beta readers were invaluable.

Thank you to developmental editor Jacquelin Cangro for helping take this story to a new level, and to cover designer and illustrator Mary Ann Smith for bringing Mia and Luca to life.

And to my husband, Michael, thank you for inspiring my love of racing and for showing me the true meaning of romance. I love you more.

ABOUT THE AUTHOR

Darci St. John is a long-time freelance writer and editor. She lives in the US Midwest with her husband, Michael, and a rescue pup, Pippa, and enjoys travelling, hiking, and, of course, auto racing.

www.darcistjohn.com
@darcistjohnwriter

Bedford Square Publishers

Bedford Square Publishers is an independent publisher of fiction and non-fiction, founded in 2022 in the historic streets of Bedford Square London and the sea mist shrouded green of Bedford Square Brighton.

Our goal is to discover irresistible stories and voices that illuminate our world.

We are passionate about connecting our authors to readers across the globe and our independence allows us to do this in original and nimble ways.

The team at Bedford Square Publishers has years of experience and we aim to use that knowledge and creative insight, alongside evolving technology, to reach the right readers for our books. From the ones who read a lot, to the ones who don't consider themselves readers, we aim to find those who will love our books and talk about them as much as we do.

We are hunting for vital new voices from all backgrounds – with books that take the reader to new places and transform perceptions of the world we live in.

Follow us on social media for the latest Bedford Square Publishers news.

@bedsqpublishers
facebook.com/bedfordsq.publishers/
@bedfordsq.publishers

https://bedfordsquarepublishers.co.uk/